MORE
The

"Smart fun for those curious about the madness of what is still the world's largest country."
—*Kirkus Reviews*

"Thriller fans will want to follow [Nowek] every step of the way." —*Booklist*

"Riveting... [Nowek is] even more captivating than he was in his debut." —*The Monterey County Herald*

PRAISE FOR ROBIN WHITE'S
Siberian Light

"Powerful." —*Entertainment Weekly*

"White creates a psychological setting that is as lurking and dark as anything conjured up by John le Carré."
—*The Atlanta Journal and Constitution*

"Exhilarating." —*The Washington Post*

"A true find, a book that makes an exotic locale come to throbbing, pulsating life while telling a story that blasts across that landscape like the Trans-Siberian express."
—STEPHEN HUNTER, AUTHOR OF *Time to Hunt*

"[Robin White's] expertise shines through *Siberian Light*, giving its plot and setting the weight of authority."
—*San Francisco Chronicle*

"Robin White is an exceptionally gifted new writer who is brilliant at creating characters, atmosphere, and suspense. Great writing and wonderful reading." —NELSON DeMILLE

Also by Robin White

Siberian Light

The Ice Curtain

Robin White

A DELL BOOK

THE ICE CURTAIN
A Dell Book

PUBLISHING HISTORY
Delacorte Press hardcover edition published February 2002
Dell mass market edition / January 2003

Published by
Bantam Dell
A Division of Random House, Inc.
New York, New York

This is a work of fiction. Names, characters, places, and incidents either are the product of the author's imagination or are used fictitiously. Any resemblance to actual persons, living or dead, events, or locales is entirely coincidental.

Library of Congress Catalog Card Number: 2001047312

Dell is a registered trademark of Random House, Inc.,
and the colophon is a trademark of Random House, Inc.

ISBN: 0-440-22624-4

Manufactured in the United States of America
Published simultaneously in Canada

OPM 10 9 8 7 6 5 4 3 2 1

For L.—trapped by crystal,
and freed.

Whether we fall by ambition, blood or lust,
Like diamonds, we are cut with our own dust. . . .

—JOHN WEBSTER
The Duchess of Malfi

MIRNY, SIBERIA

August 19, 1999

CHAPTER 1

The Dead Zone

BLUE, WHITE, GOLD, AND BLACK. IN SIBERIA, the seasons are colors, though not the ones you'd expect in a land the imagination keeps buried under eternal ice and endless snows.

The sunless days of black winter yield to blue spring when the new shoots of larch, cedar, and pine emerge, their pale leaves the color of an arctic dawn. By July, Siberia steams under a sun that hardly sets before rising again. The sky hazes to humid alabaster, and from Novosibirsk to Magadan, white summer has begun.

Summer teeters on a knife edge in the far north, where it can snow any month of the year. The calendar might say August, but the hard frosts have already arrived in the arctic mining city of Mirny. In Mirny, summer is an incandescent flash of light and heat. In Mirny, the ground stays frozen to the depth of a kilometer. The people marooned there call the rest of Siberia *The Earth*. When the world hears Siberia's name and conjures up a desolate, treeless hell of ice and barbed wire, it's Mirny they're imagining.

Alexei checked his watch. The crystal was covered with

the same gray dust that covered everything in Mirny. It was shattered kimberlite, a soft volcanic rock in which diamond, the hardest of gems, was found. He licked his thumb and rubbed the face until the numerals appeared. *Nearly three.*

Alexei had a commanding view of the world from the cab of a Belaz 7530, an ore truck the size of a three-story house. From up here he could look over the motor pool's barbed-wire fence, across the roofs of the old log cabin dormitories to the lip of the open pit mine and beyond, all the way to a sunset horizon fired deep ceramic red.

It was August nineteenth, Alex's twenty-first birthday. His mother had prepared a picnic lunch with good bread, cheese, and smoked fish. Even his father, a big boss at the company, had taken off work to join them. Alex had told him the truth and now it terrified him to think it had been a mistake. After all, Kristall owned everything in Mirny. Everything and everyone. He flicked his cigarette out the window. The third shift at the mine came up at three. *Any minute.*

A Belaz 7530 was more like a ship riding on giant wheels than a truck, and Mirny was more like an island than a city; a remote atoll of dirty, spalled concrete surrounded by a sea of tundra as dangerous as any ocean. It was an impassable mud bog in summer and absolutely lethal in winter when deep cold shattered rubber tires as though they were made of glass. No one would live here if it weren't for the diamonds.

A quarter of the world's supply came from the mines of Mirny. Not that the miners saw much in return. In Soviet times, Mirny had been a "chocolate city" where luxuries that were scarce even in Moscow could be found. There were no shortages, no black days when the central generating plant was shut down to save oil. Movies played in the theater. The clinic was well equipped. Best of all, miners' pay was "double arctic." Back then, a miner earned more than an army general. More than even a Moscow bureaucrat.

All of that ended when the Soviet Union died. The state diamond enterprise became a private company named Kristall, though the same men still ran it. Their faces were about the only thing that hadn't changed.

First, fresh produce disappeared from the company stores. Then the theater was shuttered. Electricity became unreliable. The clinic ran out of antibiotics, out of everything except aspirin. Then aspirin became rare and even rubles fled, replaced by company scrip worth only what the company said it was worth, and only in Mirny. Meanwhile, diamonds were leaving by the ton.

Call it inertia. Call it stupidity. Call it hope. People stayed on. Mirny was stuffed with diamonds. If things seemed bad here, what must the rest of Russia look like? By the time they learned the truth, it was too late. The trap had snapped shut.

Alex watched the wind sweep across the waist-high reeds in hypnotic, shimmering waves of green and gold. The northwest wind promised a cold night of bright stars and bitter frost. He was about to check the time again when the portable radio on the seat beside him squealed, then a voice, spattered with static, said, *"Chainik."*

Teapot. A slang expression used to describe someone new to the world of computers. Alex was no chainik. He'd played with computers for years. First because they were cool, then because they were an astonishing window to the outside world. "On the stove." He clicked off the radio, reached into the breast pocket of his denim shirt, pulled out a plastic identity card, and swiped it through a small scanner bolted to the ore truck's dash. He'd altered the digital data file on the card to change his job description from *safety supervisor* to *haul truck driver*.

A red light on the scanner winked yellow. A computer was deciding whether or not Alex belonged here. If the answer was *no,* an alarm would go off and that would be the end of everything.

The yellow light turned green.

Alex smiled, savoring the last few moments of silence and peace. The setting sun was still warm on his bare arm. It had been the kind of day to spend with friends and family, enjoying the end of good weather, not a thousand meters underground, ripping into the eternal ice for the even colder glint of diamonds. And for what? *Nothing.* But that was going to change.

Alex pushed the big red start button. A powerful jet of compressed air turned the 7530's engine over. Slowly at first, then faster, until the five thousand–horsepower monster rumbled awake. He revved the engine until the ragged idle smoothed. The fuel gauge showed half. A Belaz would drink diesel fuel anywhere but Mirny, where the deep cold of winter turned fuel oil to stone. *This* truck's tank held two thousand liters of arctic-blend gasoline.

Time was the enemy. He'd fooled the computer once. But there was no way to keep it from reporting the truck's movement when he passed a security gate. Then it would be a race. He jammed his boot down on the clutch, selected first gear, and with a roar, the Belaz began to roll.

The gates were open. He saw the red laser light of the scanner twinkle and flash. A report was about to pop onto a screen at Security. Maybe the duty officer was asleep. Maybe he was reaching for the alarm button even now. Either way, the race was on.

The Belaz rumbled out onto a wide, dusty street. The center of Mirny was to the left. Alex swung the giant ore truck to the right.

The concrete buildings gave way to tundra, the paved road to gravel. Other than mounds of mine tailings, the landscape was flat, the road empty. The ore trucks weren't needed much anymore, and there were few cars in Mirny. Where would you drive? There were no roads out, no way off this arctic island at all except by river barge or plane, and like the Belaz, like the mine, they were all owned by Kristall.

He shifted up and accelerated. There was nothing in the side-view mirror but a cloud of ore dust raised by his wheels. Directly ahead, a tall black tower rose ten stories against the dimming sky. Slender as a modern office building, but windowless. Inside were ore lifts, elevators, fans. Radio masts spiked its roof. The black tower stood over the throat of a kimberlite ore pipe, an ancient volcano with deep roots and impossibly rich with diamonds.

Just how rich was a closely held secret, even from the miners, though everyone knew something of the truth. Most diamond miners never saw a diamond outside a jewelry store. They didn't come like raisins in a bun. Back when the open pit was in production, a Belaz would carry one hundred tons of kimberlite, and in all that blasted rock there would be a single carat of diamond, half the size of a pencil eraser. The deep mine should have changed everything. Mirny was never going to be heaven. But there was no good reason for it to be hell.

A double row of fencing surrounded the black tower, both topped with dense coils of razor wire. He pulled over to the side and stopped. The dust cloud enveloped him, then drifted over the third-shift miners waiting between the inner and outer security fences: a kind of purgatory dividing the underworld from the surface known as the Dead Zone.

The inner gate would open to allow the miners through. It would close and only then could the outer gate open. A security measure, though Alex thought, *Why?* Leave the mine with your pockets filled with gems and what would you do? Selling them meant leaving Mirny, and leaving was not easy. For most people here, it wasn't even possible.

Alex heard the tinny bleat of a horn. He looked in the side mirror. The crew bus was flashing its lights, its driver probably wondering what the devil a Belaz was doing here.

Alex rested his finger on the hard black knob of the ore truck's horn. The outer gate began to open.

Now. Alex leaned on the horn. An ocean liner's blast froze all movement. The silence lingered, ripened, broke.

A miner pulled the cover off a green metal rubbish bin chained to the fence and reached in. Out came a fat, tightly rolled sheet of white fabric. The banner unfurled as it was passed hand to hand down the line of miners. It took ten men to keep it off the ground, and on it a single word written in letters tall as they were:

ZABASTOVKA!

The word came from the Italian *basta,* for *enough.* A subtle complaint. In Russian, it was simpler: *STRIKE!*

The miners began throwing slips of paper into the metal trash bin. They looked like confetti, but they were *veskels,* official company IOUs that promised that sometime, somehow, the bearer would be paid something. What Kristall had been handing out to its miners while the company stole billions. When the bin was filled, Alex trumpeted the horn again.

The blast brought the miners out of the Dead Zone at a run. They ignored the bus, making straight for the Belaz. They clambered up the ladder mounted to the front grille. It was twenty rungs up to the broad balcony mounted over the engine compartment. The men fastened the banner to its railing.

ZABASTOVKA!

Alex didn't need to count heads. If it wasn't the entire third shift, it might as well be. He saw the bus driver shake his fist, shouting something. He could guess what. *Are you crazy?*

There had never been a successful strike in Mirny. The company always learned about it in time to break it. This strike would be different. It wasn't just the miners. It was the militia, the police, the women at the ore separation plant, even some of the headquarters staff. They were *all* going to stop work. They were *all* going to meet in the city's main square, under the giant black bust of Lenin right next to Kristall's main building. They would speak with their own voices, and the word they would say was *Zabastovka!*

A miner leaned into the cab and yelled, *"Zabastovka!"*

Alex gave him the thumbs-up sign, checked in his side mirror, then threw the gearshift into reverse and backed away, spinning the steering wheel, turning the monster's blunt prow in the direction of Fabrika 3, the ore separation plant. Nothing could stop them now. He mashed the accelerator to the floor.

The Belaz began to roll, sailing over the undulating gravel road like a freighter plowing through low seas. Geared to haul a hundred tons up a thirty-percent grade, an empty Belaz could really move on the flats. The black headworks tower receded.

Alex could hear the big gears whine. *Seventh in the high range.* Beneath his boots was an engine with eighteen pistons the size of basketballs. With no ore in back, the 7530 ran light on its wheels, floating, almost *flying* above the gravel. It gave him a feeling of invincibility. A miner leaned into the cab's open window and yelled, *"Alyosha!"*

Alex grinned and shouted back, *"Zabastovka!"*

Where the road split in a broad Y, Alex turned right, away from Mirny and toward a vast steel building standing off by itself, surrounded by empty marsh, guarded by more security fences and even more coils of razor wire.

It was Fabrika 3, the ore plant where women in pocketless gowns, surgical masks, and latex gloves sifted processed ore for diamonds. Bright, unpainted steel, blocky, angular as a crystal and big as a city block. The biggest building in Mirny, and its gates stood wide open.

The crowd there was twice the size of the third-shift crew. The Belaz rolled through the gates and rumbled up to the entrance. The air brakes *whooshed*. The women of the ore plant hurried up the truck's boarding ladder, gathering their skirts for the long step up to the first rung.

The miners squatted on the catwalk balcony, making room for the new arrivals, sharing bottles and cigarettes. Someone produced an accordion. It was a company picnic, not a strike.

A girl paused at the top of the ladder. There was no place left for her to stand. Someone offered a hand. She took it, and the next thing she knew, she was being passed across the miners' heads, settling on someone's shoulders. She wrapped her legs around his neck, skirt flapping in the wind, raised her fist and screamed, *"Zabastovka!"* Fifty fists rose in answer:
"Zabastovka!"

Alex was about to shift into reverse when he saw a man

crouch down by the front left wheel. He had a stick in his hand.

It was Anton, one of the "Twelve Apostles." A dozen men with special status, special privileges, who worked for the mine director. Alex laughed. One Apostle with a stick was all they could send to stop them? He cupped his hands to his mouth and leaned out the window. "Hey! *Secksot!*" It meant "secret worker," and in Mirny, as everywhere in Russia, it was a curse. *"Are you joining us?"*

Anton paid no attention. He had the stick in both hands now. He was twisting the top of it as though trying to strangle a goose.

Not a stick, a . . .

A flare, a big one, and it erupted with the hot white brilliance of a welder's torch. He flipped open the cap on the Belaz's fuel tank, dropped the flare, and ran to a door in the building's side.

One second. Two. Alex's scream was still inside his throat when a hot yellow gust sucked the sound from his mouth, the glass from the windshield, the air from his lungs. The blast rose into the indigo sky, roped and knotted with turbulent black eddies, a hungry furnace that consumed everything, flesh, hope, the world, and turned them all to ash.

IRKUTSK, SIBERIA

Saturday,
September 25, 1999

CHAPTER 2

Golden Autumn

IN SIBERIA, AUTUMN IS THE GLINT OF A bright coin dropped into deep water. Tumbling, flashing, dim, then gone. In Moscow, summer gives way reluctantly, sweetly. Five time zones to the east in Irkutsk, fall arrives with the fury of a breaking wave.

It was seven in the morning. A ragged fog draped over the swift, icy waters of the Angara River. Fine rain spattered the broad window overlooking the runways of the Irkutsk airport. Soon, hard frost would stitch itself to the glass, and the mountains, the forest, the outside world would vanish behind an impenetrable curtain of ice.

Gregori Nowek watched the last swifts of the season cut the threads of rain apart like scissors, darting between the gray sky and the slick, wet runways. He wondered where the birds went for the winter and why they returned. Was it instinct? Choice? It made him think about his daughter Galena, due back next week from a summer spent in America. What could bring her back from heaven?

Gregori Nowek had turned thirty-eight in June. He had a thin face, dark blue eyes, and a shock of brown hair that spilled over his forehead like water flowing over a stubborn rock. He wore a green jacket Galena had sent to him from America. It was supposed to allow air in but keep out rain. He hoped it worked because the weather in Moscow would be the same as here in Irkutsk: cold rain.

"So how many diamonds did we send those bastards?" asked the Siberian Delegate, Arkady Volsky.

They stood by a window in the VIP lounge, watching a weary Aeroflot IL-62 being readied for the morning flight to Moscow. Their bags were piled around their boots in a defensive circle.

Volsky had been appointed by President Yeltsin to keep an eye on Siberia for the Kremlin. Or as Volsky preferred, to keep an eye on Moscow for Siberia. He was Nowek's boss, his mentor, his friend.

"Which bastards?" asked Nowek. "The ones in London or Moscow?"

"Funny. The ones who were supposed to pay my miners."

His miners? Nowek thought. "Kristall shipped twelve million carats to Moscow last year," he said. Kristall was the big Siberian mining company that controlled ninety percent of Russian diamonds. Kristall was to Russia what the diamond cartel in London was to the world. "A third of it was gem quality. The cartel bought all four million carats."

"Four million? It's a mountain of diamonds."

"Not even a hill," said Nowek. "How much do you weigh? Eighty kilos?"

"Maybe."

"Ninety?"

"It's not necessary for you to know," Volsky said testily. He was shorter, heavier, though he lifted weights religiously. It gave him the surprising solidity of a bulldog. "What are you getting at?"

"Four million carats is eight of you. Or seven. You've put on some weight."

Volsky looked down at his waist, then up at Nowek to see if it was a joke. You had to be careful with Nowek. "Never."

"Easily. You were a coal miner. You still think like one. Diamonds come by the carat, not the ton." Nowek held up his hands and used a thumb and forefinger from each to form an oval the size of an egg. "Three thousand carats. The *Cullinan* stone. The largest gem-quality crystal ever found."

Volsky's eyebrows arched again. "That small?"

"Arkasha," said Nowek, "a big diamond is still a very small thing."

Volsky was a square, bluff man in his late forties. He had the pink face of a serious drinker, webbed with burst veins, and a smooth, thick helmet of silvery blond hair. His fingers were stubby and powerful. Even in his best suit there was no mistaking him for anything but a man who had known hard work.

Volsky had been a coal miner, a labor brigade leader in the Kuzbass coal region, a union organizer at the rebellious Anzhero mine. His miners had led the nationwide strike that toppled Gorbachev and installed Boris Yeltsin in his place. Yeltsin rewarded Volsky with the office of the Siberian Delegate. It was a big step up from the pits, though Volsky still spoke simply and loud, like a miner shouting *Fire in the hole!*

"These four million *markovka*," he said, using the Russian word for *carrots* instead of *carat*. "What are they worth?"

A pun in two languages? "You've been studying English."

"It's the language of business. It's practically mandatory," said Volsky proudly, pleased to be able to surprise Nowek. "So?"

"In dollars, more than half a billion. Maybe more. I can't keep track of what that is in rubles these days."

"Dollars are good enough."

They're better, thought Nowek. Dollars were the eternal stars. You could navigate by them. Rubles were meteorites, streaks of light, weightless dust. Breathe and they'd blow away.

"So Moscow sold the cartel half a billion dollars' worth of diamonds and those mousepricks won't send a barrel of cold shit to the mines?"

"Moscow hasn't sold *any* to the cartel in almost a year. They're too busy arguing over price. I don't know what Kristall ships to Moscow."

"I have a colleague who says they're shipping plenty."

It was the first Nowek had heard of it. "A miner?"

"Let's just say colleague. The *mafiya* slits throats for twenty dollars. Just think what they would do for half a billion."

Once, Nowek had been a petroleum geologist. In Soviet times, the oil business had been absolutely corrupt. Nowek assumed diamonds worked the same way now. "Which *mafiya*?" he asked. "The ones on the street or the ones in the Kremlin?"

Volsky sighed. "It's a distinction without a difference."

Yes, but Nowek was surprised to hear him say it. Volsky was the one with dreams of a better Russia, a Russia of laws. A Russia that might one day actually be normal. It was a dream that was becoming hard to sustain. "Moscow will say they can't send money to Siberia when they haven't sold any rough to the cartel," he said.

Volsky shrugged. "Let them. I have a plan."

It better be a good one. Winter was coming, and the lowest temperature in history, minus one hundred sixty degrees, had been recorded near the diamond mines. "So?"

"We're meeting Yevgeny Petrov, the chairman of the State Diamond Committee. They call him *Prince of Diamonds* for a reason. He controls the state diamond stockpile. It's a *real* mountain of gems." He gave Nowek an impish grin. "He's going to sell some and send the money to my miners. It's simple."

Nowek thought that what seemed simple in Irkutsk might not seem that way in Moscow. "How will you make him do it?"

"First I'll use reason," said Volsky. "But if reason doesn't work, I have other tools of persuasion."

"A club?"

"The President. My miners handed him his job in ninety-one. That's why I have a direct number to the Kremlin duty desk today. I even have my own password. Maybe you forgot?"

"It's his memory I worry about." Yeltsin was fast becoming an invisible man. The papers were full of rumors that he wasn't even alive. "I hear he's not in such good shape."

"I don't care if he's made of wax. He's still President and if he says do something, Petrov will obey." Volsky looked out the window, too, then said, "Galena is really coming back home next week?"

"She can't stay in America. Her visa runs out. Besides, she's only eighteen," said Nowek. But he didn't sound convinced. "I want to be back in time to meet her plane."

"Don't worry. You will be."

Nowek turned. "Not you?"

"I'm going up to Mirny with my pockets full of Petrov's money, or with his head. It will be up to him which. I've never been there. It should be interesting."

Desperate. Dismal. Marooned. These were the words that came to Nowek's mind when he thought of Mirny. Not *interesting.* "You're not giving Petrov much time to be reasonable, Arkasha."

"I gave the miners my word."

Nowek knew there was no arguing. Once Volsky said he would do something, Nowek had never known him to back away. Volsky could be maddeningly evasive. But heaven help *anyone* who stood between him and his word. You might as well stand in front of the Trans Siberian Express and try to flag it down with a handkerchief.

"Relax," said Volsky with a smile. "I know what I'm doing. Besides, three days in Moscow is long enough. More and we both might contract some disease."

Nowek knew his friend wasn't speaking about the flu. Moscow wasn't another city so much as a black hole, a whirlpool that drew in Siberia's wealth and magically made it disappear. Moscow, florid with corruption, radioactive with greed.

They watched a fuel truck rumble up to the old jet. A worker got out and tugged a hose from a reluctant reel. He was smoking a cigarette, but out of respect for the fuel left it burning on the truck's fender. A breeze sent it into a rain puddle.

Volsky saw Nowek was preoccupied. He thought he knew his friend's mind. Sometimes he did. "You've talked with Galena?"

"By *electronka.*" E-mail. "I asked what she missed from Siberia. You know what she said? *Get serious.*"

"It's not easy growing up without a mother."

Nowek didn't need reminding that it was right here, at this very airport, that he'd last seen his wife alive. Nina had boarded a plane bound for Moscow. It went down twenty-seven minutes later. Years later, the potato field still reeked of jet fuel and burned plastic.

"You know," Volsky continued, "if you decided to go . . ."

Nowek looked up. "Where?"

"To America. With Galena. Live a normal life. I could help."

"No thanks," said Nowek. "What would I do there? I'm a troublemaker. There are no troubles in heaven. Only money. Everything in America is about money."

"Everything is about money here, too, Gregori."

"Yes. But we still tell ourselves it's not."

The window dripped with condensation. Its edges were alive with mold, the panes fogged. Nowek cleared a circle in the glass. A face appeared in the cockpit windows, peering up at the leaden sky.

"About your diamond figures," said Volsky. "They're reliable?"

"They're reliable estimates. We know how many gem diamonds ended up in London last year because the cartel published the figures. No one knows how many were really mined."

"Petrov knows."

"Not even Petrov. By law, Kristall reports only total diamond production. Gem quality and industrial. The gems sell for a lot. The industrials for a little. You see the problem?"

"Fuck." Volsky grunted. "If no one knows how many *good* ones actually come out of the ground, anyone with access . . ."

"Exactly." Access was what Russian politics was all about. From access came influence, from influence control, and from control? Plunder. "Your miner friend says gem diamonds are being shipped to Moscow? Petrov can—"

"Skim off as many good ones as he pleases. And nobody said anything about a miner friend."

"Fine. Just so you know that when it comes to how

many stones were mined, it all depends on your assumptions."

Volsky snorted. "It doesn't pay to make assumptions when it comes to Moscow. These days, nobody has any fucking answers."

"In Russia, answers can be harder to find than diamonds."

"I'll tell that to Petrov."

A flashing beacon began to strobe from the wings of the jet.

"Amazing," said Volsky. "They're going to be on time."

"It doesn't pay to make assumptions about Aeroflot, either."

"They're better now."

"Russian Darwinism," said Nowek. "The survival of the luckiest. You know what Americans call it? *Aeroflop.*"

"*Shto?*"

"*Flop.* It means *disaster* in the international language of business."

A tinny loudspeaker announced the morning Moscow flight.

Volsky grabbed his suitcase and hefted the strap onto his broad miner's shoulder. "Be honest. Could Aeroflot get any worse?"

Nowek had to smile. BE HONEST: COULD I DO ANY WORSE? was the slogan Volsky had suggested for Nowek's campaign for mayor of Markovo. It had proven popular. Nowek won the election. But not durable. Russia's economic collapse in 1998 had claimed millions of victims. Nowek had been one of them.

Volsky flashed their official passes to a bored clerk. They walked through the control gate, through a grimy hallway and out into the rain. They skirted a Brownian mass of passengers pushing their way to the plane. The boarding stairs were blocked by a wet, grim stewardess who allowed the Siberian Delegate and his assistant in ahead of the herd.

"Petrov has a lot of power," said Nowek as they stooped to enter the musty cabin. "You don't become chairman of the State Diamond Committee without friends."

"No. Petrov has *collaborators*. *I* have friends."

The rising scream of four jet engines drilled through the cold rain. They dumped their bags in the open compartment in the tail, and found their seats in front. The passengers filled the cabin with the smell of wet wool, cigarettes, dried fish.

The stewardess slammed the hatch shut. The engines roared, the brakes squealed, and the IL-62 trundled off to the long, concrete runway. The engines roared again, louder. A lurch and the big jet began to roll, accelerating, the seams in the concrete a fast staccato, then silence as the ground fell away.

Noisy, inefficient, and cursed with an unquenchable thirst for fuel, the 62 was graceful in its way. The four engines at the tail and slender fuselage gave it the appearance of a long-necked goose in flight. And it was fast: they chased the morning westbound at better than 800 kilometers an hour.

Cities, islands of gray concrete in a green, rolling sea, fell beneath the wing. Novosibirsk, Roschino, Bolshoye Savino. Nowek peered down through the scratched plastic porthole as a low, sinuous hump of hills appeared. The Ural Mountains, dividing Asia and Europe. They weren't much to see from the ground. They were even less impressive from above.

"You were once a geologist. Tell me about diamonds."

Nowek looked up. "How much do you want to hear?"

"I'll say when to stop."

Nowek shifted in the seat. "Pure carbon exists in just three states: graphite, amorphous, and diamond. The first two are almost worthless. The last is not. What makes a jewel instead of something you put in a pencil is the environment of extreme heat and pressure found deep inside the earth. Okay so far?"

"Keep going."

"On their way to the surface, most diamonds burn up. Those that survive take on trace elements from the surrounding rock. These give color to the pure crystals. Nitrogen makes a clear diamond yellow. Boron turns it blue. Greens have been irradiated. Reds are very rare. No one knows what turns a diamond red. Reds are mysterious."

"Maybe to you."

"Red *diamonds*. The crystals get caught up in flows of lava that erupt at the surface in a kind of volcano of diamond."

"Grisha, this is just rocks. . . ."

"So are diamonds. That's the secret the cartel doesn't want anyone to know."

"Fascinating. Now tell me what I need to know."

"Take a lump of coal, squeeze it with tremendous pressure, bake it under extreme heat, blast it to the surface, and dig it up and it becomes something you put in a vault, not a furnace."

"Thank you. Now what about *our* diamonds?"

"Discovered in northern Yakutia in 1947. The Mirny mine was opened in fifty-four. Siberia is the number-two producer of diamonds in the world. More than South Africa."

It aroused Volsky's competitiveness. "Who's first?"

"Australia by weight, Botswana by value. Siberian diamonds go straight to Moscow, to Petrov. He's supposed to sell them to the highest bidder. That's always been the cartel. Now they want to pay us less and so nothing has been sold. No one can force Petrov to act. He's under nobody's thumb."

"He's under the President's thumb."

"Maybe." Nowek had his doubts. In a bankrupt country where influence came from money, who had more power? A sick President or a man who controlled billions?

"So all our gem diamonds go to the cartel?"

"*Everyone's* gem diamonds end up there. They control ninety percent of the world trade. When Mirny was discovered, the cartel's stock went down twenty-five percent overnight. They flew to Moscow the next day because they were afraid we would flood the market, drive down prices, and break the cartel."

"So then why aren't they afraid of us now?"

"It's a good question. You should ask Petrov."

"I will." Volsky turned away. In a minute he was snoring softly.

Four, five, six hours. It was already time for dinner by Nowek's watch when the roar of the engines quieted to a whisper, and the airliner tilted steeply down. The stewardess reappeared and busied herself with powder and lipstick at a mirror.

Outside Nowek's porthole, a deck of clouds swiftly rose up to meet them. The jet slipped through into gray, bumpy murk. Lower, lower, the view below darkened, then cleared, revealing rich green earth, almost wild-seeming, with only the occasional dacha, surrounded by summer gardens gone fallow.

Ahead, the dark spires of Moscow pierced a smoky horizon, ominous and black in the smudged light. City of Dead Souls.

The old terminal at Moscow's Shermetyevo I Airport

was part circus, part mob. Traders from the south in Italian clothes, gangsters from the west in leathers, northerners already in fur. Western tourists with backpacks and running shoes, homing beacons for pickpockets, thieves. A poster showed a busty blonde wearing an old leather aviator's helmet and nothing else. An advertisement for a club. Across the top, in block letters: YOU WILL DO IT TONIGHT.

"The Kremlin sent a car. It's probably at the VIP terminal," said Volsky as they pushed through the crowds. "I'll wait. You go look."

Nowek found a uniformed guard and asked for directions. He got a cold look for an answer. Either Nowek already knew where VIPs should go, or there was no reason for him *to* know.

Outside, a fine mist fell from pearl-gray clouds. Taxis dove and darted, ignoring Nowek and Volsky, competing for foreign passengers. Mercedes sedans floated by on invisible currents, the *biznismen* within hidden behind tinted glass, shepherded by Jeep Cherokees bristling with gun barrels.

A loud *blaat,* followed by a crunch, then the almost musical tinkle of a shattered taillight lens, made them turn and look.

A big black dinosaur of a car, a Chaika 10, backed up, disengaged from a cab's rear bumper, and rolled forward again in a cloud of blue oil smoke. You could hear each beat of its engine.

"Brezhnev's ghost," said Nowek. The Chaika looked like an American car from the fifties with prominent fins and a toothy grille.

"I wonder who . . ." Volsky began, but he stopped when the Chaika rolled up to the curb and stopped. The driver got out, put a blue flasher on the roof and turned it on.

He was young, dressed in a leather jacket and an officer's

wide-brimmed cap. A long dark ponytail dangled from be-neath it, halfway down his back. "Gentlemen! I'm Gavril."

"So what?" said Volsky.

"I'm your driver. This is your car. Chairman Petrov sent me."

Volsky looked at Nowek, then back.

Gavril smiled, then said, "Welcome to Moscow."

CHAPTER 3

The City

GAVRIL MANEUVERED THE OLD CHAIKA INTO the stream of traffic heading for the M10 highway. Theoretically, the blue flasher on the roof was reserved for official traffic, though you could buy one on any street corner. It might make Moscow's famously corrupt traffic police hesitate before requesting a bribe. Then again, it might not. "You really work for the President?" asked the driver. "Normally they send his people to the Metropole."

The most expensive hotel in Moscow and so tightly controlled by the *mafiya* it appeared *mafiya*-free. Volsky said, "We're not?"

Gavril looked into the rearview mirror. "You're booked at the Rossiya. It's not the Metropole, but it's very convenient."

"Convenience is important," said Nowek, earning him a dirty look from Volsky.

Everyone knew the Rossiya. Built in 1967, the concrete monster was proclaimed the world's largest hotel, eight hundred seventy-five rooms on eighteen floors. Now the Rossiya was famous for being the very worst place to stay in Moscow.

Its endless corridors and gloomy halls had become a kind of vertical slum.

"Chairman Petrov uses the Rossiya for foreign visitors of a different rank...." Gavril let his words trail off into a cloud of implication.

Volsky said, "Which?"

"Visiting diamond men from Angola, Botswana. You know..."

"Africans," said Nowek.

When Gavril nodded, his ponytail slithered up and down his leather-clad back like a puppet's string. "I hear the restaurant on the top floor still has a great view."

"We'll be sure to look." The radio was tuned to Radio Orfee, the best classical music station in Moscow. Nowek recognized one of the Bach "English Suites," though he wasn't sure which one. A violin was individual, full of character and innuendo. A piano was a machine made from hammers, pulleys, wires. A piano dominated. A violin insinuated, seduced. A violin sang.

They turned onto the highway, heading southeast. The Chaika slowly gathered speed. It might be a derelict, but it still moved with exaggerated dignity, as though it were carrying a Politburo member to an important meeting. The announcer identified the piece as the Suite Number 6 in D Minor.

"*Look* at all this traffic," Gavril chatted. "And a Saturday. Did you know there are more cars in Moscow now than in all of Siberia?"

"In Siberia," said Volsky, his voice like rocks rumbling down a steel chute, "we say the same thing about thieves."

Through the outer MKAD Ring Road, by the giant tank trap sculptures commemorating the defense of Moscow, they rolled by the sparkling new IKEA furniture store, marooned in a muddy field.

"The Swedes should have known better," Gavril chatted amiably. "They built their store just outside city limits so they wouldn't have to pay off the mayor. No one told them all the roads came from the Moscow side. The mayor said if the Swedes want customers, they can fly them in by helicopter."

Volsky gave Nowek a look that said, *Moscow*.

They crossed the inner Garden Ring. The Chaika lumbered on into the heart of the capital. Coming out onto Ulitsa Varvarka, the windshield filled with an extraordinary sight: a cluster of attractive sixteenth-century stone buildings dwarfed by an overhanging tidal wave of cracked, filthy concrete: the Hotel Rossiya.

Across the street, partially blocking the view to the domes of St. Basil's, a billboard advertised an American cigarette with A TASTE OF FREEDOM!

"Here we are," said Gavril.

Nowek peered up at the hotel's stark facade. There were windows missing, smashed, covered over with plywood sheets.

Gavril docked the old limousine under the Rossiya's swooping concrete canopy, scattering a few prostitutes out working the afternoon shift. "The Chairman is expecting you at six-thirty. He's booked a private room at *Ekipazh*. It's the best club in the city. What time would you like me to pick you up?"

Volsky looked at the Rossiya's forbidding entrance. "Early."

"Good idea. It's safer in daylight. We'll say five-thirty. And one piece of advice about the elevators . . ."

"Don't worry," said Nowek. "We'll walk."

Outside, the rain had settled into a spitting mist. Inside, the Rossiya looked depressingly normal to Nowek. It could be any one of a hundred hotels scattered across Siberia, only bigger.

Their rooms were on the fifth floor. They took the stairs.

"So," Volsky huffed as they climbed the stairwell. The carpet had once been red. It was now stained to an Oriental complexity of yellows, purples, browns, and whites. It seemed less a carpet, more like something that once was alive and might be still. "It's almost four. You've got some time. What will you do?"

Nowek carried his own bag and one of Volsky's. "There's a record shop called *Melodiya* that stocks old recordings. My father thinks they have some of his. I also want to check my mail."

"Mail?"

"*Elektronka.* I can connect by phone to the Internet."

"Is it expensive?"

"It's free."

Volsky looked puzzled. "How is that possible?"

"To be honest, I don't think anyone knows."

They opened the fire door to their floor and hunted for the *dezhurnaya,* the keeper of the keys, the minder of everyone's business. The Rossiya might be owned by *mafiya,* but the fifth floor was hers. They found her in an empty room, passed out on the bed, the television on. They claimed their keys from her desk.

Nowek's room was reassuringly normal. The window had glass, triple-paned and with a tiny operable portion caulked shut. The bed was monkishly narrow. He hoped the bathtub stains were rust.

Nowek unpacked his laptop computer. A Pentium, so it elicited sighs and substantial offers whenever it was seen. Nowek tried to keep those occasions to a minimum, for of all sins, envy was the most Russian. He switched it on. The screen glowed soft, cool blue. He picked up the telephone. There was no dial tone. He tapped the receiver a few times. Nothing.

He put the machine away and knocked on the communicating door to Volsky's room. It was unlocked. The room reeked of cologne. Volsky was taking a shower. "Arkasha!"

". . . believe it? There's no fucking hot water."

"The phone doesn't work, either. I'm going out."

"The car arrives at five-thirty. Don't be late."

"Arkasha, why are you going to war over diamonds? What about coal miners? Teachers? None of them have been paid, either."

The water splashed a steady *sshhh,* then Volsky said, "They're killing them. It has to stop. I'll tell you more after we beat up Petrov."

Killing them? "If I'm not back in time, I'll meet you at the club."

"There's a business card by the phone. Read it."

Nowek found it. On the back was a telephone number with a 095 prefix, followed by 661-18-94, and a word. *Buran.* Blizzard.

"If you need help, call that number and use the code word."

Yeltsin's private number was easy enough to remember; *661* was June 1961, Nowek's birthday. *18* was Galena's age. And *94*? The year his wife, Nina, had died.

"Don't get lost. I need you there tonight, Grisha," Volsky called out.

Nowek slipped the card into his jacket. "I'll be there."

THE MUSIC STORE *Melodiya* was on Nikitinskaya Street. The rain had stopped and it wasn't far, so Nowek walked. He spotted it beyond a dour brick building that proclaimed itself the Soviet Home for Working Artists. A small jewelry shop called *Eleganza* had been carved into a corner of its first floor.

Nowek was drawn to the golden light of its window. Beyond the thick glass were coiled heaps of necklaces executed in thick, heavy gold. Just the thing for a warrior princess, or a *mafiya*'s girlfriend. Behind them, under a hot spotlight, were the diamonds. A small sign shouted A DIAMOND FOR EVERY WALLET!

Maybe they were diamonds, maybe not. It took serious science to tell the difference between a cubic crystal of silicon carbide and a cubic crystal of pure diamond. Both were clear, colorless gems. Both superbly hard. Both filled with brilliant, refractive fire. One was industrial waste, the other a priceless gem signifying eternal love. But that was psychology.

Eleganza was closing. The shopkeeper peered out at Nowek, then tossed a cloth over the display and switched off the lights.

It began to rain. Nowek turned and headed for the music store.

Melodiya didn't look like the sort of place that specialized in old recordings. Teens in black leather and polychromed hair lounged against the windows, blocking the door. Advertisements behind the glass touted acid-jazz, Caribbean ska, and something called house.

Nowek pushed his way inside.

The shop was bigger than it seemed. The main room was filled with long tables stacked with CDs. A half-dozen kids in headphones tested music in a separate listening room.

They swayed, eyes shut. The air vibrated with heavy bass notes.

The smell of coffee wafted over from the bar. The price for a cup was a breathtaking one hundred twenty-five rubles. A fifth of a teacher's monthly pension, when he got one. There were computers there, too, turned on, probably connected to the Internet. He could check for messages from Galena if there was time. He made his way to the counter.

A girl in a forest-green tunic stood behind a computer screen. Her shoulder-length hair was lank yellow, pinned back with tiny black headphones. Her face was hidden behind enormous glasses set with rhinestones. Her nose was decorated with a ring. In her matching green tights she looked like a forest elf gone bad.

"I'm looking for . . ."

"Classical's over there," she said, briefly looking up.

"What makes you think I was looking for classical?"

"Just a lucky guess. Is there something in particular?"

"The Dvořák Violin Concerto in A Minor. It's performed by the Czech Philharmonia."

Her fingers poised at a keyboard. Her fingernails were painted a bright, acid green. "Violinist?"

"Tadeus Nowek."

"Your name?"

"Gregori Nowek."

She looked up, focusing on his face. The light made her eyes seem almost violet. She entered the name into the computer.

"Has this store been here long?"

"My grandfather opened it." She peered at her screen. "I'm not showing anything in current stock."

"It wouldn't be current. It's an old recording. My father thought you might have some left."

"Maybe upstairs. It will take a little time to check."

He'd have to leave soon. "Ten minutes?"

She nodded over in the direction of the coffee counter. "Buy a cup of coffee. I'll be back." She disappeared behind a door.

He bought a cup of coffee, found an open computer, and logged on to his *elektronka* account. There was a message from Galena.

His daughter was staying in America with Anna Vereskaya, an American woman of Russian parents, and a biologist at the University of Idaho. He'd met her when she came to Siberia to save the last few hundred Siberian tigers. Once, they thought they might be in love. Anna's Russian was fluent, but underneath she was one hundred percent American. It was a gap too wide for either one of them to cross.

From: Gail Nowek <4tigers@uidaho.edu
To: Gregori Nowek <gnow@russet.ru

Father:
You probably already could guess, but I won't be coming back to Irkutsk next week. Please thank Uncle Arkasha for everything he did to get me into the university. But there's not one student in Irkutsk who would stay if she had the chance to live here. It's like switching on a TV and instead of black and white, everything is now in color. I know what you'll say, but you haven't seen America so you don't have a clue. Sure, I could study for years in Irkutsk. Then what? Don't be too mad. Even better, why don't you come? If you do, you'll never want to go back, either.
Gail

Gail? Nowek stared into his expensive cup of coffee. He started typing, slowly at first, then faster, then pounding.

> To: Galena Nowek <4tigers@uidaho.edu
> From: Gregori Nowek <gnow@russet.ru
>
> Galena:
> I read your letter. "Gail" can stay in America but Galena must come home. Your classes will begin soon and your visa will run out. If you are still in America when that happens, they can arrest and deport you. I am in Moscow now. I will be in Irkutsk next week. Make sure you are, too. It's autumn now, the trees are beautiful. There are colors here, too.
> Your father

"You're in luck." It was the girl in green.

He followed her behind the counter, through the door, and up a narrow set of stairs. "What's your name?"

"Tatiana."

"Have you read Pushkin's *Onegin*?"

"It's a book?"

"Never mind."

She knocked on a door, and then opened it.

The air smelled of must and age and old vinyl. The walls were hidden behind thousands of records carefully racked in specially built shelves. Thin, dusk light came through yellowed lace curtains.

An old man sat in a padded chair. There was a cardboard record sleeve on his lap. He had a pink face and a fringe of white hair. He wore a loose cardigan of indeterminate color, a white shirt and tie, maroon corduroy pants. His eyes were magnified behind thick lenses. They were pale, watery blue.

"Your granddaughter said she found a copy of the Dvořák. . . ."

"The A Minor. It's rare. I have just the one." The old man peered at the back of the old record. He handed it to the girl. "Show him."

It was the Dvořák A Minor, Tadeus Nowek with the Czech Philharmonia. The picture on the back, taken in the early sixties, was of a young, intense man. It could be Nowek's own face looking up at him from the old, fragile cardboard.

"The Wild Siberian. He came out of the snows with a strong arm and a fast bow. He *glided*. He *flew*. He was remarkable."

"He still is."

The old eyes gazed up. "Tadeus Nowek is alive?"

"Absolutely." Though he meant, barely. Nowek's father was nearly blind, nearly immobile. He could hardly stumble, much less glide. Though he still made life miserable for the young students Nowek hired to look after him. "He practices an hour a day."

The old face wrinkled into a grin. His teeth were stained yellow with tea and time. "Put on the Dvořák," he commanded his granddaughter. "We'll listen to some *real* music."

Nowek looked out the window. Daylight was fading fast. He should be going back to the hotel to meet Volsky. "I'm afraid I can't stay. I'd like to buy the record as a gift for him."

"You can't. I'm *giving* it to you. Now listen."

The old turntable began to spin. There was a scratch, and then, from large speakers Nowek hadn't noticed, his father's music, his father himself, poured forth and filled the dim room with light.

———

THE BLACK CHAIKA pulled away from the Hotel Rossiya. It left behind a few determined prostitutes huddled beneath the hotel's concrete canopy, shivering but still hopeful.

Volsky thought, *Where is Nowek?*

"The Rossiya has had three managers this year," said Gavril.

"Why did they leave?"

"They weren't given a choice. They left in body bags. Contract killings." Gavril paused. "Where is your assistant?"

"Why?"

"Just making conversation."

"Don't."

The car turned right onto a wide boulevard scaled for parading tanks. Still known as Marx Prospect, the road was swarming with rush-hour traffic: charcoal-gray Mercedes, ministry Volvos with rooftop flashers blinking pinball blue, *mafiya* Lincolns. And at the edges, Russian Ladas cowered and darted, shouldered aside by sleek tons of victorious foreign steel. The red stars atop the Kremlin walls disappeared behind a curtain of freezing rain.

"How about a magazine?" asked Gavril. "Cigarettes?"

"What I'd like," said Volsky, "is not to be late for my meeting."

Gavril stepped on the accelerator and the Chaika bounced more enthusiastically.

They turned onto Tverskaya Street, outbound.

"Winter's coming early. They say it's going to be a cold one."

"Really?" said Volsky. "How cold?"

Gavril was encouraged. "I'm not complaining. Moscow looks cleaner in snow. But in a month it will be minus twenty," he said with civic pride. "Maybe lower."

"In Siberia, *sixty* degrees of frost is typical. Your breath freezes to crystals, and when the crystals fall to the snow there's a sound. We call it the 'whisper of stars.' " He breathed in, then let it out. "*Sssssshhhh*. Like that. So how long have you worked for Petrov?"

"Three years," Gavril answered. "I'm leaving to start my own livery service soon. I have a used limousine lined up."

"Your job must pay well."

Nobody in Russia admitted to that. "Not well, but reliably."

"In Siberia, a lot of people aren't getting paid at all."

"I'm not familiar with the situation outside Moscow."

"Neither is your boss." Volsky sat back against the faded red upholstery. "That will change."

The driver braked hard, then swerved for a side street.

"You know where you're going?"

"*Ekipazh*. This way is faster."

"*Ekipazh*." Volsky snorted. A fancy word for a saddle and reins, it carried a whiff of elaborate country manors staffed by armies of diligent serfs in red felt boots. "Is it a restaurant or a horse farm?"

"A private club. No horses. No bulls, either." Gavril used the word *byki*, slang for *mafiya*. "They have strict rules. It costs plenty to join. Businessmen of the first rank only. The *bandity* can't get in."

"Even if a bandit can pay the membership fee?"

"In that case," said Gavril, "he's a businessman."

They lumbered by the Pushkinskaya Metro station, dodging potholes and nimble BMWs. Streetlights burned inside halos of cold rain. A fast-food restaurant blazed triumphant yellow.

They turned off onto a narrow street lined with five-story flats. The lane ended at a sturdy iron fence. The Chaika rolled to a stop at a gate. The rain was solidifying into hard beads. Beyond, a luminous wall of white marble was bathed by incandescent lamps. There were no guards. In a few seconds, the gate began to open.

"How do they know who we are?" asked Volsky.

"Chairman Petrov made the necessary arrangements."

The Chaika passed a row of parked Mercedes, their engines idling, exhaust puffing steam into the chill, wet night. The red glow of cigarettes illuminated the drivers' faces.

They stopped beside the white marble wall. There was a single wooden door with fancy brass coach lights to each side. A television camera peered down from above it, its red eye steady and unblinking.

Volsky grabbed his briefcase and put his shoulder to the door. The door squealed open. "You'll take us back?"

"You're my only customer tonight."

Volsky stopped. "Your what?"

"*Customer.* Listen. You gave me an idea. *Whisper of Stars* is a perfect name for a livery service. A whisper is very discreet, and we'll cater to stars. It's a hot idea. What do you think?"

"I think it's like pissing down your leg."

Gavril blinked, then again. "Excuse me?"

"You think it's hot, but no one else does." Volsky slammed the door.

CHAPTER 4

The Prince of Diamonds

SLEET BOUNCED OFF VOLSKY'S BROAD SHOUL-
ders as he glared up at the security camera above the club's
front door. He knocked and his knuckles struck steel. The
door only looked like wood; it was artfully painted armor
plate. He knocked again.

Still no answer.

Volsky took a deep breath and shot a jet of steamy air up
at the camera. The night was too warm for the whisper of
stars, but it was plenty cold enough for a little people fog.
Another breath, a second cloud, and the lens went opaque.

The response was immediate: a loud buzz and a click
from the electric locks. Volsky pushed and the door moved.
Heavy as a bank vault, it was balanced well enough to swing
easily.

The door closed behind him with a solid, jailer's *clank*.

"What did you do to the camera?" demanded a guard
with a submachine gun slung over a shoulder.

Some say the bottle is the basis for all relationships in
Russia. It's not. What's most important is this: Who beats
whom? Who has more power? Who has less to fear? Volsky

would no more bend before a guard than he would show fear to a yapping dog. "Congratulations. You're one stupid question away from guarding the Irkutsk sewer plant. What were you asking about?"

It worked. "Nothing. Please step through the detector."

Volsky walked through the arch. "Are you worried about someone bringing in a gun, or leaving with the silver?"

A nasty tone warbled. A guard passed a wand down Volsky's jacket, his pants. It began to squeal as it came to his briefcase.

"Would you please open the case, sir?"

Volsky placed it on the table and cracked it open.

The metal detector stopped at a plastic vial. Inside it was Volsky's emergency collection of tiny fifteen-kopeck coins.

"What are these for?" the one with the weapon asked as he shook them. They jingled. "Nobody uses them anymore."

"They do where I come from." Kopecks weren't worth much even when a ruble was a ruble. In Moscow, in the Carriage Club, their value was microscopic. But not in Siberia, where most public phones still used them. Anyone wanting to use an "automatic phone"—a misnomer to be sure—had to buy them from street vendors for three American dollars each.

The guard handed them back. "You can go in now."

At the far end of the corridor, the Siberian Delegate came to a door made from real wood. Volsky reached for the handle, but it was pulled open from the other side before he could touch it. There, waiting, was a doorman with enough gold braid swinging from his shoulder to pass for an admiral on Fleet Day.

"I'm here to see . . ."

"Yes. Please follow me."

The admiral led Volsky into a warm, low-ceilinged dining room that swarmed with waiters dressed as ... what else? Medieval serfs in red tunics and red felt boots. The dark paneled walls were hung with paintings of leaping horses, dogs in baying packs. Stuffed partridges strutted along glass shelves. Trophy heads peered down from their mounts; the greedy snouts of boar, the placid gaze of reindeer, the frozen snarl of wolf, though his wide glass eyes made him look more startled than fierce.

Saturday was a big night at *Ekipazh,* but it was still early, and the room was barely half full. The customers were young. The men wore business suits. The women were feathery, perfumed creatures dressed in shimmering, close-fitting fabrics.

"This way, please."

As he followed, someone grabbed his elbow.

"Hullo." A short, wiry man with iron-gray hair, dark suit, blue shirt, and a brilliant yellow bowtie was now attached to Volsky's arm with a crab's pinch. His skin was tanned the color of expensive leather. There was enough alcohol on his breath to melt ice. "You're a new face. You speak English? My name's Wilson. Willie's good enough." He spoke with a British accent. He pulled a card from his pocket. *"Vot maya visitka."*

Volsky read the business card. Willie was a lawyer from the Cayman Islands, one of the *mafiya's* favorite parking places for illicit hard-currency earnings, a string of palmy islands overgrown with holding companies, offshore banks, shadow incorporations, all diaphanous covers for Russians interested in exporting funds abroad with a verisimilitude of legality. "I don't need your services."

"Maybe not today. But what about tomorrow?"

"In Russia, you never know what you'll wake up to."

"That's my point *exactly*."

"Excuse me." Volsky slipped the business card into his breast pocket as the headwaiter swept open yet another oak door.

The private dining room beyond contained a long banquet table heaped to overflowing: platters of white sturgeon with fresh lemon slices; sausage and pungent charcuterie; gilt-rimmed bowls brimming with fresh cherries, shrimp, crab; red and black caviar mounded into pyramids worth four hundred dollars apiece. And to drink there were glittering bottles of Rowanberry Vodka, Golden Ring Vodka, Amber Vodka, Martini Bianco, Sovietskaya Champagne, three kinds of cognac, two brands of wine, and a supply of mineral waters, chilled and unchilled, carbonated and plain. A feast put on for two dozen very important men.

Who else is coming? Volsky wondered. For there was just one man present. Near a blazing fireplace, at a table set for four, beneath the spreading antlers of a prize elk, the Prince of Diamonds sat alone.

OUTSIDE, THE RAIN HAD TURNED into heavy, wet snow. Gavril could hear the flakes strike his windshield. He had a copy of the *Moscow Times* open on his lap. It was an English-language paper read by almost all the Americans in town. The kind of people any entrepreneur wanted as clients. He was circling their addresses when lights flashed across his face. He looked up.

A dark gray Land Rover had parked directly in front of his Chaika, blocking the view of the main door. He flashed his lights and then, for an exclamation mark, gave his horn two quick jabs.

The Rover didn't budge.

Gavril leaned on the horn again.

Nothing. He was about to roll his window down when the Rover's dome light came on. Someone was getting out.

Gavril reached under his seat and felt the reassuring weight of a heavy steel crowbar. It was fine to think in new ways, so long as you didn't forget the old ones.

A man approached. He was short and powerfully built, dressed in a dark raincoat and no hat, which was odd on a night like this. His hair was either close-cut, or else he was bald. He flicked a cigarette away as he walked, the red ember arcing to the wet street like a dying meteor. He came up to Gavril's window and rapped it with a heavy gold ring adorning his right hand.

Gavril rolled down his window. He hefted the crowbar into view. "Who the fuck do you think you are parking there?" Gavril snapped.

He reached into his coat and pulled out a wallet and let it flop open to show an identity card that bore the white, red, and blue stripes of the PSB. Boris Yeltsin's Presidential Security Service.

Who beats whom? "Okay. What do you want?"

The man put the wallet away and walked around to the other side. He opened the door and got in beside Gavril. "I'll show you."

"WELCOME TO *EKIPAZH*," said Petrov. The Prince of Diamonds was younger than Volsky but looked older. His brown hair was wispy thin, his long, oval face was sallow. His eyes were red. A poor impression of health, but calculate the worth of his accessories, and a different view emerged.

His pin-striped suit was cut in London from the best

wools. His glossy leather attaché carried the logo of a famous designer. His gold Swiss watch was the biggest, his Nokia cell phone the smallest. Petrov was a blend: Russian, European, East and West, a sum that tried very hard to equal its expensive imported parts.

He nodded to a bottle of vodka sweating on the white linen tablecloth. "Drink? I know how you Siberians like to celebrate."

"I'll wait for a reason." Volsky took off the raincoat and draped it over the back of a chair and sat.

"Perhaps I can tempt you with something from the kitchen."

Volsky hadn't eaten a real meal all day. He eyed a hillock of black caviar set in a bowl surrounded by ice. The roe was fat and glossy, as big as ball bearings. "You can tempt me with some answers," he said as he dredged a piece of bread through the caviar and popped it into his mouth. "I have a friend who says that in Russia they're rarer than diamonds."

"It's an odd thing to say."

"I find he's usually right."

Petrov filled his own glass, took a sip. "I've heard you have some thoughts about the state diamond stockpile."

That was fast. How? Volsky wondered. He'd only arrived this afternoon. "I have no thoughts." He loaded his toast with a thousand rubles' worth of roe, ate it, then said to Petrov, "I only have demands."

"Demands?" Petrov took a sip of vodka. "What sort?"

"You've blocked an agreement with the diamond cartel for almost a year now."

"If two parties disagree, which one is guilty of blocking?"

"I don't care. What matters is that the cartel isn't buying our diamonds. That means no money is going to my miners."

"*Our* diamonds? *Your* miners? You're the Siberian Delegate. Not the delegate from Mirny. You don't speak for them."

"I'll fight for them. Winter's coming in case you forgot."

"You traveled all the way here to beg?"

"To inform. It's time for you to do your job before any more miners die."

"Someone died?"

Volsky stared at the Prince of Diamonds, then said, "Ask your friends in Kristall what happened in August. See if they'll tell you the truth. Fifty dead, and it's just the start."

"I heard nothing about an accident."

"Who said it was an accident?"

Petrov looked disappointed, as though a puppy he'd petted had turned around and nipped. "I'm sorry, but mine safety is not my responsibility. My job is to obtain the most value for the stones so that your miners, as you would say, can live."

"What have you obtained for them lately?"

"Listen. I understand your concerns," said Petrov. "I share them. But I'm like a general. I have compassion for my troops, but I must never hesitate to use them to win the war."

"Let another week go by without sending the miners their pay and you'll have a *real* war."

Petrov's expression hardened. "Forgive my bluntness, but the sale of Mirny diamonds is not your affair, Delegate Volsky."

"The survival of the people who dig them *is*. They're already rationing electricity. Do you have any idea what it's like when the lights go off in the middle of a Mirny winter?"

"I'm sure that life will become more normal when . . ."

"When there's *no fucking heat and no fucking electricity* because some fat-faced prick in Moscow is keeping four million carats under his warm ass?"

Petrov looked surprised. "Who gave you that number?"

"Tbye ne nuzhna znat." It wasn't necessary for Petrov to know. "Now *you* listen. I'm going to Mirny in a few days to bring them their money. Every ruble they're owed. I'll do it with your help or over your head. It's up to you which it will be."

"You don't need to make threats. The miners will be paid."

"All right." Volsky crossed his arms over his barrel chest. "When?"

"Eventually."

"Eventually we'll be dead."

Petrov wagged his finger at Volsky. "I have more faith in Siberians. You know how to survive. Fishing, trapping, the *dacha* garden. You're good at making do. Making do is what you're best at."

"Actually," said Volsky, leaning close, "telling Moscow to go fuck itself is what we're best at."

Petrov stared. "What did you just say?"

"If Moscow ignores Siberia, how long will it be before we return the favor? They won't send us money? We'll sell our own stones."

"They'll *never* get paid unless they keep mining diamonds."

"And they won't keep mining them unless they get paid. It's a circle. Do I need to speak with Boris Nikolaevich to break it?"

"President Yeltsin is aware of the situation," said Petrov. "Believe me. I wish the problem were more simple."

"Here's something that's simple enough: if you refuse to send an emergency payment to Mirny, I will ask Yeltsin to release a portion of the state diamond stockpile by decree.

Stones will be sold. The miners will be paid. You won't even get a chance to pocket a commission."

"He'll throw you out if you suggest it."

"You think so? I don't. Let's find out who's right."

Petrov looked up at Volsky as though he were seeing him for the first time. "If the stockpile is raided you'll flood the market and drive down prices. The stones won't be worth as much. Maybe only half what you think."

"Half a sausage is better than starving."

"Not when you take the larger view." Petrov smiled indulgently. "You don't understand the world of diamonds." He picked up the bottle of Baikalsk vodka again, its raw alcohol only slightly diluted with the pure waters of Lake Baikal, the Sacred Sea. He poured his glass full. "People think it's about mining rare gems and selling them. Well, it's not."

Volsky thought, *Where is Nowek?* Petrov was about to throw sand in his eyes. "What are you saying?"

"For two thousand years diamonds were actually rare. There was just one mine in India for the entire world. But then came Brazil, then Africa, and suddenly diamonds were no longer rare and everyone knew it. That's when the cartel was formed. They *control* the supply to *transform* a diamond *into* something rare. That's why a diamond is worth only what people *think* it's worth. It's all image. And when it comes to image, you come to the cartel."

Petrov placed the bottle back down onto the table. "London has kept hold on the diamond world for nearly a century. It's practically the world's oldest monopoly." Petrov paused, sipped, looked up. "World wars. Great depressions. Countries come and go, but the cartel survives."

"What does this have to do with paying my miners?"

"Everything. We're at war with the cartel. A war for independence. They're a powerful enemy. They deserve the greatest respect. We must be careful, and, frankly speaking, so should you. It's no exaggeration to say that there is nowhere on earth they can't reach. Not even the Kremlin is beyond their grasp."

The fireplace crackled. A shower of golden sparks rose up the sooty flue.

Petrov took a sip of vodka. "For years, Russia *had* to follow the cartel's lead. We had enough diamonds to destroy them. But what did we know about selling them? Less than nothing. The agreements we made with them were not always in our best interest. When you dance with an elephant, crushed toes are to be expected."

Damn it! Where is Nowek? "So?"

"Now *we're* the elephant. We're free to sell diamonds anywhere, and we have plenty to sell. The cartel has no choice but to come to our terms. When they do, *everyone* will live a better life."

"All I know," said Volsky, "is that they haven't signed anything so far. What will make them do it now?"

"Think," Petrov said. "How do you get a monopoly's attention?"

It didn't take much thought. "You threaten to break it."

"Exactly." Petrov pushed a tumbler to Volsky, then refilled his own. The vodka's oily surface was nearly convex. He raised the glass to Volsky. "A toast to the Siberian Delegate. A man who should not be underestimated. May you be buried in a coffin made from an oak tree that I will plant from an acorn with my own hands tomorrow." He drained it in a gulp.

Volsky left his drink untouched. "In other words, you're already selling our diamonds, just not to the cartel."

Petrov gave Volsky a sly, confirming smile. "Now we're moving into areas I'm not permitted to discuss."

"So where's the money?"

"Money?"

Volsky grabbed Petrov's arm. "You're not giving our stones away."

Petrov tried to pull his wrist from Volsky's grip. It didn't budge. "I can have you thrown out."

"Do it. I'll bring your arm with me. It will look good over my fireplace." Volsky squeezed once, very hard. "So?"

"All right!" Volsky let go and Petrov rubbed the blood back into his hand. "For the last year, diamonds have been sold under the direct authority of the Kremlin. And *not* to the cartel."

"Where?"

"Where the money is. America. We started our own company there to market them. If the cartel won't negotiate, we'll keep doing it. But they'll come to heel. They have to."

"This company. Its name?"

"Golden Autumn. The cartel will have to choose. Pay us more, or we'll break your back. The Kremlin is running the whole show. I'm just a small gear in a big—"

"A minute ago you were a general. Now you're just a small gear. Next you'll tell me you just sweep the floors."

"Listen. This *must* be kept secret until everything is in place. You think the cartel doesn't have friends in America? Officials they can buy? Diamond brokers they can threaten? You could destroy years of planning. Then it will be your fault if your miners freeze."

"Unless I keep silent and wait?"

Petrov sat back. "I'm glad we finally understand one another."

"I understand. I wonder. Does our president also understand? Does he realize his diamonds are being sold out from under him?"

"It would be impossible to move those diamonds without his approval. You must trust me when I say—"

"I wouldn't trust you with a piece of colored glass. Tomorrow, I'll go to Gorky-9." It was Yeltsin's suburban retreat. "If I'm wrong you'll have my apologies. But if I'm right"—Volsky leaned close and smiled—"we'll go back to Siberia together. Only you'll be in chains."

Petrov slapped his open hand to the table, exasperated. "What makes you think the President doesn't already know everything?"

"I know Boris Nikolaevich. He's no criminal."

Petrov laughed. "You've been in Siberia too long. You know the difference between a criminal and a businessman? A businessman has more imagination. Listen. The rain falls down. It doesn't fall up. This matter begins above all our heads."

"We'll see who still has a head tomorrow."

Petrov stood. "Good evening, Delegate Volsky. I wish you a night of sober contemplation and a safe trip home." Petrov opened the door and left.

Volsky scooped up some caviar, put it to his mouth, then stopped. He tossed it to the table, grabbed his raincoat and briefcase, and walked to the door. Outside the private room, the main dining area was slowly filling. Petrov was already gone.

The rain falls from above. But from how high? If someone at the Kremlin was involved, some termite who had burrowed into a position of power and influence, Volsky would have to be careful.

It reminded him of the Siberian Dilemma.

It's winter. Minus forty degrees. An ice fisherman falls through into frigid water. If he stays in, he'll die in a minute. If he pulls himself out, he'll freeze to a statue in seconds. Which will it be? A minute of life, or a few seconds?

Forget Siberia. Here was the *Russian* Dilemma: official, unofficial, law and crime, businessman, politician, president, thief. They were *all* becoming distinctions without a difference.

The headwaiter noticed him and hurried over.

"Was there something you needed, sir?"

"A phone."

"Our members usually carry their own."

Volsky spotted the foreign lawyer. He was no longer sitting alone. Another man was with him. Another foreigner. A blue blazer, an oxford shirt. Khaki pants. A Russian would have to work up a hard sweat to appear so casual.

Volsky joined them. They looked up. The second man was much younger, and there was something odd about his eyes. Then Volsky saw what it was; they were not quite the same color. "It seems that I need your help after all," he said to the drunk lawyer.

"That's what I'm here for. Meet my friend—"

"Sorry. There's no time. You have a cell phone?"

Willie seemed puzzled, or just too drunk to understand.

"Please." The second man reached into his rain-dark Burberry and handed his cell phone to Volsky. "Use mine."

The green light was still blinking, whatever that meant. "And you are?"

"Eban Hock. You're the Siberian Delegate. I'd like to talk with you if you have a moment to spare."

"I don't." Volsky walked to a corner away from the tables and punched in a private number that rang in the Kremlin.

The line clicked.

"This is A.V. Volsky. The Siberian Delegate. *Buran*."

Buran. Blizzard. The code word that was supposed to prove that Volsky was Volsky. There was a long silence as a list was scanned one finger at a time. Finally, "Listening."

"I'm requesting an immediate inventory of the state diamond stockpile. Tonight if possible. Tomorrow if it's not."

"That's the responsibility of . . ."

"I've spoken with Petrov." That was technically true. "It's a big job, so we'll need some help. We'll need a representative from the Finance Ministry, one from the Presidential Administration, and, naturally, someone from the FSB." The last was the Federal Security Bureau, the successor to the old KGB. "Have you got it all?"

"Yes. But—"

"I also want a report on an American company licensed to sell Siberian diamonds. It's called Golden Autumn. There's paperwork someplace that authorizes it. I want it found and ready for inspection by tomorrow morning. Have you got all that or do I have to call Gorky-9 and have the President repeat it for you?"

"Everything is noted!" the desk officer said.

"See that it happens." Volsky folded Hock's cell phone closed and returned back. "Thank you."

"Now, if you have just a few moments . . ." said Hock.

"I'm staying at the Rossiya. You can call me tomorrow."

"I won't be in Moscow tomorrow, I'm afraid."

"Count your blessings." Volsky turned and walked back through the warm, intimate dining room to the guarded outer hall.

The guards were gone. The telephone at the guard's desk was ringing, a light on it flashing. He ignored it and found the button that unlocked the outer door. He pushed it.

There was a loud buzz, then the click of steel tongues

retracting into oiled slots. He grabbed the lever. The heavy door moved and a wave of cold, wet air flowed in.

The temperature was dropping fast. Big flakes were falling through the glow of the outside lights, large and soft as eiderdown. He stepped outside. The door locked behind him. Where was Nowek? *He'd better have a good reason.* For that matter, where was his fucking car and driver?

There. The Chaika's engine turned, turned, then caught in a roar and a cloud of steam. The headlights switched on. The tires spun in slush, the car approached.

Volsky held out his hand and caught a flake in his palm, really a cluster of flakes welded together. Neither one thing or another. A dishonest snow, perfect for Moscow.

The Chaika pulled up. Volsky got in back and slammed the door. "Forget the hotel," he said. "We're going to the Kremlin."

The old limo began to roll.

Volsky looked at the back of the driver's neck. There was no ponytail. "Where's Gavril?"

"THIS IS AS FAR as I can go," the cabdriver said. They were outside the iron gates to Club *Ekipazh*. The windshield went opaque with snow. The wipers struggled to keep it clear.

Nowek saw two headlights turn in their direction. He paid the driver off, tucked the fragile record under his coat, and got out. The pavement was slick and treacherous. The cab spun its wheels as it backed up. It swung around, disappearing down the narrow lane.

Nowek took one step, then stopped. He heard the engine. BMWs, a row of Mercedes. One Chaika. It had to be Volsky's car. *Don't be late.* He'd let Volsky down for an old recording. He stepped into its headlights and waved for Gavril to stop.

VOLSKY COULD FEEL THE SPRINGS in the Chaika's seat poking his thigh. He leaned forward. "Where is my driver?"

"He had another passenger to meet."

You're my only customer tonight. . . .

They were almost to the gate.

Volsky saw a figure standing in the headlights. Finally. Nowek. "Stop here."

The driver jammed his boot down on the accelerator.

Volsky lunged for the handle and pulled. It didn't budge.

The Chaika's threadbare tires began to lose their grip. The car slid through the gate sideways. Nowek jumped a half second late.

The rear bumper caught him on the knee. A light brush for the old limousine, a caress, but enough to send him tumbling to the street. The Dvořák A Minor went flying.

The Chaika was halfway down the narrow lane when the red brake lights flashed. It swerved to one side and stopped.

Nowek saw one of the rear doors fly open.

VOLSKY LANDED HARD, slid and scraped to a stop on wet concrete. He struggled to his feet. He could see traffic passing by at one end of the street. He could see the luminous wall of *Ekipazh* at the other. And Nowek.

"Arkasha!"

The driver jumped out of the Chaika with a shotgun. Its short double barrel rose. Volsky slipped, fell, then struggled to his knees.

"No!"

Volsky heard Nowek cry out, and then something swept his legs out from under him. He flew back against a brick wall.

The blast reverberated, echoing like thunder.

Volsky gasped for air. He was on his back. Snowflakes fell on his face, melting, running down his cheeks. Something warm was spreading across his chest. One shell. He could survive that so long as the man didn't shoot again. He heard Nowek shout. A barking dog. The warble of a distant siren. The driver was standing over him with the gun. Two barrels. *Don't shoot again and I'll live. I'll live.*

"Arkasha!"

It was Nowek, and the sound of running feet was unmistakable. *Fuck.* Volsky saw the shotgun rise, level, point at his friend. *Fuck.* He lunged and grabbed hold of the hot barrel, using all his strength, all his determination, to pull it down.

His world. Endless Siberia, Moscow, his friends, his work. Everything narrowing, narrowing. All he had to do was hold on to those two barrels for another moment. A lifetime.

A blast. The barrel flew out of his grip like a rocket on a tail of fire, and Volsky was moving again, swept up in a wave of pure light. A *buran,* a blizzard, not of snow, but of flame. Nowek's face. White against the black sky. Volsky tried to speak. To whisper. Nowek leaned close. His face was wet.

Volsky summoned up something from inside him, some force, some pressure, and a word, a name, rose up. *"Grisha . . ."*

"Don't talk. They're coming. Don't say anything."

There was a lot to say and no air left in his ruined lungs. He swallowed, tasted blood. *"Idi . . . k'gorizontu . . . Idi . . ."*

"Arkasha!"

Had he said it? Spoken the right words? It was all receding now. Fading behind a gentle curtain of falling snow, buried under the soft whisper of a million, million stars burning bright in a sky so infinitely deep he could no longer hear the siren's wail. So vast, it swallowed the voice still calling out his name.

CHAPTER 5

The Punishment

THE MILITIA SERGEANT SAID, "NAME."

Nowek looked up. "I've already told you my name."

"You've got something better to do? Tell me again."

Nowek's hands were cuffed together behind his back. He squatted at the sergeant's feet, his thighs numb, the snow collecting on his hair, melting down his cheeks. "Nowek. Gregori Tadeovich Nowek."

"City of registered residence?"

"Irkutsk."

"A little snow shouldn't bother a Siberian."

It didn't. Nowek was numb. His clothes were turning stiff with Volsky's blood. Gavril's cap was beside him. So was the shotgun. The Dvořák was a mess of sodden cardboard trampled beneath the shuffling boots of the militia. The headlights from their patrol cars slanted across new snow.

A photographer bleached the scene with a flash, arresting the heavy flakes in mid-fall, then released them to the dark.

"Let's begin again. You were driving the Chaika...."

"Gavril was driving," he said. "I'm Volsky's assistant."

"You admit you knew the victim." The militiaman had a clipboard in one hand, a pencil in the other. The urgent blue flash of a strobe illuminated his face. The ambulance with Volsky inside was already gone.

"Of course I knew him. I was supposed to meet him here."

"Now tell me why you shot him. Was it *razborka*?" A criminal settling of accounts. "Who paid you?"

Nowek looked up. "Nobody's paid me in months."

"So you decided to get even your own way...."

"No." Nowek looked at the shotgun, a Baikal 27. Volsky owned one very much like it, maybe the same model. What did he feel? Anger? Fear? Numbness. "This was a professional murder."

"You're an expert? Well, not such a good one. Volsky was shot twice. The *kontrolniy vuistrel* was unnecessary." The control shot, the coup de grace. "Volsky was already dead. It's the sign of an amateur. If it wasn't money, then why did you do it?"

"For the last time, it was Gavril. They were leaving the club. They passed me at the gate. I thought they'd stop, but they didn't. They swerved and I was knocked to the ground. Halfway down the alley, Volsky jumped out. Gavril stopped the car and came around with the gun. He backed Arkasha against that wall and ..." Nowek stopped talking. His breath wouldn't come. His heart tried to hammer its way through his ribs. He looked at the dark spray of blood, the pitted brick, remembering the flame, the thunder. "I started to run. Gavril pointed the gun at me and ..."

"You ran at a man with a loaded shotgun?"

"I wasn't thinking. Then I saw Volsky grab the barrel and ..."

"Volsky was dead."

"He was alive. That's why he shot him again. Gavril dropped the gun and ran. There was a GAI patrol," he said, meaning a car belonging to Moscow's traffic police. "I thought they were coming to help, but he jumped in. Why aren't you hunting for them?"

"So now the police are accomplices to murder?"

"Why bother to ask? You already know the answer."

The sergeant kicked Nowek backward into the wet snow.

"I'll tell you what *else* I know, citizen Nowek. We aren't looking for Gavril because we know exactly where he is. We found him where you left him in an alley with his throat cut so badly his head came off when we picked him up off the street."

Nowek struggled to sit. "Gavril is dead?"

"You're the only healthy one left. Here's the gun. Here's the body. Here you are. Everything fits. You're in trouble. You can still help yourself." The pencil was poised next to a final line marked *Confession.* "Is there anything you want to say?"

"If Gavril was already dead, who was driving Volsky around?"

"You."

"I took a cab here from a record shop. The *Melodiya.* The proprietor will remember me. The cabdriver will remember me, too. Nobody let me in through the gate. The security cameras will show that. So how did an amateur assassin end up inside the gates and inside that Chaika?"

The pencil moved away from the last line. "A thorough investigation will answer these questions."

"You're an optimist. The Moscow militia hasn't solved a contract killing in years. Why would you? You'd have to arrest your friends."

The boot lashed out again. It lifted Nowek off the pavement, sending him hard against the Chaika's fender. "As of tonight, your information is out of date," said the sergeant. "You'll be our first."

Another first. He'd ridden in militia cars before, even in prisoner vans. But always in front. Never in back. The locked cage was mustard-yellow fiberglass, windowless, reinforced with wire mesh. It was airless, lightless, cold as a meat locker. The chill did nothing to hide the smell of vomit, urine, the unmistakable rusty odor of blood. His clothes no longer felt wet. Volsky's blood was coagulating into a glue that cemented his pants to his skin.

The walls were slick with condensed breath. It beaded up and dripped as the jeep swayed and jounced its way to the district militia headquarters, and its annex: Gagarinsky Detention Facility 3.

There, Nowek was photographed and X-rayed. He had his blood drawn with a thick needle blunt with use. The bruise on his left leg from the Chaika's fender was lurid and purple. It was duly noted against future prisoner claims of torture. Finally, Nowek was processed into the Preliminary Detention Area.

By law he could be kept in PDA for seventy-two hours. As mayor of Markovo, he'd enforced that law over the objection of the militia. Practically, he knew he'd remain in Gagarinsky 3 until the militia obtained a confession, or someone wanted him moved.

He was escorted down a long flight of concrete stairs decorated with enthusiastic posters. At the top was WHO DOESN'T FULFILL SOVIET LAWS WORKS AGAINST THE PEOPLE! and THE PEOPLE OF THE USSR ARE EQUAL! and farther down, THE PARTY IS THE HONOR OF OUR EPOCH!

At the bottom, nothing had changed in over half a century. Even the air was old. It was a large, bare room of wooden benches, caged incandescent lights, a single armored door. Nowek was led through it to a corridor lined with bars.

"Lend me your boots," came a voice from the darkness. "I'm going in front of the judge! For one day only!"

"Cigarettes? Come on, cookie. Let's make a trade."

"I need your fucking boots!"

"You're in luck," said his escort as he unlocked a cell. "Tonight you have a private room. Tomorrow we'll give you the honeymoon suite." He unfastened Nowek's belt, then unlocked his wrists and pushed him in. The door pulled shut. Nowek could hear the locking bar drop.

Nowek examined his cell. It was larger than the prison van, but not by much. There was a poured slab for a bunk, a foul hole in the floor for a toilet, a single bulb burned overhead behind thick glass. On the wall someone had written in marker pen, TECHNOROCK RULES!

Technorock. Ska. House. Classical. He thought of *Melodiya,* the music shop, Tatiana, her grandfather. The Dvořák A Minor.

Petrov, he thought. Volsky vowed to sell off some of his cache of diamonds. Was that a motive for murder? Volsky had been right. In Russia, a twenty-dollar bill was reason enough.

Nowek replayed the night again and again. The car, the struggle, one flash, another. Volsky had been alive after that first shot. Dying, he'd saved Nowek's life.

Again.

In America, you can call someone you just met your friend. Friendship is harder to earn in Russia, but once kindled it burns for life. Volsky had always lived up to his end of the bargain. And Nowek?

Four years ago Nowek's wife, Nina, was dead, and he

might as well have been. He was numb with grief, sleep-
walking, a zombie. He'd just been fired from his job as a petroleum geologist at the Samotlor fields. He'd caught it in
the neck for daring to speak the truth about the potential
for a catastrophic oil spill that happened just as he said it
would. Being right had doomed him. Volsky invited him
out to hunt eiders. In truth, he wanted to tempt Nowek
back to the world of the living.

A fire crackling in the woods. A cold, still afternoon, the
sun draining away low to the west, more glare than heat.
The smell of snow in the air. A metal flask placed near the
fire to keep the tea inside from freezing. It was silent, as only
the northern taiga can be silent in the grip of deep cold.
And then, the shot.

The dense air carried the shotgun blast up from the lake.
It arrived like a slap. A minute later, Volsky clumped through
a stand of frozen reeds, a gorgeous white eider in one hand,
the shotgun broken over his shoulder. "*This* is what we can
do to them." He tossed the bird to the ground. His breath
puffed white.

There was very little blood, just a pink fringe to the
snowy white neck. The eider had been neatly decapitated.
Nowek said, "Not bad."

"Not bad?" Volsky pulled his own flask from inside his
jacket and toed the eider with his boot. "It's fucking *perfect.*"

Nowek looked at the bird. The long-tipped feathers
were slowly opening like a fan. "That depends on what you
were aiming at."

"What I aim for, I hit." He handed Nowek the bottle.
His eyes had a calmness to them. "Let's talk about you. The
All-Siberian Reform Party is getting organized. We're
looking for candidates." He leaned over. "Your name has

come up for the position of mayor of Markovo. It's an oil town. You have the necessary experience."

"My experience was brief. They fired me."

"People say you're stubborn, that you don't care if you make trouble, only whether something is right."

Nowek unscrewed the top. He tipped it back and drank. Vodka. It was cold, then hot, then good. "Have you considered these might not be compliments?"

"They are to us. To *me*."

Nowek drained the flask and turned it upside down. A crystal droplet appeared, hung, and fell. "You think they'll let me just walk in and win an election?"

"No. We'll fight and *take* it from them. I'll watch your back," said Volsky. "You watch mine. From now to the end. Wherever it leads. Do we have a deal?"

Volsky had lived up to his word, even as his life was draining away into the gutters. And what had Nowek done? He'd dawdled over a Dvořák symphony.

He leaned against the cold prison wall. *I'll watch your back, you watch mine.* Volsky had stood by him, even as he whispered something that made no sense: *Idi . . . k'gorizontu . . . Idi . . .*

A command: *Go to the horizon.* To take up Volsky's cause? His life? Or did he mean the horizon that divided life and death? Maybe it was a place where all that was wrong in this world was made right, all that was crazy made sane. He thought of Galena. If he could send her a message now, what would he say? Stay. Become Gail. Live a normal life. Russia is a madhouse, a psychiatric ward run by the inmates.

Forget horizons. Nowek wasn't going anywhere. He remembered Volsky's *visitka,* his business card, the one with President Boris Yeltsin's phone number. They'd taken it, but he'd memorized it. The code word, too. *Use it if you get into trouble.* Only, what would he say to Yeltsin tonight? *I didn't kill Volsky?*

Nowek leaned back against the cement wall and felt it yield, felt it soften, felt it draw him in. Deeper, falling back through layer on layer. A *buran,* a blizzard, howled overhead as his arms closed around soft white pillows of new snow.

CHAPTER 6

... and Crime

IT WAS THE KIND OF MORNING THAT MADE Major Izrail Levin wish for a real snow. Not a "walking" snow, but a rushing snow, a rioting snow. A snow that buries things and keeps them safely buried. Instead, the bright morning sun had already melted most of last night's flurry, and Moscow's millions of ineptly tuned engines were fast turning what remained a sooty black.

A bus roared by, sending filthy water across Levin's windshield. He cranked down his window and wiped the glass clear by hand. His 1986 Zhiguli was over a decade old and looked twice that. The little car lacked windshield wipers, its body was held together with rust, but its engine always sparked to life no matter what the Siberian winds threw at it, and it was completely self-insured; no car in Moscow dared to tangle with it.

Levin's entire Investigations Directorate was supposed to be driving new Volvos. As government vehicles, they could be imported without the usual tax, which only made them more profitable to steal. It was a matter of market forces. Somewhere between Sweden and Moscow, the cars vanished without leaving so much as a spot of oil behind.

Market forces were in control of Russia now. Not ideology. Not the Kremlin. Not even Levin's own Federal Security Bureau, successor to the once-feared KGB.

Of middling height and more than middling weight, Major Levin had the stout, pugnacious physique of a wrestler whose glory days had receded faster than his appetite. His dark blond hair was turning prematurely silver at the temples. He kept his mustache nicely trimmed. His eyes were as brown as olives.

Levin joined the FSB during a period of reform. That was one strike against him. He was a Jew, which counted for two more. Yet at thirty-three, he was a young, fast-rising officer. Why?

Market forces. In Russia, investigating corruption was a growth industry and Levin had a talent for it. He'd even earned minor fame, and an odd nickname.

Before the great ruble meltdown of 1998 annihilated them, storefront banks dotted Moscow like mushrooms after an autumn rain. Their lure was simple: you handed over all your money and they paid back enormous rates of interest, so long as ever-greater numbers of depositors agreed to hand over *their* money.

Friday's interest payments came out of Thursday's deposits, with the principal going straight to the bank's branch office in Cyprus. A classic pyramid scheme, and Levin was assigned to investigate one with a peculiar name: the Eynabejan Bank.

It was the name that intrigued him. Vaguely Armenian, not quite Caucasian. Was it a village? A lake? It was a puzzle, and eventually he figured it out: *Eynabejan* was

Najebanye backward: Russian for "Fuck You." The baldness of it forced the FSB to act.

One week after Fuck You's board of directors moved en masse to Cyprus, the bank was raided by troops wearing ski masks and carrying machine guns. The Fuck You Bank had left a few accounts behind and Levin stubbornly tracked them down. A few small depositors actually got some money back, and Levin became "Fuck You Levin," a populist hero.

Levin passed the Old Arbat. It might be Sunday morning, but the daily coal miners' rally was getting under way. They'd descended on Moscow from the catastrophically dreary coal cities of the Kuzbass. Their pockets were empty. They vowed to stay put until someone filled them. Levin thought they might as well leave now. The government's pockets were empty, too.

He turned left and entered a maze of small streets whose general trend was in the direction of the Kremlin.

He checked the time. *Almost eleven-twenty.* Would the powerful chairman of the State Diamond Committee be punctual? An even more interesting question: Why send Levin out on a Sunday morning to interview him about a murder that should be in the hands of the militia, a murder with a suspect already in a cell?

The Zhiguli rattled by Manezh Plaza, the mayor's new shopping mall where fat, balding thugs wearing leather by the meter paraded with tall blondes wearing leather by the scrap. In other words, a New Russian sort of place. Here, just one block from Lenin's Tomb, were stores with names like *Eleganza, Prestige.* Even *Vendetta.* The churches might be half-empty, but the shops were filled with customers anxious to buy something, anything, expensive.

There were times Levin missed the Communists.

Levin turned onto Elyenka Street and entered the heart of Moscow's governmental district, all but abandoned for the weekend. The five-story buildings were painted in pastels and soot. The Kremlin walls loomed at the end. Snow still hid in their shadowed cornices.

He steered left onto Ulitsa Razina. The offices of GOKHRAN, the state repository for treasure, were out near the monument commemorating the Battle of Borodino. But beneath this street, buried under ten meters of concrete, reinforced with steel and stiffened with the bones of the men who dug it, was the treasure itself. Here, comfortably close to the Kremlin, safe behind steel doors proof against even a nuclear blast, was the complex of tunnels and vaults known as the Closet.

Built by the Tsars, expanded under the Soviets, the Closet was filled with gold bars, ingots of platinum, carved panels of solid amber, Fabergé eggs, looted art, and heaps of precious stones; a thieves' cave scaled for an empire. Above it stood an ornate masonry building with walls the color of thin tomato soup, the headquarters to the State Diamond Committee.

The building also dated from Tsarist times. The keystones above the north-facing windows still showed the old double eagle. The tall arched panes on the second floor had been ruthlessly bricked over in the interests of security. Steel bars covered most of the main entrance as well as all the first-floor glass. The effect was an elegant old dowager held hostage, blindfolded and gagged.

The parking area in front was chained off. There was a red-striped kiosk for a guard, and a sign warning that deadly force was authorized. Levin pulled up to the chain, rolled down his window, and flashed his official identity card. It carried the red diagonal slash of the FSB. "Major Levin. Investigations Directorate. I'm here to meet Chairman Petrov. Where should I park?"

The guard palmed the ID and trudged back to his kiosk.

Levin straightened his blue tie in the cracked rearview mirror. With the gray suit and denim shirt, it gave him the raffish, *mafiya* look so fashionable in Moscow these days.

Levin had arrived in the first class of recruits following the collapse of the Soviet Union; a period known as the Bakatin Interregnum. Bakatin, the first post-Soviet head of the KGB, splintered the all-powerful security agency into five bite-size services, then handed over total authority to the President. He ordered probes into past misdeeds of the KGB, fired thousands of senior officers and even appointed a close friend of the dissident physicist Sakharov to head the Moscow office.

Those were times when anything seemed possible. Levin had seen the great grim statue of Feliks Derzhinsky, Iron Feliks, founder of the KGB, hauled away to a dump as crowds cheered. He'd stayed long enough to see it remounted in Gorky Park.

Bakatin was first absorbed, then expelled. His reforms followed the same ballistic arc. Levin's Investigations Directorate was abolished, then reestablished. Now only the KGB's name was new. Everything else about it had become, like the Tsarist double eagle, recycled, more familiar.

The guard returned and pointed. "Pull onto the sidewalk down the street and wait."

Levin parked the Zhiguli with two wheels up on the curb. He had to slam the sprung door twice to keep it from falling open.

As he turned, a sapphire-blue Mercedes 600 series glided

soundlessly up to the chain barrier. The guard all but genu-
flected to it as he rushed to pull the stanchions aside.

Levin walked over. Petrov's driver got out. He wore a
dark leather coat that came down to his knees. Levin had
seen the likes of him in those ceramic figurines on sale in
places like Manezh Plaza. They came in collectible sets: the
miniskirted moll, the dark-suited *biznisman,* the leather-
jacketed security bull. The vendors would arrange them in
realistic tableaux, authentic right down to tiny cell phones
glued to the ear.

The back door of the Mercedes swung open. Petrov unfolded his legs and got out. "You're from Goloshev's department?"

Levin nodded. "Major Izrail Levin."

"Petrov. Chairman of the State Diamond Committee."
Petrov was dressed in a long tweed overcoat. Snowy white
cuffs peeked from his wrists. A gold watch. Cuff links.

The businessman. The guard. Levin glanced into the glittering blue Mercedes. *An incomplete set. Where's the blonde?*

Petrov said, "I assume it's about Volsky. You know, I was
with him moments before he was killed. The thief was
caught?"

"What makes you think it was a robbery?"

Petrov gave him a long look, as though measuring Levin's
sanity. "*Ekipazh* is the best club in Moscow and every thief in
the city knows it. Anyone associated with it becomes a natural target."

"You weren't."

"And how would you know?" Petrov didn't wait for an
answer. "What exactly do you want from us, Major?"

"You met with Volsky last night. What was it about?"

"I'm chairman of the State Diamond Committee. We

talked about diamonds. Is that why Goloshev sent you? Or do you have a personal interest?"

"Personal?"

"With a name like Levin you must have a relative in the jewelry trade."

Levin's family had been Russian for centuries, yet in his passport, under *race,* the word *Jewish* appeared. "My father worked at a submarine shipyard. My mother was a surveyor. My personal interest is in the murder of Delegate Volsky. You were one of the last people to see him alive. I have been assigned the case."

"Another mystery. Why should the FSB investigate street crime?"

"The assassination of a high-ranking official is a matter for state security. Sometimes, things work as they should."

Petrov caught the use of the word *sometimes,* and reevaluated Levin accordingly. "You know, I invited him to stay for dinner. It's a tragedy he didn't accept. Who knows what would have happened if he had?"

He would have died with an expensive stomach. "You set up this meeting at your club. Why not here at your office?"

"For Volsky's sake. A person from the regions has no opportunity to experience a place like *Ekipazh.*"

"But is it as safe?"

"*Ekipazh* is like a diamond vault. No one enters without close screening. So far, the club has kept crime outside the gate. But for how long? It makes you think."

"Which thoughts, Mister Chairman?"

"The usual ones. I left only moments before our dear Siberian friend. You say I wasn't a target? Allow me to disagree. These days we're *all* targets. How do you guard yourself from random violence? A bulletproof vest? They'll poison you. An armored car? They'll use rockets. You see what I mean?"

"The driver you assigned to the Siberian Delegate was ambushed and murdered. The killer took the car back through the gate and waited for Volsky. These are not random acts."

"And Gavril was one of our best drivers, too."

Petrov was odd, *Ekipazh* was a crime magnet, but also safe. Volsky's murder was to be expected, but also random. Levin thought of him as an image seen through a pair of binoculars, coming in, then slipping out of, focus. "Who else knew of your meeting with Volsky?"

"We received notification of his arrival from the Presidential Administration, so naturally, they knew. My secretary assigned Volsky a car and driver and booked an appropriate room."

At the Rossiya? "What was the purpose of the meeting?"

"I expected Volsky to make a report on conditions in the diamond zone," said Petrov. "I was wrong. He was after money."

"For the miners?"

"At first I thought so. But when he said money had to appear right then and there, I knew I was facing a more familiar problem."

"Extortion."

Petrov pointed his finger at Levin. "The *exact* word. Unless I paid him off, he threatened to sell Siberian rough diamonds without bothering to send any to Moscow."

Could he do that? "And you refused."

"Naturally. Volsky became quite crude. In his own words, he would tell Moscow to go fuck itself and he would keep the stones."

"What did you tell him?"

"That Siberian diamonds are owned by Russia, not by

Siberia and surely not by *him*. That their sale is a matter of interest in the very highest ranks of power. He became irrational. He grabbed my arm so hard I'm still wearing a bruise. I was an instant away from calling the guards, but I decided to simply leave him with a bottle of vodka. With Siberians, it usually works."

"Could Volsky have carried out his threat to sell the diamonds?"

Now Petrov looked troubled. "We've worked shoulder to shoulder with Kristall ever since they took over the mines from the state. Not one pebble has ever gone astray. But I don't need to tell you that times have changed. Volsky hinted at a 'black' connection in Mirny. Such a person could have had access to diamonds, so I had no choice but to take his threats seriously. My committee has authority over the diamond reserves. If there are problems, they're my responsibility. That's why I ordered an audit of our diamond stocks. The killer. You said he's in custody?"

"The militia arrested Volsky's assistant." But Levin thought, *Amazing.* It usually took an act of God to force a bureaucrat into taking responsibility for anything. Petrov was volunteering.

"So." Petrov's cuff links glittered.

"Are you aware that Volsky made a phone call to the Kremlin a few moments before he was killed?"

Petrov's expression shifted to something like interest. "What about?"

"He asked to have the diamond stockpile sealed and audited. He also asked for the files of a company licensed to import Russian diamonds. A company named Golden Autumn."

"There is no such company," said Petrov. "As for his other request, there's a difference between *sealing* and *auditing*."

"I'm not sure I understand the distinction."

"You audit something when you're suspicious. Sealing is something else, something more like"—Petrov paused, then found the word he was hunting for—"hiding."

"What could Volsky wish to hide?"

"It's an interesting question. Perhaps we'll all find an answer when the audit is complete." Petrov glanced up at the Repository building. "I assume you can be trusted around loose diamonds? Come. We'll walk together." Petrov dismissed the driver.

Levin followed him. "Your car is an unusual color."

"When they made it bulletproof, I had them repaint it the precise color of the Hope Diamond. You've heard of it?"

"Only that it was supposed to be cursed."

"The world's most valuable gem. When they moved it they had armored trucks, troops. A real show of force. Meanwhile, they'd already sent the diamond to its new home. You know how?"

Levin shook his head.

"By mail. In a simple box." Petrov smiled. "The world of diamonds is filled with fascinating stories."

So it seemed. *Volsky asked for records about a diamond company, Golden Autumn. Did it exist? If it didn't, why would Volsky think it did? And if it did, how could Volsky know about it and the chairman of the State Diamond Committee not?*

They walked into a security antechamber big enough for just one person to pass. A fat bureaucrat in a heavy winter coat would be a tight squeeze. Levin handed over his identity documents and keys to a Ministry guard sitting behind thick bulletproof glass.

Petrov walked straight through without stopping. He

motioned Levin toward an elevator. "We're using the sorting area for the audit." The door opened with a rattle.

Levin looked at the stairs. Elevators in old buildings were notoriously unreliable.

"Don't worry," said Petrov. "The elevator's function is absolutely normal."

Levin reluctantly followed him in. *Absolutely normal.* It reminded him of a story. Ivan and Oleg went looking for a place to eat lunch and discovered that the cafés, restaurants, and kiosks were all inexplicably closed. It was lunch hour. The biggest meal of the day, and everything was closed. Complaints could be risky. You never knew who was listening. Ivan shrugged his shoulders and said, "The situation is normal." Not to be outdone in case someone *was* listening, Oleg replied, "The situation is *not* normal. It's *perfect.*"

The elevator came to a stop. Petrov opened the door. The corridor beyond was guarded by another Interior Ministry officer seated at a desk. He smiled a gold-toothed grin at the boss.

Petrov paused at a set of enormous double oak doors. "Have you ever seen half a billion dollars sitting on a table?" With that, he pushed them open.

The room beyond was high-ceilinged and softly lit from a wall of arched windows. The glass block Levin had seen from the street cast a diffuse, but penetrating, glow. Shadowless and powerful, it filled the vast sorting room with a cold clinical light. A dozen women in white laboratory smocks and nurses' headbands were seated at long tables pushed up close to the windows, bent over heaps of colored pebbles. Guards were stationed at a desk with several television monitors. Cameras peered from above.

"In a normal year, two and a half billion dollars' worth of Siberian rough comes through here. Technical diamonds make up two thirds of the carats. Gems, two thirds of the value."

Levin said, "I understand this year hasn't been so normal."

"True. We're battling the diamond cartel for fair treatment. Who will give in first? They say Russia. I say *they* will."

"The cartel is very powerful, isn't it?"

"But they need diamonds. *Our* diamonds. Take a look at those tables, Major." Petrov nodded at the heaped sorting tables. "The stones come from just our Transit Room. We have thirty-three other rooms at the State Repository. Each year, another four million carats of gem diamonds arrive. We're hanging them over London's head. If the cartel doesn't want to be crushed, they'll start buying again and they'll do it at *my* price. Not theirs."

"The diamonds. They're safe here?"

Petrov smiled. "Nothing has disappeared from the Closet in *centuries*. The diamond boxes are verified, then locked away in the Transit Room until the stones can be sorted by color, quality, and size. What you see taking place now. The eye is still best for that work."

"How are the diamonds verified?"

"The stones are sorted in Siberia by Kristall, then packed into containers and sealed. A detailed manifest accompanies them. We check the containers by weight when they arrive. Naturally, we also examine the seals to make sure they're intact. In normal times, the stones are on their way in a matter of a few days. But as you said, this year has not been so normal."

In other words, thought Levin, *nobody knows what's really in the boxes.* "Is it wise to trust Kristall that much?"

"The world of diamonds is *built* on trust, Major. A billion-dollar deal rests on a handshake. It's a tradition. As for Kristall, our relationship goes back many years and not one—"

"Mister Chairman!"

A young man in a suit bustled over with a sheaf of papers.

"My sorting room manager." Petrov leaned over and whispered, "Someone's useless nephew. You know the kind?"

Levin nodded. His office teemed with them.

"So?" Petrov said brusquely. "Have you finished?"

"The weights all match. The seals were intact. We're checking the contents against the manifests now."

Petrov asked, "How much longer?"

"One moment while I check."

"Splendid idea." Petrov turned to the FSB officer. "Come with me, Major. I'll show you something."

The translucent glass panels spilled a cold gray light over the sorting tables. A woman used a tiny rake to sift through the rough diamonds. There were three piles of sparkling gravel before her, each with a paper label: *specials, sizes,* and *smalls.* From each pile, thinner lines radiated containing stones of similar size and color.

Ice clears, yellows, silvery grays, browns, a few startling blues. Some diamonds showed classic crystalline form. Others were flat triangles, or cubic, or even double pyramids joined at their bases. It looked like nothing so much as the colored gravel children put in the bottom of aquariums. It took an effort to remind himself what these pebbles really were, and what they were worth.

"Siberian rough is among the best in the world," said Petrov. "Australia mines more carats, but most of it is junk."

"So many pieces," said Levin, looking over the table with its piles. "I thought diamonds were hard to break."

"Diamonds get their name from the Greek *adamas*. It means *unconquerable*. It's not really true. They're hard, but strike them along a crystal plane and they'll shatter. We learned that the hard way," said Petrov. "Kristall's ore tumblers once used iron balls to help break the ore. But they were breaking *everything*, including the diamonds. Now we treat them more carefully. Like eggs."

Levin had never been so close to something worth so much. Each pebble on the table was worth more than his annual salary.

Petrov reached over and plucked an especially large yellow crystal from the *special* pile. "Go ahead. Take a closer look."

Levin cupped his hand and Petrov dropped the rough diamond into it. It was a big octahedron, though its points were rounded. The color was a brownish yellow, with dark smudges trapped within. It felt like ice, as though some of Siberia remained inside. "It feels cold."

"Atomic density," Petrov explained. "Nothing absorbs heat so well as a diamond. It literally pulls it from your skin, so naturally it feels cold. What do you think? Perhaps your wife would enjoy wearing something like that on her finger?"

"Very big." He handed it back, nervous about dropping it.

"*All* special stones are *big*. But size is not the whole story." He turned to the sorter. "What would *you* say?"

"Strong yellow. Eleven point four carats," the woman said rather mechanically. "Many carbon inclusions."

"In other words, not gem quality," Petrov explained. "A crystal like this is worth no more than ten thousand dollars. If it were a flawless D or E, the same stone would be worth perhaps one million dollars to the right buyer."

"You think Russia will find a buyer soon?"

"Diamonds aren't sausages, Major. They don't go bad."

"Mister Chairman!" the sorting room manager hurried back, his hair plastered to his brow.

"Finally." Petrov turned and held out his hand for the report. He reached into his suit jacket and pulled out a pair of reading glasses. He handed it back to the manager. "This is a listing of technical diamonds. Where are the stones of the highest rank?"

The floor manager looked as though he'd swallowed a diamond, and a big one. "The weights match the manifests...."

"You've haven't counted any gem rough. Why?"

"Mister Chairman ..."

"Well?" said Petrov. "Go finish up and be quick about it."

The manager looked at Petrov, then Levin, then back at the chairman once more. "Sir, the *weights* are all correct. But when we broke the seals and opened the boxes, we found only technical stones. The gem rough ... it's ..." he stammered, "it's gone."

CHAPTER 7

The Buzzard's Egg

LEVIN PULLED THE ZHIGULI UP TO THE LOCKED gates of *Ekipazh* and parked. The street was strewn with sodden trash, some of it vaguely medical. Bandages and wrappers left by ambulance workers still in a hurry. Some empty cigarette boxes. The sleeve to an old vinyl record. How long had that been sitting there?

He thought about the big industrial diamond he'd held back at the Closet. Worth what? Ten thousand dollars? Petrov had dismissed it as mediocre. How much would *a year's* supply of *gem* diamonds be worth? Four million carats. Millions? *Hundreds* of millions? And how had they been siphoned away? A disgruntled miner didn't do it.

Would the head of the State Diamond Committee pick his own pockets? Would the Siberian Delegate make himself rich from Siberia's treasure? They weren't even serious questions.

But why would Petrov be so eager to perform an audit if he already knew the stockpile had been raided? Why would Volsky demand the stocks be sealed and examined? They both should be on some warm, secluded island that lacked an extradition treaty, drinking tea with the board of directors of the Fuck You Bank. Anywhere but Moscow.

He paced the length of the narrow street to where the brick wall was gouged and blasted by buckshot. The red surface was pocked with craters. Lead beads could still be seen in them. Pellets that had rocketed through the Siberian Delegate's chest. Their spread was remarkably small. The gun had been fired at zero range. He faced the gate.

Petrov's driver, Gavril, murdered three blocks away. Had he driven away from *Ekipazh* after dropping Volsky off? Parked by an alley to smoke? Met Volsky's aide Nowek? Then Nowek cut his throat and drove back through those locked gates. Who let him back in? A guard would pay more attention to the car than the driver. Who would inconvenience the occupants of a new Mercedes? But a *Chaika*? The guards should have met it with pistols drawn.

A lot of questions. There had to be a camera record that would provide some answers. He walked back to the fence and stared across the empty courtyard. He saw a camera in a hooded box above the club's front door.

Levin quickly found three more. One was mounted on the corner of a building across the street, another tucked beneath a streetlight fixture. The last was just a small glass porthole beside the brass call button outside the gate. As he looked into its eye, he saw the optics within shift, focus. He was being watched.

He pressed the button.

"What do you want?" the speaker squawked.

"Major Levin. FSB. General Goloshev's department."

"Documents."

He held up his card to the tiny eye. It focused in, then back.

There was a pause, and then the gate began to open.

The front door was already buzzing when he reached for the polished handle. Inside was a corridor, a desk, a metal detector, and a guard sitting in front of a television screen. Multiple switches allowed him to select different views, different cameras, and a joystick permitted him to pan the cameras at will.

The door closed behind him with a solid clank. Levin noticed a video recorder and a bookshelf of videotapes, all carefully labeled, and one unmarked cassette on the desk.

"Here." The guard pushed the videotape forward. "Take it."

First Petrov taking responsibility. Now a guard offering important evidence. Neither one had demanded a bribe to do the right thing. What was Russia coming to? "Thank you for your cooperation."

"The general already sent his thanks." The guard smiled slyly. "The militia wanted it too. I slipped some hot stuff into a blank case and gave it to them instead."

"Hot?"

"German," said the guard. "Women with men, women with dogs. Levin. I've heard your name somewhere."

"I doubt it. About the tape. That was good thinking."

"Be sure to tell Goloshev. Do they still call him the Toad?"

Levin slipped the tape into his coat. "Still."

LEVIN DROVE DOWN Vladmirova Street, noting that a line had already formed outside *Na Skoruyu Ryku,* "At the Quick Hand." It was a Russian version of a fast-food restaurant, a small, stand-up café where the city's best borscht was made. Levin made a mental note to stop there on his way home.

Why shouldn't Goloshev ask for the tape? Goloshev was leading the FSB's investigation into Volsky's murder. And it made sense to keep the tape away from the militia. They were hopeless clowns. The only killer they'd bothered to catch and arrest in years was Volsky's aide, and he'd been standing next to the body, covered in blood, a shotgun at his feet. All Nowek lacked was a union card from the Society of Amateur Assassins.

Petrov's quick audit. Goloshev's quick request for the security video. Intelligent, responsible steps. Normal in any rational place. Only in Russia was normal suspect.

He turned off Bolshaya Lubyanka onto Furkasovky Perelok.

The entrance to the FSB's underground parking garage was an unmarked arch set into the gray Lubyanka Annex. He swung off the street and down the long ramp to the garage level beneath the street.

Beyond a single concrete wall was the basement of the old Lubyanka Prison, the last stop for untold thousands of doomed men and women. The lucky ones would be taken out to the Moscow River, a pistol put to their heads and shot. The unlucky ones went east to where the tracks ran out and the snows began.

Levin parked and walked to the elevators. They were guarded by two sentries in plain clothes. Levin showed his pass and was allowed through. He pressed five, and with a lurch and a whine, the cab began to rise. A charred smell filled the air. A fire had broken out two years ago, and it still smelled like a burning chemical dump.

A lieutenant "guarded" the fifth-floor hallway. Sherbakov, Levin's assistant, had the duty for the weekend. A newspaper was open on the desk. Friday's *Moskovsky Komsomolets*.

Sherbakov had tousled red hair, a bony, angular face. He

wore glasses with fashionably small black frames. He loved computers best. He'd lose himself fixing, tweaking a database, improving some program. Levin gave up assigning regular administrative tasks and let him work on an encryption system for electronic mail. At least it was remotely related to his work.

"Anything interesting?" Levin asked him.

Sherbakov showed Levin the big headline: COMMERCIAL DIRECTOR ALMOST SLAIN!

It was the *almost* that Levin found compelling. The subtitle, BUSINESSMAN CATCHES BULLET WITH HIS TEETH, was even better. Of course, there were so many contract killings these days that every conceivable statistical probability was taking place. A victim catching a bullet in his teeth? Why not? "Here," he said, tossing the videotape to him. "Make a copy and send the original up to General Goloshev."

"What format is it in?"

"How should I know? It's from a security system."

"It could be PAL, VHS, even something like . . ."

"Whatever's normal." Levin could see the disappointment on Sherbakov's face, but he was not going to get drawn into a technical discussion of videotape formats. "How's the e-mail project coming?"

Sherbakov brightened. "Still a few bugs. Sometimes it works perfectly, sometimes it crashes. I'm hunting for the glitch."

"You think you'll find it?"

Sherbakov looked offended. "It's a *computer*, Major. I've got a *killer* name for it, too: *KGB*. As in, *Let KGB keep your secrets!* What do you think?"

"Don't take forever about the tape." Levin rode the elevator up another two floors, where Goloshev's private secretary, a plush blonde of about forty, escorted him down a long corridor. She had the short, overripe shape of a carved fertility fetish. Levin imagined her in *Soviet Agriculture*, Miss Kolkhoz, 1985.

She knocked on Goloshev's door. There was a grunt from the far side. She opened it. Levin tugged at his tie to straighten it, then walked into General Goloshev's office.

"We have a real buzzard's egg, Levin. It started small and hatched into something big and ugly. Sit."

The air was hazy with cigarette smoke. At least it made the char smell easier to ignore. Levin pulled a wooden chair over.

General Goloshev sat a conference table covered in crimson baize. He was short and fat. His white shirt was stained yellow with sweat. His heavy winter uniform jacket was draped across the back of his chair. He had loose jowls, a neckless neck, and small, suspicious eyes. The young officers called him the Toad, though not too loudly.

Levin thought of him as one of those desert amphibians that digs into the sand and waits decades for the rains. Goloshev had dug himself deep during the FSB's brief flirtation with reforms. Now that the old ways were back in style, the rains had returned and the Toad was free to croak again.

"So?" said Goloshev. "How did Petrov seem to you?"

"Worried."

"He won't have anything to worry about if those stones aren't recovered. His neck is on the block."

Levin thought, *We're not going to protect him?*

Goloshev lit another cigarette, sat back, and sent a long stream of smoke jetting at a picture of Brezhnev. "How many diamonds are missing?"

"One year's supply of gem rough. Four million carats." He thought of the glittering piles in the sorting room. "It's got to represent billions of rubles."

"That's just the beginning." Goloshev tapped ash into a

red ceramic tray. "And his meeting with Volsky? What was it about?"

The beginning? "Petrov expected a report on conditions in the diamond zone. Instead, Volsky threatened to stop shipping diamonds to the State Committee unless payments were made."

"Typical." He sucked down the last of the cigarette. "Then?"

"Petrov turned him down and left. Volsky followed a few minutes later. He was shot by someone posing as his driver. Possibly Volsky's own aide."

"Also typical. What about the real driver?"

"Already dead. His body was dumped three blocks away. The murder weapon was a Baikal 27 shotgun. No ID."

"Again, no surprises." Goloshev toyed with a pencil. "What about the audit? Why did Petrov perform one?"

"He was worried that Volsky's threats to siphon diamonds off directly from the mine might be real. The Siberian Delegate had a connection there."

"We'll have to find Volsky's man, of course. Now let me ask you. Do you think Petrov is guilty?"

"He's guilty of trusting Kristall too far. He's been accepting boxes of stones for a year without bothering to look inside them."

Goloshev nodded gravely. "Kristall. Volsky. Inside connections. All these fucking *Siberians*. Petrov trusted Kristall too far all right. As for Volsky, he did everything but admit his guilt. There's the matter of offshore accounts."

"Petrov's?"

"*Volsky's.* He met with a foreign lawyer at *Ekipazh*. His card was found on the body. We've interviewed him and learned that he managed accounts in the Cayman Islands in Volsky's name."

So Volsky was dirty. It wasn't exactly a distinguishing characteristic these days. "Then who ordered the killing?"

"Whoever was taking the stones. Volsky was going to ruin things with his demands. Bang. What's one corpse in this city?"

Levin thought, a threat. A foreign lawyer's confession. A killer dispatched from the wild east. It wasn't proof, but it was believable. "Has the foreign lawyer been detained?"

"It's better. He's cooperating."

"Then we should be able to recover Volsky's account."

"Dust." Goloshev opened a file folder. "Volsky tore a billion-dollar hole in the state's pockets and we don't have much time to mend it. Two weeks, actually."

"You said a *billion*?"

"*Fourteen* billion, fourteen days," said Goloshev. "The International Monetary Fund is supposed to send us a loan next month. Before, they trusted us to use their money correctly. Now they're playing a more political game."

Too late. "What's the connection to the missing diamonds?"

"The IMF demanded the new loan be secured with something real, something valuable. Something like . . ."

"Diamonds?"

Goloshev squinted as though Levin had switched on a bright light. "You'd think our President would *look* at the Closet before he pledged it. But no. He does things his own way, and we'll all have to live with it. Two weeks from tomorrow, the IMF arrives. Do I need to spell out why they must not find the Closet empty?"

No. It would be another August 1998. Another ruble meltdown. Could Russia survive a second blow like that? Levin had his doubts. "But the Closet isn't empty. Petrov said there were another thirty-three rooms filled with diamonds."

"What do you think Russia has been living on since 1998? They're empty, Levin. That's why the world must never learn these four million carats are missing."

"But they *are* missing, General."

"*We* know it. *They* don't. We must proceed quickly to recover them. Petrov's pointing his finger at Siberia. He's probably right."

"There's just one thing that doesn't fit."

Goloshev raised his eyebrows. "Well?"

"Volsky made a call to the Kremlin before he was killed. He requested the records for an American company licensed to import Siberian diamonds. Petrov told me it doesn't exist."

"He would know, wouldn't he?"

"Then why would Volsky demand its records? If Volsky was trying to cover his tracks, and those tracks lead to America, we could contact the FBI for help. They have a Moscow office now and . . ."

"No. American assistance means American interference. Think. The IMF is located in Washington. So is the FBI. You want to tell one hand what must be kept secret from the other? There must be *no* mention of the missing stones to *anyone*. Especially not to any Americans. I hope that's completely understood."

"Yes." But he thought, *Well, no.* If someone was sending diamonds to America, wasn't it wise to find out who? "Then we're left with Volsky's aide."

"Keep me informed."

"Yes, sir." He'd been dismissed. Levin was out in the hall again and stopped. He'd forgotten to mention the tape.

CHAPTER 8

The Evidence

LEVIN PARKED THE ZHIGULI IN AN OPEN-SIDED metal shed behind his apartment house. He grabbed the copied security videotape from the seat, the Styrofoam container of borscht from *Na Skoruyu Ryku*, and slammed the door shut.

Another 1998. Levin remembered August of that year only too well. The IMF turning its back to Russia, the wild scramble to withdraw money from banks already emptied by those in the know. The equally mad rush of foreigners to the airport, willing to buy a ticket to anywhere, at any price. The "young reformers" who'd steered the economy to a cliff and then, with an almost drugged stoicism, driven it over the edge.

True, things were different now. Russia owed the IMF billions. They might not wish to see their biggest debtor collapse. If Russia went down, it might take the IMF along.

It was a curious kind of hope.

The back door to his five-story building was protected by two heavy locks and thick steel-plate bearing marks from an arms factory. Levin was amazed the weight didn't pull the door off its hinges. Maybe they were tank hinges.

Inside, the entry was cold and dark. The floor was made from yellow-and-black linoleum, cracked and peeling, gritty with decades of dirt. Light came down from a single fixture up on the third floor. His own floor. His own bulb, too, scavenged from his office. He trudged up the stairs. He could pick out the odors of boiling cabbage, sizzling oil, the heavy smell of lamb.

The building had once been a *kommunalka,* a dingy warren of rooms overcrowded with people and underequipped with plumbing. A contractor had converted it to separate apartments, two to a floor, though the walls were so thin they only suggested privacy. Noises and smells were still community property.

His door was covered with sheet metal bought at an open stall at the building materials market at Kashky Dvor. The bazaar was patrolled by police and run by the Solntsevo *mafiya,* who made sure the goods were the best, and the customer always left happy. It was better than a government seal of approval.

As he grabbed the doorknob, he heard a heavy thump.

"Sasha?"

He opened the door and reached in to feel for the light. He heard a second thump, this time from the small bedroom. He toggled the switch on.

It wasn't the elaborate lair of a New Russian *biznisman.* But it had come a long way from its days as a bleak communal flat. There was a sofa, a low table, a cabinet with a good stereo, a Sony television. The kitchen held pots and dishes, neatly stacked.

And on the floor, a corpse. A tangle of shredded flesh, a protruding bone, strips of metal foil, a spreading stain.

"*Sasha!*"

The basset hound poked a nose from Levin's bedroom. His tail thumped against the wall.

"What have you done!"

The thumping slowed.

Once, the corpse had been a roast chicken. Levin examined the body with a forensic eye, and concluded there was more to this crime. He placed the container of borscht on the counter, tossed the security tape from *Ekipazh* onto the table, and looked into his bedroom.

Bones littered the floor. The blanket was splotched with grease. He heard a thump from beneath the bed. "Stay there all night," he said, and left to assemble dinner. It was amazing, when you thought about it. If Levin shared his flat with a person who behaved like this, he'd have him arrested.

Soon, Levin was on the sofa with crackers, cheese, sliced sausage, and a container of borscht. He drank it straight from the cup. Levin picked up the remote control. The television hummed to life. Next, the VCR. The screen glowed blue. He hit play.

A snout intruded in the space between the back of his knee and the sofa, pushing at his leg.

"You're out of prison, but you're still on probation."

Sasha leaped onto the cushion and curled against Levin.

The blue screen went black.

It was the gated entry to *Ekipazh*. The tape was stop-action, the movements jerky, sudden. A small split screen showed a second view taken from a camera Levin hadn't noticed that afternoon. One mounted low, meant to record license plates.

The soundless scene had a dreamlike quality, or perhaps a nightmarish one, since Levin knew what was going to happen.

A lumbering black Chaika appeared in the wide-angle view. The close-up showed an official license plate. The wide-angle shot narrowed to examine the face of the driver,

Gavril. The time was shown in small white numbers at the bottom right of the screen.

Where's Nowek? He wasn't in the car. He hadn't arrived with Volsky, unless he was hiding from the camera.

The basset edged closer to the dinner plate, stretched.

Several more arrivals were recorded, the cars, and the people in them, conforming absolutely to type: *BMW. BMW. Lincoln. Jeep. Mercedes.* Inside each, a New Russian and his expensive girlfriend.

Levin sped through them, then stopped and backed up. A difference. A black Land Rover, tall on its suspension, ready to prowl the Moscow savanna. Inside, a different face. Not Nowek. A foreigner. Levin could tell without knowing how he knew. Maybe it was the lawyer Goloshev mentioned? He jotted down the plate number and let the tape run again.

An empty stretch of tape, a street slowly turning white with snow, and then, the Land Rover. This time, leaving. He checked the elapsed time. Five minutes. It wasn't much of a stay at the fanciest club in Moscow. Perhaps a drop off? The tape rolled on.

Chairman Petrov's Mercedes hurried out through the gates. If the IMF wanted some *real* collateral, the government could seize every official Mercedes in the fleet.

Seven minutes later, a small car turned down the snowy lane. A cab. It left dark tracks in the street. It stopped a respectful distance from the gate. The back door opened.

Levin leaned forward. The security camera didn't zoom. It didn't pan. It didn't budge. It had become a fixed, dead eye. Where were the guards?

A figure approached the gate. He was carrying something under his arm. A newspaper? Levin paused the tape. *Nowek.*

He let the tape run. The low camera recorded Nowek's legs. The main screen showed the cab backing away, disappearing down the street, hopping from frame to frame like a flea.

One second, two. Levin was about to press fast-forward when something black hurtled through the low camera's field of view. A black Chaika skidded into view across the small, split screen. Halfway down the lane it slammed into the curb and came to a stop. A person jumped out, then fell. The nightmare accelerated. The driver emerged carrying a shotgun.

Levin held his breath, not even blinking his eyes. One moment Volsky was halfway to his feet. The next, a white flash, a mist expanding from Volsky's body. The next frame, and the Siberian Delegate was down, the gunman standing over him. There was Nowek, running. The weapon rose. Volsky stirred. The barrel pointed back down. Levin watched. Another frame, another flash, another gray cloud streaked with white.

The killer dropped the weapon and ran down the lane. A militia patrol car appeared. He got in. The car vanished.

Nowek held Volsky in his arms. There he remained until the flash of another militia car made him raise his head.

Levin stopped the tape. There had been just two departures since Volsky arrived: Petrov, and the Land Rover. Gavril, the driver found knifed a few blocks away, had to have been in one of them.

He stared at the screen. He didn't know about the lost diamonds, or Volsky's role in their disappearance, or what Golden Autumn might be, if anything at all. But the man the militia arrested for his murder hadn't pulled the trigger.

Levin reached for another cracker. He looked down. "*Sasha!*" The plate was empty. The basset hound was gone.

CHAPTER 9

The Resurrection

NOWEK KNEW WHAT WAS COMING, BUT IT WAS still terrifying. Unlike other, simpler nightmares, this one had been real.

It was two years ago, the second warm night of spring. Winter was dying, and mounds of plowed snow had congealed into rock-hard ice that blocked the gutters and drains. The streets flooded, overflowing onto the sidewalks. It was the small town of Markovo, down by the River Lena, in the rundown industrial district called the Black Lung. He was still Mayor Nowek, not that it meant much. Clearly, the man trying to kill him was unimpressed.

The water was numbingly cold. Nowek scrambled to rise, but then something slammed against his head and he was under. Gelatinous bubbles streamed from his lips, his nose. Nowek managed to get a hand beneath him. He clawed at the boot on his chest. Struggling only used up his air faster.

The puddle was barely half a meter deep. Not much compared with Lake Baikal, or the River Lena, or even a bathtub. But plenty enough to drown in.

One minute, maybe two. How long can you hold your breath? There are scientific terms for what is about to happen, but what it comes to is this: a desperate brain steps up to the roulette wheel and plays the odds. Open your mouth and you might die, keep it shut and you *will*. And so there's just one last bet to make, and it's almost never a good one.

An involuntary gasp. A slug of water rushed down Nowek's throat. It filled his chest with cold weight. He tried to spit it out. More water flooded in. The gag reflex was uncontrollable. With each spasm, his lungs grew heavier, colder. He was drowning. His ears roared. His forehead burned.

Nowek woke with a gasp, his face soaking wet with *real* water. He panicked. His heart stumbled. The harsh glare of a white bulb burning behind heavy glass poured down into his eyes. Gray concrete everywhere. Ceiling. Floor. Walls. A black scrawl: TECHNOROCK RULES! A cell. His. He looked up. A militiaman held an empty bucket. A single drop formed at the lip, quivered, fell.

"Impossible." A voice from out in the hall. "He belongs to us."

"Not anymore. Here."

"So what? It's our prison."

"I don't want your prison. I'm taking your prisoner."

A pause, then "Major Levin, it's not even nine o'clock. Contract Murders hasn't talked to him yet."

"They can talk to him at the Lubyanka. We're taking Nowek to our P-4 facility. Maybe you've heard of it."

"Never."

"Let's just say that when something sinks to P-4, it never rises. You can come and see it yourself if you'd like. I'll give you a private tour."

Nowek listened for an answer.

"On your feet." A boot prodded Nowek.

Major Levin. Nowek burned the name into his memory, husbanding the information. *And from the Lubyanka.* That made Levin FSB, or whatever they were calling themselves this week.

A youngish man with stylishly long blond hair, dark eyes, and a dark mustache appeared at the door. He was dressed in a suit, but no tie. He looked at Nowek. "Okay? Let's go."

Nowek's pants were brown with dried blood. It flaked off as he bent a knee to stand. He held his hands out in front and the militiaman snapped the heavy cuffs back on. Nowek's leg ached badly. He could scarcely put weight on it.

"What happened to his leg?" asked Levin.

"We didn't do it."

As Nowek limped down the corridor, a prisoner grabbed the bars with both hands and thrust his face, his tongue, his lips, into the gap. "Give me your boots, cookie. You won't need them now."

The militia sergeant waited at the stairs. He tossed a sheaf of official-looking papers at Nowek.

He stopped. Was he supposed to pick them up?

"Keep moving. You belong to Major Yid now."

Two militiamen in winter greatcoats waited at the top of the stairs. One carried a leather-wrapped truncheon, a *demokratizer,* sent by a police organization in America. Who said humor was dead?

The front door to Gagarinsky Detention Facility 3 opened, and Nowek caught sight of the street beyond. He stopped, staring. The normal world. One day in Gagarinsky 3 and he'd already lost his sense of connection to it.

The snow was gone. Monday morning traffic choked the streets. It was warm enough to smell the rankness coming from the back of an open prisoner van. Its blue lights flashed. A small white car, a Zhiguli, was parked in front of it. A thin young man with unruly red hair sat in front.

Nowek paused, savoring the normal world, the light, the air. What was P-4, if not a hole in the world?

"What are you looking at?" one of the militiamen asked.

"The snow is gone. It's not winter yet."

"The flowers will be out before you see daylight again."

HOW LONG WAS THE TRIP from Gagarinsky to the Lubyanka? Long enough to recall Volsky's words shouted from the shower, to remember Galena's message waiting for him at the music store *Melodiya,* to hear the music rising from an ancient LP. The blast of a shotgun, and words whispered through melting snow and blood.

Idi k'gorizontu . . . Go to the horizon.

Once, Nowek had been a geologist. A geologist is accustomed to chaos, to fragments. The world is like an old building remodeled so many times that nothing makes any sense. The basement is on top, the windows are in the floor, the attic is buried below your feet. A geologist looks at chaos, at nothing. But sometimes if he looks long enough, chaos becomes order, nothing becomes something.

But not all the time. A well-ordered life, a friend, an obligation, meaning, hope. Try putting those pieces back together. Stare all you like. A life can shatter and stay shattered.

The van tipped down. Soon, it came to a stop. The door opened. They were in an underground garage.

The young red-haired officer was carrying a suitcase. Nowek recognized it as his own. His possessions. They really were going to make him vanish down the hole of

P-4. What would his daughter say when she found out her father no longer existed?

Levin joined them. "You can walk?"

"Yes." But then Nowek put too much weight on his injured leg and almost fell. The FSB major helped him to the elevator bank. Nowek scanned the buttons. They were at P-1. The last button at the bottom was labeled P-4.

"My name is Major Levin. I'm with the FSB Directorate of Investigations."

"Levin's not a name I would expect to hear in the Lubyanka," said Nowek. "At least, not on this side of the bars."

"Times have changed. Nowek is also an unusual name. It's Polish?"

"Siberian."

"That used to be the same as Russian."

"Only in Moscow."

Levin raised his eyebrows, then nodded at his colleague. "This is Lieutenant Sherbakov. Give him your hands, please."

Nowek held the cuffs up, and watched in astonishment as Sherbakov unlocked them and took the heavy steel rings off.

Levin pressed five. The elevator began to rise.

"We're not going to P-4?"

"P-4 is dead records storage." He nodded at Nowek's suitcase. "Nothing is missing. You can check."

Floor three. Sherbakov handed him his suitcase. "I hope you don't mind. I drove your machine around the block a few times," he said. "It's a Pentium. Where did you get it?"

"A friend gave it to me."

"You want to sell?"

Sell? It seemed like an odd question to ask a man whose wrists were still red with cuff marks. "Am I under arrest?"

Sherbakov was about to answer, but Levin spoke first.

"That depends."

Nowek opened his suitcase. It was intact. Fresh pants, a shirt. His shoes, the laptop computer Sherbakov had admired. He looked at Levin. "Why did you take me away from the militia?"

"You're innocent, aren't you?"

"When did that make a difference here?"

Levin smiled. "We'll discuss the details of your situation after you change."

Nowek felt certain they would. The FSB didn't rescue accused murderers out of kindness. Were they trying to reassure him into a confession? "I didn't kill Volsky."

"We know that."

Nowek waited, and when there was no amplification, he said, "You *know*?"

The elevator stopped. The doors opened onto a hallway. No one moved. Finally, Nowek said, "Then I'm free to go?"

"That also depends. The washroom's the second door on the right," said Levin.

A lot of things seemed to depend on something, but what? Nowek went in. Sherbakov followed. Nowek walked to the window.

"You could speed up the machine if you partitioned your hard drive," Sherbakov said. "And don't stand too close to the window."

"Don't worry. I won't jump." Nowek let the tap run hot, and scrubbed the crusted blood from his hands, from beneath his fingernails, from his cheeks. The white porcelain swirled with Volsky's blood. It ran dark, then pale, then fainter, then clear.

"If you did, it would be much more efficient."

Nowek looked up into the small mirror. "If I jumped?"

"If you partitioned your drive. I could do it. Programs here, files there. I could make it really *scream*."

It was an odd thing to say in the Lubyanka, where experts in screams had always found work. Sometimes he missed the old days when irony still had a purpose, when it still had a bite, when the world was terrible, but at least it made sense.

Nowek piled the bloodstained clothes on the floor tiles. He kicked them away and put on fresh pants, a clean shirt, socks, his Nikes. The air was deliciously steamy. He smelled cleaner. His leg was purple with bruises. It throbbed, but he could walk. He was innocent. He was free, but not too free. It all depended.

Sherbakov knocked, then opened Levin's door. He didn't follow Nowek in.

Levin had a small office with one window facing a broad, open square. On the far side, Nowek spotted *Detsky Mir*. The world's largest toy store. Levin sat behind a cluttered desk. Two file cabinets, one gray, the other black. A picture of an old woman hugging Levin was mounted on the wall. Her face was radiant with unabashed pride. There was a plastic dog with a pivoting whip of a tail on his desk. Levin motioned for Nowek to sit. Two files were open on his desk.

Nowek could see a photo clipped to the one on top. His.

"This is your first visit to Moscow in some time," said Levin.

"I try to avoid it."

"The file says the last time you were here was when the Oil and Gas Ministry accused you of selling state secrets to the foreign press. You were fired."

"It was an oil spill, not a secret. I said it would happen and it did. Nothing was sold. A journalist interviewed me. He was doing his job. I thought I was, too. The Oil and Gas Ministry disagreed."

"Butting heads is your pattern." Levin turned a flimsy page, translucent as onion skin. "As mayor of Markovo, you accused high officials of making improper deals with a foreign oil company."

"They weren't in Markovo for oil. I thought they should be."

"Again, removed from your position as mayor."

"The Irkutsk Prosecutor General was removed from his position to a prison cell. He's still there."

"Then, after Markovo, you joined Delegate Volsky's staff." Levin looked closely at something on the page, then up at Nowek. "What amazes me is that every time you get into trouble, powerful people end up in prison and you rise. What's your secret?"

"Sometimes things work the way they should."

Levin peered. *Sometimes things work the way they should.* It was more or less what he'd said to Petrov. Maybe the exact words.

"Now I have a question for you," said Nowek. "If you know I'm innocent, why did you bring me here?"

Levin refocused. "I said you didn't shoot Delegate Volsky. I didn't say you were innocent. You were his colleague."

"And he was my friend. It's not a crime."

"Don't be so sure. You wrote a report for him on mining operations in Mirny."

"Volsky wasn't killed over a report."

"No. Most probably it was over the diamonds themselves. What was your purpose in coming to Moscow?"

The diamonds themselves? "Delegate Volsky was going to meet with Chairman Petrov of the State Diamond Committee."

Levin flipped a flimsy page and pretended to read, letting the silence ripen. Then "To report on conditions in Mirny?"

"Yes, but also to ..." He stopped. He was going to say *force*, but thought better of it. "... to urge Petrov to send money to the miners so they can make it through the winter."

"Maybe he was more interested in the diamonds."

"Arkasha wouldn't know a diamond from a piece of glass." Levin tossed the file to his desk. "You were a geologist."

"A *petroleum* geologist."

"Why did Volsky need diamond production figures?"

"To know how many diamonds Kristall shipped to Moscow so that he would know how much money the miners were owed."

"Four million carats. It's correct, by the way. How did you obtain the figure? It's supposed to be a state secret."

"Only in Russia. The cartel publishes accurate numbers on the Russian diamonds they buy. I found it there."

"You received no help from Volsky's associate in Mirny?"

"No." *Careful.* "I used nothing from Mirny."

"I'm confused. Why would Volsky ask you to hunt for something when he could pick up a phone and find out himself?"

"I don't know."

"He told you nothing about his contact in Mirny?"

"He called him his *colleague*, that time was running out and he'd given his word to bring the miners what they were owed."

Levin shrugged. "Well, even friends keep secrets from one another. Now tell me about Golden Autumn."

"It's already over in Siberia."

"Not the season," said Levin. "The diamond company."

Nowek shook his head. "I've never heard of it."

"Volsky's friend in Mirny has been sending them Siberian diamonds *na lyeva*." Literally, *On the left*. Under the table. "He never mentioned Golden Autumn to you?"

"Volsky had no reason to know about diamond companies."

"Or is it that Volsky had no reason to know of Golden Autumn unless he was helping his colleague sell diamonds?" Levin reached into his desk drawer and pulled out a small tape recorder. He pushed it across the desk. "Hit the play button."

Nowek touched the silver Sony recorder with the tip of one finger, as though an electric current might leap across space and burn him. It was cool to his touch. He saw that a tape was loaded, partially spooled. He touched the play button and the spindles sprang into motion. The original recording was very high quality. His friend's voice was both clear and unmistakable. Each syllable was a blow, straight to the heart.

"I also want a report on an American company licensed to sell Siberian diamonds. It's called Golden Autumn."

"Everything is noted!"

The recording continued, but Nowek wasn't listening.

"Well?" said Levin. "It seems your good friend kept some secrets from you after all. Maybe there are more."

Golden Autumn? "Arkady Volsky had nothing to do with selling diamonds under the table."

"A great many missing stones suggest otherwise." Levin closed Nowek's file. "Kristall ships diamonds to Moscow on a special flight that operates under a regime of maximum security. For the last year, while Chairman Petrov has negotiated with the cartel, these flights have continued."

"What's missing?"

"Volsky threatened Petrov with selling Siberian stones right from the mine unless money appeared on the table. Petrov was worried enough to order an audit. The audit revealed that Mirny's shipments contained only industrial diamonds. Four million carats of gems were never sent. Where did they go? To Volsky? We don't know. But we will."

Four million carats? Nowek let the idea of that percolate. Not a mountain, as Volsky had thought. His weight times eight. Or seven. You could put it all in the back of a small truck. But immensely, dizzyingly, valuable. "Volsky wasn't involved."

"He didn't know about Golden Autumn, either." Levin opened another file, this one with a photo of Volsky clipped to the corner. "You missed his meeting with Petrov, so perhaps you don't know. But Volsky met with a lawyer at *Ekipazh*. A lawyer who specializes in setting up offshore bank accounts."

"Arkasha kept his rubles in a pillow."

"His card was found on Volsky's body. We've talked with him. He's already admitted to managing offshore accounts in Volsky's name. Where did Volsky get the money? Perhaps it's time to face the fact that you didn't know your good friend so well."

Accounts? Nowek replayed Levin's words. Missing stones, overseas accounts, calls to the Kremlin. *Volsky?* Nowek shook his head. "Whatever you're trying to prove, you're wrong."

"Then let me tell you where we're right. You and Volsky worked together. Whatever he's done, people will believe you have also done. I'm giving you a chance to help yourself."

"By proving Arkasha was a diamond thief?"

"Was he?"

"*No!*"

"The Siberian Delegate's pockets were full of unexplained cash. He tried to squeeze the chairman of the State Diamond Committee for more. He met with a representative from an outlaw bank. He made a suspicious call to the Kremlin demanding that incriminating records be placed under his control. A net will be cast and I don't see how you can avoid it. Think about that."

"I have. I'll tell you a story. It happened in my home city of Irkutsk. A truck left a factory one day and took a shortcut across the Angara River instead of driving to the bridge. It's winter, and the ice is usually five meters thick, but sometimes it's thinner, especially near Lake Baikal. The river is deep and the current is swift. Halfway across, the truck broke through."

"What does this have to do with Volsky?"

"I'm coming to that part. Investigators came to find out what was on the truck. They did an inventory. They toured the factory. It was the end of the month. Quota time. A regular panic. The inspectors asked each department, *What did you have on that truck?* By the end of the day they added up everything. It was no wonder it broke through the ice. That truck weighed nine hundred tons. Every department had met its quota and loaded its parts onto it. Nobody could prove otherwise. With the truck sitting on the bottom, the figures were balanced."

"You're saying that because Volsky is dead . . ."

"You'll put four million carats of Siberian gem diamonds in his pockets. No one has to worry. Especially not the real thieves. And speaking of that, what about Petrov? Who *else* knew of Volsky's meeting? Who *else* assigned us a car and a driver? I wonder. Was it Petrov who discovered the diamonds were gone?"

"Of course. But . . ."

"And now Petrov has someone to blame. Someone sitting on the bottom. Someone who will never be able to clear his own name. All the books balance. Life goes on, at least in Moscow."

Levin scowled. "I don't know what will happen to Petrov. But I can tell you that if those diamonds aren't recovered soon, life will *not* go on." Levin stopped. "You have family in Irkutsk?"

"My father lives there."

"Not your daughter?"

"She's not in Irkutsk."

"Why be modest? She's in America. Visas are hard to come by. Volsky obtained one for her, didn't he?"

"They're close. She calls him Uncle Arkasha."

"Did Uncle Arkasha pay for her trip, too?"

"No."

"Travel is expensive. When were *you* last paid?"

"She's staying with a friend."

"Did I say that Golden Autumn is in America, too?"

Levin was piling up building blocks. Stone to stone. Volsky, Nowek, Galena. *No.* "You know, for the first time I'm glad Galena is out of the country. It's comforting."

"Don't be. The Americans would deport her tomorrow if we asked. Don't think that I would hesitate for even one second."

Nowek believed that. "What do you want from me, Major?"

"We know Volsky was planning a trip to the diamond zone. What was the purpose of this visit? To meet with his colleague? Maybe Kristall is a bank run by thieves. Maybe you and Volsky were the only honest men in Siberia. All we can say with certainty is that the Siberian Delegate will not be able to fulfill his plans."

"Plainly."

Levin turned to face Nowek. "But you can go in his place."

"To Mirny? Why should I?"

"To find where the trail of missing diamonds begins. To uncover Volsky's connection at the mine. To learn where the diamonds go and who is responsible for their theft."

"You admit I had nothing to do with Volsky's murder. *I* know Volsky had nothing to do with losing four million carats of diamond. Why shouldn't I just walk out of here?"

"Go." Levin pointed at the door. "The Moscow militia hasn't caught a contract killer in years. You'd never make it to the train station."

"You'd make sure of it."

"I wouldn't have to. Let me suggest an even better reason to go to Mirny. You think Volsky is innocent? You may be the only man left in all of Russia who does. Think of it as an opportunity to prove all of us wrong. It's the kind of work you're best at, I think."

Idi k'gorizontu. Volsky's final words, his last command. Go to the horizon. What more distant horizon was there than Mirny?

Levin leaned forward. "I'm giving you a way to clear the name of your friend. There's no time for deep thinking. There's no time for weighing options. To be frank, you don't have many."

Nowek sat back. "You said life would not go on if the stones aren't recovered. What did you mean?"

Levin tapped the black receiver with a finger, then moved his hand away. "You told me a story of your city? I'll tell you one from mine. Moscow. Do you remember 1998? August?"

The collapse. "Everyone does."

"I was at work that Friday. There were rumors about financial troubles, the ruble would fall, that the rich were getting their money out of the country. But then Yeltsin went on television and promised our savings were safe. The ruble would never be devalued. He said the IMF was sending billions of dollars. Everyone figured Russia might explode in November, but for one weekend we could relax and enjoy the sun."

"I remember."

"On Monday morning, you could still buy a dollar for six rubles. Then, at eleven in the morning, the IMF said it was holding back funds. The Kremlin allowed the ruble to fall. Excuse me. It didn't just fall. It *imploded.* Now it took twenty, thirty rubles to buy a single dollar. The big thieves had all weekend to dump rubles and send their dollars overseas. For everyone else, the story was different. Everything they had vaporized. I went to my own bank. You can probably guess what I found."

"A line?"

"A mob. The doors were open, and people were inside tearing everything apart like animals. Not just the old men and women who'd put their money there for safekeeping. Tellers. Secretaries. Managers. They were taking computers, lamps, lightbulbs. They were prying marble off the walls and pulling the glass from the windows. There was no one to stop them. If anyone had tried, they would have been torn apart, too."

"If I don't go to Mirny, it's going to happen again?"

"The IMF is supposed to send us fourteen billion dollars

next month. This loan is secured by diamonds in the State Repository. They're coming in two weeks to inspect their security. The Closet is empty. The diamonds aren't there."

Good, was Nowek's first thought. Who trusted banks anyway? But then he thought, *What would be left?* A country that was struggling to find its way in the world, a country that might be slowing down like an unwound clock, but was still ticking? Or a pile of smashed gears, snapped springs, rusted wires?

"It's not a matter of helping yourself," said Levin. "Or proving Volsky's innocence. You want to know something? I shouldn't be telling you any of this, but you claim to care about what happens to your country."

Nowek should have found it difficult to trust the word of an FSB major. But he believed Levin. Another mystery. "Two weeks?"

"Two weeks. What's your decision?"

"I would say," said Nowek, "that it depends. If I go, it has to be with the authority of the Siberian Delegate's office."

"Volsky is dead."

"Mirny's the moon. It would be easy to vanish. I'd rather not. Find a way to get me official standing."

"Incredible. You were in a cell an hour ago and now you want to be authorized by the *Kremlin*? Nothing more?"

"Yes. I think Petrov murdered my friend. I want the investigation taken wherever it leads. However big the names. Do I have your word on that?"

Levin tapped the cover sheet of Nowek's file. "If I tell you I will do everything in my power, you'll go to Mirny for us?"

"How far will you go, Major?"

Levin looked out the window. "I can only give you my word that I will pursue it as far as I can." He turned. "Will that do?"

"I wouldn't have believed you if you'd said anything else." Nowek stood. "I'd better start making arrangements."

"We'll take care of your travel to Mirny."

"Not Mirny. Irkutsk," said Nowek. "I'm taking Volsky home."

CHAPTER 10

Barbarian's Hour

"GOLOSHEV." THE VOICE BOOMED WITH AU-
thority and impatience.

"Good afternoon, General. This is—"

"I know your voice, Levin. Is there progress on the diamond front?"

Progress on the diamond front. It had a nice ring. "Nowek
agreed to go to Mirny."

A grunt, then "I was hoping for something substantive."

Like what? A confession? "He didn't shoot Volsky."

"You thought Petrov was white as snow, too."

"Actually, I said he placed too much trust in Kristall."

"Now you put your trust in another Siberian?"

"I'd prefer to let the evidence speak for itself, General."

"I have yet to hear any evidence."

"Chairman Petrov said no Americans were licensed to
import our diamonds. That Golden Autumn didn't exist.
He was wrong."

"How do you know?"

"I spoke with a colleague at the Ministry of Finance.

They have records there on Golden Autumn. Quite a few, actually."

"There must be a dozen companies with that name."

"But only one that imported Russian diamond-cutting machinery to the United States. Only one that received a loan directly from the state treasury. It's why they're so worried."

Goloshev was silent, then "How much of a loan?"

"A deposit was made to the Bank of America last year in the amount of one hundred forty million dollars. So far, nothing has been repaid."

"Who approved it?"

"The request came straight from the Kremlin. General, you asked about evidence. I think *this* is evidence of—"

"Stop." Goloshev took in a deep breath, then let it out. "A good investigator pays attention to more than just evidence. You must remain focused on what is vital. Tell me. What is that?"

"Finding the diamonds and recovering them before the International Monetary Fund representatives arrive."

"*Pravilna.* Suppose this Golden Autumn exists. You'd have to go to America. What are the chances of your finding anything useful in the time we have?"

"It might be difficult."

"Or impossible. And this loan authorized by the Kremlin. Suppose it *does* smell? This will make the IMF want to send *more*?"

"No."

"Exactly. Plow your own fields, Levin. Before you dream of America, remember we have plenty of criminals to track down right here. Volsky. His connection in Mirny. And before you pronounce Nowek innocent, remember that he traveled a long way to meet with Petrov. When the bullets began to fly, where was he? This is also evidence. What did you do to get him to agree to go to Mirny?"

"He wanted official status."

A pause. "From us?"

"No." Levin took a breath, then said, "From the Kremlin."

A longer pause. "This is a joke?"

"No, and I can see his point. Documents signed by the Presidential Administration would give him some protection."

"From whom? If he's worried Volsky's accomplices will throw him down a mine shaft, let him tell us who they are now."

"He says he doesn't know."

"Let me guess. You believed him?"

Yes. "It doesn't matter. Nowek was Volsky's assistant. If Volsky does have a black connection at the mines, it would be only logical for Nowek to come in his place. We'll be there when he does. Even more, if the Kremlin appoints him Delegate *pro tem*, whatever happened would be their responsibility."

"You'd have them appoint one thief to replace another."

"Yes," said Levin. "Exactly."

You could hear the creak and gnash of Goloshev's reluctant gearing. "And if Nowek is just as dirty as Volsky . . ."

"It will cast a shadow on them. Not on us."

"And if by some miracle he's clean . . ."

"We've been absolutely fair."

A final *clank,* and Goloshev chuckled. "You're a devil, Levin. Mind that you watch out who you're being a devil around. When do you leave for Mirny?"

"Sherbakov will travel with Nowek to Irkutsk tomorrow. I'll meet them in Mirny later. I've asked our Irkutsk office to arrange a cover for Sherbakov."

"Why? There are good security people at Kristall."

"What if one of them was Volsky's connection?"

Goloshev grunted an agreement. "All right. What else?"

"I'd like to meet that Cayman Islands lawyer. I want to know how far back his relationship with Volsky goes."

"Leave him to me. You concentrate on Nowek. About the security tape," said Goloshev. "How many copies were made?"

"One. It's in my office safe with the original."

"Who else has seen it?"

"Only the guards at *Ekipazh*. And Sherbakov."

"Don't make too much of it, Levin. The eye is not always the most reliable witness. Stick to Nowek. Don't let him out of your sight." With that, the Toad hung up.

Levin put the phone down and turned to face his window. Across Derzhinsky Square, a man dressed as *Ded Moroz*, Grandfather Frost, braved the chill outside *Detsky Mir* wearing his traditional thin blue robe.

You'd think a Russian would be better dressed for the cold.

AT FIRST NOWEK THOUGHT it was a riot. The street outside the music store *Melodiya* pulsed with young men pushing, shoving, arguing. Above it all, a chorus of raucous female voices blared across the crowd from a pair of giant loudspeakers in the alley next door. They were singing loud and belligerently off-key. The song was as recognizable as it was unexpected.

> *"Great Russia has forged an inviolable union of free republics. Glory to you, homeland! The great, the powerful Soviet Union!"*

The old Soviet anthem elicited images of scarved peasant blondes joyously thrusting pitchforks into hay, of hearty proles wrestling glowing hunks of steel out of forges, of tractors rolling off assembly lines. As Nowek listened, the stirring tune changed into a call to action of a different sort.

"We will, we will, ROCK you!"

The men surged forward. Fists flashed. Bottles sailed through the air and crashed against the wall of what had once been the Soviet Home for Working Artists. It was like watching the turbulent flow of some thick liquid, with eddies of hot violence spinning off into the cold night.

The steaming mass poured into the alley, where the men were pressed together like atoms approaching critical mass. The zone of maximum density occurred at a velvet rope blocked by four bouncers in military fatigues. Behind them, an open door throbbed with heavy bass notes. A sign flashed in English above it all, HUNGRY DUCK.

"We will, we will, ROCK you!"

A roar, and the men at the head were shoved against the ropes.

"Hey *you*!" Someone grabbed Nowek's shoulder with a hard pinch. "Buy me some vodka!"

Nowek turned. The man fastened to his shoulder was already drunk. What more did he want? "What did you say?"

"I want to drink vodka with you!"

Nowek took in the coarseness of his language, the bandit haircut and figured he was a second away from a mugging. Who would he report it to, the militia? "Why should I buy you anything?"

The drunk leaned into Nowek's face. The air was rank with *peregar*. Was there another language that had a word for the smell of alcohol on breath? "I'm *bandity*," he said with a menacing jut of his jaw.

Nowek laughed in his face. "*Bandity* without money?"

The drunk deflated. "I'm just starting out."

"Get lost." Nowek pushed him into the crowd, then made for the music store.

Inside it was quiet as a library. A young man with vivid yellow hair and a glittering violet jewel set into a nostril stood behind the counter.

Bodies slammed hard against the plate glass window. Nowek watched it bend like a fragile bubble. It didn't break. "What's going on?" he asked.

"It's Ladies' Night at the *Utka*."

Utka. The Duck. "Is Tatiana around?" Nowek thought she should be warned. If the militia really wanted him guilty, they would have to deal with any witnesses to his innocence.

"Forget it. She's unconscious."

"What happened to her?"

"She's next door. Ten rubles gets a girl in on Ladies' Night. Then it's free drinks until ten. Half of them are up dancing on the bar tearing their clothes off. The rest are passed out on the floor. At ten, they let the guys in. They call it Barbarian's Hour."

Nowek looked at his watch. Almost ten. He could imagine what would happen. Men drunk with anticipation, add violence and pour into a closed container filled with steamy, semiconscious, half-naked girls. Like two hypergolic liquids, they'd explode on contact. It wasn't a dance club. It was organized rape. Except the girls had paid the equivalent of fifty American cents for the privilege. "I'd like to use one of your computers."

"Take your pick." He waved at the empty cybercafé.

Nowek went over to a table with a small screen. He

tapped in a password, and his free *elektronka* account appeared. He started to type.

> To: Galena Nowek <4tigers@uidaho.edu
> From: Gregori Nowek <gnow@russet.ru
>
> Galena:
> Something huge, something terrible, has happened.
> Your uncle Arkasha is dead. They shot him and he died
> at my knee in Moscow. They're calling him a thief, which
> is ridiculous, but Russia has become a ridiculous place.
> The situation is very complicated. I don't even know
> where the story begins, much less how it might end. But
> I do know this, and it's important: Do not return to
> Irkutsk until I can say that it's safe. If you can arrange
> an extension for your visa at the university that would
> be best. But if you can't, just stay and we'll worry about
> laws later. I leave for Irkutsk tomorrow. I'll send word
> when I can. For now, know that I love you, and that
> Volsky loved us both. I don't know what will happen,
> but thinking of you there, safe, makes it possible for
> me to keep fighting, to keep breathing.
> With all my love,
> Your father.

LEVIN LEFT WORK as the sun flattened into an orange band on the horizon. He maneuvered his wheezy Zhiguli around lumbering electric trams and diesel-spewing buses bursting with people returning to drab, cramped apartments their parents would have had no trouble recognizing.

Lights flashed in his mirror. Levin looked. Here was something that had changed. He moved over to let a large

American car roar by. *Mafiya,* and he wouldn't be alone. *There.* A jeep, so filled with weapons the barrels poked out the windows, appeared, then passed. Only then did Levin move back into the correct lane.

Once, you knew who to be careful around. Now the world was a lot less familiar, a lot more dangerous. The Soviet monolith had been carved up into one hundred and fifty slices, each controlled by its own criminal organization. Moscow alone was home to eight.

The bottom layer of each was occupied by the runners and lackeys. A half step up were the small-time speculators and smugglers who depended on *mafiya* connections for both supply and demand. The third rung made the headlines: the *khuligany,* the hooligans and hitmen who made sure debts were paid on time, troublemakers discouraged and competitors eliminated. At the top were the chiefs, the "Red Barons": district party men, factory managers, ex-KGB officers. Men who combined the power of their old-time Party connections with freelance *mafiya* enforcement.

The various clans were in competition, and their fortunes waxed and waned. Levin had an infallible measure of their status: the Planter's Cheese Ball Index. The imported snacks were wildly popular in Moscow, and so, in short supply. Kiosks that still stocked them were blessed with a reliable supplier. That meant the most powerful *mafiya* clan. You could chart their ups and downs by how scarce Cheese Balls were on its turf.

He came to Kalinin Prospekt. His apartment was to the right. Levin turned left. He was heading for Number 16, a small nineteenth-century mansion that had once been the Moscow branch of the British Merchant's Bank. The Revolution sent the bankers packing, and the small Moorish mansion with its turrets and arches became the House of

Friendship with Peoples of Foreign Countries; a front for supplying Third World revolutions with guns and money.

Then diamonds were discovered in Siberia, and the property was sold to a foreign enterprise: City East West, Ltd. It was a wholly owned subsidiary of the diamond cartel, and like the House of Friendship, it was a front.

The Communists were anathema to the rich capitalists of the diamond cartel. The cartel was anathema to the Communists. It was in everyone's interests that City East West's purpose, the quiet transfer of Siberian rough gems out of Russia and the equally quiet transfer of funds in, remain well cloaked. Two billion dollars in a regular year. In exceptional times, advances three times as large were made against future diamond sales. That was why the Kremlin called the small mansion at Number 16 Kalinin Prospekt the House of Friendship with Currencies of Foreign Countries.

Levin parked in an old tour-bus stop down the street. He shut down the rattling engine and fished out a flashlight from under his seat. He checked the battery. *Weak.* He tapped it against the dash, and the bulb brightened. He got out.

The street was almost deserted. His shoes rasped the gritty sidewalk, as though it were made from sandpaper, not concrete. The mansion had a tall, arched entry. Columns carved in ornate spirals flanked the marble staircase leading up to a pair of wooden doors. Soft light filled ivory curtains drawn across curved windows. There was a small garden to the left of the mansion, fenced in wrought iron with brick piers topped with polished golden globes. He poked the feeble flashlight through the bars.

Four Range Rovers were parked inside, their gray paint black in the fading light. One of them had appeared in the security camera tape taken outside *Ekipazh*. The plate number he'd scribbled down, KZ131, was registered to City East

West, Ltd. He aimed his light at the first Rover's plate: KZ128.

An electric tram rumbled down the street beneath a shower of white-hot sparks. Levin checked the next car. KZ116. He was about to check the third when the tall doors opened, and a light so thick and golden it could be bottled and poured over *blini* spilled down the marble stairs, across the sidewalk, out onto the dirty street, and into Levin's eyes.

"Don't move." A loud voice.

Levin saw two dark figures silhouetted in the doorway. One carried a large bag. He dropped it and ran down the stairs, reaching into his jacket as he came. Levin stepped back and let his hands fall to his sides, trying to look unthreatening.

The guard wore a dark leather aviator's jacket, unzipped, over a pure white shirt. "What are you doing?"

"Wondering how much you have to steal to be able to afford one of these cars."

Levin remembered a writer of the sea describing how a storm wave "picked up his small boat in a giant's fist." This was the same. The guard rushed him, spun him, and slammed him chest-first against the iron bars of the fence. There was nothing to be done about it. Levin was carried along. His flashlight cracked to the sidewalk and went out. The bars were cold against his cheek.

The guard patted Levin down with one hand, quickly, professionally, while pressing the short barrel of a snubnosed pistol deep into his ear.

"*Bandity?*" asked the other man.

Foreign accent. Levin tried to turn to see, but the guard mashed his face back against the cold iron and jammed the barrel halfway to his eardrum.

The guard fished out Levin's wallet and flipped open his identity card. "Police."

"Then let him go, Sergei."

The cold chrome barrel in his ear withdrew. Levin pushed away from the fence, turned, and saw a tall man in a tan raincoat and dark slacks coming down the marble stairs. The light from the open door surrounded his head with an icon's golden halo. His breath flagged white in the chill, dank air. He held out his hand to the guard, took Levin's wallet, and let the streetlight illuminate it.

The foreigner picked through the wallet until he came to a picture of a dog. "Basset. Female?"

"Male," said Levin.

"I used to raise them. Small for a male. What's his name?"

"Sasha. Now that we're friends, how about you?"

He flipped the wallet shut and handed it to Levin. "Eban Hock. Forgive me for taking precautions. It's Moscow. You can't be too careful." Hock fished out a small business card from inside his raincoat and handed Levin his *visitka*, his card.

Eban Hock
Strategic Resources, Ltd.
Lynnwood, Pretoria
South Africa

When he turned, the light from the streetlamp washed across Hock's face. It was the face Levin had seen on that security tape, the foreigner in the Land Rover being ferried through the *Ekipazh* gate. Short sandy hair. The dark tan of a European who spends a lot of time under an African sun. Wide-set eyes. Hock had arrived at the club in one of the two cars Levin had seen leave just before Volsky was murdered. Hock surely wasn't the one to pull the trigger. Was he the one to pay for it? "Just what is your business, Mister Hock?"

"Law enforcement. You and I are alike. The FSB keeps order in Russia? *We* keep order in the world of diamonds." Hock said to the guard, "Get my bag, Sergei. We don't want to be late."

"You're leaving Moscow?"

"You haven't said why you're prowling about."

"One of your vehicles was involved in a crime." *And you were there.*

"I've always thought Moscow was a model of efficiency when it came to law. In London it can take all day to resolve a parking ticket. Here a fine can be paid on the spot. In cash. It's much simpler, really."

"In Moscow, murder is still a little more complicated."

"You must mean Delegate Volsky."

Now it was Levin's turn to register surprise. "Yes, but—"

"I was there the night it happened. I thought the militia already had someone in custody. Am I mistaken?"

Levin was prepared for evasion, for denial. For lies. Not the truth. "*They* were mistaken. What were you doing at *Ekipazh*?"

"I was there for a meeting." Hock checked his watch. "I wish I had more time to talk, Major. But as I said, I do have a plane to catch." He nodded to the guard. A combination was entered into a keypad, and a section of fence began to open.

"In Russia, airlines are subject to all kinds of delays. Weather. Mechanical difficulties. A request from state security. It doesn't take much to keep them on the ground."

Hock looked up and down the street, then at Levin.

"Usually the FSB is noisier when it makes an arrest. Guns. Men in black ski masks. All I see is you."

"Times are hard. We run a leaner operation these days."

"Ah. Then you're looking for money."

"I'm looking for information. Who were you meeting at *Ekipazh*?"

"Yevgeny Petrov. They call him the Prince of Diamonds. The meeting didn't come off. Anything else you'd like to know?"

"Why were you meeting Petrov?"

"Why?" Hock chuckled. "Because your Prince of Diamonds has been breaking the law."

"Why would you care if he broke our laws?"

"Not your laws. *Ours*. Petrov is supposed to be working out a new purchase agreement with London. Instead, he's been selling diamonds hand over fist. Rather a lot of them, too. That makes life difficult for everyone."

Levin had the odd sensation of suddenly being in deep, dangerous waters. One moment your feet are touching sand. The next, there's nothing below. "You were going to tell him to stop?"

"Well, it would be in everyone's interests if he did."

"You mean the cartel's interest."

"The cartel, Russia. The company that mines the diamonds. The miners. Everyone. Diamonds are being leaked to the black market. *Flooded* is more like it. They're bringing world prices down. Not just for the cartel, either. Leaks are bad for everyone and we've traced this one to your Petrov."

"How were you going to stop him?"

"We're not terrorists, if that's what you're getting at. There's no point. In Russia, everything is bought from the top to the bottom dirt cheap. It's always been that way. Even in 1917. When Tsar Nicholas was shot, his diamonds were packed in fourteen cigar boxes and sent to London in exchange for cash, and not very much at that."

"You were going to pay Petrov to stop?"

"Cooperation is our bread and butter. Maybe you and I could find a way to work together, too." Hock opened the tailgate.

"I don't think so, Mister Hock."

"No?" He tossed in his bag.

"Petrov broke your laws. Not Russia's. Petrov's job is to sell Siberian diamonds to the world. Not to the cartel. Unless he's putting them in his pocket. That would be different."

"Not to us." Hock let the tailgate fall with a *thump*. "Maybe when I come back to Moscow, we can meet again."

"You're going to London?"

"No." Hock opened the back door. "I'm going to Mirny."

"Mirny?"

"My client's Kristall. It's their diamonds that have gone missing, after all. You'd better go home, Major Levin. It's getting late. The streets can get dangerous." With that, he got in.

When the car's lights came on, Levin could read the back plate perfectly: KZ131.

HE'S WORKING FOR KRISTALL. Levin turned off Kalinin Prospekt, heading home. *Not Petrov.* Like Levin, the cartel thought Petrov was guilty. But not of the same crime. Petrov had been up to something with Golden Autumn, and whatever that something was, whoever had authorized it, a lot of diamonds were gone. All the cartel cared about was that Petrov was selling the stones to someone *else*. Hock had just confirmed what Levin already suspected. Yet the possibility that he and Hock might be on the same side left him uneasy, left him less sure of what he knew.

It was nine when Levin pulled up and parked the Zhiguli behind his apartment building. His neighborhood was reasonably safe, but Levin preferred to be behind a solid door.

He unlocked his apartment. "Sasha?"

The basset raised his heavy head from the arm of Levin's couch and gazed back soulfully.

Levin held out the collar and leash. "Walk?"

At the word *walk,* the dog bounded to life, tail swinging.

They went down the front stairs, out to the street.

His breath smoked. The wind was raw and sharp. The next time it snowed it would last until April. He let the basset take him on the usual route. Up one side of the narrow street. Across, then back, each lamppost properly anointed. Another tram rumbled by the intersection. The cold ground trembled like struck steel.

He crossed the side street for the last time and headed back. Ahead, two figures hurried in the opposite direction. When they passed under a streetlight, he saw they were dressed in dark pants, dark jackets. Heavy boots. Wool caps. Not a pair of New Russians. They looked like what they were: *Khuligany.* Leaving the scene of a crime, or hurrying to one.

Levin's grip tightened on the leash. He was already thinking how he would describe them to the militia after he handed them his wallet. One was tall, with the thin, hollowed face of a serious drug addict. His arms swung curiously out of rhythm with his steps. The other was short, almost plump. He walked with his arms well out to his sides. They were the cheap *bandity* Levin thought of as "flatheads" for their distinctive, brush-cut hairstyle.

The short one was carrying something. A cane? Levin stepped aside to let them pass.

They didn't. The basset looked up, his back hairs stiff, a low growl issuing from his throat. "Quiet, Sasha. There's a good dog." Levin bent down to reassure him, and unhooked first his collar, then removed his muzzle. "Looking for an address?"

Their only answer was the puffing of their breath.

"Let me suggest another possibility," said Levin. He reached into his jacket for his wallet. "You're thirsty. Maybe you're low on cash. Here." He opened the wallet. "Buy yourselves drinks on me."

The tall, hollow one said, "We don't want kike money."

In other circumstances, Levin might have wondered what made them think he was Jewish. He wasn't wearing a yellow star on his sleeve. But he was paying closer attention to the length of steel reinforcing bar in the short one's grip. It was thick as a thumb, the tip crudely broken and sharp.

He held up his wallet. A whizzing sound, and his hand flew away, stung. The wallet fluttered to the street ignored.

"Stay away from the Closet, Jew," said the tall one.

The Closet? He would have asked, but Sasha lunged and clamped his jaws around the nearest available leg.

It belonged to the tall one. "Fucking dog!" All four of the basset's legs flew off the ground as they spun. Sasha wouldn't let go. They twirled and danced, ears, legs, arms flying. "Fucking *dog!*"

The steel rod rose, stopped, poised. Levin didn't think. He didn't measure. He drove his shoulder into the short one's gut.

They tumbled off the curb together, slammed against a parked truck, tangled, fell. The rod clattered to the street. Levin tried to pin him against the tire, but a bare hand, scarred, decorated with tattoos, wriggled free and stabbed at Levin's eyes.

He jerked his head back. The fingers missed an eye, caught an ear. Warm blood gushed down Levin's cheek. He rolled and made a grab for the rod, but the short one was quicker.

He kicked Levin hard enough to stun him, grabbed the steel and whipped it down across Levin's shoulders.

Levin rolled away, then up onto his knees. He was almost on his feet when the rod caught him squarely in the mouth. His front teeth cracked. Levin felt another warm gush of blood. He fell hard and crawled under the protective bulk of the truck. Let them whip his legs, his back. They'd get tired eventually and he'd be hurt, but alive.

The rod struck methodically, scientifically flaying the coat from his back, his shirt from his skin, his skin into torn, bloody sheets. He heard his attackers' heavy breathing, as though this was hard work to be taken seriously, to be finished properly. He felt himself rise away from the pain. They'd have to stop. They'd have to stop.

It was Sasha that brought him back.

The tall one pulled the dog off by the ears, and swung him hard against a light pole. The basset yelped. A kick and Sasha bellowed, the air was filled with the dog's frantic cries, the thud of boots, of snapping ribs.

It wasn't smart, but he wasn't thinking. Levin crawled out from under the truck and grabbed the tall one's legs. His hands closed around torn pants already slick with blood. A kick flicked Levin away, depositing him on his raw, bloody back.

He looked up into the streetlights, the sky, the stars. He sensed the boot coming too late. It snapped his head back and speared his vision with jagged streaks of light. When it cleared, Levin saw the rod.

It came down like a lance. Instinct threw his arm up. Instinct closed his eyes. But instinct was not enough.

The tip caught the corner of his right eye. It was cold, granular like the frozen sand of a winter beach. Levin wrapped a hand around the shaft and tried to push it away, but with a determined grunt, the thug put his weight behind it.

The rod pushed, the skin stretched inward, then ripped. Levin sensed only a brief, invading pressure before the world dissolved, shattered to jagged pieces. Steel grated on bone. The whole world pulled in around him to what he could feel, what he could hear. A world illuminated by incandescent flashes of pain, punctuated by the rumble of iron tram wheels, echoing like distant thunder.

IRKUTSK, SIBERIA

CHAPTER 11

The Trapper

SENIOR ENGINEER IVAN BEZDOMOV SAT ON the steps of his summer bunker, watching clouds race across the face of a three-quarter moon. The air smelled of winter, wet and heavy. It would snow tonight. Not a blizzard, but enough to stick and stay. That was good, and bad. Good because snow made tracking stray dogs easier. Bad because it meant winter, killing winter, was back.

Across an empty street and beyond the abandoned factory, Bezdomov could see the dark wall of the Irkutsk airport terminal. It might as well be abandoned, too. Nothing moved. Not a single light burned. He might be the last human left alive by some strange, slow-motion apocalypse that left buildings standing and people alive, but stripped them of their normal lives, their everyday dreams, their simple hopes.

Bezdomov's summer house was an old bomb shelter built in the middle of a field of wild grass across from the Irkutsk airport, equipped with rotting bunks and sturdy bombproof doors. But let's call Bezdomov and his home by their real names: He was one step away from being a stone-age hunter living in an unheated cave. He looked at the bricked-up hulk of the old optical plant.

Once, he'd worked there as a senior engineer. Now he trapped stray dogs for their fur and sold their skins at the city's main bazaar. If a fortune-teller had told him he would live like this he'd have laughed in her face. Or killed himself.

He was halfway down the cracked concrete steps into his bunker when a sudden flicker of light made him stop and look back. The moon was gone, but the once-dark airport was ablaze with light: blue lamps outlined the runway, red and green beacons flashed from atop the control tower, brilliant white strobes lit the undersides of the clouds. Lights were expensive. *Some big shot on a tour.* Whoever it was, it had nothing to do with him.

He went down the steps and pulled the blast door shut behind. The bunker was lit by candles. The curved walls were rough, unfinished concrete. The skinning business had been good this season. A lot of dogs had been kicked out of their homes, and more than a few had fallen into his wire snares. Two carcasses, fresh enough to bleed, were on the floor; a black Alsatian and a big husky. The husky was the real prize. Its lush, thick fur banded in black and gray, frosted with silver, would sell as wolf.

If only the bunker were heated, he'd stay here year-round. But it wasn't, and so it was time for Bezdomov to move to his winter den. He left the carcasses. The cold would freeze their meat more reliably than any refrigerator. He slipped a nest of wire snares under his belt, slung the un-cured skins over his shoulder, picked up the candle, and made his way to another hatch set low into the side wall. He climbed through. Ahead lay a hundred-meter tunnel that ran under a field, beneath a road, and into a storage closet in the basement of the old optical plant. *His* building.

The low passage had been well engineered. Half of it was sloped downhill. At the precise midpoint, a floor drain, and then uphill to another, final blast door. He pulled the door in and stepped through.

The brick factory held on to the meager heat of the day. It was still freezing, but a good five degrees warmer inside than out. And he hadn't even turned on the heat. That was next.

In the corner of the storage room, two pipes penetrated the foundation wall, turned ninety degrees, and ran straight up to the floor above. An iron wheel that looked straight off a submarine operated the main shutoff. Bezdomov touched it. Warm.

The factory used to be heated with steam from the central airport system. The boilers were shut off in summer, but now that it was getting cold, the main supply pipes out in the street were filled with steam, free for the taking.

He grabbed the big wheel. It hadn't been touched in a year and so it turned reluctantly, but soon he heard the hiss of pressure coursing through rusted pipes. A bleed valve spat air, then bubbles. The pipes went from cold to warm to hot. Forget airport lights. Free heat in a Siberian winter was the real miracle.

Bezdomov pulled off his heavy rubber boots, put on the warm felt *valenki* he wore inside as slippers and went out into the old shipping area. Candlelight revealed bare brick walls, a set of doors that opened onto the airport ramp, a grimy linoleum floor. He hung the pelts on a pair of metal hooks and started for the stairs that led to the administrative offices, but for the second time tonight, something new, something curious, stopped him.

The old sable trappers up in the Barguzhinsky Mountains could look at a set of marks in the dirt and deduce from it not just an animal, but an entire history. Bezdomov wasn't that good, but he didn't need to be to know that someone had been here.

Two days ago the floor was blanketed in dust, as unmarked as new snow. Tonight it wasn't. They'd tracked grit in from the loading ramp door. How many boots? One pair was too many. And look. *Skid marks.* Something had been dragged, or rolled, to another door that opened onto an equipment storage yard that held wrecked electrical equipment of some kind. Probably with valuable metals, since the yard was fenced with electrified wire. Who had been here? And why?

Bezdomov spotted something small, something white, by the ramp doors. He walked over to it, wary as a deer who has heard the snap of a twig in a forest that should be silent. A small white pouch. Cigarettes? He picked it up carefully, as though it might explode.

The pouch was made of several plies of paper. There was a kind of plastic Ziploc closure at the top. He opened it. No cigarettes. Nothing. He turned it inside out. The inner layer was napped like felt. The outside was woven from something waterproof and tough. The engineer in him wondered what it had been designed to hold. Lenses? Something small, something valuable, surely. Something that needed cushioning. He held up his candle, letting its light shine on some writing at the bottom.

There were three lines of script. The first was easy to decipher: VIGOR. A brand of cigarette? Next a size: **95.3 × 50.8 mm**. Point three? It seemed unnecessarily exact. The final line was a surprise: *gemstone supplies*.

Gemstones? Bezdomov moved the candle to read it better, when he heard the scream of jet engines growing louder, closer. *The big shot,* he thought. He waited for it to pass, but it didn't. Instead, the sound grew to a piercing whine, then fell away to a whisper, right outside the factory wall.

He blew out the candle, stuffed the pouch into his belt, and ran upstairs, taking the steps two at a time. Eight risers. A landing. Eight more. At the next level, Bezdomov stopped and listened. Around him, the building echoed with the thump of filling steam pipes. Inside, his chest hammered, too.

There was a window up in the director's old office. The glass hadn't been washed in a decade, but it was clear enough to see the jet. A short, stubby plane with three engines in back was parked right below. A cargo ramp at the tail descended with the controlled grace of a ballerina flexing a leg, and then a man stomped down to the tarmac. He looked around, then motioned impatiently to someone inside. He had a shotgun over his shoulder.

Bezdomov reached down and touched the handle of the pelt knife he kept in his boot.

A second man emerged from the jet. He guided a large rolling cart down the ramp. Some kind of metal box was strapped down to it like a body going to an autopsy. It didn't seem heavy, but the man moved it so slowly, so carefully, it might be filled with fresh eggs. Together, they rolled the cart toward Bezdomov's building and disappeared beneath the canopy over the door.

He rushed to the stairs and heard the rasp of turning locks, the squeal of reluctant hinges, and a loud, booming voice.

"... boxes. One pebble and we could live like two pashas."

"Or die like two idiots."

"Don't say you've never thought of it."

"Slava, don't even make jokes. You never know."

"Relax. He's not here." The door slammed shut.

But Bezdomov was, not that he had a clue what they were talking about. Pebbles?

"It's fucking cold in this tomb. What time is it?"

"What does it matter? He's never late."

Bezdomov eased back from the stairs, not even breathing. He'd wait them out. Whoever they were, whoever was coming, they would leave. There was no reason for them to stay.

Just then, a bleed valve popped open over the trapper's head with a sharp, loud *clack*.

"What the fuck was that?"

"Wait here." The stairs flashed bright with the beam of a powerful lantern. "Who's up there?"

Bezdomov slipped the pelt knife from his boot. Run or fight? It seemed ridiculous to put a knife up against a shotgun. That left escape. There was another floor above, and a roof. But getting to them meant running in front of whoever it was with the . . .

"Who's there?" the voice called again, louder now. The light shifted. He was coming up the steps.

Bezdomov retreated into the empty director's office. There wasn't even a desk to hide under. Jump out the window? He might be able to smash it with his knife, his fists, and run. The canopy would break his fall and from there it was a short drop to the ground. He thought of all the animals he'd trapped. Simple, tame pets who should have run when they saw the snare, but who let their hunger for fresh meat, their trust in the human race, lure them to their deaths.

Bezdomov had seen the paper pouch. It should have set off an alarm. He should have run back into his tunnel and sealed the blast doors. Instead, the lure of a safe warm haven for the winter had drawn him in. Not to a refuge, but a trap.

He flipped the pelt knife around and smashed it against

the window. The entire pane jumped from its rotted molding and fell out. Bezdomov pulled himself into the eyeless opening. It seemed like a bigger drop than he'd imagined. He looked and thought once, again, and then it was too late. A beam of light caught him.

"Don't turn. Don't even fucking *breathe*. Get back down and drop what's in your hand."

He swayed, the decision to jump draining away second by second, muscle by muscle.

"Do as I say! Now!"

"Please," he said, easing down from the open frame. "It's a mistake. I thought the building was empty. I'll go."

"It's a mistake, all right. Don't make another. Drop the blade *now*."

Bezdomov wasn't brave. If he had been, he'd be living in a flat with people, not in a bomb shelter with dead dogs. His fist opened. The knife clattered to the floor. He heard the one with the shotgun approach from behind and kick the knife away. "I won't cause you any trouble. Please. I used to work here." He thought of the husky he'd trapped. Someone's pet. Used to humans. Used to being taken care of. With his leg snared in Bezdomov's wire, he'd looked up and wagged his tail. Didn't he *know*? It mystified Bezdomov then. Now he understood.

The man with the gun snatched the wire snares from the trapper's belt. "What the fuck are these?"

"For animals."

A snort. "How did you get in?"

"I'll show you. I didn't mean to make things difficult."

"Don't worry. You won't."

From below "Anton?"

"It's a squatter." To Bezdomov he said, "Hands behind you."

Bezdomov did as he was told and felt cold metal around his wrists. His snares! Of all the . . . A kick in the small of his back sent him sprawling. The shotgun barrel pressed against his neck.

Anton searched him. He found his old identity card. A piece of plastic with a picture, a job title. "Senior engineer, eh?"

"That was a long time ago."

"Fucking engineers. What's this?" The paper pouch drew the gunman's interest. "Where did you get it?"

"I saw it on the floor downstairs. When I first came in. I swear I won't, I mean, I didn't think it was . . ."

Anton tapped the back of his skull with the barrel. "You're giving me a headache, Engineer."

In the silence that followed, Bezdomov heard a second jet approaching. The sound of its engines swelled, then died. A few minutes later, he heard the door scrape open downstairs, low voices conferring, then someone called up, "What is it?"

Bezdomov listened. A different voice. Impatient and full of authority. And an accent. Who was it? A foreigner?

"A squatter. It's under control," Anton replied.

"Stay. I'm coming up."

No wonder they turned on the airport lights. A foreigner meant that Bezdomov had stepped in really big shit.

"So," said the foreigner. "Who is it?"

"He says he used to work here. He had a card and this." His tone was deferential.

"Senior Engineer Bezdomov," said the new voice. "What were you doing snooping? You left something in your desk drawer?"

"I wasn't snooping," said Bezdomov. "I was only looking for a place to sleep." Whoever this foreign voice belonged to, he was clearly the *nachelnik*. The boss. His hopes rekindled. A Russian would kill him, but foreigners were different. Softer.

"The building is under new ownership."

"I swear. If I had known I would never . . ."

"Where did you get the diamond pouch?"

"Diamonds?" said Bezdomov. "I don't know *anything* about diamonds. Lenses, ray paths. Skins and snares. Just ask. But diamonds? Nothing. I was just . . ."

"How did you get in? The doors are all bolted and locked."

"Don't worry. No one has a key. There's a tunnel. . . ." Bezdomov explained everything without omitting the smallest detail. When he was done, he said, "I don't know anything and that's the way it will stay. You can count on me."

"He's lying. Tomorrow everyone will hear," said Anton.

"No! I'll take your secret to the grave! *Please!* Life's a kopeck here, but you're not Russian, I can hear it. You're not . . ."

"We're all loaded up!" came the call from below.

"Well," said the foreigner. "Now what?"

There was a long silence, then Anton said, "Throw him over the yard wire. Twenty thousand volts. People fry trying to steal copper cable all the time. No one will wonder."

"Gentlemen, I'm looking for a solution. Not a light show."

Bezdomov felt a surge of hope. "I knew you'd understand."

"You've made an honest mistake, Senior Engineer Bezdomov," said Eban Hock. "You were just looking for a warm place to rest? I think we can accommodate you."

CHAPTER 12

The Eternal Ice

LIKE ROME, IRKUTSK IS A CITY OF HILLS, though you can live here all your life and hardly notice them. But then Rome was never buried by an ice sheet nine kilometers thick. When the last glacier retreated, it left behind hills barely high enough to contain the swift Angara River. The hills of Irkutsk aren't dramatic, but like the people who live among them, they're survivors.

Cemeteries occupied the high ground. One was still called Jewish Hill, though it had been paved over in Soviet times and turned into an amusement park. To this day you can still walk twenty paces away from the big Ferris wheel at the top and be surrounded by old gnarled trees, mushrooms, and mossy headstones capped with pebbles.

The Orthodox Church fared better under the Soviets, and so the graveyard beside the Church of Our Savior remained sacred ground. It was here Nowek brought Volsky home.

It was a clear, bitter morning, the last Saturday of September. Last night's snow dusted the hard ground. The winter sun was dazzling. A glittering "white frost" was in the air. The tiny crystals flashed with prismatic fire.

The Angara swept north through the city from nearby Lake Baikal. This morning it was covered in "water smoke"; thin fog spawned when cold water met even colder air. It made the gray river look like it was boiling.

The Church of Our Savior had three bell towers painted in bright green, fiery red, and rich gold. The nineteenth-century French aristocrat who proclaimed Irkutsk the Paris of Siberia described them as embroidered cantaloupes. To Nowek, they were colorless as a faded photograph, gray as the river.

He listened to sweet, resonant music rising from within the church. It was the "Canon for Repentance." Nowek's mother had insisted he attend the Polish Catholic church on Kirov Square. But then she found his father and a young voice student together, superimposed, on a couch. It wasn't the first time, but it was the last. She left Irkutsk for Leningrad, and a few years later, Leningrad for a cancer ward.

Nowek stopped attending masses, but he still was drawn to the church by those deep, rich voices. If heaven existed, Nowek hoped his mother would be listening to music exactly like this.

"You'll never find out who did it," said Chuchin. He had Nowek's suitcase resting against his leg. A fresh Prima dangled from his lips.

"Maybe." Nowek was still wearing the clothes he'd changed into at the Lubyanka, though in deference to the cold Chuchin had come up with a proper winter hat of dark wool karakul.

"Even if they do you'll never learn who ordered it."

"Probably."

"What's amazing is that they let you leave Moscow."

"Definitely."

"Pah." The Prima flared, glowed. The raw, unfiltered cigarette smelled even more toxic than usual.

Chuchin's leather jacket was new, but the rest of his outfit was so old it seemed more like skin than clothes. An ancient gray wool hat, heavy felt welder's pants, scuffed work boots. His face was weathered and lined, his fingers cured yellow with nicotine. He turned sixty this year and looked older. He wore cheap plastic sunglasses tinted absolute black. Chuchin had been a citizen of the gulag for twenty years, and two decades of felling trees and trekking across fields of blinding white snow had seared his eyes.

When he did take them off, a surprise: his eyes bore a distinct, Mongolian fold. Chuchin was Slav enough to let you know he was up to something, and Asian enough to keep you guessing what it was. He'd been Nowek's official driver in Markovo. When Nowek lost his job as mayor, he'd followed him to Arkady Volsky, and to Irkutsk.

Chuchin said, "The militia came to your office yesterday."

"What for?"

"What else? You. I said I was just a pensioner. I go where they tell me, I raise flags and sweep floors. What could I know?"

A lot. When it came to knowing things, Chuchin was an acknowledged master. He carried a map of the world in his head, remarkably wrong at the rim, dead right at the center. Still, Nowek doubted the local police had been convinced any more than he believed the Moscow militia had given up on rearresting him.

But the flags, thought Nowek. Volsky had insisted on flying two in front of his office. One, the white, blue, and red of Russia. The other, the Siberian flag, green below for the endless taiga, white above for the snow. "They took you at your word?"

"They're militia," said Chuchin, as though that should explain everything. "If they were smarter they'd be *mafiya*. Though they're good enough at avoiding trouble when it bites them on the ass."

"You're worried about something, Chuchin?"

"You haven't said why they let you go."

"I'm innocent. How could they hold me?"

Chuchin peered at him from behind his dark lenses.

Nowek glanced back at the church and saw a young priest hurrying from the monastery. The black wings of the priest's *ryasa* flapped in the wind. His beard was full and long.

The priest bustled up, waving impatiently to the driver sitting on his rusty bulldozer. It chuffed sooty exhaust, the dented blade rose. Lengths of chain dangled from it. They drew taut, and Volsky's plain wood coffin, suspended on iron hooks, floated up from the back of an open truck, into the air.

"It's good," said Chuchin. "Just a simple machine made for work. He'd like that." He saw Nowek looking back to the street. "You're expecting someone?"

Nowek saw just the militia jeep and a dark Volga sedan. The governor of Irkutsk, the mayor, the head of the All-Siberian Reform Party, they all should be here. Volsky hadn't just fought for them. He'd died for them. Where were they now? "They've forgotten him already."

Chuchin shrugged. "They didn't want to get close and risk catching the same disease."

"He was murdered for speaking the truth. It's not catching."

Chuchin replied with a cloud of smoke.

The wind carried it to Nowek's face. He waved it away. "There was a fire in the Lubyanka that smelled better than that."

"Go back and breathe the KGB's air then."

"It's the FSB now."

"Different name," Chuchin said with a snort. "Same smell." He sucked it down to ash and ember, then flicked it away.

The young priest hurried over to them. He wasn't dressed for the cold. Clearly, a very quick service was in the works. "The *Metropolit* sends his—"

"Choirboy," Chuchin interrupted. "What's the matter? He's too busy praying with his *mafiya* friends this morning?"

Nowek glared Chuchin silent, then said to the priest, "Forgive my driver. He's not himself. There's no reason to wait."

The priest waved to the bulldozer driver. The engine chugged. The treads slipped, then dug into the half-frozen earth. The bulldozer began to move.

Chuchin picked up Nowek's bag. "So much for speaking the truth."

"You have something against priests now?"

"I'm Russian," said Chuchin. "I have something against everybody."

They walked slowly behind the bulldozer, across a low shoulder of open ground dusted with gray snow. The ground was still bare beneath the trees. Ahead, the view opened to the Angara River. The river smoke was barely ten meters deep. The wind ripped holes in it, revealing plates of thin, new ice spinning north.

The bulldozer headed for a cluster of white birches and a mound of fresh, dark earth.

Chuchin said, "What will you do about Galena?"

"I told her to stay."

"For once she'll be happy to obey." Chuchin took another drag, let it out, then said, "You know, just because they let you leave Moscow doesn't mean they won't throw you to the wolves later on. What did the militia want from you, anyway?"

"To send me back to Moscow." He felt the cold of the frozen earth coming through the soles of his shoes. Siberia on the cusp of winter. He should be in boots, not shoes. "But they won't. Not while I'm still needed."

"For what? You don't work for Volsky. Neither do I."

"You can work for his replacement."

"Never. I'd rather hang for being loyal than be rewarded as a weasel." Then "Who will it be?"

"Why should you care? You'll be hanging."

"I still have standards."

Nowek waved away the foul smoke. "Not many."

"Smoking is cheaper than eating. So? Who is it?"

Nowek drew in a long breath, and let it out slowly. It was snatched from his lips by the brisk wind. "Me."

Chuchin looked at Nowek long, hoping it was a joke, afraid it might not be. "You *agreed*?"

"I made a deal."

"With the devil. Which one, Mister Mayor?"

"You saw the car parked behind the militia jeep?"

"Black Volga, killer plates from the Interior Ministry." *Killer plates* put the occupants above local law. The term was quite literally true: a car with killer plates could run over a squad of grandmothers and drive away. "The engine is leaking oil badly." Chuchin screwed up his face. He looked like he'd bitten into something sour. "I can't believe you're working for the KGB."

"It's *FSB*. He's a lieutenant who works for a major

named Levin. Levin is keeping the militia off me. I think I can trust him."

Chuchin raised an eyebrow. "They say Siberian tigers are rare. You could put this Levin behind glass and charge admission."

"It's complicated."

"It's simple. Volsky is dead. You're still breathing. Take his job and you take on his enemies." Chuchin looked back at the Volga. "What does the KGB want?"

"Volsky was going to Mirny. I'm going in his place."

"Alone?"

"You want to come?"

"I've seen snow, thank you. Why Mirny?"

"Volsky was murdered over diamonds. Mirny is where they come from. I know Volsky was in touch with someone there. He called him his colleague. I'm going to find him."

"For the glory of the KGB?"

"No," said Nowek flatly. "For Volsky."

The bulldozer clanked to a stop, blade raised high. The two groundsmen swung the coffin around to line up with the rough hole. The priest began reading from a prayer book, his back to the wind and the water. He finished, then said, *"Mir prachu tvayemu."* Peace upon your dust. He looked at Nowek and cleared his throat.

Nowek walked to the front of the earth-moving machine and gripped one of the cold, rusty chains that held Volsky's coffin.

The open grave was lined with giant crystals of ice. Soft, feathery, white as eiderdown. Moisture had risen from the river, settled into the hole, and frozen where it touched the ground.

Both ice and diamonds grew in response to changes in temperature. The slower the change, the larger the crystal.

The process inside Volsky's open grave had been slow. The crystals were extravagantly big. Nowek thought, *Fifty, sixty carats* at least. They looked terribly fragile. A warm breath would shatter them.

"Arkasha," he said softly, "I wasn't going to say anything this morning. What for? Maybe it would have made no difference if we had been together. Maybe we'd *both* be dead. I don't know. But now they've blessed your dust, so your soul is safe enough."

The young priest shivered and wrapped his *ryasa* around his shoulders against the biting chill.

Nowek ignored him, and continued to speak softly, softly. "You once said we'd look out for each other. You kept your word. You also promised you would help the miners. Whatever it took." The ground seemed to tilt. He grabbed the chain to steady himself. "I want you to know, I will keep your promise for you. Whatever it takes. And though it's a little late, I'll keep mine, too." He looked up and nodded.

With a clank of a clutch, the bulldozer blade began to drop.

Nowek guided Volsky down, down, into the soft bed of crystals, down into the eternal ice. When the coffin bottomed, he unfastened the iron hooks and pulled the chains up hand over hand. They rattled against the coffin. His palms were rust red.

"There aren't many people in this world worthy of trust," Nowek said as the distant voices from the church climbed higher into the air, then, from beneath the trembling alto came a low, powerful bass. The voice of the river.

"Today there's one less."

The first shower of dirt thundered against the wooden coffin. The next was softer. Nowek couldn't hear the third at all.

On the way back to the battered white Land Cruiser, Chuchin said, "So how soon do we have to leave?"

Nowek took him by the shoulder. "The diamond company will send a plane to meet us tomorrow. Thank you, Chuchin."

"I'm not busy. What now?"

"My apartment. I want to see my father."

THE TRAUMA SURGEONS AT Moscow's Municipal Hospital Number 31 were experts when it came to bullet wounds, picking bomb shrapnel, stitching knife slashes. When a businessman ended up on the wrong side of a deal and couldn't afford the gleamingly expensive American Medical Center, Number 31 was where he would hope the ambulance drivers would go. Sometimes it was a matter of luck. Levin was lucky. Not once, but three times.

He woke up on the street, covered in blood, cold, his body rigid, his face a shell, a mask. He forced himself to move. First an arm, then a leg. He pushed himself upright and felt cold air on the bare, raw skin of his back. He could see with only one eye. He didn't know why, and that was luck paying its first call.

If he'd known his right eye was attached only by a slender, violet thread of optic nerve, he might have given up, sat down, and quietly frozen to death. Instead, Levin found Sasha, carried him to the front door of his apartment building, and collapsed.

Luck came again. A neighbor's daughter had a fight with her boyfriend and returned home early. She found Levin clutching the broken body of a dying dog, screamed, ran upstairs, and called 02.

An ambulance was dispatched. When it arrived, the

medics took one look at Levin and decided it didn't matter where they took him. But Levin was lucky one more time: someone followed the trail of blood back to the street, and there they found his wallet and, inside, his FSB identity card.

That changed the equation slightly, but enough. Whether they were calling themselves KGB, FSB, or the Monks of the Holy Name, the organs of state security could make your life miserable. This FSB officer might die, but nobody was going to say they didn't take him to the best trauma center in Moscow. And so the ambulance screamed off into the night, siren wailing, lights flashing, heading for Number 31.

The duty surgeon was accustomed to Moscow's nightly harvest of murder and mayhem. He coiled the optic nerve back into the bruised socket, casually pushed the eye in and stitched the torn flaps of muscle and skin closed.

The nerve would either work or not. The eye would either stay put or not. And if the damage extended into the brain itself? Levin would never regain consciousness.

But he did, and when he did, Levin found himself floating on a flat sea of white sheets. His face was hot and swollen. His left eye saw through a narrow slit. When he closed it the world went black. A steady drip of anesthetic left him feeling nothing, which just added to the confusion. He tried to reach up and touch his face, but his arm would only go so far.

The memory of the attack was beyond recollection. All Levin knew was what he could see: a light fixture, a clock, a radio without a dial that played just one station, a green wall.

Then a face.

"He's awake," said General Goloshev. "He moved."

"He's not really awake," said a gaunt, sad-looking doctor.

"I'm looking at his eye. It's open. *I* say he's awake."

"And I'm on the faculty of medicine at the Lomonosov Institute at Moscow State University. How about you?"

General Goloshev loomed in Levin's monocular view. "Levin?" The general leaned over close enough for Levin to smell his breath. It was sweet and minty. "He'll remember nothing of this?"

"If he does he won't know what it means."

Levin blinked. Adding Goloshev to the scene didn't help him identify it. He looked around the room, to see some clue, something, anything, familiar.

"How long will he have to stay here?"

"We should be able to move him to a recovery area tomorrow. Of course, hidden damage is a possibility. The eye is not far from the brain."

"He's one of our top boys. We want him taken care of. Let him have all the rest he needs. What are you using?"

"Scopolamine and opiates."

"It's safe?"

"There can be reactions." The doctor placed a tray on the table beside Levin's bed. It contained two syringes. "That's why we keep Antilurium close by. It counteracts the sedatives." He pointed to the other syringe. "We'll know by Wednesday if he'll recover."

"Whatever is required. Just take good care of him."

Levin thought, *What day is it?* He tried to move, to speak. It came out as a moan. But it brought the Toad back into view.

"You see? They said you could be out for days. I said, Levin? Not a chance. You're at Hospital Number 31. You have a concussion, some nasty cuts. Frankly speaking, your face has looked better. Scars give a man character. You'll have to beat the girls off with a stick."

A stick! "My eye . . ."

"You were robbed and beaten."

Stick. Beaten, yes. But robbed? Was that right? Levin fought to clear the mist, to see, to remember. An indistinct shape materialized, just out of reach.

"Remember next time to keep your pistol handy when you go out for an evening walk . . ."

Sasha! The memory sharpened, slowly, emerging from the murk and the shock like a developing photograph.

Hock . . . Kristall . . . Petrov . . . Images began to come at him faster, clearer, piercing the shock, the drugs. A face, no, *two* faces. The flow of memory rushed ahead, a river surging between narrowing cliffs.

Stay away from the Closet!

They didn't want his money. They wanted him to stop his investigation. *Petrov?* Who else *could* it be? "What day . . . is today?"

"Tuesday."

He took in a sharp breath. He was supposed to meet Sherbakov in Mirny . . . tomorrow? How was he going to do that?

"The hooligans who attacked you. Can you describe them?"

"Sherbakov . . ."

"He's already flown east."

"A man . . . South African . . . Hock . . ."

"Relax, *boychik*. You're the lucky one. If you knew what it was like where Sherbakov is going, you wouldn't be anxious to follow. For now, rest. Everything is taken care of. You can sleep like a gopher."

Levin felt the bite of a needle.

Stay away from the Closet!

Goloshev leaned over and patted Levin's arm. "We'll get

these two bastards. You rest. We need you back at work as soon as possible." He winked, turned, and left.

Levin's tongue tasted swollen and metallic. The drug was rising, and he was falling. How could Goloshev get them if he didn't know what they looked like? Levin had their faces memorized. He could picture them in detail. Their heights, weights, their nationalities . . . Nationalities?

We don't want your fucking kike money.

They'd known he was Jewish. It was on his passport, but they never saw it. They might infer it from his name, but he was just a man out walking a dog. *How could they know?*

Levin struggled to think clearly, precisely. Either they'd seen his personnel file at the FSB or were hired by someone who had. Who sent those two flatheads his way?

"We'll get these two bastards. . . ."

Levin felt his face throb with each beat of his heart.

And who told Goloshev there'd been *two?*

CHAPTER 13

The Violinist

THE MILITIA JEEP FOLLOWED THEM ONTO BOU-
levard Yuri Gagarin. Sherbakov's ailing Volga struggled to
keep station at the rear, its sick engine spewing blue smoke.

Chuchin glanced into the rearview mirror. "Your FSB
friend is having troubles."

"Slow down. I can't afford to lose him," said Nowek.
"He's the only thing keeping the militia away."

Chuchin slowed. All three vehicles rolled at a more majestic pace down the frost-heaved boulevard.

They followed the river from the center of Irkutsk to the
university district known as *Akademgorodok,* Academics'
City. The wide avenue named for the first cosmonaut to or-
bit the earth looked more like a relic from the eighteenth
century than something from the age of space. The street
had been abandoned to the elements. Now it was an obstacle course of potholes.

The deepest had been filled with straw and water, then
allowed to freeze over. It worked until the temperature
really dropped, and then, when the ice expanded, so did the
hole.

Chuchin carefully steered the white Toyota Land Cruiser around the worst of them. He was a master when it came to scrounging for parts. He'd grafted Russian headlights, wipers, and wheels onto the sturdy Japanese car, but replacing something major? Out of the question.

Nowek had received the car as a gift back when he was still mayor of Markovo. A group of Japanese businessmen wanted his permission to log the taiga around the city. They'd done business in Russia before. They knew a facilitating payment was expected. What happened was not.

Nowek accepted the car and denied their request. Back then only the *mafiya* drove nicer vehicles. Now, after two years of Siberian roads and Chuchin's surgeries, Nowek's Land Cruiser looked like the survivor of a great tank battle fought in mud.

They passed streets named for Lenin, for Marx, even for Derzhinsky, the founder of the KGB. In Moscow, the old names had been erased. They persisted in Irkutsk, though whether out of nostalgia or indifference was difficult to say.

The ten-story apartment towers of Academics' City rose in orderly chevrons from the river embankment to the top of a hill. The old steam ferry *Baikal* was moored where the buildings met the river. The ship, built in Britain, disassembled and hauled across two continents by rail, was wreathed in river smoke. The mist swirled around its single black smokestack as though ghostly stokers were shoveling soft coal into its great, silent boiler.

Chuchin pulled into the drive that led to Nowek's building. "When do you want me to come back?"

"An hour will be more than enough," said Nowek as he opened the door and grabbed his bag. He walked up the cracked concrete stairs, through the glass door and into the cold lobby.

What was the old joke about the drunk who fell asleep on a train? He woke up in a different Siberian city, but emerged onto the same Square of the Soviets, walked down the same Lenin Street, up to an identical building on Marx Prospekt, climbed a matching set of filthy stairs to a floor he knew by heart, and only discovered something amiss when his key didn't fit?

Nowek paused and turned. The militia jeep was parked on the street. As Nowek watched, the Volga appeared.

All was right in the universe.

The flat was on the sixth floor. He ignored the elevator. The stairs might be reliably grim, but they were also grimly reliable. It was cold enough for Nowek to see his warm breath rising in a thick cloud. Soon long daggers of ice would hang from the walls, the ceilings, like dripstone in some underground cavern.

He came to the sixth-floor landing. The metal door that opened onto the hallway was streaked with ribbons of dark rust. As he pulled the handle, he heard a shout, punctuated by the *bang* of a door slammed hard.

Nowek opened the door and came face-to-face with a young woman, a girl, hardly older than Galena. Jeans, boots with fashionably thick heels, a tight red turtleneck that was nothing if not an invitation to admire. She had short, wheat-yellow hair. The sweater's neck gaped to one side, pulled out of shape.

"Paulina?"

"He's an *animal*! Look what he did!" She grabbed the neck of her sweater. "It's ruined! Who will pay for another? Him? *You?*"

"What happened?" Though he could guess.

"He said it was time to take his medicine. I knew it's really just vodka, but I played along. I was pouring him a glass and he grabbed me like a snake. You said he was blind!"

It wouldn't help to tell her he was only *nearly* blind. "I'm sorry about the sweater. He's old and he doesn't know what he's—"

"Oh, he knows what he's doing. At least, he knows what he'd *like* to be doing. Go to the Intourist Hotel and hire a professional."

"Paulina, let's—"

"You don't even have to pay me. I wouldn't touch the money." With that she pushed by him.

Nowek listened to the angry stomp of her boots as she fled downstairs. Paulina had been the fourth girl Nowek had hired to care for his father. She'd lasted longer than the first, shorter than the last. He walked to his apartment and stopped, listening.

Sweet violin music came from inside, the notes soft and rich as old wine. He recognized a Khachaturian "Nocturne," a duet for violin and piano. The playing was so full, so devastatingly elegant you'd never know the piano was missing.

A mystery. How could those stiff, arthritic fingers summon a universe from just a faint constellation of notes? Two mysteries: What would the crippled seventy-six-year-old have done if he'd actually *caught* Paulina?

He went in.

Tadeus was a commanding figure with a violin tucked under his cheek and a bow flowing gracefully back and forth across bright strings. Music charged the air like ozone. The instrument fell lightly into perfect position, his head just so. His expression was one of complete confidence and control. The tiny room vanished, and Nowek's father was in front of an orchestra in a hall packed with people holding their breath, waiting for the final note.

The "Nocturne" was short. The final note rose to a musical question, then fell away to answer it with silence.

When he stopped and turned his thick lenses in Nowek's direction, Tadeus underwent a second transformation: to a tired old man in an overheated room.

"Welcome home, Gregori." He put the old violin down. He felt along the tabletop for a brimming glass. Medicinal herbs tinted the liquid a dubious green.

"Hello, father," said Nowek. He carefully closed the door behind him. It wouldn't latch. "I didn't realize you heard me."

"Your disapproval was deafening."

"You're wrong. I was admiring the piece."

Tadeus had a full head of snow-white hair. His face was bright pink, especially after a drink. His eyes were magnified behind thick, useless glasses. He wore a white shirt buttoned all the way to his neck, a woolen vest, and old black pants faded to eggplant. He wore slippers. "That's all you can say?"

"I just came from a funeral. It's the best I can do."

"You'll get used to them." Then "Whose?"

"Arkady Volsky died."

"Your boss?"

"My friend." Nowek tossed his suitcase to the couch. What would he need for Mirny? Coat. Sweater. Boots. Everything.

"Dead friends," said Tadeus. "It's nothing new. There was a time when you didn't dare to make a friend. You never knew who would be around one day to the next."

"The war?"

"Stalin. That student you hired. What was her name?"

"Paulina."

"She has a very sweet voice."

"Not when I heard it."

"Well." He turned to face Nowek in that disquieting, upturned way of the blind. "And how was Moscow?"

"I didn't bring the Dvořák."

"Didn't, or couldn't?"

"Both." He cracked open the suitcase, pulled the blood-stained clothes out and tossed them into the sink. He ran cold water on them. The colors began to swirl in maroons and reds.

"What are you doing?"

"I have to leave again tomorrow." Nowek put his hands under the tap, turned the hot water on full, and scrubbed hard. "I won't be back for a few days. Maybe longer. You'll have to be on your own. Can you manage?"

"I lived through wars. I lived through Stalin. I'll survive a few days more." Tadeus answered by picking up the violin again. He drew the bow and played a single, high, lonely note.

The opening note unfurled. It was the sound of a winter sunset fading to deep night. But then, from underneath, a more intimate theme, pulsing, filling the darkness with light.

Nowek recognized it immediately. It was *Luchinushka*. "The Rush Light." A folk melody that honored a primitive oil lamp once found in every Siberian house. A slender reed filled with cottony fibers, soaked in melted fat. No matter the cold, the isolation, the rush light held back the terrible tide of winter, of night.

Nowek turned off the tap and listened. A single flame that overcame the dark. What was that if not hope? A man who stood for what was right, no matter the cost. What was that if not Volsky?

Nowek pulled his computer out of the suitcase and

plugged the phone line into the wall jack. He turned it on.
The screen glowed a soft blue. A message was waiting.

> To: Gregori Nowek <gnow@russet.ru
> From: Galena Nowek <4tigers@uidaho.edu
>
> Father:
> When I read your letter, I had to close my eyes and think
> that it was all some mistake, that you were saying one
> thing but meaning another. You know how you do that.
> Then I read it all again. Of course I will stay. But now
> even you say that living in Russia is ridiculous. Yes. I al-
> ready know, thank you. Why would you stay there now?
> What is left to be loyal to? Your friend? Your country?
> Americans don't want to hear about us anymore.
> Nothing good is expected to come from Russia. It's
> only for gangsters and vodka and, yes, diamonds.

Nowek stopped. *Diamonds?* He read the last lines.

> Did he tell you he'd sent them to me? The delivery truck
> brought this tiny box. I had no idea what it was. I mean,
> only you and Uncle Arkasha knew my address here.
> Diamond earrings!? Inside was a note: *From Siberia's
> eternal frost. Uncle Arkasha.* I'll wear them for him but
> please. You say that thinking of me safe in America al-
> lows you to breathe. Imagine what it's like for me to
> think of you still there. Please come out. If not for you,
> then for me.
> Galena

Volsky sent diamonds? Nowek felt his pulse begin to race.
Was that even possible? *No.* But neither were Volsky's words

captured on Levin's tape recording. Who *else* knew where Galena was? If not Volsky, then it had to be someone who could find her—and find her terrifyingly fast. She was safe in America. Safe. It allowed him to think, to live. Was she safe still?

Levin? He knew she was in America, but not where exactly, and *he* was FSB. It had to be someone else. Someone *else* who was sending Nowek a message: *No one is beyond our reach.*

Pressure and heat turn carbon to diamond. The same forces were turning Nowek's fear into anger, his anger to fury. His best friend shot dead.

They were threatening his daughter.

Mirny, he thought as he shut the computer off. A city on the tundra, run by Kristall, totally controlled, sitting on a mountain of diamonds. A place beyond the world's horizon. It would be so easy, so impossibly easy, to turn away, to stop. To pretend. They knew it. More, they were counting on it.

Corruption. Theft. Murder. These were everyday crimes in Russia. But someone had plundered the Closet, someone had pocketed half a billion dollars in rough Siberian gems and the IMF was set to pull the plug on the whole mess. It was crime on a scale that made the larceny of the oligarchs, the men who'd already stolen everything in Russia worth stealing, look like shoplifting.

Nowek always suspected that everything Marx had said about communism was a lie. Who could have guessed that everything he'd said about capitalism would turn out to be so right?

CHAPTER 14

The Entrepreneur

CHUCHIN PULLED UP AT THE APPOINTED TIME with neither the militia jeep nor the smoking Volga in sight.

Nowek got in. "What did you do?"

"Do?"

"The militia. The FSB. They didn't just quit for lunch."

"Why would they tell me their plans? I'm just—"

"I know what you are." Nowek glanced at the empty street. Losing a tail almost always made them angry. And if the militia found him alone without Sherbakov to intervene, what would happen?

They'll send me back to Moscow.

"Your father's all right?"

Nowek looked up. "You know, when I haven't seen him for a while, I think he's just a sad old man who can't keep his hands off young girls. Sad and lonely. Then he picks up his violin. I forget how much I admired him."

"You play the violin."

"Not like he does."

"Enough to be invited to Moscow."

"Only because Tadeus had a friend who ran the Moscow

Conservatory. He never told me that he'd arranged it all. He just *assumed* I'd go. I was seventeen. Galena's age. What did I know? I thought geology was more exciting. Siberia wasn't going to be tamed by musicians. When the invitation came, I threw it in the trash." Nowek shook his head. "He never forgave me."

"You've heard something from Galena?"

Nowek didn't answer. Instead he said, "I need someone to look in on my father while we're in Mirny. Someone tough."

"You need Gosplana."

Gosplana. A name from Soviet times, when mothers actually named their daughters for GOSPLAN, the central planning agency in Moscow. "Tell me more."

"She lives in my building. She was shift brigade leader at the hydroelectric project in Bratsk. She's on a pension now, so she could use some money. You can pay her, can't you?"

"How old is she?"

"Old enough to handle your father. The only problem is that working around heavy machinery left her a little deaf. Her voice . . ."

"Loud?"

"It peels the paint off a cement wall."

"Perfect," said Nowek. "You can go find out if she's willing after you drop me off at the airport."

"What's there?"

"An old friend."

"You don't mean . . ."

"Don't talk. Drive."

"Pah." Chuchin put the Land Cruiser in gear and moved off from the curb.

For most Russians, the collapse of the Soviet Union was the end of normal life. The collapse of the new Russia in 1998 was the end of everything else. Everything they'd counted on, jobs, salary, a future, vanished. But for Yuri Durashenko, president of White Bird Aviation, the new, wild Russia offered opportunities not seen since the age of the robber barons.

The young pilot started off with a single AN-2 bush plane borrowed from Aeroflot's arctic division. For the price of a drum of paint to cover the words AEROFLOT with WHITE BIRD, Yuri was open for business.

"Since when is that thief one of your friends?" asked Chuchin as they turned off the rolling Lystvyanka Highway and onto the airport road. Spears of tall dark evergreens stood out against the bare winter forest.

"Yuri and I understand one another."

"He'd sell you for the right price."

"You see? You understand him, too."

Chuchin slowed, then pulled over to the side of the road. "You didn't answer when I asked about Galena."

Nowek let out his breath. It fogged the cold window glass. "They found her, Chuchin."

"Who?"

"Whoever had Volsky killed. Whoever's been stealing diamonds from Mirny. They found her in Idaho. They sent her a pair of diamond earrings."

"Jewelry?"

"And signed Volsky's name to them." Nowek looked into Chuchin's sunglasses and saw his own double reflection. "You understand what it means?"

"We aren't going to Mirny?"

"Just the opposite. There's no way I *can't* go. Listen. In Russia, stealing is an old game. Oil. Timber. Tigers. Diamonds. It makes no difference. Everyone plays it. Murder? How many contract killings happen in Moscow each week? It's not even news anymore."

"But this is Galena."

"*That's* what makes everything different. This isn't Russia. That's Levin's worry. This isn't my head. It's my heart, my blood. They're threatening her, Chuchin. They're telling me to turn my back and if I don't, no place is safe. Not even *America*."

"So why not turn your back?"

Why not indeed. He'd thought of it ever since he'd read Galena's message. Each time, a single word stopped him cold. A name. Nowek said, "Volsky."

"He's already dead, Mister Mayor. You can't save him."

"He trusted me with his life and I let him down. I won't do it again. And I'm not mayor anymore."

"You could still resign. You could go join Galena and tell the KGB to go fuck itself. That way no one would bother you or—"

Nowek smashed his fist on the dash. The glove compartment door dropped slack-jawed, its catch broken. "I'm not running."

Chuchin shrugged. "It was just a suggestion."

They turned onto a road leading to a tall, arched military hangar. A sign displayed the ubiquitous "brick," a white circle and red rectangle warning drivers that deadly force was not only authorized, it should be expected. A bronze statue of a Soviet hero pilot stood beside a pair of glass doors, an arm wrapped around a propeller stuck into the ground like a grave marker. The pilot's face was gallantly upturned, the deeply set eyes scanning the skies for enemies of the people. A wooden sign had been applied to the base of the figure: WHITE BIRD INTERNATIONAL.

They pulled up to the doors.

"Go see about Gosplana." Nowek got out, slammed the door. The white Land Cruiser drove off. It was no longer an air force base, but the doors were still guarded. Not by a soldier in fatigues, but by a young man in a navy-blue tracksuit. He lounged in a padded leather chair, the kind so heavily upholstered you didn't so much sit in it as sink. A Kalashnikov lay across his knees. Nowek rapped on the glass. He didn't want to startle him. Eye contact established, he went inside.

The room was cold and dark. The guard's hair was jet black and tightly curled in fine ringlets. His profile hawk-like, his skin the color of polished wood. The rifle's stock was decorated with the intricate, Oriental designs of a tribal *kilim*. A Chechen.

"Turn around and walk away. Whatever you're looking for it's not here." The guard's hand stroked the AK's stock with intimate familiarity.

Hiring a Chechen was either very foolish, or very smart. Some Russians considered them savages. All Russians feared them. "My name is Nowek. Yuri and I are old friends. He'll want to see me."

The guard lifted a telephone. "Stay," he said, as though to a dog who might not remember his training.

A display case drew Nowek's eye. "It's all right to look?"

The guard shrugged as he waited for Yuri to pick up.

The case was a corporate shrine to White Bird Aviation, and, more specifically, to Yuri Durashenko.

Yuri as a child with a paper airplane, arm back, ready to throw, face alight with fierce longing for the skies. Yuri astride a motorcycle, wearing the uniform of Frontal Aviation. Yuri in a pilot's high-altitude pressure suit standing with one foot on a Mig's boarding ladder. Next a group photo taken next to a small, expensive-looking jet. Note the faces: Yuri, of course, the governor of Irkutsk, and in between them? Boris Yeltsin. *Amazing.*

Then, finally, a religious relic, a piece of the true cross: Yuri's actual leather jacket, creased and scuffed with use.

Nowek smiled. Yuri hadn't just invented an airline, he'd invented himself. He'd never been a military pilot, though he once ran an air base motor pool where he swapped rides in jets for items tossed off the backs of his trucks. The leather jacket looked familiar, though. He'd seen Yuri wearing it in the days before he'd traded leather for Armani.

The guard said, "Any weapons?"

"A pocket knife. The blade is dull."

The Chechen nodded at the stairs.

Nowek went up. The stairs ended at a dimly lit corridor. Nowek flipped the light switch. Nothing. He walked to a window.

An interior window. It looked down to the floor of a cavernous hangar. Below, Nowek could see people moving around an airplane using flashlights to see. The hangar doors were cracked open to let in light without letting out too much heat.

"Welcome to my disaster."

Nowek turned. "Did you forget to pay your electric bill?"

"Just the opposite. I *paid*. That's *why* they shut me off."

Yuri was as tall and gawky as an adolescent. His dark hair was cut closer than before. His clothes had taken a sharp turn for the better. Instead of jeans and leather, he wore an expensive suit made of some shiny blue fabric.

"Can you believe it?" he said. "The airport hasn't sent a ruble to the power company in years. Because we have income, they left the airport's power on and shut me off."

"They think you can afford to pay both bills."

Yuri scowled. "You're saying this makes sense?"

"I'm saying that in Russia, things don't have to make sense."

"It's no wonder the world is turning its back on us. Enough of my troubles. I understand congratulations are in order." Yuri walked to Nowek, hands out. One for Nowek's hand, the other for his shoulder. "*Delegate* Nowek."

Yuri's cologne was strong and green. *Like the dollar,* thought Nowek. "How did you hear so fast?"

"Siberia's a village." Yuri paused. "It's true about Volsky?"

"That he's dead? Yes."

"That he stole half the diamonds in Siberia. That he had a fortune hidden in some island bank. That—"

"He was going to force Moscow to pay some miners what they're owed. That's all. Someone stopped him first."

"They say the militia can't touch you because you're working for the FSB."

"Can you imagine me working for them?"

"It's just what I said, too. Well, there's no point in standing in the dark." He took Nowek by the shoulder. "It's dark in my office, too, but it's warmer."

Yuri's office had double windows overlooking the hangar floor. Enough light trickled in to see that the furniture was heavy and rich. Nowek's shoes disappeared into thick Oriental carpets. "The guard downstairs. He's Chechen?"

"Like his whole family. I hired Mahmet, his two brothers, and his cousin. They're my new security team. They're very motivated."

"I can imagine." The army had turned Chechnya to rubble. Mahmet and his brothers weren't motivated. They were exiled.

Yuri smiled as he uncapped a bottle and poured two glasses full. "You know, if Volsky did pocket a few diamonds, going to Moscow wasn't smart." He handed a glass to Nowek.

Nowek put his down untouched. "Why?"

"Too many thieves. Too much competition. But let's not talk about money. There's the future to consider."

"What future?"

"Ours. You know, we're in a golden position in Irkutsk. A hundred tourists a day would come if the airport conformed to international standards. By that I mean a new terminal, clean bathrooms. New customs officers. The old ones are used to being paid with bribes. There would have to be a new hotel, naturally."

"You wouldn't want them to realize where they were."

Yuri pointed a finger at Nowek and said, "I *knew* you'd understand. Americans want to see Siberia. They don't want to live it. You might ask, would such an investment pay off?"

"I didn't ask."

"It's not even a question, not with Lake Baikal right next door. The biggest lake in the world. A quarter of all the fresh water on the planet. Rare and endangered animals and plants. To us it's just green slime. To them? Believe me, they *love* this stuff."

"Yuri . . ."

"We're closer to Tokyo than Moscow. We're closer to *Chicago*. You see where I'm going with this? We could rename the airport *Baikal International*. In a year we'd be bigger than Disneyland."

"Lake Baikal is already bigger than Disneyland."

"Exactly. So what's holding us back? Psychology. People are afraid to invest in Russia. Who can blame them? Even the big bankers are robbed. Even the *IMF* thinks Russia is a rathole."

"Yuri . . ."

"And if the IMF can't do business here without getting plucked, what chance is there for anyone else? But with the right political support behind the right development package—"

"I came to talk about diamonds."

Yuri blinked. "You said Volsky was innocent."

"He is. What do you know about Mirny?"

"Mirny? It's *chertovy kulichki*."

It meant *where the Devil throws pancake parties*. The middle of nowhere. "You've never been there?"

"It's not permitted."

"That's not what I asked." Nowek sat back in the chair.

"Ah." Yuri wagged his finger at Nowek. "You look like a crocodile waiting for something to walk into his mouth."

"I'm not feeling that patient."

"Why are you so interested in Mirny?"

"Volsky was murdered over diamonds. Mirny is where they come from. So Moscow isn't where they should go? Where would you sell them?"

Yuri poured himself another glass. "You have some to sell?"

"Consider it a theoretical question."

"I'd run to the Chinese as fast as I could."

"Because of the FSB?"

Yuri laughed. "They're amateurs. If we're talking quantities, then the cartel is going to wonder who you are and where you got them. They might try to make a deal with you. Then again, they might not. The Chinese are safer. You won't get top dollar, but you'll live to spend it. Those diamond bastards call smuggling *leakage*. They plug leaks with dead bodies. Exactly how many diamonds are missing?"

"Four million carats of Siberian rough. All of it gem quality."

Yuri's hand shook slightly. "Do you know what that—"

"Half a billion dollars. Volsky didn't take it."

"But you know who did?"

"Let's just say the stones grew wings. You're an expert when it comes to things like that."

"You aren't suggesting I had anything to do with it?"

"No," said Nowek. "At least, not yet."

"Not yet? Listen. If I flew four million carats of rough out of Mirny do you think we'd be sitting in a cold, dark office in Irkutsk? Forget it. I'd be sitting on the beach."

Or under one. "Who could fly them out?"

"Mirny is a forbidden city. Company planes are the only ones allowed in or out."

"Could Kristall do the entire operation alone?"

"They have the diamonds. They make the rules."

"You've broken rules before."

"Ransha." It meant *earlier.* "White Bird is a completely legal joint stock company. We're even registered and pay taxes."

"Really? Where's Plet?" Plet was Yuri's original partner. He was well over six feet tall. Short hair, bull neck. Hands like dinner plates. Plet frightened the men Nowek found frightening.

"Plet is conducting negotiations with the power company."

"Then you should have your lights back soon." He remembered something Volsky had said on their trip to Moscow. If Russian mines were so rich, how could the cartel afford to turn its back on them? "If Kristall is stealing its own diamonds, why isn't the cartel stopping them?"

"Simple. They're going from Mirny and into the cartel's pockets. Kristall. The cartel. Everyone wins."

Except for the miners, Moscow, and, soon, Russia.

"I'll say this," Yuri went on. "If the cartel made its own

deal with Kristall you can forget about getting to the bottom of it. First, they're in London. Second, they're everywhere else. Well, maybe not China. As for Mirny, you won't get anywhere near it."

"I'm going there tomorrow."

Yuri whistled. "If they're letting you in it's because they want you there. You'd better hope they don't change their mind."

It was the very reason he'd demanded some sort of official status from Levin. The piece of paper he carried was from the Chief of Staff of the Presidential Administration. "So you've never done any business with Kristall?"

"I tried. I offered to handle their Irkutsk operations. They completely ignored me."

"What Irkutsk operations?"

"They used to fly equipment here for repair."

It was the first Nowek had heard of it. "To *Irkutsk*?"

To which Yuri said, "To Sib-Auto."

Of course. Sib-Auto made mining machinery, computer analyzers and controls that were state of the art, circa 1976. It was another industrial zombie, the walking dead, in business only because it was willing to accept oil, timber, and as a last resort even rubles for its equipment.

"Kristall flew in broken machines," said Yuri. "Sib-Auto had a work yard across the airport. I haven't seen anyone actually working there in a year. It's a junkyard now."

Nowek thought, *If Kristall flew broken machines to Irkutsk they were breaking more than machines.* One of the oldest rules in diamond mining dictated that once a piece of equipment arrived at the mine, it never left. *Never.* There were too many nooks and crannies to hide something so small, so valuable. "I'd like to see it," he said.

"There's nothing there to see but junk."

"Then it shouldn't take long."

YURI KEPT A SMALL JEEP in the hangar. They drove out into the light and down a line of Aeroflot jets. Most had panels removed, engines stripped, window glass missing.

"These planes all belong to you?" asked Nowek.

"More or less. Your daughter. How is she?"

"In America."

"Congratulations."

They bumped across the uneven concrete ramp and headed to the far side of the field. They pulled up to a steel-roofed shed surrounded by a tall fence.

Nowek looked in. Yuri was right. There wasn't much to see. The yard was filled with disemboweled X-ray diamond sorters spewing colorful electric wires from their ripped bellies. A tall fence topped with electrified wire formed three sides of the yard. The solid, windowless wall of an adjoining building sealed the fourth. "Who owns the building next door?"

"*Sovah.*" It meant *Owl.* "They used to make binoculars for the Army. The company privatized. The workers owned all the vouchers. They were going to sell their equipment to the world. It was nice stuff and dirt cheap."

"What happened?"

"Two guys from Armenia bought up all the vouchers for dollars." Yuri slapped one hand across the other. "*Sold.* So what do they do? Invest in the factory? Find new markets? No. They changed the name, bricked over the windows, and fired the workers. That was eleven months ago. It's been dead ever since."

It was a typical enough story, one that played itself out

across Russia in any one of a thousand dismal variations. Nowek looked at the structure more carefully. Four stories high. A flat roof. There were no windows. They'd all been bricked over. A flag of white steam rose from a rooftop vent.

Yuri's company couldn't keep the lights and heat on, so how could a bankrupt company? "What did they change the name to?"

"Golden Autumn."

CHAPTER 15

The Kingdom of Dust

SHERBAKOV SHIVERED IN THE DARK VOLGA. It was barely eight o'clock, and already there was ten degrees of frost, maybe more. In Moscow, winter was something you could adjust to. Irkutsk was like being shot forward into mid-December and Mirny was a thousand kilometers north. What was that going to be like?

The windshield was fogged over with his breath. He wiped an area clear. The car's heater worked as well as its engine. Turn either one on and the interior filled with oil smoke. Sherbakov weighed his options. Asphyxiate warm, or breathe clean air and freeze?

Welcome to Siberia.

He blew warm breath into his bare fist. He could feel the cold of Siberia close in around him, layer by layer.

The entry lights at Nowek's building dimmed, brightened. Sherbakov watched Nowek walk across the frozen, bare ground to an idling Toyota and get in. Its brake lights went out and the car moved away from the curb. The militia jeep followed.

Sherbakov started the Volga and glanced in the rearview

mirror. No oil smoke? Either the engine had cured itself, or else it was out of oil. He didn't care. He turned the heat on full blast, released the brake, and followed the militia jeep's single red taillight.

A trickle of warmth escaped from the dashboard vents.

The caravan turned left onto the Lystvyanka Road. A two-lane highway that ended on the shores of Lake Baikal, some thirty kilometers distant.

Sherbakov had hardly gotten up to speed when Nowek's Land Cruiser swerved to the side of the road, heading for a liquor kiosk that was open for business. There was a naked lightbulb burning over its window, dangling from an electric cord. A delivery van was parked beside it, two of its wheels over the curb. The sign on its side said KHLEB, *bread*.

Sherbakov parked well back, but still close enough to see Nowek's driver get out. The old man headed for the kiosk, shuffling with a curious, gliding step, as though he might break through a thin crust of ice and sink into deep, deep snow. Or perhaps he was just accustomed to walking in chains. The file said Nowek's driver was an old *strafnik,* a gulag survivor. People said once you spent some time behind the wire, you never felt warm again, you never threw away the last crust of bread, and you never felt free. Seeing Chuchin walk, he could believe it.

Chuchin stood in front of the kiosk's window, his breath steaming in the cold, still air. Was he after more cigarettes? Was it even *possible* for one person to smoke so much?

Then an answer: *vodka.* Nowek's driver reached in through the open window, came back with two tall, clear bottles, and shuffled off in the direction of the Toyota. But he kept walking. All the way to the jeep.

———

CHUCHIN APPROACHED THE MILITIA *bobyk* and clinked the two bottles together like bells.

The window rolled down. "What do you think you're doing?" Warm breath spilled out in a steamy cloud.

"It's cold. I brought you a little warm water." Chuchin wiggled one of the bottles. It was Baikalsk vodka, premium stuff or at least a premium *bottle*. You never knew.

"Drinking on duty is not permitted."

"Too bad. I'll have to give both to your friend from Moscow."

"Wait." An arm extended. A gloved hand closed around a bottle. "For later."

"Sure. We all breathe air and piss water, right?" Chuchin turned to leave.

"Wait." The second bottle was reeled in. "*Fuck* Moscow."

"Fuck Moscow," Chuchin happily agreed. When he returned to the Land Cruiser, Nowek was gone. *So far,* he thought, *so good*.

THE BREAD VAN GRUMBLED up to the side of the hangar and stopped, its diesel engine clattering like a bucketful of loose change. Nowek got out, rapped on the door. "Thanks."

A hand hoisted a bottle. Nowek's fare. "Any time." The van departed, weaving along the airport road.

Yuri was waiting inside along with the Chechen guard. Instead of his customary Kalashnikov, Mahmet was armed with a pair of heavy cutters and a stout pry bar.

"I made arrangements," said Yuri. "You're late."

"There's a schedule for burglary?" asked Nowek.

"Absolutely. I'll show you what I mean on the way over."

The little open jeep was waiting, engine running, head-lights off. Yuri drove right out onto the concrete runway and accelerated. On the far side, the Sib–Auto junkyard was bathed in bright orange-sodium light.

"What about the lights?"

"Watch."

Nowek wondered what Yuri had in mind, but then the lights went out with an audible *pop!* Not just the security lights, but every light at the Irkutsk airport. "How did you do it?"

"Plet can be a persuasive negotiator." Yuri swerved onto a taxi way and rolled up to the chain-link fence. "We have twenty minutes. You think they're keeping diamonds in there?"

"No," said Nowek. "But I'm prepared to be surprised."

"Electric." Mahmet pointed to the ceramic insulators on top of the fence. It didn't keep him from attacking the steel links with his cutters. He worked fast, and soon a panel was free.

Nowek crawled through first, then Yuri. Mahmet was last.

They threaded their way along a row of rusted steel cabinets. In the east, undimmed by lights, the stars of Orion rose above the eastern horizon, bright as an airliner's landing lights.

"What are these things?" asked Yuri. "Computers?"

"X-ray sorters," said Nowek as he looked at one more carefully. "They use radiation to separate diamonds from ore."

Yuri stopped. "They're dangerous?"

"Only when they're running. Diamonds glow under X-rays. There's no shielding. Stand close enough and you'll glow, too."

Ahead was a solid brick wall with just one door made

from steel plate. There were no handles, no obvious locks. Not even a place to insert a key. Apparently it was designed to be opened only from the inside. Mahmet used the pry bar to attack the cement joint around the frame.

The mortar was of poor quality. Chips flew, then whole chunks. The more space the pry bar had to work, the more leverage Mahmet applied. A red brick wiggled like a bad tooth.

Mahmet shifted his attack. Now he used the pointed end as a pick. With each blow, the loose brick was driven farther in. Then, with one last stroke, it toppled through to the room beyond. Mahmet thrust his arm in, feeling around for a latch.

With a solid *click,* the door swung open.

They left Mahmet behind and walked into the cold, dark space beyond. Yuri switched on a flashlight.

The empty room smelled of cold, dead air and dust. The floor was paved in cracked linoleum tiles. An old felt boot was frozen to sculpture. The ceiling was webbed with pipes and conduits. Three walls were bare brick. One was covered in clear ice.

Yuri's light lingered on two fur coats hanging from nails. "Someone left in a hurry," he said.

"A water pipe must have burst," said Nowek. It reminded him of the scene from *Zhivago,* the return to the abandoned manor house at Varykino, the walls, the chandeliers, the furniture, an entire lost world preserved in ice. He walked to the ice wall.

The two coats weren't coats at all, but raw animal pelts. One black, the other silver gray. The gray fur was frosted with big ice crystals like those inside Volsky's grave.

Yuri joined Nowek. "I thought dogs were getting scarce. A squatter's been living here. Most probably he sold fur hats down in the bazaar. Some poor guy with a sign, GENUINE SABLE." Yuri stroked the frozen fur. "Here's Sable. See how well trained he is? Not even one growl."

Nowek wondered how the dog skinner came and went. *Not through the door we broke through.* Even if he'd had a key, there was no lock on the outside. Was the old felt boot his, too? "Hand me the light." He examined the floor. It was covered with dust, but a large area was disturbed in wide, wild sweeps, as though a child had played with a mop. A darker, grittier path marked where someone had tracked in mud from the double doors leading out to the loading ramp.

"Seen enough?" asked Yuri.

"No. Here." Nowek handed the light to him and pulled out a handkerchief. He went to the place where the gritty tracks crossed the floor. He got down on his knees, breathed warm air onto the rough, muddy surface to melt the ice bond, then pressed his handkerchief down hard.

"What are you doing?"

"Seeing if Locard's Law can help us," said Nowek.

"Who?"

"Edmond Locard. He was a French geologist in the early twentieth century. His law states that whenever two things come into contact, material is always transferred from one to the other. You may not be able to see it, but there's always something."

"All I see is dirt."

" '*Vast is the kingdom of dirt.*' That's how Locard's Law begins." Nowek carefully folded the handkerchief and put it away. "The police called him in to investigate the murder of a young woman. There was reason to suspect the father, but no proof. Locard found dirt under his fingernails. Just dirt. Under a microscope it became bismuth, iron oxide, magnesium, and zinc."

"So what?"

"Her face rouge. He was convicted. Let's go upstairs."

They followed the path to the back of the big room. Open steel stairs went up to the next level. Nowek began to climb. Eight risers. A landing. The temperature rose a little. He remembered the plume of steam he'd seen coming from the roof. Eight more steps and he came to the next floor.

The flashlight revealed a sizable room with doors leading off to other rooms. Offices, perhaps. A steam pipe ran along the wall, turned and disappeared through the ceiling. Nowek touched it. *Hot.* A closed steam loop that was still connected to a main might be warm. Only one that was still circulating could be hot.

Nowek looked into the first office. Empty. The others were the same. One was missing a window, and it was cold as a meat locker. He shut the door.

"The water leak must be upstairs," Yuri said.

"Let's keep looking." Nowek went back to the stairs and started to climb. Free water trickled down the bricks. The air was wet and heavy with sulfur, like rotted eggs. It reminded Nowek of something he'd smelled up in the oil fields. A drill pipe penetrated the permafrost and struck a lens of water bubbling with the dissolved gasses of decomposing plant material. A toxic, sulfuric champagne came roaring up from the hole, sending everyone running, cloths over their mouths.

The last flight of stairs ended at a door.

He opened it and heard the *hiss* of escaping steam. The flashlight beam lanced through a fog of it. The floor was sheeted with water, gray with bird droppings. There was a small sound, a shuffling of papers. He swung the light and caught a startled pigeon. The bird had found a warm place to roost. How did it get in? He pointed the light up.

A glass skylight was partly open. Not much, but enough for a bird to enter, for steam to escape. Nowek followed the pipe to where scalding-hot vapor billowed, and found the second felt boot.

"Fuck," said Yuri.

The steam pipe was suspended from the ceiling by wire anchors. A section had ripped loose and snapped under the weight of a man. Steam blasted him squarely in the face.

The dead man wore long underwear, a dirty white shirt pulled up at the waist, plastered to his skin by steam. He dangled from the pipe by one arm, his hand shackled to it by steel wire.

Yuri said, "Leave it. Mahmet will take care of things."

Nowek didn't move. He let the light follow the pipe to the skylight, then back. In geology, getting the rock sequence right was key to understanding the bigger picture. From a well-chosen outcrop, vast forces, collisions, entire continents, could be deduced. Nowek put this sequence together layer by layer.

There'd been a struggle downstairs. The skinner had lost a boot. They'd tied his hands with wire, dragged him here, hooked him to a pipe, and left him to die. Somehow he'd managed to pull one hand free. He'd worked his way along the pipe to the skylight. Somehow, he'd managed to open it a crack. What for? To cry out and be heard, to be rescued? Screaming himself hoarse, his arms growing weaker, weaker, he must have known there was no time left for hope. He must have decided to try something else. Something desperate.

He'd struggled back to the middle of the span, hoping the pipe would break, that the wire around his wrist would slide off the broken end and he would fall to the floor. Maybe it would yank his arm from its socket, but he'd live.

It almost worked. The pipe pulled free and snapped. But

in the wrong place. A poor connection, a bad weld. Who knew why the pipe broke where it did? Instead of dropping him to the floor, he slid forward against the final fitting. The wire wedged tight. An instant later, steam exploded in his face. He'd thrown his free hand up to protect his eyes. How long could bare flesh stand it? Long enough to cook his palm bright red. When it finally dropped, the steam struck him again.

Nowek found an isolation valve and spun the wheel. The steam hissed, sizzled, spat, then went silent. Nowek breathed through his mouth. He could feel death cascade down like a shower of fine, corrupt particles. It made his skin prickle.

He saw the plastic card in the dog skinner's waistband and gently pulled it free. The dog skinner had a name: Ivan Bezdomov, an optical engineer who once worked for Sovah. *He must have kept a key to the building.* He showed it to Yuri.

"An engineer skinning dogs like a savage," said Yuri. "It makes you wonder what made him do it."

"His pension." Nowek pocketed the card.

A whistle came from downstairs. It was Mahmet.

Yuri said, "In five minutes the electric fence goes hot. I don't see any diamonds. Have you seen enough?"

A yard filled with derelict diamond machinery. A squatter, a dog skinner who picked the wrong place to be. Nowek looked up at the dead man. The oil business left spills. The diamond business left bodies. "Yes," said Nowek. "I've seen enough."

NOWEK CAME HOME expecting to see his father asleep in the chair, a drained bottle of medicinal vodka on the table beside him. Instead, there was only silence. He turned on the lights.

Gosplana, the tough old woman Chuchin had hired to look after him, had struck the apartment like a *sarma,* the autumn hurricanes that shrieked in off Lake Baikal. Instead of tearing things apart, this *sarma* had put them back together.

His father's chair was empty. A clean cloth had been spread over the headrest, replacing one grown black with use. The table was cleared and polished. It glowed with a honeyed luster. Clean dishes were in the sink. The blood-stained clothes he'd rinsed out had been dried and folded. There wasn't a bottle, a glass, in sight.

Where was Tadeus? For that matter, where was Gosplana? Not on the couch. He went to his father's bedroom, cracked the door open enough to let in a little light, and looked in.

Tadeus was in bed, his slippers neatly placed on the floor, ready for his feet to discover the next morning. His snoring was loud and deep. Of late, his father had spurned bed, preferring to remain in his chair. It worried Nowek. He thought his father's world was slowly closing in. First to the apartment, then the chair. The old man had fought all suggestions to sleep in a bed.

Nowek watched his father's chest rise and fall, then looked more closely. Some of the snores were in synch with his breathing, some not. Nowek could tell a solo performance from a duet.

An almost blind musician. A deaf hydroelectric dam builder. The mysteries of love were unfathomable. Who could ever explain them? He quietly shut the door and went to the kitchen.

There Nowek turned on the electric ring for some tea, and opened the cabinet by the window. Nestled between a canvas sack of flour and a brick of tea was his binocular microscope. He took the microscope down, broke off a chunk of pressed tea and dropped it into the kettle, then went to his desk in the living room.

The desk was dusted, the papers aligned. He plugged in the scope, switched on the stage illuminator, then carefully unfolded the handkerchief he'd slid into his pocket.

The dirt from the floor of that not-quite abandoned building looked even less impressive under the microscope. The pale tan powder flecked with brown grit was transformed into a yellow beach paved in soft, crumbling plates. A few broken sheets of mica sparkled from it. In other words, a kind of common clay found on the bottom of any lake in the world. He moved the cloth to the area of darker grit.

The landscape shifted. The pale yellow beach was gone. Nowek now looked down on a field of jagged, deeply colored shards. The individual fragments were no bigger than grains of sand. Unlike sand, they weren't rounded.

The teakettle shrieked.

Nowek got up and poured the pot full, then brought it out to his desk to steep. He selected higher magnification. The view darkened. He adjusted the lamp to throw more light.

Now he floated above the remains of a shattered stained-glass window. Some fragments were emerald green, some wine red, others amber. A few glowed with the azure blue of a tropical sea. Their edges were wickedly sharp, and that was the key.

What Russian geologist didn't know the story? In the 1930s, the geologist Sobolev noted that the rocks of Siberia and South Africa were very similar. His reasoning was simple: If there were diamonds there, why not here?

Sobolev mentioned it to a student, Larisa Popugayeva. They were more than just academic friends. They planned a joint prospecting trip that was also to be a honeymoon, but then the war came. Sobolev died in the siege of Leningrad. Larisa survived.

In the summer of 1947, she traveled to the northern Siberian province of Yakutia. Larisa began her hunt in the rivers, where diamonds might collect. Summer came and went. Autumn was near, and the snows not far. She set up her final camp near the banks of a small river. A barge was due that afternoon to take her back to Yakutsk.

No one knows why she bothered to take one last sample. Whatever the reason, she found fragments of ilmenite, garnet, pyrope, and green diopside, *indicator minerals* that formed alongside diamonds. Like Sobolev, her reasoning was also simple: the more crystals she found, the closer she was to the diamonds.

She sent the barge away and drove up the banks of the river. Snow swirled around the prospecting party. The river froze solid. The indicator minerals grew more plentiful. Their source, and the diamonds, *had* to be nearby.

Then, in February, with the thermometer down to seventy degrees of frost, she discovered the banks of a frozen river *paved* with perfect crystals, still shiny, their edges new and sharp. She set off across the marsh and found a shallow, frozen lake two kilometers across. It was the mouth of an ancient volcano. The indicator crystals had summoned her straight to the first of the great Siberian diamond pipes, *Mir*.

The crystals under his microscope, the dirt he'd collected from the floor, were a veritable rogue's gallery of indicator minerals. New and fresh, they could only have been left by someone who'd walked the same ground Larisa Popugayeva had walked. And like the crystals she found that day, like Galena's diamond earrings, they were summoning Nowek to the very same place: Mirny.

MIRNY

Wednesday,
September 29

CHAPTER 16

The North

KRISTALL'S TWIN-ENGINE AN-24 WAS THE NIC-
est plane Nowek had ever been allowed to sit in. The carpets were unstained. The toilets worked. The seats were
upholstered in gray leather. The captain himself had ush-
ered Nowek and Chuchin aboard in Irkutsk, and then
waited while they got settled in the small VIP cabin. It was
separated from the cockpit by a paneled wooden door and
from the simpler accommodations in back by a red curtain.

Lieutenant Sherbakov had been exiled to the wilds of
the aft cabin, which only grew wilder when they picked up
a dozen returning miners in Yakutsk, capital city of the
Republic of Sakha, a weightless balloon of a state kept in-
flated by diamond taxes.

The returning miners had stomped aboard looking like
Vikings returning from a successful raid. Their shoulders
were draped with net bags bursting with meat, fruit, dispos-
able diapers, stereos. And, of course, vodka. When the plane
banked, the aisles clinked with empty bottles. The party grew
until celebration and riot merged, became indistinguishable.

How had men who hadn't been paid in months been able to afford it all?

Nowek looked out the window at a rolling, empty landscape of bare mountains and struggling forest. The trees were dwindling, the open marsh of the northern tundra growing. Roads were few, signs of settlement fewer; an occasional power line, the equally identifiable one-kilometer-square clearing that marked the ruins of an old prison camp. Mirny was still half an hour away, and soon Siberia's true north would begin. Once it did, it would stretch unbroken all the way to the polar sea.

"Are you listening to me?" asked Chuchin. He had a deck of cards out on his lap. They were smudged and dog-eared. He started to shuffle them.

Nowek turned. "What?"

"Let's play *Durak*."

Durak meant *The Fool*. Nowek said, "Have you ever wondered why a game where there are no winners, only losers, is so popular in Russia?"

"No." Chuchin shrugged. "It's just a game. Unless you make more of it, but that's looking for trouble. In *my* opinion," he added.

"Meaning?"

"You know what they did to Volsky. You know about the building in Irkutsk. You saw what they did to someone they didn't like. You can make a report to your KGB friends and say I did my job. It's not like you'd be turning your back on anything."

"It's like poison ivy, Chuchin. You don't cut off a leaf. You go for the roots, where everything begins, and you pull it out of the ground until there's nothing left. The roots aren't in Moscow. They're in Mirny." He lowered his voice.

"Someone was feeding Volsky information. If I can find him, I might find some answers."

"Unless they find you first. Then what?"

"Then I'll think of something else." He glanced out the window. The landscape had changed. The mountains were gone and so were the trees. In their place was a level marsh that went to the horizon and beyond. True north. "Those miners bought a lot of things in Yakutsk for men who haven't been paid. Don't you wonder how they did it?"

"It's not my business to wonder." He lit another Prima.

"Cigarettes might be scarce in Mirny. You brought enough?"

Chuchin looked offended. "It's not even a question."

"They probably have some back there to sell. It's just a thought."

Chuchin sighed and stood up. "I'll see what I can find out."

"I don't know why I didn't think of it first."

Chuchin went aft through the red curtain. Nowek pulled a book out of the seat pocket. It was Kristall's *To the Diamond Frontier!*

Exclamation marks were the giveaway. The Soviets used them to inflate common things with great purpose. A photo of some poor fisherman mending a net would carry the dead weight of *Fulfilling the Nation's Demand for Fish Protein!* A soldier stuck in a wooden shack on some nameless rail bridge became *Eternal Vigilance Guards the Rails!* At least *To the Diamond Frontier!* was better than *To the Pole of Cold!*

He opened the book. First came pictures of unspoiled arctic wilderness *(Nature!)*. Then, scouts leading pack-laden reindeer up a shallow river. In the background? Helicopters *(Progress!)*. Next came four pages of bureaucrats *(Planning!)*.

Those of the lowest rank held microphones to their lips. Higher up, fountain pens and telephones appeared. You could tell right away who the big boss was: he used a pen to conduct a meeting while holding a phone to an ear.

Nowek came to a picture of a young woman. Larisa Popugayeva, the geologist who had actually found the diamonds. No pens. No telephones. She held a well-used rock hammer. He turned the page. The machines grew bigger. The holes deeper. The first diamond glittered in a miner's cupped hands. Then, that pinnacle of Russian enterprise, the hydroelectric plant.

Next came Mirny "street scenes" showing pretty girls out for a stroll *(Sex!)*. Pretty girls getting married, pretty girls pushing baby carriages *(Young Siberia!)*. Schools. Cultural facilities. Parks of Rest and Relaxation. Clinics. Squads of skiers joylessly marching across snow *(Mirny! A Winter Playground!)*. Mirny. Paradise on earth, minus a few details.

The last page showed a photograph of a large white bird in flight against a frigid-blue sunset. It was a stork, and probably real, though in books like these even real birds looked stuffed, even the sharpest, brightest eye became a bead of glass.

The red curtain parted, and Chuchin returned with a carton of Marlboros, a greasy envelope filled with smoked *omul*, a small oily herring found only in Lake Baikal, and a wad of paper notes.

Nowek raised an eyebrow at the Marlboros. "You're developing expensive tastes."

"It's all they had." He tossed the familiar red-and-white box down. "Cartons. *Boxes* of cartons. And not that fake Hungarian shit. The real thing. Forget diamonds. They have enough Marlboros on this plane to *buy* Kristall."

"So what did they use for money?"

Chuchin handed him the paper notes. "They changed my rubles for these. They said where we're going, they're all we need."

They were *veskels,* company IOUs inscribed with Kristall's logo. Legally, you could only use them in company stores, which meant Mirny. Anywhere else and they would have to be converted into something slightly more believable.

Veskels were usually issued by bankrupt companies who still had something worth bartering for. A steel company needing tires for its trucks would swap *veskels* with a tire factory needing steel. The tire plant needed rubber, so they'd trade steel IOUs with a plant that made elastic bands. The elastic band factory got paid in brassieres. The bra maker ended up with steel company *veskels,* which, if they were lucky, they could exchange for something *they* needed. At best, it was freelance feudalism. At worst, a game of musical chairs where anyone left standing at the end lost everything.

Marlboros, a currency second only to dollars. Yet some shopkeeper had been willing to sell his valuable cigarettes for something that he had to know was almost worthless. There was no way Nowek could make that exchange plausible. But the logical alternative, that the miners had used dollars, was even more fantastic.

Chuchin bit off some fish, crunched the bones with a thoughtful expression. "You're hungry?"

Omul came cold smoked, hot smoked, raw, and even rotten. The best Nowek could say about these was that like him, they were a long way from home. "Not enough."

"You know Levin is using you to find out how the stones are leaking. So long as he catches his fish, who cares what happens to the bait? You'll still climb on his hook?"

If it meant finding Volsky's contact in Mirny? If it meant

clearing his name? If it meant finding out who had sent those gems to Galena? "Yes," said Nowek. "I'll climb on the devil's own hook."

THE MINERS at the back of the plane roared, clinked bottles, and toasted one another. Sherbakov wondered how much they could drink and remain conscious. He wondered when Levin would show up in Mirny, and how soon they would be able to leave. One day? Two?

Sherbakov's travel papers said he was an engineer from Sib-Auto, a mining equipment company, coming to Mirny for a survey of Kristall's major equipment in order to "make recommendations." It was the best cover the threadbare Irkutsk FSB office could come up with on short notice. Once, the KGB had run the entire security apparatus in Mirny. Now the FSB had to lie to get him in.

He tried to shut the din from his ears as he worked on *KGB,* his e-mail security program. He'd finally found the software bug that had been driving him crazy.

KGB was a kind of virus with a purpose. Once introduced to a host computer, it took up residence there. Infect two computers, or as Sherbakov preferred to say, *vaccinate* them, and they could communicate with one another in perfect security. The encryption program was 126-bit, making it more secure than the nuclear release codes Boris Yeltsin carried in his suitcase.

But the virus had proven to be less than reliable. Sometimes *KGB* worked perfectly. But other times, half the message was rendered into jibberish, or worse, sent unencoded. Test versions of *KGB* were encoding his own e-mail messages, plus Levin's and Nowek's. Now he knew where the problem was, he could correct it. Then forget Siberia. Forget

Moscow. He'd be a millionaire sitting on a California beach. *KGB* would be his ticket to . . .

Something jabbed his shoulder. He turned.

"Hey engineer!" It was a gold-toothed miner with a half-dead bottle. He pronounced *engineer* with a sneer. "We're almost there. It's your last chance." He sloshed the vodka in Sherbakov's face. "This will keep your prick from freezing." His name was Anton.

Anton's breath could defrost a runway. Sherbakov pushed the bottle away. "No thanks."

"You don't care if your prick falls off?"

"I'm not worried."

"You must have nothing to worry about." With that, Anton stumbled back to his mates and flopped down. He said something to them, and they roared again.

Apes. Sherbakov put away his notebook and pulled out his new Game Boy. Its transparent case was tinted a color called *Radioactive Purple.* He played Tetris with the volume turned low. Alexei Pajitnov, the game's creator, was Sherbakov's hero. If a Russian mathematician could become rich with a computer, why not an FSB lieutenant?

THE PLANE FLEW surrounded by the unearthly brilliance of the far north. The endless marsh below was shot through with a silver filigree of ice. Nothing, not a hill, not a telephone pole, not a tree, broke the tundra's geometric flatness.

Chuchin leaned over to see. "Where's all the snow?"

"Mirny is a kind of frozen desert. The world's lowest temperature was recorded here," said Nowek. "Minus one hundred and sixty degrees. The air has to be very dry for cold that deep. When it does rain, the water just gets locked up in the permafrost. It doesn't go anywhere. It melts, it freezes. Nothing changes."

Chuchin looked outside. "Something's changed."

Nowek leaned over. Chuchin was right. The tundra was gone, buried under mounds of bare, broken rock. *Mine tailings.*

Suddenly, the Antonov flew across a sheer cliff that plunged to a shadowed bottom. The AN-24 could have easily flown circles inside the vast, stepped crater. Apartment buildings crowded the south rim. They looked like a child's set of dominoes next to the open-pit diamond mine. A tall black tower rose from the opposite rim.

The plane dipped a wing. Nowek had to fight a moment of vertigo as he stared down at the bottom of the pit. Then the wing came level, the engines throttled back, the wheels rumbled out, and they were down on Mirny's runway, raising clouds of dust.

The taxi was short. The terminal was a drab, two-story concrete-and-glass building, dirty and spalled, the windows fogged over with condensation. Old vehicles were parked in a way that suggested haste or abandonment. It could be any Russian airport, except for the sign on its roof: MIRNY. A blue-and-white bus was parked in front.

The engines died. The propellers spun down, stopped. A pair of boarding ladders thumped against the plane, one at the nose, the other at the tail.

The bus pulled up to the rear, escorted by a car. A white van hurried across the windy ramp. The forward hatch opened, and a flood of cold air swept in. The red curtain billowed. The pilots appeared at the cockpit door and stood. Usually, the crew on a Russian plane got off first, and only then the passengers. But they were VIPs, Nowek reminded himself.

He put on his heavy coat, grabbed his hat, collected his bag from the small compartment next to the door, and stepped out onto the stairs.

It was a good twenty degrees colder than Irkutsk. Cold enough to freeze skin, but not yet Mirny's deep cold. Winter was just practicing. A fine, crystalline glitter made the very air sparkle. Not like the white frost he'd seen in the air down in Irkutsk. These were real snowflakes. Where was it coming from? There wasn't a cloud in the sky. The concrete ramp swirled with yellow dust devils kicked up by the brisk wind.

The van's side door slid back. Nowek expected Levin, but instead, he saw a woman. She wore a scarf around her head, tied under her chin. Red, cream, white, and blue, its bright colors stood out against the vista of concrete and dust. Like those old hand-colored photographs. Everything is black, white, and gray. But here, something is different. Something is bright.

She looked up and waved. Her teeth seemed very white. You could see by the cut of the coat that she was slender. Her boots had enough of a heel to suggest fashion without hobbling her in real snow. Blond hair spilled out from around the scarf. He turned to Chuchin. "What do you think of the reception committee?"

"Her?" Chuchin lit another Prima. He was hoarding the Marlboros. Who could put a match to money? He let the smoke out slowly. "More bait."

SHERBAKOV WAITED for the miners to gather their bags before putting on his fur *shapka* and making his way back to the baggage hold. Except for an old canvas mail sack, the compartment was empty. His suitcase with all his warm clothes was gone. Had someone taken it by accident? Or was it another little joke? He walked to the open hatch. It was snowing from a clear blue sky. The cold air froze the hairs in his nostrils. The blue-and-white bus was idling below.

The bus belched sooty exhaust and rolled away.

"Hey!" Sherbakov started down the stairs at a run.

Two men got out of the car to intercept him. One wore a heavy blue uniform, the other, a gray business suit.

The one in the suit was small and dark-skinned, a native Yakut. His black shoes were polished to a gloss. He disdained the cold by going without a hat, without gloves.

Sherbakov came face-to-face with the guard. "Someone took my bag." Where was Levin? *He should be here.* "It has to be on that bus."

The guard said, "Documents." Kristall's crystal-in-a-circle insignia was sewn to his padded sleeve.

"If anything is lost, you will be responsible." Sherbakov handed over the papers that proclaimed him a mining engineer.

"No," said the Yakut. "I am responsible." He read them slowly, then handed them back. "I'm Kirillin. The mine director. Relax. Your bag is in my car. You can begin your work right away."

"Right now?"

"We can't afford to delay another hour. DRAGA 1 has been misbehaving. We need it back in operation. Is there something you need to do first?"

Sherbakov looked off in the direction of the terminal. *Where is Levin?* "No." He slipped the papers into his coat. He'd studied enough to know that DRAGA 1 was the ore dredge at the bottom of the open pit mine. "What's wrong with it?"

"Let's go. You can make your own determinations."

"DELEGATE NOWEK? I'm Larisa Arkova from Kristall's Technical Information Department. Welcome to Mirny."

She was tall and slender in the Western fashion, or perhaps just naturally starved in the Mirny fashion. Larisa was in her mid-twenties. Her wide-spaced eyes were pale blue. Her hair was pulled back tightly beneath the scarf, but even so a few loose strands caught the struggling sun and glimmered like white gold.

"*Ochen priyatna,*" said Nowek. "This is my associate, Chuchin."

Her eyes shifted, then returned. She made a slight motion with her mouth that hinted at displeasure. "You should know that the mine is a restricted area. It takes special permission to tour it."

"Don't worry," said Nowek. "My associate would prefer a tour of your city." He turned to Chuchin. "Isn't that so?"

Chuchin spat out a jet of smoke. "I can hardly wait."

She was relieved. "After the mine, you'll meet with our mine director. He can answer almost any question you might have. Do you have some special area of interest?"

Nowek looked up. "This snow."

She cocked her head slightly and tiny wrinkles appeared in the corners of her eyes. "Fairy Dust?" she said. "The winds pick loose snow up from the north and carry it here. Usually, it means there's a storm coming." She opened the sliding door. "Why don't we start?"

SHERBAKOV WAS IN TROUBLE. He was supposed to be here to survey the condition of Sib-Auto equipment. Anyone could sleepwalk his way through that. But to actually fix DRAGA 1, the world's biggest ore dredge? "I should tell you, my training was in automation."

"My training was in law. We can't afford specialists in Mirny. When there's a problem, we fix it with the tool at hand. That's you."

The car sped along a dusty road. Mounds of broken rock blocked his view to the sides. Ahead, the road began a gradual rise. As the car neared the top, it slowed, slowed, then came to a stop at a closed gate.

Kirillin slid his card through a magnetic card reader. The gate opened and they were through. Ahead, the world ended at an impossibly sheer cliff. There were no rails, nothing to stop a vehicle from sailing out into space. They turned hard left onto a descending ramp. The view out Sherbakov's window took his breath away. DRAGA 1 looked like a yellow matchbox. The giant ore trucks, even smaller.

He gripped the door handle. The far terraced wall of the open pit mine was hazy with distance. Black scars plummeted straight down the sides. What had fallen? Rocks? Trucks? Illegitimate engineers?

"First we have to be sure no one is coming up," Kirillin explained. "There's no room to pass. When a Belaz is loaded with a hundred tons of diamond ore, it can't afford to even slow down."

The way clear, the car headed down. The road was ten meters wide and cut into the wall of the open pit. Like the rim road, it was unguarded. Showers of loose pebbles fell in streams. The edge was eaten away in broad scallops. The whole wall looked ready to collapse.

"Normally, it takes an ore truck half an hour to reach the bottom. Go off the road and the trip is considerably shorter."

Sherbakov could feel the tires slipping on loose gravel. He tightened his grip on the armrest and closed his eyes.

They must have taken the road at breakneck speed. It didn't take anything like half an hour to reach the bottom. Sooner than he expected, Sherbakov felt the car slow. When he opened his eyes, a tall yellow building sat astride their path. The car rolled up to it and stopped. Then, with a low rumble, the building began to move. Sherbakov looked straight up and saw an enormous, gaping jaw. It wasn't a building at all. It was DRAGA 1.

CHAPTER 17

Dirty Business

NOWEK HELD ON TO THE HEAVY, RUSTED chain that guarded the edge of the observation platform; a spindly structure that projected over the rim of the mine like a diving board designed for suicides. It was nearly noon, and a brisk northwest wind drew the smell of rock dust and burned explosives up from below. The pit boss draped his heavy frame across the chain as though he couldn't possibly imagine its breaking. Nowek had a better imagination. The bottom of the mine was half a kilometer straight down. He stepped back.

Biologists call Siberia a thin green skin stretched over immutable ice. If so, then the open pit mine was a bullet wound two kilometers across and so deep the bottom was already in shadow. It might be a crater on a dead lunar sea except for the truck parks, the equipment sheds, the ten-story tower on the far rim, the people.

A low thud shook the ground like an earthquake.

Maxim Boyko nudged Nowek and said, "Watch."

Nowek thought the pit boss could have stepped right out of *To the Diamond Frontier!* Boyko was enthusiastic about nearly everything. The north wind only "cleared the air for hard work." The movements of the ore dredge and ore trucks were "like ballet." The deep cold of winter made "the cheeks of young girls blossom like flowers." Nowek had met men like Boyko before. They could be counted on to point out everything inconsequential, and nothing of importance. That would be his job, and Boyko looked like a man who took his job seriously.

Nowek watched as a curtain of rock collapsed in a graceful waterfall of yellow dust. From where they stood on the rim, the ore dredges, the trucks, the bulldozers far below were battered toys. The men operating them were invisible. He watched a car go round the spiraling terrace road, a tiny black marble in a gigantic race.

A chuff of black smoke, and DRAGA 1 began to swivel.

"One bite. A hundred tons," said Boyko. "*Now* you'll see something."

Yes, but what? Painted in rust and yellow, DRAGA 1 looked like a derelict factory riding on tank treads. Its boom rose fifty meters from the operator's cab. Its jaws opened onto a pile of blasted ore, clamped shut, rose, and carried the load to a Belaz 7530, an ore truck the size of a house. The boom swayed. There was a moment's hesitation before the jaws opened, and then gray boulders tumbled into the ore truck.

Nowek counted one second, two, then heard the low rumble of distant thunder as sound caught up with distance. The cold wind whipped his canvas parka. He put the fur-rimmed hood up.

"You're cold?" Boyko asked.

"I'm adjusting." One morning in Mirny and Nowek was already thinking of Irkutsk as the sunny south. The northwest wind was steady and strong. Northwest was the direction that went on forever in Mirny. There were no barriers, no line of trees, not even a fence to slow it down.

Boyko was dressed lightly in a wool sweater under a dark blue windbreaker that sported a white Nike swoosh on the back. He was cut from a classic Soviet mold: thick-waisted, heavy-jowled, "stylish" oversize glasses that kept slipping down a small, stubborn nose. He wore a red pin that proclaimed him a HERO OF SOCIALIST LABOR. In Moscow, young people wore them in irony. One look and you knew Boyko wore his in earnest.

Nowek's wool pants flapped around his legs. "You blast with nitroglycerin?"

"We had to switch. Nitro burned too fast. We use Dynagel now," said Boyko. "Dynagel burns slow. It breaks ore, not diamonds."

"How much ore do you process?"

"The standing quota is twenty thousand tons a day."

Nowek saw only two ore trucks. There were several derelicts and a second ore dredge, smaller and painted a different, brighter yellow, parked far from the blasting. The big ore separation plant, Fabrika 3, was about three kilometers away. Its blocky, cubic mass loomed from the dust and haze like a graceless container ship run aground on the endless marsh. A large black scar marred one face of the building. A fire? "You make your quota?"

"I wouldn't be pit boss if we didn't. Once, you could pretend to work and no one knew, no one cared. You know the old saying. . . ."

"I'll pretend to work, you pretend to pay me?"

"Now everything is measured by results. No results? No pay."

Nowek believed the no-pay part. He wasn't so sure about results. "It looks like there was a fire at the ore plant."

"No essential equipment was damaged."

"What about people?"

"Mining is a dangerous business. We just have to work a little harder to make our quota. But we're not afraid of hard work."

Nowek was prepared to doubt almost everything he encountered in Mirny. But for men like pit boss Boyko, the quota was a holy number against which their own worth was measured.

Twenty thousand tons. Each Belaz could hold a hundred tons. That meant two hundred round trips a day. Nowek could see only two trucks. "How much diamond do you recover a day?"

"We have a saying," said Boyko. "You have to blow up a lot of rock to find a little diamond. This pit isn't new, so we just have to blow up even more. Each year, it gets harder and harder."

Nowek watched a Belaz 7530 laboriously climb the perimeter road. The daily quota added up to seven million tons a year, more or less. A vast number. Or was it?

Every open pit reached an age, a depth, when it had to be abandoned. Not because the diamonds weren't there. It was a matter of geometry. The deeper you went, the wider the perimeter had to be to keep the walls from collapsing on top of you. But a diamond pipe was shaped like a carrot, narrowing with depth. Inevitably, you spent more and more effort reaching less and less ore. At some point, you either walked away or converted the pit to underground operations.

Nowek looked off to the far rim.

The tall steel tower out there marked just such a point. Nowek could hear the throb of powerful fans, and it was a long way off. A plume of steam rose from its antenna-spiked roof. According to everything he'd read, the conversion of the Mirny pit to deep rock mining had been a victim of bad timing. Begun as the Soviet Union collapsed, abandoned when Moscow's support dried up, the deep mine was like so many other half-built projects that dotted Siberia, a relic, a tombstone that stood over a buried time, a lost era.

Twenty thousand tons a day year-round. He knew the cartel bought four million carats of high-quality gems a year from Russia. That meant this open pit was yielding nearly *two carats per ton.* Not quite an impossible number. But close. "Is anyone still working in the underground mine?"

Boyko dismissed the very idea with a snort. "Only a caretaker crew to keep it pumped out."

"Why bother pumping if you aren't mining?"

"A lot of blood went into Mirny Deep. You don't just turn your back on that," said Boyko. Then "What do you think of my pit?"

"Very impressive." The wind flattened the shock of dark hair that escaped the wolf-fur ruff. He thrust his hands into his parka pockets. "Like Lake Baikal, only without the water."

"There's plenty of water locked up in the eternal frost. The aquifer complex is deep. Stop pumping in summer and it *would* turn into a lake." Boyko stopped, then said, "If I may ask, what is the purpose of your visit?"

Now we can start, thought Nowek. "Delegate Volsky was coming to see Mirny and bring the miners their pay. I'm here instead."

"Without any money."

"Without it," Nowek admitted. "I wanted to see things with my own eyes. I'm hoping to go back to Moscow and do something to help."

"To be frank, we try to ignore Moscow."

"You, or Kristall?"

"Everyone thinks the same way. Moscow waters the leaves and forgets about the roots. You tell me. How long will the leaves stay green if the roots are dead? But we'll manage. We always do."

"You're not worried about winter?"

"Every miner has a garden. The shops aren't empty. Kristall makes sure they accept credit."

The veskels. "Who arranges credit for Kristall?"

"Ask Mine Director Kirillin when you see him. I'm just a worker. I know how to break rocks. As for winter, we're not afraid. Once the autumn snows stop and the deep cold comes, it's like another world."

To the Diamond Frontier!

"Life has never been easy. It's always been a place to work, not to live. But we have reasons to be proud." He swept his arm out, with the palm open and up. The wind came up as if on cue, whipping Boyko's jacket. "Thirty years ago this was a valley with reindeer and a few Yakuts in felt tents. Now look. Who else could have done all this?"

Boyko's pose reminded Nowek of those classic statues of Lenin, wind-whipped jacket, upthrust goatee, arm outstretched, palm up, as though feeling for rain. "Russia leads the world when it comes to digging holes."

"Absolutely," Boyko said with honest enthusiasm. "You know how this pit was started? With an atomic charge."

"A *nuclear* bomb?"

"It vaporized the ice. We were working with diamond ore in a week instead of a year. Talk about *results.*"

"What about radioactivity?"

Boyko shrugged. "First the muscle, then the hair spray.

We brought in DRAGA 1 and we were storming. Tons, tons, and more tons. Even the Americans admit it's the world's biggest excavator."

"They say that about our microcomputers, too," said Nowek. Why worry about radiation when there was winter to think about? Strontium killed slowly. A deep cold could freeze your lungs with one breath. "What will you do when it really gets cold here?"

A shrug. "What we always do. Work."

It wasn't a boast. Steel shattered, concrete cracked, the hardest rock spalled. Everything failed under intense cold. Everything except for men. Men survived. Even in Mirny.

"Naturally, there are limits," Boyko explained. "When the temperature reaches minus fifty-two, the engine exhaust is too thick down at the bottom of the pit. We have to stop."

Nowek nodded at Mirny Deep's tower. "It's a shame the deep mine was never put into operation. You could have worked warm."

"Below the seventh horizon the rocks are hot to the touch."

"Seventh horizon?"

"The levels of the mine. They're called horizons. Who knows what we might have found if we'd kept on? Mirny Deep was supposed to be the future. Of course," Boyko continued, "the deeper we went, the more difficult conditions became. It's not like an open pit. Deep mines are warm mines. No matter how cold it is up here, the ice melts fast down *there*. Imagine an iceberg one kilometer thick and it's melting on top of you. Turn your back and it would fill with water and gas overnight. Maybe it's all for the best that it was shut."

Boyko was going on about how the deep mine was

warmer, but that no miner in his right mind would give up the open pit with its air and sky. Nowek was no longer listening. Instead, he was remembering Volsky's last words: *Go to the horizon.* He looked over at the tower standing above Mirny Deep. Could it be?

Nowek watched the lone ore truck grind its way up. "Have you ever found a diamond?" he asked Boyko.

"Most of us never see one except in pictures. But the largest stone ever found was pulled from a tailings pile by an honest miner with a sharp eye. One stone, over three hundred carats. The *Star of Yakutia.* He thought it was a bottle of vodka sticking out of the dirt."

Another thud, another waterfall of rock dust.

"What about a miner who's not so honest?"

"Diamonds don't grow legs. Where would they walk to?"

"In South Africa they have elaborate security. Cameras. Guard posts. Electric fences. I don't see them here."

"We don't need them. We have two things they don't have." Boyko swept his arm out. "We have space."

"They have space in Africa."

"Nasha bolsha." Ours is bigger. "In Mirny, legs aren't enough. Not even wheels. Here, you would need *wings.*"

"That's also happened. An African mine was leaking diamonds to the black market. The company used scanners, X-rays. Guards searched everything, everywhere. They quarantined the workers for three days and examined the toilets to make sure no one swallowed a stone. Diamonds were still finding a way out."

Boyko took a professional interest in the story. "How?"

"Pigeons. They'd strap a diamond to its leg and let it fly over the fence. There was a roost on the roof of an apartment building in town. The off-duty miners would go up with a bucket and collect diamonds like eggs. *Plink, plink, plink.*"

Boyko chuckled, appreciative of their invention and not at all concerned. "There are no *stukachi* in Mirny."

Stukachi. Boyko had used a very specific word, one that meant both *pigeons* as well as *informers.* "You said Mirny has two things they don't have in Africa. What's the other?"

"Mine Director Kirillin," said Boyko. "When you meet him, you'll understand."

THE AIR WAS CHOKED WITH yellow dust and oil smoke. Sherbakov could hardly breathe. They'd set off two thunderously loud blasts close by, each one a bright flash, followed by a roaring avalanche of blue-gray boulders that looked like nothing so much as a crashing wave of rock. Minutes afterward, the hard-frozen ground still trembled like a struck tuning fork.

High overhead, DRAGA 1's operator peered down from the slanted windows of his cab. His orange hard hat gave an exaggerated bob. An instant later the huge boom swiveled, the bucket opened, then closed around a hill of ore. It swung the load above a Belaz 7530. Another nod of the helmet, and the boulders rumbled out.

"You don't mind getting your hands dirty?" said Kirillin. He stood next to the dredge's tank treads, waiting. "Get ready!"

The bucket elevated, then stopped. The operator looked down. His orange hard hat bobbed again.

"Now!" Kirillin scrambled up using the links as broad steel steps. They were treacherously slick with mud and grease, but he didn't slip. "Hurry!"

Sherbakov climbed up onto the first tread and reached for the next. His hand slipped on grease. He had to thrust his fingers between the treads to find a grip. It was not where his imagination wanted his fingers to be. One shudder, the smallest of movements, and his fingers would be crushed.

The engine rumbled from inside the hull. The dredge trembled.

Kirillin looked back. *"Bistra! Bistra!"* Faster! Faster!

Sherbakov didn't need encouragement. He put his imagination on hold and clambered after Kirillin as fast as he could climb.

At the top of the treads, a short ladder led to a perforated steel deck. Kirillin nimbly jumped onto the ladder and pulled himself up and to his feet.

A fat belch of soot clouded half the sky. The ore dredge shuddered. Sherbakov reached up to grasp the first rung. The treads began to shake underneath him.

Kirillin's greasy hand closed around his wrist and hauled him up to the deck as the treads clanked into motion. DRAGA 1 advanced into a slope of blasted ore.

Sherbakov stood on the decking, feeling the machine tremble. Or perhaps it was his legs. The bucket lowered for another bite.

"Hey!" Kirillin shouted. He stood next to an open hatch leading into the dredge's hull. He held a dark blue towel and a pair of thick ear protectors. He cleaned his hands, then tossed the cloth to Sherbakov. Then the hearing protectors.

Sherbakov put them on and followed Kirillin through the oval hatch, into the dredge's dimly lit hull.

It was bedlam inside DRAGA 1. His eyes slowly adjusted to the dark. Screeches, roars, the hum of wire cables running under strain. It wasn't *noise*. It was a physical pressure that assaulted Sherbakov's body. Loud with the ear protectors, deafening without.

An oily engine the size of a boxcar sat in the middle of the enclosure, fed by fuel lines thick as Sherbakov's wrist. Catwalks surrounded the motor. Ladders led up to the operator's cab, down into the clanking bowels. Steel beams supported a maze of cables, gears, pulley blocks, and hydraulic lines. The dim light came from naked bulbs strung along bare wires. When the dredge moved, the lights blinked off, back on, their dull orange filaments trembling.

The machine swiveled, sending Sherbakov reeling against a catwalk railing slick with spilled oil.

"Careful!" Kirillin had to bellow to be heard.

Below the engine deck was a flowing river of cables. All were rusty.

Kirillin pointed down. "One of the bucket control cables is our troublemaker. What do you think?"

Sherbakov leaned over. One cable was badly damaged. A section had blossomed into a nest of tangled wire strands.

With an earthquake's rumble, the worn cable was swept away.

Sherbakov tried to keep his eye on it as it threaded through a turning guide, then up to a pulley. The broken strands slammed against a guard plate. Hot yellow sparks erupted. The broken wire strands glowed red with friction heat.

Sherbakov laughed. Sometimes he forgot just how stupid the rest of the world really was. This wasn't like a software bug. You could spend days, weeks, tracking one of those down. Here was a problem that advertised itself with sparks, and they couldn't fix it?

He motioned for Kirillin to join him. *"Watch!"*

Sherbakov had to shout to be heard. *"The plate needs to be moved."*

Kirillin peered, cursed, then headed for the hatch.

"Tell them to bring a socket wrench!" Sherbakov called after him.

A minute later the diesel stumbled, then loped to an idle.

"Hey engineer!"

Sherbakov turned.

It was Anton, the miner he'd met aboard the plane. He was carrying a big wrench.

BOYKO LEANED OVER THE CHAINS, looking down. The steel poles visibly deflected. "They say you were once a geologist."

"That's true," Nowek said.

"Here, every miner is a geologist. We know rocks, not from pictures, but by their taste."

"I worked in the oil fields. Tasting wasn't a good idea."

Boyko kept staring down into the pit. "What made you leave?"

"It turned out to be a dirty business."

"And then you were a mayor."

"Politics is another dirty business."

He looked back at Nowek. "Now you're the Siberian Delegate. To be frank, it's an odd choice for someone allergic to dirt."

"Volsky wasn't dirty."

"One man."

"You heard what happened to him?"

"Stories."

"Here's a true one: Volsky cared about getting your miners paid. He cared so much he went head to head with some powerful people. It scared someone enough to have him murdered. Now you want a real story? Moscow is missing some Mirny diamonds. They say Volsky sold them *na lyeva*."

Boyko looked up sharply. "That's ridiculous."

Nowek was surprised. He hadn't expected this from the pit boss. "Then who do you think took them?"

"Who? Take a look." He nodded at the earthmover. "DRAGA 1 is still digging after twenty-five years. To survive all that time it must know a few things."

"Like you."

"And that one." He pointed down to the other yellow earthmover, a tenth the size of DRAGA 1, parked away from the working face of the mine. "It's from America. A Caterpillar. A visitor."

"Like me."

"Exactly. The American machine was supposed to be cheaper to run. It lasted one week. You see what I'm saying?"

"I'm beginning to."

"Ask about mining and I'll answer. Ask about tons and I'll give you facts and figures. You want to know what happened to Delegate Volsky? You want my view about stolen diamonds? I'll tell you a big secret." He took out a neatly folded handkerchief from the breast pocket of his windbreaker and mopped his brow. The white cloth turned ruddy brown. He held it up and smiled. "You see? Diamonds are a dirty business, too."

ANTON JUMPED DOWN to the catwalk. "What's the problem?"

"Loose bolts." Sherbakov motioned for him to bring the

wrench. The catwalk shook as Anton shambled up in his heavy boots.

Anton stopped, the wrench still over his shoulder. "So?"

"The plate needs to be moved away from the cable, then the bolts have to be tightened." Sherbakov could see the dull gleam of his gold teeth in the light of a naked bulb. "You think you can do it?"

Anton's breath still reeked of vodka. His gold teeth made his mouth look like a machine, an excavator, meant for chewing rock. He hefted the heavy wrench, letting the massive end bob. It seemed light in his hands. "In my sleep."

"BEFORE MIRNY?" said Boyko. "I came from the Kuzbass."

"Coal?" Nowek asked.

"My father, my uncles. Everyone worked in the mines. I was sick of breaking my back for tons. I thought I'd come here where they measure results in carats."

"You still have to move tons to get at the carats."

"But who knew? They also offered double arctic bonus pay. So I moved my family here. Back then you could find almost anything in the shops. They had to keep us happy because who else would work in a place like this? Your question about radiation? You're not the first to ask. The government sent in a military team to analyze the problem. They were supposed to stay a week. They left in two days. We never heard the results."

"But you stayed."

"I was making good money. In five years I'd be on a beach on the Black Sea. That was the plan. It didn't work out."

"Don't take it personally," said Nowek. "Those five-year

plans were never too dependable." He watched a black car race around the perimeter road, heading for the surface at breakneck velocity.

A fresh chuff of black soot rose from DRAGA 1's stack. The boom swung over a pile of boulders, then opened its jaws.

Nowek watched DRAGA 1 take another bite. The bucket rose, then started to swing, but it stopped so abruptly the jaws gaped open and car-size boulders tumbled and fell with a dull rumble.

Boyko was already reaching for his radio when a thin wail pierced the silence of the vast pit, the constant rattle of loose stones, the steady whisper of wind.

Boyko had the radio out. "What's wrong?"

A rush of words came back from the tinny little speaker. His face clouded. "Is he hurt?"

"What happened?" Nowek asked.

Boyko snapped the radio off. "Some idiot was inside DRAGA 1 trying to fix something while it was running. An engineer from Sib-Auto."

"What happened?"

"He died."

A white van pulled up on the gravel road that circled the pit. It was the one that had met them at the airport.

An engineer from Sib-Auto. Who else could it be?

"There's your ride to town. I'm afraid I have sad matters to deal with, Delegate Nowek. I won't be able to answer any more questions."

"I have just one more. What are the chances of seeing Mirny Deep?"

Boyko squinted. "Poor. You can ask Mine Director Kirillin if you don't believe me. You'd better go. You don't want to be late."

He thought, *Sherbakov*. They weren't afraid of the FSB. What *were* they afraid of ? The Siberian Delegate?

Nowek took a last look into the pit. DRAGA 1 was silent. What would happen when the pit shut down for good? DRAGA 1 was far too big to haul up to the surface. The terrace roads would collapse under it. It was doomed, condemned, a mechanical monster digging its own grave, roaring as it descended, resolutely swallowing the frozen earth.

CHAPTER 18

Back to the Past

THE PIT BOSS THREW BACK THE VAN'S SLIDING side door and cigarette smog poured out. "Who are you?" asked Boyko.

The driver wore a black leather jacket and sunglasses. He waved a cigarette at Nowek. "They told me to come here and pick him up."

"Who told you to come?"

A thumb jabbed back in the direction of town.

Mirny was a place where everyone knew everyone, at least by face and the pit boss was quite sure he didn't know this face. Boyko kept staring into the van, as though he could force the unexpected back into line. A stranger, but how could there be one in a city so tightly controlled as Mirny? Boyko knew the answer, even if it left him uneasy: there were no strangers. Everyone was known, everyone was here for a reason. This driver was here for a reason, too, even if nobody had told him what it was. Still . . .

"Is something wrong?" asked Nowek.

"No." Boyko turned to Nowek. "Be sure to ask Miss

Arkova from Technical Information about the history of Russian diamonds. You may be surprised."

"Russian history can be very unpredictable."

The pit boss slid the door shut.

The van rolled off, trailing a billowing cloud of rock dust.

"I heard there was an accident," said Chuchin. He took a deep drag. The tip glowed cherry red. "I'm glad you're still breathing."

"If you want me to keep breathing, open your window," Nowek said. "It was Sherbakov."

"I figured." Chuchin rolled down his window. "How?"

"Boyko said he fell into some machinery."

"Maybe your honest friend Levin decided to go out for a walk on his flight from Moscow, too."

The thought had already occurred to him. Levin was supposed to be here already. Nowek didn't know if he'd ever arrived. He was beginning to hope he hadn't. "How did you hear about Sherbakov?"

Chuchin pointed to a radio mounted beneath the dash.

"What happened to Miss Arkova?"

"I'm not the one she was supposed to be interested in. She left me with the driver. His name is Vadim. We had a lot in common."

Nowek smelled alcohol on Chuchin's breath. It was a miracle he didn't burst into flames. "Besides a bottle?"

"Siberians are sponges. You don't know their shape until you get them soaked. He was an old *strafnik* like me." A citizen of the gulag. "I let him do the talking. Me, I hardly wet a tooth."

"So he gave you the keys to the van."

"Strictly in the interests of safety."

"I see." Nowek figured that he would hear more about this later. "Did he tell you anything useful?"

"That Kirillin is no one to play games with. He'll tie a knot in your tongue and ask how you like pretzels. He also said I should think twice about working with you. What about Boyko?"

"He said he was just a simple worker. I believe him. He said diamonds are a dirty business. I believe that, too."

"That's it?"

"No. He's boss of the pit. But there's another mine. An underground mine beneath that tower. It's called Mirny Deep." Nowek nodded at the tall, black structure. "There are levels in it. They call them horizons. It's not a term I was familiar with until today."

"Who cares what they call them?"

"Volsky's last words were *Idi k'gorizontu*. Go to the horizon."

"He could have meant anything."

"He could have meant Mirny Deep."

They came to a gate marked NO. 5. Chuchin stopped by a card reader, slipped a plastic card from his jacket and scanned it in.

The gate began to open.

Nowek held out his hand. Chuchin gave him the plastic card. It had a photo of Vadim. Boyko's regular driver. "Chuchin."

"I didn't steal it. It came with the keys." He was about to drive through, when an ambulance screamed by, heading in the opposite direction. He let it through, then drove off. "The city museum was very interesting. A *babushka* runs it. She took one look at this"—he held out the Marlboro—"and practically begged me to sell her more."

"The miners on our plane had cases of Marlboros."

"Those miners aren't miners. Or at least, they're not just miners. They used to be miners. They've earned special privileges."

"From Kirillin?"

Chuchin seemed surprised. "How did you know?"

"That's how it was in the oil fields back in Soviet times. I think Mirny hasn't changed much."

"They're Kirillin's *mafiya*. In Mirny if you need something you go through them or you go without. The company stores are almost empty, Mister Mayor. I know. I looked. Pockets are empty, too. Volsky was right. People are worried."

"Boyko said that things are tough, but people are eating."

"Well, he's a boss. Did he mention the fire?"

"He called it an accident."

Chuchin snorted. "The only accident was that the miners didn't burn the fucking city to the ground. They were sick of working without pay, so they stole a Belaz. Maybe they were going to drive it to Moscow. Who knows? Someone had the idea of going to the plant. They ran over a gas pipe. There was a spark. *Boom.*"

"Why would anyone stay in Mirny and work for nothing?"

"He said it wasn't possible to leave. They'd lose their accounts."

"What accounts?"

"Kristall pays half their salaries with *veskels*. The other half is in dollars they deposit overseas. Or so they say. If a miner leaves, all he gets to keep are the *veskels*. The miners who aren't miners? They get paid in dollars. It's why they can afford these." He held up the Marlboros. "Everyone else gets a little envelope every month saying how rich he is. Every fucking miner is worth forty, fifty thousand dollars. Except he can't spend it. It drove Vadim's wife crazy. She didn't bother with a divorce. She just left. That's when he started crying and handed the keys over. He wanted to join her, but he couldn't. He said he wasn't brave enough."

It was another pyramid scheme. Stay and work for promises or leave penniless. Nowek sat back in the seat as the dusty road unfurled. Were the dollars even real? Even if they were, he doubted they'd ever find a way into the hands of a miner. No. The miners here weren't just unpaid. They were prisoners. Not of barbed wire or ice. But of their own hope.

Chuchin's leather coat was zippered to the neck, as though winter never left his bones, which, in a way, was true. He glanced at Nowek and said, "You have that look. You're thinking."

"Boyko said their quota was twenty thousand tons of ore a day. A Belaz can carry one hundred tons. That's two hundred trips from the pit to the ore plant."

"I haven't seen three trucks on the road."

"So how are they making quota?"

"They're not."

"Then how could the cartel in London buy four million carats of gem diamond from Kristall? If they aren't coming from the pit, where *are* they coming from?"

Chuchin paused. "The other mine?"

Nowek looked back at Mirny Deep's tower. White vapor streamed from the top. A cloud, a ribbon drawn out by the wind, then gone.

Could Kristall pull it off? Nowek knew it was common practice to keep as much of your business off the books as possible. That's why every businessman, from factory chief to the owner of the corner liquor kiosk, put on paper only what he was willing to have confiscated by the tax police.

But Kristall wasn't a corner liquor kiosk. It wasn't a factory. *It was the source of a quarter of the world's gem diamonds.* Could Kristall run an entire mine off the books? Could they just decide to cut Moscow out of the deal entirely, and make their own way in the diamond world? With the cartel?

The van left a trail of rising dust, a gritty plume that flattened in the wind. They bumped up onto the paved road to Mirny. It was made in typical Soviet fashion: huge precast slabs of concrete dropped like oversize dominoes onto the ground. The permafrost shifted beneath them, sagging, melting, buckling the panels into an obstacle course.

Nowek sat back.

"We try to ignore Moscow."

"That look." Chuchin scowled. "You're thinking again."

"Have you ever heard of a Potemkin village, Chuchin?"

"I don't like travel."

"This was in 1787. Prince Potemkin was governor of Crimea and Empress Catherine was coming on an inspection tour."

"Like you."

"Things were a mess."

"Like now."

"Potemkin couldn't let her find out, so he built a false-front village so she could see how wonderful everything was. Houses, stores, well-dressed peasants. Bread baking in the ovens."

"What are you saying? Mirny is one of these Potemkin villages?"

"No," said Nowek. "That the open pit might be a Potemkin mine. Only here it's backward. They send the gems to Irkutsk and the junk to Moscow, and if anyone comes here to look . . ."

"They can say *From this mine? What diamonds?*"

"Sure," said Nowek. "Meanwhile the good diamonds are sold. Those overseas accounts get bigger."

"Who do they belong to?"

Nowek didn't have to think long. "When I find that out, we'll know who murdered Volsky."

"If you ask me, Volsky would have figured this out."

"Probably."

"And they stopped him. Why do you think you'll do better?"

"Volsky marched into a minefield. We'll take it step by step."

"When it comes to mines, one step is all it takes."

They entered a district of raw, ten-story concrete apartment flats that blocked the view to the mine. Piers elevated them above the permafrost. The unpainted concrete walls were streaked in red rust and grime, the corners gnawed by wind, chipped by cold.

Chuchin said, "You're right. Nothing much has changed in Mirny. It reminds me of a story."

"No stories, Chuchin."

Chuchin was unimpeded. "Lenin, Stalin, Brezhnev, and Gorbachev are riding the train together to the future when the tracks suddenly stop. They hit the brakes and scratch their heads. Lenin says, *Organize the villagers to cut wood for ties! The steelworkers will forge tracks! The rail crews will hammer it into the ground! Shoulder to shoulder, we'll roll on to true communism!*"

Chuchin's eyebrows curved down, tricky and sinister, his accent syrupy Georgian. "Stalin says, *It's the engineers' fault. Arrest them and shoot them. Who needs tracks? We'll run the train across their bodies.* He's about to give the order when Brezhnev interferes. *Comrades! I have an even better idea. We'll pull the shades down and pretend we're moving.* But then Gorbachev says, *Who needs rails? We'll just call the train a bus, drive ahead, and see what happens.*

"The train moves. It's almost off the end when Yeltsin jumps out of the woods with a bottle and says, *Stop! Forget the future! Everyone! Back to the past!*"

"And so?"

"That's Mirny," said Chuchin. "You don't need a nose to smell it."

"I'm surprised you can still smell anything."

"Pah."

The administrative center of town was built around an open square that looked both ceremonial and ominous. A place for parades and executions. In its center, what else? A black, heroic bust of Lenin almost two stories high. It was surrounded by a grizzled fringe of park, all stunted trees and gap-toothed fences. To the right was the mayor's office and the militia station. To the left was a small hotel, the *Zarnitsa*. The name meant *first light of dawn*. At the back of the square was Kristall's *apparat*, its headquarters.

Chuchin slowed as they approached the statue. The ground at its base was studded with broken vodka bottles. Executed in smooth black stone, Lenin glared down at the few people hurrying by. His forehead was bizarrely pronounced, as though ready to burst and spread the seeds of revolution across fallow land.

Chuchin lit a new cigarette from the smoldering tip of the old, then flicked the stub out the window.

Nowek asked, "Do you ever wonder what your lungs look like?"

"Never." Chuchin pulled into a reserved parking spot at Kristall's front door. The *apparat* was modest for a diamond company. Plain concrete stairs beneath a projecting concrete awning. A simple revolving glass door at the top. All the windows were covered by heavy steel security screens. "So." He killed the engine.

Nowek paused, looking at the shabby building.

"You have that look again," said Chuchin.

"How could someone here know where Galena was staying in America?"

"They couldn't."

"So who sent her those diamonds?"

"Someone bigger. Some Moscow shit like Petrov."

"Maybe." Nowek slid open the side door and got out. "I shouldn't be long. Find a quiet place for me to call Moscow. If Levin is still there, he has to know what happened to Sherbakov."

The revolving door swept Nowek into an air-lock entry guarded by men wearing the old uniform of the KGB. They sat in glass booths, their hands poised, waiting for Nowek's papers.

Nowek gave them up and was allowed to pass.

Kristall's *apparat* was two buildings masquerading as one. The bleached, broken exterior blended with Mirny depressingly well. Inside, the lobby looked and felt more European, less Russian. It was orderly, with only a hint of the normal Russian odors of cigarettes, boiled cabbage, and sweat. It took a lot of effort to establish the illusion of order. It took even more to keep Russian smells at bay. Squint, and it might be Berlin.

The vaulted atrium was filled with light. A cascading waterfall of crystals hung from the skylight beams, catching the light and flashing in imitation of a diamond's fire. In the center, a fountain splashed over wet, blue rocks. Not just any rocks, but kimberlite ore, the native rock of diamond.

Nowek walked over to a glass display case.

Inside it, bathed in spotlights, big rough crystals sparkled against black velvet. They couldn't be real, not sitting behind just a thin sheet of glass.

The stones had names. *The Larisa Popugayeva* was the biggest at a full 336 carats, followed by the *Pushkin* at 320 carats. Next the *Star of Yakutia,* the diamond Boyko said was found in a rubble pile, at 304 carats. There was even a *Twenty-Sixth Party Congress* stone. It was a lumpy, egg-shaped chunk with a crack up one side. Someone had a sense of humor, though back then he'd probably been shot for it.

"Delegate Nowek!"

He turned. Larisa Arkova was hurrying in his direction, long legs striding, feet kicking forward, awkward in her heels. Her neck was flushed. She swept a loose strand of hair off her forehead. "I'm sorry to be late. There was an accident at the pit."

"The Sib-Auto engineer."

"He wasn't from Sib-Auto. Director Kirillin called Irkutsk to inform the company. They had no one on today's flight."

Nowek was surprised. That she knew. That she was willing to say. "Perhaps this is not the best time to meet with the mine director."

"No, please. It's all been arranged. We can wait for him in his office. Would you follow me?" She turned away and began walking to the stairs, her heels making that familiar, determined rhythm, one that allowed for no disagreement, no indecision, no alternative.

The elevators each had a sign that read, NE RABOTAYET. Not working. Finally a detail amidst the cool, uncluttered lobby that made Nowek feel like he was still in Russia.

"I understand you were once a geologist," she said as she paused at the foot of the stairs. "So instead of the usual information about our mine, I prepared some notes on the history of the diamond industry. I think history can be helpful in understanding the future."

"Do you really believe that, Miss Arkova?"

"Sure. Don't you?" She didn't wait for an answer before starting upstairs. "The first diamond pipe was mined in an open pasture at Colesberg Kopje, South Africa. That was in 1871."

"It makes you wonder. The deserts of Africa and Australia. Northwest Canada. Siberia," he said. "Why do diamonds show up in such places? Why not New York? Paris? Why not *Minsk*?"

"I'm sure you would know," she said, unwilling to be drawn too far from her script. "The first South African pit was divided into approximately five hundred claims, each ten meters square with narrow borders used as access roads. As the claims went deeper, the roads became less dependable. Kimberlite is not well suited to bearing heavy traffic or loads. The roads collapsed. Mine claims were buried."

"But no miners?"

"Loss of life is expected under unregulated conditions."

"The pit here is safer?"

"The period of individual claims was marked by irrational development. When Cecil Rhodes acquired all the holdings in 1889, those problems vanished. The company he formed was named for the farmer who owned the original pasture. De Beers."

Their slow ascent seemed carefully timed. He felt obligated to throw her timing off. "Have you ever met someone from the cartel?"

"An Oppenheimer. The young one. Nicky. They call him the Cuban because he wears a bushy beard. To be honest, he seemed unhappy."

"All that wealth must be a great responsibility."

"I suppose he was unhappy in his own way." Her steps came fractionally faster, as though to make up for lost time.

"You like Chekhov?"

"You mean Tolstoy. *Happy families are all alike, but every unhappy family is unhappy in its own way.* Or am I wrong?" She knew she was right and dared him to deny it.

He didn't. Couldn't. "What keeps you in Mirny? The bracing winters? You're a skier? A student of permafrost construction?"

"My husband was hired by Kristall."

"So it was love."

"He's been in Angola for the last three years."

"So much for love. My daughter once said she would do anything to get out of Russia. I told her it wasn't so easy. She did it anyway."

That stopped her. Her expression opened slightly. "How?"

"A student visa. She's in America."

"But how was it arranged? You have to be sponsored."

"She was. I have an American friend. Her name is Anna."

Larisa seemed honestly excited, as though Nowek had gone shopping for soap powder and discovered a cache of chocolates hidden behind the box. "Maybe she would sponsor you, too."

"She offered," said Nowek. "I turned her down."

Larisa stood by a closed door. She knocked on it, then took hold of the knob. "So much for love," she said with a smile, and opened it.

CHAPTER 19

The Mine Director

"DIRECTOR KIRILLIN? I'M GREGORI—"

"I know your name." Kirillin had a telephone pressed to his ear. His hand covered the mouthpiece. "Now I'm learning who you *are*. Give me a moment. I wouldn't want to miss anything."

His name might be Russian but the mine director looked like a Korean businessman, dressed in a silver-gray suit, white shirt, and striped tie. In his mid-forties, the native Yakut had nut-brown skin, a black helmet of hair streaked with silver, and the compact, muscular frame of a boxer. With his telephone, his brace of pens, Kirillin could have stepped out of the pages of *To the Diamond Frontier!*

Nowek looked for a place to sit. No chairs. Apparently, Kirillin wasn't fond of long meetings.

There was a bookshelf with volumes so neatly arrayed you knew they hadn't been touched in years. There wasn't a hint of anything personal, anything that suggested a world beyond the immediate grasp of the mine director. A map of the Mirny pit occupied one wall. A polished silver hard hat hung from a peg. Next to it, an overcoat smeared with grease. A window framed a view of drab concrete walls. A snowflake tumbled by.

"That's the general view of the situation," said Kirillin. He glanced up at Nowek. "When can I see a copy of the decree?"

Nowek thought, *There are two kinds of meetings in Russia.* The first, when something is actually expected to happen. There will be a table covered in green baize, one glass for water that no one will touch, one for syrupy sweet soft drinks for sipping, and a small tumbler for endless congratulatory rounds of iced vodka.

Then there is this kind of meeting.

"Tomorrow is soon enough," said Kirillin. "We have weather coming in. Yes. I know. It's Mirny. *Pakah.*" Kirillin hung up and pushed back from his desk like a man finishing a meal. "You were with Boyko a long time."

"Like you, I didn't want to miss a thing."

A quick flash of anger radiated from the mine boss, then vanished. Kirillin pressed a buzzer on his phone and said, "Bring in a chair for Delegate Nowek."

Outside, the snowflakes fell like fat confetti dumped from an upper-story window. "It's snowing."

"It can snow any month of the year in Mirny. You found Boyko informative?"

"Not especially. But I found him reliable."

Kirillin turned slightly, as though trying to catch a faint sound with a bad ear. "Reliable?"

"Like DRAGA 1," Nowek explained. "He told me how long it's been at work."

"Decades."

"And how the American machine broke days after it arrived."

"He said the Caterpillar *broke*?"

"It didn't?"

"It was sabotaged. You want to know why? There was an instrument on it, a kind of a clock that measured the hours of operation. You couldn't run it four hours and get paid for eight, so Boyko's men made sure it didn't run at all. That's how reliable he is."

"Well, he didn't go into details."

"Allow me to," said Kirillin. He nodded at the phone. "That was Moscow. Nobody seems to know why you were appointed to be the new Delegate. Or what you're doing here, for that matter."

"I was appointed by President Yeltsin to take Delegate Volsky's place. I'm here to fulfill his obligations."

"The Kremlin Chief of Staff doesn't know your name."

The Kremlin Chief of Staff was the former mayor of Mirny. Why had Nowek not remembered that until now? "The Kremlin can be a complicated place."

"I'd also like to hear how a man the Moscow militia charged with murder manages to become Siberian Delegate."

"Moscow is a complicated place, too."

Kirillin eyed Nowek with the look of a man seeing a natural enemy. "Mirny isn't so complicated. Here, you are trusted or not. I don't trust you. There were two serious breaches in security today. One was your fault, and the other one might be, too."

"What breaches?"

"A man with false documents arrived on the—"

Two shy knocks came from the door, as though someone was worried it was booby-trapped, as though it might explode.

"Come!"

Larisa brought another chair in, slid it to Nowek, smiled, glanced at Kirillin, then left without saying a word.

"Did you have a problem finding our headquarters building?"

Nowek shook his head. "None."

"I'm surprised. It was your driver's first day on the job."

Nowek thought, *That breach.* "He had a good sense of direction."

"He got one of our employees drunk, took his identity credentials, and then stole his van. Did you think it wouldn't be discovered?"

Not this quickly. Nowek asked, "Where is Chuchin?"

"We're holding him downstairs in case he feels like stealing something else. As for the regular driver, he's been fired. You have yourself to blame. He'll be sent out on the first available flight."

"Maybe he'll be able to join his wife now."

Kirillin cocked his head. "You collect odd pieces of information."

"You never know when something will turn out to be useful."

"You'll find these useful." He reached into his suit jacket and pulled out two paper vouchers. He waved them at Nowek. "Two passes out of Mirny on a special flight to Moscow. As soon as the snow is cleared from the runway tomorrow, you will leave."

"I have no reason to travel to Moscow."

"You will. As Siberian Delegate, you had special privileges. . . ."

"I still have them."

"Excuse me. A decree is being prepared by the same Presidential Administration that appointed you. Your nomination will be rescinded tomorrow. When that happens, you will have no official standing and no official immunity. Mirny is a closed city. It requires permission from Kristall to stay. I can promise you that permission will not be forth-coming." Kirillin held out the vouchers. "Well?"

Nowek didn't touch them. "And if I stay?"

Kirillin tossed them to the desk. "The Moscow militia requested we hold you until they send someone out. If you're here without immunity, I'll have no choice but to comply with this request."

Nowek eyed the vouchers. Leave tomorrow for Moscow and hope Levin could keep the militia off his back, or end up in a cell here until Kirillin decided to send him to Moscow in chains. *Where was Levin?* "What about Chuchin?"

"If you stay, there are additional charges of theft to consider."

Nowek reached over and took the vouchers.

"My opinion of you rises," said Kirillin. He checked his watch. "Lunch is being served at the hotel. If you hurry, you'll find a table."

"I should probably work on my report first."

"Report?"

"The one Volsky was going to write about conditions in Mirny."

"You've only been here a few hours. What could it say?"

Nowek stood. "That a diamond mine that's supposed to be the source of a quarter of the world's gems can't be."

Kirillin's face was a perfect, impassive mask. "How did you come to such a fantastic conclusion?"

"Like you, I keep things simple. The cartel is buying Mirny diamonds? They didn't come from your pit."

"No gem rough has been sold to the cartel in a year."

"No gem rough was sent to Moscow, either."

"Then why did our shipping manifests say otherwise?"

"I was wondering about that, too. I'd like to speak with the person who made out those manifests."

"Take it from me. There is no crime in Mirny."

"Well, that's reassuring. Then there's the ore plant. Fabrika 3. I think Moscow would want to know what happened."

"Some drunk miners in a stolen ore truck? Moscow has better things to worry about." Kirillin reached into his desk drawer. He took out a pack of Marlboros and got one lit.

"That cigarette reminds me of Kristall's *incentive* program. The dollars you stuff into overseas accounts. I believe that's illegal under currency laws."

Kirillin let out a long stream of smoke. "The Finance Ministry does it. The President and his family do it. Why shouldn't a simple worker have the same opportunities to get ahead?"

"There's a difference. The miners can't spend their dollars."

Another cloud of smoke. "It's a bag of feathers. Not a report."

"You're probably right." Nowek started to leave.

"Wait." Kirillin looked grave, serious, even believable. "Let no one accuse us of hiding from legitimate questions. As you said, today you're still Delegate."

Nowek sat back down. "Four million carats of gem-quality rough is missing. Yevgeny Petrov says you filled boxes with industrial stones and kept the gems."

"And who neglected to inspect the shipping containers for the better part of a year? I wonder. Could it be Petrov? Our view is that if Moscow lost them, it's Moscow's problem."

"If they're lost, Kristall won't get paid. Isn't that your problem?"

"Our problem. Not yours. So? What else?"

"I'd like to see Fabrika 3."

Kirillin considered it, then said, "The shift changes at three this afternoon. Boyko will take you through."

"And also Mirny Deep."

"It's been shut down."

"I'd like to see it anyway."

"It's unsafe."

"I'll take the risk."

Kirillin was about to speak when the door clicked.

Larisa Arkova came in, smiling shyly. "Yes?"

"We're finished." Kirillin faced Nowek. "Miss Arkova can answer your questions about Mirny Deep." Kirillin glanced at his watch. "Boyko will pick you up at the hotel at two-thirty. And don't miss your flight in the morning. I say that with your own interests in mind."

"Please," Larisa said to Nowek. "Won't you follow me?"

Out in the hall, Larisa went to the barred window at the end of the corridor. Gray, north light flooded the corridor. Swirling knots of snow danced across the open, deserted square. "What were you hoping to see in Mirny Deep?"

He looked down across alleys, onto a vista of dirty rooftops, plumes of steam, wood smoke. "You have a suggestion?"

She laughed, but then said, "Your daughter. What's her name?"

"Galena."

"Like the mineral?"

Nowek looked up with his surprise. *Galina* was a common girls' name. *Galena* was a metallic, blue-gray cubic crystal of lead sulfide. "How did you know?"

"I think you like things that are unexpected." Her whole face seemed to take on the cool radiance of the north light. "I've planned a surprise for you."

"Mirny Deep?"

"Not that big a surprise."

CHAPTER 20

The Spear

LEVIN ROSE UP OUT OF THE DARKNESS, THE deeps, like a bubble rising through oil. Slowly, slowly, to the light, the air, to a world that only gradually assumed recognizable shape. He rebuilt it detail by detail. A door. A clock. A small plastic radio. The sharp smell of antiseptic. Half his face felt stretched and hot, dangerously thin, a balloon filled almost to bursting. The other half felt nothing at all.

They'd moved him off Hospital 31's busy trauma floor to a recovery area. His new floor was quieter. There were no more screams. Just an annoying American song playing from the bedside radio over and over again. There was a volume knob, but he couldn't reach it.

"Raindrops keep falling on my head. . . ."

He had to think, and think clearly. How had Goloshev known he'd been attacked by *two* flatheads? Had he told him? *No.* From a militia report? *Unlikely.* A witness? *Possibly.* Because he'd arranged it? Four possibilities, two very different implications. For the investigation. For Levin. Most of all, for Sherbakov and Nowek. Levin kept worrying about it like a tongue unable to stay away from a chipped tooth.

Stay away from the Closet!

That had to be a message from Petrov. Yet Goloshev had seemed perfectly willing to pin the loss of all those diamonds on him. If the Toad had sent those two flatheads, didn't that mean he was working for Petrov?

"Nothin' seems to fit . . ."

Either way, he had to get word to Sherbakov, to Nowek, that the man in charge of the entire case might well be working for its principal suspect, that everything about their mission to Mirny might be compromised.

There had to be a telephone on the floor. He tried to move his arm, but it was fastened to the side rail with rubber surgical tubing. He couldn't see out of his right eye. He heard the doorknob rattle, then a voice.

"Wait. This one is due."

The sallow-faced doctor walked up to the bed and beamed a bright light into Levin's eye.

The room vanished behind blinding sparks, galaxies, rainbows. Levin blinked. His dry lips felt welded shut. His tongue was a swollen sock, a cotton towel rammed into his mouth. Levin recognized the "desert mouth" brought on by the sedative scopolamine. It used to be a common interrogation drug until someone noted that even a willing confessor couldn't get the truth by a thick, dry tongue and parched throat. Not that they were looking for truth.

The doctor placed a tray on the table beside Levin's bed. It contained a syringe and two vials. One filled with scopolamine. The other with Antilurium, its antidote.

The doctor picked it up and jabbed the needle into a bottle of straw-colored fluid. He pulled the plunger down, filling it with sleep, with time. He unfastened the surgical tubing that bound Levin's wrist, the better to allow the free flow of sedative.

The sharp prick of the needle almost made Levin cry out. He fought the impulse. The needle slid deep into his forearm. Levin felt the familiar burning. The pressure behind the syringe flowed through it and into him. Pushing, pushing him back down to that dark, quiet place.

A new voice. "We're ready for you, Doctor."

"I said I'll be right there." The needle came out. The doctor stood by, watching.

Levin blinked, fluttered his eye, then closed it.

The doctor left. The door clicked shut.

Levin could feel the deadness. A finger drooped. Another. Sherbakov. Nowek. They had to be warned. He opened his eye.

The rubber tubing had not been refastened. He didn't have much time. His arm was already numb. His fingers were loosening, untying themselves from his bones, dissolving.

As the poison raced for his heart, he clumsily grappled the second syringe from the table. It felt like he was wearing mittens. He brought the needle to his mouth, bit off the cap and spat it out. Light glinted from the sharp tip.

He commanded his thumb to press down on the needle's plunger. A round, milky drop formed. As the ground began to tilt, as he was about to slide off an invisible cliff, down into deep silence, into darkness, he rammed the needle into his belly.

He squeezed the plunger until his fingers no longer obeyed. His arm flopped to his side. The needle, still in him, swayed like a metronome to the beat of his heart.

THE PUNGENT AROMAS OF boiling cabbage, frying onions, and meat filled the ground floor of Kristall's headquarters. It reminded Nowek that he hadn't eaten since

Irkutsk, that Kirillin hadn't invited him to the company cafeteria.

"I'll meet you outside the hotel in a few minutes," said Larisa. "Your colleague is in there." She pointed out a small door tucked behind the hanging waterfall of crystals, then left to retrieve her coat.

Nowek went to free Chuchin. Thousands of diamond-shaped prisms streamed down from the high atrium, like big raindrops frozen in the flash of a strobe. They shifted in currents of air, sending patterns of refracted color across the balconies, the floor, the walls. Nowek touched one. Not crystal. Not even glass. What else would a Russian company that mines a quarter of the world's diamonds use? Plastic.

A small camera stared down from above an unmarked door. A red light glowed below the black lens. He pushed inside.

"It's about time," said Chuchin with as much dignity as a man with bound wrists could muster. His face was flushed red. He perched on a bare wooden bench. A braided cord bound his hands together. It was looped through a steel ring set into the wall. The geometry forced his body into what had to be a deeply uncomfortable position. Not that it showed. With his dark sunglasses still on, Chuchin looked like royalty surveying a room of commoners. He even had a smoldering cigarette pinched between his yellowed fingers. A Marlboro at that. "Did I miss lunch?" Chuchin asked.

"We had to restrain him," the guard apologized. He sat behind the desk. A row of small televisions was mounted on one wall. The dirty window behind him was filtered by steel bars. "We couldn't let him wander around the building. There are diamonds here. You understand."

"Perfectly," said Nowek.

"You'll sign for him?" The guard spun a thick bound notebook around and offered a pen.

Nowek hesitated, considering. "If he's willing to reform."

"Pah," Chuchin snorted. "I've been places where sitting in a warm room was something worth slitting a throat for. This is a vacation. Forget lunch. Bring me a bowl of *balanda* and I'll stay all night." It was a prisoner's soup made with subtle hints of vegetables, distant memories of meat.

"You'll have to earn your *balanda,* zek," said Nowek as he signed, then tossed the pen to the desk. "Vacation's over."

Outside, a high cloud layer veiled the sun.

Chuchin looked up and sniffed. "I smell snow."

"Kirillin said a storm is due in tonight."

"I met him. One look was all it took to know that you can forget about seeing that underground mine. What did he say?"

"That we're leaving tomorrow morning for Moscow."

Chuchin seemed surprised. "How did you convince him?"

"It wasn't hard. He was talking to someone at the Kremlin when I walked in. They're issuing a decree tomorrow to strip me of my title. If I'm still here, he'll arrest me. Us."

"You think Kirillin scared Levin away?"

Nowek thought about young Sherbakov. "I hope so."

Chuchin reached into his jacket and took out his cigarette lighter. It was made from a machine gun cartridge. Chuchin smoked enough to let the dying embers of one cigarette light the next, so it was rarely needed. "Take it."

"I don't smoke."

"You don't drink, either. Sometimes I wonder if you're even Russian. I've had it ever since I was *na narakh*." Behind the wires. The gulag. "And I'm still breathing. It's for luck."

Once, Nowek thought he might learn enough to clear Volsky's name, maybe enough to find out who had taken those diamonds and though it was a very long shot, return them in time. Now his aims were simpler: to leave Mirny alive, to somehow evade the Moscow militia long enough to find Levin. And if he couldn't? How long would he stay alive before he was found dead? What was the current word for it? *Suicided?*

He took the butane lighter, pulled the nose cap off and thumbed the wheel. A spark, a tiny blue flame. Fragile like a man. Temporary, easily blown out. He snapped it shut and slipped it into his parka. "Thank you, Chuchin."

"Don't lose it."

They continued across the open square, heading for the dingy hotel. A stand of slim birches huddled together at the base of Lenin's black marble bust. Their trunks were secured with wire and stakes to keep them upright. They looked like shackled prisoners caught out on a forced march, swaying, an instant away from collapse, too stubborn to die.

The Hotel *Zarnitsa* appeared to have struck some invisible reef and foundered, sinking slowly into the eternal frost that lived a few meters under the earth. The front facade was cracked, grimy concrete. Entire panels had come loose and remained attached only by habit. The stairs leading up to a pair of glass doors tilted wildly.

The double doors made an air-lock entry. The inner door was also made from glass. It was attached to a weight and a pulley. You pushed it open, the weight rose. You let go and the weight fell, slamming the glass panel shut with enough force to make you wonder why it hadn't shattered long ago.

Inside, the lobby was dim. Two women sat at the reception desk behind thick glass panels, watching a small television. There wasn't enough work for one. Why two?

There was a guard, of course. Usually, their main function was to protect the exclusive franchise of the house prostitutes. This one was cut from the common pattern of square shoulders, heavy torso, leather jacket. His hair was trimmed very short, his temples shaved. He sat at a low table, legs apart.

The dining room was brightly lit and booming with loud, excited voices, punctuated by laughter. Nowek listened. A foreign voice. He walked to the doorway and was immediately blocked by a middle-aged woman with a clipboard in one hand and a soiled napkin in the other. The hostess.

"You can't come in unless you're on the list."

"I am. My name is Nowek." Her minor rudeness made him feel better. Almost at home. In Russia, keeping people out is the primary task of a "hostess." Her black hair was alloyed in silver, her bosom the prow of an icebreaker. She wore a red vest and a red skirt, a snowy-white blouse. The toes of her shoes were so sharply pointed they looked dangerous.

"I will check. Wait." She went to her table and called the front desk. A glass bowl half filled with red-and-white striped candies was on her desk. Chuchin reached for them but she shot him a fierce look that stopped him cold.

Nowek scanned the dining room. Several men were eating and drinking together. A large table in the center was threatened by a lurid chandelier made from the same plastic crystals he'd seen at the headquarters building. To one side a stuffed bear reared up, claws extended, slightly more welcoming than the hostess. Waitresses in short black skirts and spotless white blouses floated by the tables with full pitchers of water, impervious to eye contact, deaf to all requests.

The hostess opened her notebook and used a stub of a pencil to write in a name. She snapped it shut. "One of you is Nowek." It wasn't a question. More of an accusation.

"I am."

"Come with me." She turned without wondering whether Nowek might follow.

He didn't.

On the far side of the room, walled off on three sides by ornamental screens, a smaller, private party was eating. Or drinking. Nowek couldn't see everyone at the table. The view was blocked.

"Over *here,*" the hostess said impatiently.

A man in the uniform of the militia, a colonel, no less, was offering a toast. His arm was outstretched, a glass tumbler in his hand. Seated next to him was a man in a poorly cut business suit, his face already pink and rapt with interest as the militia officer spoke. A foreigner sat next to him. He wore a casual sport coat and no tie. What was it called? A blazer? The skin of his face was deeply tanned.

Nowek walked over. The colonel sputtered on for a moment after he saw Nowek, then let his arm with its brimming glass of vodka slowly sink to the table.

Nearer, Nowek could see around the decorative screen and into the partitioned space.

A plate of pickles, onions, and carrots was on the table, flanked by more plates of cheese, salami, and bread. A silver bowl sparkled with the fat black marbles of expensive caviar. Two bottles of vodka stood guard beside it, along with pitchers of untouched fruit juice. And one more guest, a woman.

It was Larisa Arkova.

THE WORLD OUTSIDE HIS WINDOW was pitch dark, but Levin was wide awake. He put the used syringe back on the table in time for the night nurse to find it. He listened as she made her final rounds. His ears were acutely tuned. Approaching feet, the slight rattle of a knob. The tiny squeak his door made just as it was opened.

He closed his left eye and relaxed. The room light went on with a sharp snap. The night nurse didn't bother checking Levin's pulse. Apparently that was secondary. She tugged on the rubber restraints. Left arm, right. Both ankles. Soon the lights snapped off, the door shut. Levin opened his eye.

The room was lit by a sliver of yellow light coming in beneath his door. He kept listening. There was a narrow window of opportunity between the night nurse's last check and the arrival of the morning staff. When he heard the nurse shuffle by his room, when he heard her chair squeal as she settled back into it at her station at the end of the hall, he twisted his right arm, exposed the slipknot, threw off one restraint, another, and pushed himself up.

His head swam. Levin fought it by staring at the bar of light beneath the door. His horizon. At first it tipped, tumbled. But then it steadied and stopped. Blood returned to his head.

He could reach his ankles. He pulled loose the last two knots that kept him bound, then swung his legs out into space and felt for the floor. A toe. A foot. Both feet. He let his weight accumulate, gram by gram, until he was standing.

The mirror drew him. It was three steps away. One step

steadied by a hand on the bed, another by the sink beneath the mirror. In between, a bottomless black chasm to be crossed unaided, alone. One step. He took a deep breath and crossed it, proud as though he'd run a long race. There was a fluorescent tube above the mirror. He switched it on.

His first thought wasn't a thought, but a spasm. Someone else was in the room. Someone with half a face covered in bandage, tape and gauze, and the other half a bruised balloon ready to burst. Purple, red, gentian violet, ghastly white. A monster. But when Levin blinked, so did the monster. He tried to gently peel away the bandage over his right eye, but the gauze was stuck to something deep. When he pulled harder, flashes of jagged light stopped him, as though everything inside his head would come spilling out.

He turned the light off and went to the window. Snow, glowing under streetlights. The sky the charcoal gray of old, cold ash. What were the chances of getting out dressed in a white sheet and bare feet, with a face like *his*?

Levin went to the door and cracked it open.

The hall was empty. Silent, except for the soft snores of the night nurse. Her head was on a crimson pillow she'd placed on top of the desk. Levin looked closer and saw the telephone.

With one hand on the wall for balance, he started to walk. He stopped every few steps to listen. Only the hum of lights, the whirring of fans, soft snores. When he drew near, he saw the name tag on her white cap: L. Pavlova. Lydia? Lena? She was more the Ludmilla type, he decided. He could call Sherbakov's voice mail at the office, and if he checked in, he could be warned. He reached for the telephone and . . .

"*Shto?*" It came out in a sleepy slur.

Levin froze. She swept a lock of hair off her cheek, briefly considered waking, shifted in her chair and pinned the coiled phone cord with her elbow.

An elevator rumbled up from below. Air whistled out through the crack between the doors. It kept going. He waited until the snores returned. The phone was not going to help. He looked around for another, and saw the computer.

He went around her desk. The screen was dark. He tried to see where it was connected, but where it was connected was hidden behind two ample thighs. He touched the keyboard.

The screen snapped, buzzed, filling with bright blue clouds and symbols. Yellow file folders. Unknowable hieroglyphs, runes. Where was Sherbakov when he needed him? Sherbakov was probably saying the same thing of Levin.

In one corner of the screen was something more recognizable: the time, the date. *Wednesday. At least it's still September.* Then, in the opposite corner, another familiar symbol: a blue globe. Levin sent the cursor skittering to it. He placed it over the blue sphere and clicked.

A cascade of fervent notes rose from somewhere beneath the desk. A connection was made. There was a new icon on the screen. Levin had used it only a few times before, but he knew it. Levin began to type.

To: wizard-private@russiamail.com
From: ivl-private@russiamail.com

Levin knew Sherbakov checked his *elektronka* hourly. He'd be attached to it by an umbilicus if he could. He only hoped the security program, his *KGB* "virus," kept the message he was about to send from being read by the wrong eyes.

If you are still in Irkutsk, stay there. . . .

When he was done, he moved the cursor over SEND, but then stopped. He went back to the box that sent a copy of the message to others, and began typing again:

CC: <gnow@russet.ru

It was more than he'd hoped for, and less than he'd wanted. But it was everything Levin could do. He heard the elevator rumble again. Air whistled through the shut doors, higher, higher, and then stopped.

The doors opened.

Two nurses. White uniforms, faces rumpled from rising too early. Hair pinned beneath white paper caps. They were almost to the desk before they saw him.

"What are you doing out here?"

"Call an orderly!"

They didn't need one, for when the nurses rushed him, Levin fell into their strong, snowy arms.

LARISA ARKOVA WHISPERED SOMETHING to the foreigner, then stood, gathering her coat, smiling her apologies. "You're early," she said to Nowek. "We're just finishing."

"Am I too early?"

"Not at all," said the foreigner in excellent Russian. "You're just in time. By tradition, the second toast is in honor of the women at the table. The third can be for the new Siberian Delegate." Navy blazer, blue oxford shirt, no tie. You didn't have to hear his accent to know he wasn't Russian.

"I'm afraid I don't have time for toasts," Nowek said.

"Delegate Volsky said almost the same thing."

The room seemed to narrow, to taper in on itself like one of those strange geometries with six dimensions, folded, convoluted, focused. Nowek stared. "Excuse me?"

"I was in Moscow last Saturday. I was visiting a club called *Ekipazh*. I ran into your predecessor and invited him to join our table but, like you, he was too busy."

Nowek felt the chill of that night invade his bones again. The cold, and the fire, too. "Who are you?"

The foreigner fingered a small business card from the inside pocket of his blazer and handed it to Nowek.

Eban Hock
Strategic Resources, Ltd.
Lynnwood, Pretoria
South Africa

There was the silhouette of a horse on it. Or was it a chess piece? "What did you want to speak to him about?"

"Business. The presidential representative for all of Siberia is a man I need to know. I'm a *konsultant abrazivanye*."

A business consultant. "What sort of business did you have with Volsky?"

"We really should be going," said Larisa.

"Why? The Delegate's plane doesn't leave until tomorrow."

Nowek thought that Mirny was like a cobweb. Touch it here, and it vibrated everywhere.

She said, "We have a busy afternoon scheduled."

Hock wagged a finger at her. "I'll be in Africa seeing your husband next week. He won't approve, Larisa."

"It's not for him to approve." But Larisa sat back down.

"Right." Hock took a bottle of ice-frosted vodka and splashed a tumbler full. He offered it to Nowek. "It's decided."

"It's not," said Nowek. "Miss Arkova is right. I have work to do, Mister Hock."

"You're the first Russian I've met who wouldn't mix drinking and working."

"You haven't answered my question about Volsky."

Hock gave Nowek's glass to the colonel. "I was in Moscow to meet with the chairman of the State Diamond Committee."

"Petrov."

"You know him?"

"We never met. What about Volsky?"

"He and Petrov had their heads together when I showed up. They were together only a short time when Petrov stormed out and said that Volsky had demanded money."

"For the miners."

"I wasn't there. Come to think of it, neither were you. In any event, Petrov left in a big hurry. A few minutes later Volsky came out looking ready to break someone in half. He asked to borrow my cell phone. I invited him to sit down and talk. But like you, he was too busy. And now here you are."

"What brought you here, Mister Hock?"

Hock sipped his vodka. "The same as anyone. Diamonds."

"You're a buyer?"

"When necessary. Generally, we're paid with them. When a mine runs into trouble, there's usually no money for consultants. But diamonds? Plenty of them."

"Kristall is in trouble?"

The militia officer was about to interrupt, but Hock said, "No. He's asking serious questions. We should give him serious answers." He took another sip and said, "Some diamonds have gone missing. My client would like them found."

Four million carats? "You mean Chairman Petrov."

"Petrov?" Hock laughed. "He's *why* they've gone missing. No. I'm working for Kristall."

He's why they've gone missing? It was exactly what Nowek thought. Why did it leave him so uneasy to hear Hock say it? "You think they disappeared from Mirny?"

"No doubt some did. Every mine in the world leaks. Diamonds are the most condensed form of wealth known to man, and who mines them? The poorest of the poor. Sierra Leone or Siberia. Poverty and wealth make a combustible mix."

"And you put out the fires."

"That's a bit overstated. The diamond world is like a country. It has rules. We remind people what they are. Usually, that's enough."

"And so you hunt down diamond smugglers if it isn't?"

"We'd rather enlist them." Hock emptied his glass, then reached for a pickle and took a quick bite. "We buy what they sell at a very fair price. That way, they guard their own turf. They keep the ones you don't know out of business so we don't have to, plus the stones end up back in legitimate channels."

"Legitimate according to the cartel?"

"What makes London happy makes everyone happy."

"So you're working for the cartel, too."

"Yes and no. Do our interests overlap? Sure. But in a way, the cartel is also our main competition. Who needs us if the machinery is running smoothly?" said Hock. "Take

Botswana. The whole bloody country is in the cartel's pocket. The phones work. There are schools, hospitals. The streets are swept. It's the Switzerland of Africa and I haven't had a reason to go there in six, maybe seven, years. Then there's Angola." Hock shoveled up a pile of caviar with a toast point.

"The Catoca Mine ships eight million dollars' of rough a month only because we guard it. If we left, the rebels would overrun it in a day. The diamonds would go to the black market, prices would fall, and Larisa's husband would end up with his hands chopped off. Chopping hands is the specialty in Angola. That and a charming custom they call *spear sitting*."

"Spear sitting?"

"It happened to one of the UN's boys. His name was Phillipe. The rebels caught him in the bush and tried to sell him back to us. Negotiations broke down while the UN decided what to do. The bandits got impatient. They decided to make an example of him."

"Eban . . ." said Larisa.

"They stripped poor Phillipe naked and tied him to a wooden pole about eight feet high. Tied him to the very top. Did I say that they'd stuck a great long spear up Phillipe's anus?"

"Eban!"

"No doubt he tried to hang on as long as he could, but his weight pulled him down. It took him all night to die. In the morning, the tip of that spear was poking right out his mouth."

"Stop it," Larisa protested. "You're disgusting."

Nowek thought, *What's the specialty in Mirny? Falling into machinery?* "You're here, so Russia must be more like Angola."

"Fewer generals. More politicians. They can be expensive, but at least you're sitting at a table and not staring into a gun."

Politicians like Petrov? Or like Volsky? "You say you enlist smugglers. Who have you enlisted here?"

The militia officer said, "That's an outrageous . . ."

"Simplification," Hock finished. "Do we look for ways to cooperate? Of course we do."

"What happens if you find someone you can't buy?"

"I couldn't tell you," said Hock.

"Because it's a secret?"

"Because it's never happened."

CHAPTER 21

The Cleaner

OUTSIDE THE HOTEL *ZARNITSA* THE FLURRIES
had stopped, but the clouds had lowered. The horizon was
soft and indistinct, with no division left between earth and
sky. The air was heavy, windless, silent.

Nowek saw a militia jeep parked on the sidewalk. On its
roof, two orange lights flanked the customary blue. "I didn't
expect to be arrested until tomorrow," he said.

"Don't worry." She seemed to think Nowek was joking.
"We're just borrowing the jeep. In Mirny, everyone has two
or three jobs. We maintain the militia's vehicles. When we
need transport, we call on them."

"Do you also have other jobs?"

The driver leaned on the horn button.

"We'll talk on our way."

To where? Nowek looked inside the jeep and recognized
the guard from the hotel lobby. He had both elbows propped
on the steering wheel. His black jacket was unzipped. It fell
open enough to see the leather straps of a holster sling.

She opened the rear door for Nowek to get in.

Nowek eased into the backseat of the jeep. He reached

to close the thin door, expecting her to climb in front with the driver. But she didn't.

Instead she carefully stepped onto the running board, slightly unsteady in her heels, then, with knees together, swung herself in. She patted her skirt back down as she settled in next to Nowek. Her perfume was sweet, but there was another, deeper note to it, a richness Nowek couldn't identify.

Her face was bright with expectation. She said to the driver, "Okay."

The jeep lurched over the curb, out onto the empty street.

"You asked about my other jobs," she said. "Besides doing technical translations for the company, I teach English in the school. I take the children on ski outings in winter. Our slope is called Diamond Hill. You have a daughter but you don't wear a wedding ring. You're divorced?"

"No. My wife died three . . . no, four years ago."

"From an illness?"

"An airplane crash. They said it was because of bad weather, but it wasn't. The pilot had his teenage son in the cockpit. The son wanted to fly. The father let him." Nowek paused. "One hundred and sixty-four people were on board. Nina was one of them."

Larisa's face seemed to deepen, become more serious. "How did you find out the truth?"

"I looked for it. Sometimes that's all it takes."

They turned off Bulvar Varvara onto Ulitsa Popugayeva, named for the woman who found that first Siberian diamond. The street was lined with almost identical eight-story apartment buildings, each precisely angled away from the street like a phalanx of concrete chevrons. They were decorated in an alternating color scheme of white and blue.

The clumsy attempt to relieve the monotony only accentuated it.

"There's my building," she said, pointing. "The first
blue one. It's not much but we're comfortable."

"I thought your husband was in Angola."

"I live with my daughter. She's six and hasn't seen her father in years. Her name is Liza. She wants me to call her
Britney. Can you imagine such a thing?"

"My Galena wants me to call her *Gail*." Bringing up
Galena made Nowek feel anxious. It was too easy to open
up to Larisa, but then, that's probably why she had this job.
"Does Hock come to Mirny often?"

"Not often. He was here just nine days ago. We were all
surprised to see him so soon."

"What is he doing here now?"

"You'd have to ask. . . ."

"Kirillin?"

"Well, what should I say?"

Nowek was leaving in the morning. She would stay behind. The answer was clear.

They came to an intersection. They turned right, and
soon the buildings stopped and a tall fence made of welded
steel bars began. Behind it ranks of Belaz ore trucks
moldered in various stages of decay. Graders, bulldozers,
cement mixers parked in rows. Kristall's motor pool, a gulag
for dangerous machinery.

"Technical information. Translation. Classes. Ski instruc-
tor. Mother," said Nowek. "Your day sounds very full."

"In summer there's berry picking. There's a small garden
plot that demands all my time. In spring, I strip birch bark
for the vitamins. The bark makes a nutritional tea."

He tried to imagine her stripping pieces of wood from a

tree, a member of some primitive, prehistoric tribe, dressed in a slim blue skirt, white silk blouse, high heels. "It sounds"—Nowek paused—"very resourceful."

They passed a knot of men standing in the lee of a kiosk. A battered white Lada sedan was parked on the curb. Its bumper rested on the wooden boards of the little shop. Six men dressed in heavy jackets and tall rubber boots. It was a liquor kiosk, open of course, with its name emblazoned over the window in bright red: NADEZHDA. As they approached, the men eased behind the kiosk, as though Nowek's presence could somehow infect them with an incurable disease.

"The liquor kiosk accepts *veskels*?" he asked.

"They could demand babies and get them. Hock is right. Everyone drinks. In Mirny, especially. Last winter, someone stole a few thousand liters of jet fuel. He mixed it with industrial alcohol and sold it on the street. Six people died, but the ones who survived were back in line the next day. You can say that drinking is one way a person can leave Mirny."

"Getting blown up at the ore plant is another."

She looked away. "Life is hard. But you can't just give in and say there are no answers. You have to make a plan and stay with it. If I thought there were no answers, I would have been on that Belaz, too."

Larisa seemed to answer serious questions casually, and casual questions seriously. "So what's your plan, Miss Arkova?"

"To live a normal life. For Liza, too."

"In Mirny?"

She suddenly reached forward and tapped the driver's shoulder. "Turn *here*!"

The jeep veered off the pavement and went bouncing

across a muddy path in the direction of a clump of sad, dispirited trees. The path ended at a rusty steel fence. They came to a stop.

She pulled out a net bag, known everywhere in Russia as a *what if* bag. As in, *what if* the store has something to sell? *What if* I happen across something that's been unavailable for months, and will be gone in an hour? She got out and made straight for the fence. The stand of dwarf cypress beyond was scarcely tall enough to block the wind, their crowns at eye level.

Nowek and Larisa were giants, approaching some secret, miniature forest.

Larisa walked along the fence, tugging at it, then stopped, knelt, and peeled up a section of chain link.

Something tickled Nowek's cheek. He looked up. The windblown Fairy Dust, the opening flurries, were done. This was the beginning of a storm.

"They'll all be covered if we don't hurry." She held the fence up for Nowek, and he knelt down and scrabbled through.

A layer of brown sawdust covered the ground. It was already turning white. Larisa moved deliberately, slowly.

Her long legs reminded Nowek of those elegant birds that stalked fish in shallow water. "What are you looking for?"

"Keep still and use your eyes." Larisa walked over to a small mound of wet, half-composted sawdust. "Here." She knelt beside it and brushed away the wood debris to expose the fleshy cap of a rising mushroom. *"Agaricus bitorquis."* The cap was gray, the gills a chocolate brown. She plucked it out of the ground, found two more nearby, and popped them into her bag.

"You brought me here to pick mushrooms?"

"The snow will bury them. The first one is hardest. Mushrooms are shy. Watch. Now they'll appear everywhere."

Nowek had never thought of mushrooms as *shy*, but she was right. Once the first mushroom mound was detected, others seemed to materialize, peeking from beneath fallen limbs, from piles of dead dry leaves, under rising crusts of half-frozen sawdust.

Spot. Bend, uncover, pluck. Her net bag began to fill.

Nowek let the snow accumulate on his shoulders. Second by second, the balance of brightness shifted back and forth between the overcast sky and the snowy earth. He enjoyed the mindlessness of the hunt and it surprised him. "I have a question, Miss Arkova."

"I've brought you to my secret mushroom patch. I think you can call me Larisa."

A secret place she shared with both Nowek and the militia driver. "Did Kirillin tell you to keep me busy this afternoon?"

She let out a derisive puff of breath. "He thinks he has a hand in everything." Her slender fingers snatched at the mushrooms now with violence. She shredded a brown cap and tossed it away. "It's best to let him think so."

Under a tangle of berry canes, he spotted something different. A mushroom of another variety. He cleared away the bramble and plucked it. "What about that one?"

"Do you drink?"

"Not much. Why?"

"It's *Coprinus atramentarius*. Tippler's Bane. If you eat it and drink alcohol, you could be paralyzed for a day or so."

"Kirillin would give you a bonus," said Nowek. "But it would probably be in *veskels*."

"No thanks," she said. "I can eat mushrooms."

Nowek smiled. Chuchin was fond of saying that under the Soviets there was nothing to buy, but at least you could afford it. Nowek didn't trust Larisa, but he understood her.

"It's enough," she said. Larisa's sack was filled almost to capacity. She brushed off the wet sawdust from her bare knees, her skirt. Snow drifted down featherlight, constant, muffling.

Nowek looked at his watch. Boyko wouldn't arrive for another hour and a half. "The mushrooms. They're good?"

"I'll show you."

"DOCUMENTS."

Levin stood in the aisle of an airliner, the way out blocked by two militiamen in heavy winter greatcoats. Their fur hats were tugged low to keep the area of skin exposed to bitter cold to an absolute minimum. Instead of the traditional red star of the militia, Kristall's blue diamond was pinned to their hats.

Levin was sweating. It was too hot for the guards to be dressed for a blizzard. His shirt was drenched and still it poured from his skin. He reached into his jacket. The pocket was empty. His wallet was gone. He looked up, confused, but then he remembered. "I already sent them."

"Who did you send them to?"

A jet was taking off nearby. Its thunder made the air tremble as it roared overhead.

"I sent them to Mirny. I sent them both to Mirny."

"Who did you send them to?" the guard demanded again.

Levin thought, *Can't you hear me?*

"Who did you send them to?"

Levin started to speak, but the words were drowned by another departing jet.

"*Levin!*"

He opened his eyes. The light was unnaturally bright. Almost bleached, as though a flash had gone off and not quit.

Goloshev, another man Levin felt he should recognize but didn't, and a third he had no idea about at all. The stranger's head was bald as a bullet, his skin fishbelly pale. Loose bags of skin underscored his eyes. All three wore dark coats. All three gazed at him with the solemn, perplexed stare of foreign tourists trying to decipher the Moscow bus schedule.

The room had changed. Levin looked to where the mirror had been. A blank wall. Where the window had looked down on a snowy parking lot, a closet door. And instead of the surgical rubber tubing, thick leather bands immobilized his wrists.

They'd moved him.

"Good. You're awake." It was Goloshev. "You gave us all a scare, *boychik*." He nodded to the one Levin thought he should recognize. "Maybe you should check him again."

Yes. The sallow-faced doctor from Hospital 31.

Another jet roared low overhead, making the glasses on a bathroom shelf tinkle merrily.

A hotel room . . . near an airport. There were no airports in the middle of Moscow. All of them were thirty, forty kilometers out of town. Which one was he near? *Shermetyevo? Domodedovo? Vnukovo? Bykovo?*

The doctor took his pulse, put a light in his eye, measured the pupil's contraction, inserted something into his ear that beeped. "His temperature's coming back down."

Sweat pooled under the small of Levin's back. He was shaking with fever. His bones ached from it. He tried to move, but he couldn't. The leather restraints had no give in them at all. A specimen mounted to a board, ready for dissection, had more freedom. He squinted against a desert-dry glare that seemed to come from inside his eyes.

"They say you'd pulled your bandages halfway off," said Goloshev. "You know what would have happened? They'd be cleaning your brains off the floor with a mop. Everyone said it was impossible. The doctor. The nurse. I told them if there was a way, Levin will find it."

Levin found that his throat was no longer stuffed with cotton. They were using something new on him. It made him feel hot and light, so light the leather straps might be all that kept him from floating away. They wanted something. What?

"Look," said Goloshev. "You know the situation. You know why there's no time. The two messages you sent? Something happened to them. Some kind of germ . . ."

The third man said something.

Goloshev waved at him impatiently. "Germ. Virus. Whatever. They were scrambled like eggs," said the Toad. "So you've *got* to tell us what was in them and who you sent them to. You must do it *now*."

Another jet, even louder, lower than the others, thundered overhead.

"Levin, we don't have forever. In ten days it will be all over. Ten days and the whole fucking country will . . ."

"He knows that," said the third man.

Goloshev stopped, then said, "I'm doing my best to shield you. But you have to help me. There have been developments."

Developments? Levin thought, *Sherbakov.*

"I went into your office safe. Materials were needed for the investigation." Goloshev leaned close. "I found the letter. I had to give it to them, Levin. I had no choice."

Letter? Levin glanced at the third man.

"He's no friend. He had the doctor give you something to clear your mind. A lot of it. If you don't start—"

The bald man touched Goloshev's shoulder. The Toad immediately stopped talking.

He outranks Goloshev, thought Levin.

The stranger reached into his jacket. "We have a lot to talk about, Major Levin. Shall we begin?"

Levin's heart jumped. But the stranger held out his identity card, not a pistol. Levin's ID carried the single red stripe of state security. This card had *three* stripes: the white, blue, and red of the flag of the Russian Federation.

He leaned close, his voice a hoarse, smoker's rasp. "I'm Chernukhin. I'm with the Presidential Security Service. Your commander found a document in your safe." He reached into his other pocket and pulled out a folded sheet of paper. "I won't waste time reading every word. I think you'll understand the situation quickly enough." With that, Chernukhin began to read.

The Office of Internal Audit and Inspection wishes to express its gratitude for your assistance in our efforts to assess the current Russian situation. As suggested, we will brief bank officers in charge of Russian accounts to make certain your information is considered in their deliberations and decisions. We recognize your help could not have come without risks, both personal and professional. It is our belief and our hope that these risks will prove small in comparison to the ultimate goal of a Russia free from the yoke of official corruption.

"Enough?" Chernukhin let the letter flutter down onto Levin's chest. He peered down, his pale blue eyes bright as polished steel. "In ten days, President Yeltsin will hold talks with representatives of the IMF. It seems you've been talking with them already. You are going to tell us all what you said."

Who wrote that letter? Levin's eyes darted between Chernukhin and Goloshev for an answer. His thinking was like a leaf caught in a gale.

The crescents under Chernukhin's eyes were shadowed, almost purple. "Now I have several questions, and I want you to answer them all in the greatest detail. Is this understood?"

Levin felt something inside his brain pry open his mouth and spit out the word, "Yes." What had they given him?

"Let's begin with your two *elektronka*. These messages were encrypted. The code is nothing we've ever seen. It's better than the nuclear codes the President carries around. I know because the person who created them told me. It's impossible to break. Who gave it to you? The Americans?"

His tongue was being pulled by strings in someone else's hands. He took a breath and said, "Sherbakov."

Chernukhin looked at the Toad.

"His assistant. A lieutenant. He's a kid."

Chernukhin took Levin by the shoulder and shook him. "Do you want to see your country go through another 1998? If it happens, who will get it in the neck first? Bankers. The media. Academics. In short, Jews. How much do the Americans know about the Closet? Where did that encryption program come from?"

"Sherbakov."

"Fuck." Chernukhin slapped the side of Levin's bed with

his open palm, then looked up at the doctor and said, "This isn't working. Give him more."

The doctor stood at Levin's side. He was frowning.

"What's wrong?" asked Chernukhin.

"I have enough scopolamine, Sodium amytal, and Pentothal to make a horse recite Pushkin. But you can't just use one after the next. They're like colors. Throw them all together and you don't get a rainbow, you get mud. His system must be flushed."

"How long will it take?" asked Chernukhin.

"Tomorrow morning should be enough."

Levin felt a tear form in the corner of his good eye. He wanted to tell them something, anything, but the truth they refused to accept.

"Levin, this is serious," said Goloshev. "Maybe you can clear it up with a few words. I know if you were yourself, this would be a joke. Try hard and tell them the truth. You have to."

Chernukhin leaned close to Levin. "We have something in common. Like you, I have a nickname. I'm known as the Cleaner. I make sure there's no dirt for the President to step in. Right now, that's you. You're a traitor. I don't need to give you chances, but I will. How much do the Americans know? What did you tell them? Is it *Israel* that you're working for? They're clever with computers. They have a big diamond industry. Is that it, Levin? Have you sold your country to the kikes?"

We don't want kike money!

Levin had no answer, truthful or otherwise. He shivered. The sweat poured out of his brow and trickled down his neck.

"Where did you send those two messages!"

Now he did have an answer. "Sherbakov."

The Cleaner turned his back to him and said to the doctor, "Eight o'clock. We'll open his head like a chestnut."

THE MILITIA JEEP PARKED at Larisa's apartment building. He followed her in. There was enough snow to leave footprints and it was falling more heavily by the minute.

"You won't meet Liza. She eats her lunch at school. It's nearby." She led him up the broken steps to the front door. The building was elevated above the ground to keep it from melting the underlying permafrost. Nowek saw that the buzzer was by the name ARKOV. Her husband. "How did you meet Hock?"

She inserted one key, turned the lock, then another key, a second lock, and the heavy wooden door opened. "Kristall sent some representatives to South Africa to negotiate an assistance package. I went along as translator."

"His Russian seems good enough."

"We didn't know."

"Besides, it was a chance to travel?"

"Of course."

The lobby was marred with graffiti on the walls. The floors were filthy with ancient grime, glittering with shards of broken vodka bottles. The elevator door opened onto black space. "Vandals. Does Kirillin know?"

"There is no crime in Mirny." She said it with Kirillin's Yakut accent. She started climbing the stairs. The dim light of the impending storm filtered down from a skylight. All the fixtures had been stripped of bulbs. The third-floor corridor was floored in chipped vinyl. She unlocked her door.

Even before he walked into her flat, Nowek knew what

it would be like. Outside, Russia can seem like an old silent movie, a bleak world where the skies, the buildings, even the people are gray. But inside is another world, another universe exploding with warmth, with life.

Larisa's flat burst with unexpected color: the bright spines of books, German magazines, gorgeous Oriental scarves draped over battered furniture, posters from an exhibition of French Impressionists, photographs of children at play in snow.

Nowek felt instantly at home. He'd grown up in this room, or one so much like it the differences didn't matter. The kitchen table served as living room, dining room, recreation area. There would be a toilet behind one door. A small bedroom behind another. An oversize closet where the babies would sleep.

Nowek could close his eyes, reach for anything and find it. His father's enormous black piano would have gone over there on that wall, far from both window and radiator, where Larisa had a couch and a coffee table with an arrangement of silk flowers faded to delicate ivory. The only jarring note was the computer and monitor on Larisa's desk. *That* was something Nowek's father would have thrown out the window.

She put a kettle on to boil for tea while he settled himself on her couch. There was a picture of her daughter, Liza, standing against a stand of deep green pines, a dark blue sky, a few white clouds. A cool day in late spring. She had a halo of golden-blond hair, tousled by wind. She was wearing a thick red jacket and holding a long pencil. Her face was illuminated by light, confident of a future that would be wonderful. Looking at her, Nowek could see why Larisa would do anything to make it so. He'd felt the same way about Galena. He still did.

Larisa melted some butter in a pan and began to chop some mushrooms for sautéing. From the tiny white refrigerator came a jar of cream cheese. From a cabinet, a tin of Kamchakta crab and a sack of kasha. The kasha went into a pot to cook. The crab was mashed into the cheese, then she tossed the mushroom caps into the sizzling butter.

A woody, nutty smell filled the apartment. When the pan turned dark, when the first smoky wisps began to rise, she removed it from the heat and began stuffing the caps with cheese and crab.

Dishes magically assembled themselves under her hands. "You'll never get mushrooms like these in a restaurant."

He joined her at the small kitchen table and took a bite of the buttery cap, the rich crab, the cream cheese. It melted to rich velvet in his mouth. "You're a good cook."

"I don't get to show off much."

"Maybe you and Liza could join your husband."

"Mirny is still better than Africa." Larisa popped a mushroom cap into her mouth. She chewed, then said, "Your daughter in America. You could join her, too."

He'd be lucky to leave Moscow. "It's not my plan."

"I would go like that." She snapped her fingers.

"What's stopping you from leaving Mirny?"

"You need money to leave. A lot."

"You really don't believe in those overseas dollars?"

"I see the statements every month like everyone, but so long as diamonds aren't being sold, they'll never be real."

"Maybe they are being sold. All those dollars might be real. Everyone in Mirny should be able to buy a ticket out."

"It's like talking about a world neither of us will ever see."

"What kind of world were the people at the ore plant looking for?"

"What did Director Kirillin say?"

"That four drunks were responsible."

"*One* man was responsible. A boy, really. But he wasn't alone. It was practically the whole *shakta*. And some from the plant, too. One man planned it. The blood is on his name."

Planned the operation? It was very different from drunks stealing a truck. And *shakta* meant *mine shaft*. The open pit was universally called *karir*. "What happened?"

"They took a Belaz and decided to stop at Fabrika 3 on their way. They were going to stage a protest against the company. They ran over a gas line. There was a spark. Thirty from the *shakta* died. Another dozen from the plant. Some right away. They were the luckiest. The driver the company assigned to you? Vadim? His wife wasn't so lucky."

So she had found a way to leave Mirny. Though not the way Nowek had imagined. What had Volsky said? *They're murdering them.* He felt like he was standing on the rim of something important. Like the open pit itself. "It's safe to tell me all this?"

She put down her fork, then reached across the table and took Nowek's hand. "Just don't bring it up with Boyko."

Her slender fingers were warm from the tea. "Why not?"

"His son was driving the Belaz."

"Boyko's *son*?"

A horn sounded from out on the snowy street.

"Don't worry." She stroked the back of his fingers lightly, casually. "He's not your problem."

"Who is?"

She made a movement with her other hand, sweeping it in an arc, as though the very air swarmed with malevolent spirits.

CHAPTER 22

The Diamond Line

NOWEK PAUSED IN THE ENTRY TO LARISA'S building, looking out on the dim street. Full dark came on fast at sixty-two degrees north latitude. The streetlamps were already on at three in the afternoon. They cast circles of sulfurous light that swirled with cold, fine snow. He put his parka hood up. In the time it took to hurry between Larisa's door and the waiting van, its fur ruff frosted white. *His son.* He slid the door open and got in.

The pit boss said, "Fucking snow. When winter starts early, it stays late."

Boyko drove off before Nowek got the side door closed. The wheels skidded, then caught, throwing him back against the seat. He could see in the rearview mirror that Boyko's hair was matted and greasy, his face smudged. There were stains on his clothes that might be red hydraulic fluid, or not. He looked like he'd spent the afternoon asleep under a bridge and had gotten up hungover and mad.

"I thought you were used to winters in Mirny."

Boyko's prominent brow was beaded with sweat. "You

spend a day picking a boy out of a pulley and we'll see what you're used to."

Sherbakov. "Did you find out what happened to him?"

"I already told you. He died. You and Mine Director Kirillin had a useful discussion?"

"He did most of the talking."

"That's Kirillin. So what did he say?"

"There's been a change in my plans. I'm leaving tomorrow morning."

"You'll be lucky to get out of Mirny, Delegate Nowek."

As the van bounced along the rutted road, the last gray light drained from the sky. The blocky, cubic shape of the ore plant appeared on the horizon, golden in sodium security lights.

"So," said Boyko. "That's Fabrika 3. The biggest building in town. Built in 1984. It swallows boulders of ore from the mine, breaks them into three hundred–millimeter chunks in a tumbler, grinds the chunks to eighteen-millimeter pebbles, sifts the pebbles for diamonds, and shits the tailings out the side." The headlights struggled through the slanting snow. "The sifting is done in stages. First centrifuges, then media cyclones, vibration tables, and grease traps."

The snow was mesmerizing in the headlights. It swept across the beams in wind–driven diagonal streaks, suggestive of furious forward speed. Like Gogol's troika, striking sparks as it hurtled across the snow. Russia, the envy of the world.

The van lost traction and started to skid sideways. Boyko wrestled it back onto the road. "The grease traps catch nearly all the diamonds in the pebble stream. Diamonds hate water but they stick to grease like glue. We boil the grease and skim it like soup. The diamonds sink to the bottom. The girls in the diamond line pluck them out with gloves and drop them into lockboxes. The last stage is the X-ray sorting hall. Trust me, you don't want to go there."

"Your driver Vadim. Didn't his wife work on the diamond line?"

"Ask Kirillin. You have some other questions?"

"One. Is there going to be anything to see at the ore plant?"

"Broken kimberlite and machines, and the machines won't be running. They're holding the next shift back until you're out."

"Then there's no reason to go."

Boyko looked alarmed. "Everything's been prepared."

"That's another reason not to go. Then there's you. My wife died in a plane crash four years ago. I can't look at the mountain where it happened. Leading a tour there would be out of the question."

There was a pause, then "I'm sorry, but why tell me?"

"Your son, Boyko. I know what happened to him."

The pit boss blinked, surprised. "Kirillin told you?"

Careful. Nowek could see Boyko's hands clenched on the steering wheel. His scarred knuckles were white. "No."

"I didn't think so. You asked to see the ore plant? You're going to see it. Let no one say we denied you a thing."

Except understanding. A son dead. Trapped in Mirny. And Boyko still could use the word *we.* How could he remain so loyal? Was it habit? Or fear? Nowek watched the snow beat against the windshield. "What was his name?"

A longer pause, then "Alexei. He died on his birthday. He was twenty-one for just two hours."

"I have a daughter. She's eighteen. She's in America."

"I already know. Be glad. At least she's safe."

You know? "I thought so," Nowek said. "Then someone

sent her a pair of diamond earrings. The note inside said *From Siberia's eternal frost.*"

"Then we're the same." Boyko turned. "They've got you by the balls, too."

"Who is it, Boyko? Who sent her those diamonds?"

The only answer came from the dry, cold snow hissing against the windshield like poured sand. A gust of wind rocked the van.

Were he and Boyko really so similar? Nowek thought, *Yes, except your son is dead and Galena is alive.* The same, except that you've given up, and I have not. He wondered whether the van was bugged, and decided it no longer mattered. "Tell me about your son."

"Alyosha?" Boyko's chest heaved. He swiped his mouth with the back of his jacket. "Everything we did, it was for him. Coming here. Staying here. So what if the whole country was fucked? We had something to point to. We had a reason. He would live a better life."

Nowek could feel something building up in Boyko. He didn't speak, he didn't want to stop it, to get in its way.

"He wasn't a miner. That was okay. Three generations breaking rocks is enough. Alyosha had a mind. He could do anything."

"In Mirny?"

"That was my mistake." Boyko's face grew stony, even more impassive. "Last year, when there was still money, we could have left Mirny. But where could we go that was better?"

"I can think of a lot of places."

Boyko didn't seem to hear. "We had our apartment, a small dacha. Our greenhouse grows melons sweeter than any from Astrakhan. There's practically no crime. Unspoiled nature. Where could you find that in Russia? I figured that so long as we had something the world was willing to buy, we'd ride out the storm."

"Diamonds."

"You asked about Moscow? They turned their backs on us and they still expected us to work around the clock. They still expected our diamonds to show up every week. How long could that go on?"

It was the same question Volsky had asked. "So Kristall started sending them junk instead."

"When you hand your wallet over to a thief and then he demands your wife, what are you going to do? It was rape. The company determined that we could make our own way without Moscow. If they wouldn't send us rubles, someone else would send us dollars."

"The cartel."

"Only we were wrong. We were just changing one thief for another. It's almost funny. Before, when we were slaves to Moscow we were more free. Now that we're free of them, we're slaves."

Nowek thought it sounded like something Chuchin might say. "Slaves can't leave. But miners can. Why don't they?"

"You know what my Alyosha wanted? A new computer. I would find him up in the middle of the night, working on the old one. Who knows what he was up to? My son could really use his head."

"Kirillin said he was drunk the night he took the Belaz."

"He was a safety supervisor. He'd no more drink on duty than piss in my pocket." Boyko had both hands on the wheel, his grip so tight he might have expected it to fly off into the snowy night. His voice was even, controlled. "Maybe it was my fault. I told him the company would stand behind us. I told him to wait, that Kristall was beginning a new chapter. It would give us everything we were owed."

"But they didn't."

"Not fast enough. My Alyosha wasn't patient. It's why he liked computers. Push a button and something happens *now*." Boyko stopped, took a deep breath. "I had to choose. Blood, or company." He turned and looked straight at Nowek. Sweat glistened on his face, though it was cold enough to see his breath.

"You chose Kristall?"

"My second mistake," said Boyko.

A white glare swam out of the darkness ahead. A double halo of approaching headlights. Someone was leaving the ore plant. Not a Belaz. The lights were too low. Boyko pulled over to let them pass, pausing at the foot of a bridge.

Nowek looked down. A fast-moving stream ran beneath the bridge. White steam rose from it. Thanks to permafrost, streams weren't rare in Siberia. But a *warm* stream had to be coming from beneath the permafrost layer, down deep where the rocks become hot to the touch. "You're pumping a lot of water out of Mirny Deep."

"I told you it would flood if we didn't."

"You also said the *shakta* was abandoned."

The approaching vehicle was a militia patrol. Shadowy faces in the dashboard light. Then it was gone, heading back to town.

Boyko threw the van into gear and steered out onto the tracks left by the militia.

The ore plant loomed out of the night, floating above the tundra, bathed in beams of bright yellow light swirling with snow. Closer, Nowek could see that its windowless skin was made from sheets of corrugated steel. Soot painted one vertical wall in long black scabs that fanned out from ground zero.

The road curved. Nowek could no longer see the damaged wall. They came to a high steel gate and stopped. He put his hand to the window. A faint but definite throb. Something was making the glass vibrate, in and out of phase. Some big turning machinery. They hadn't stopped everything for his visit to Fabrika 3.

Boyko rolled down his window. Fine snow blew in as he pulled a card from his pocket and swiped it through a reader. The gate began to open. He drove through and immediately came to a stop at a second barrier. The outer fence had already closed. The inner one remained locked. They were trapped between the two.

"Both gates are never open at once. We call it the Dead Zone."

"A gate wouldn't stop a Belaz."

"A Belaz can climb a thirty-percent grade with a hundred tons of ore in back." He used his card again. A green light flashed on, a warning tone sounded, and the inner gate began to move. "Alyosha could have taken the whole building down if he wanted to."

"What stopped him, Boyko?"

The gate was open. The beeping continued.

"He was your son."

"That's right. *My* son. Someone handed your daughter diamond earrings? They burned my Alyosha like bacon. Volsky sent your daughter to heaven? My son had to die to get there."

Nowek felt the cold flood in through the window. It cut right through his parka and lodged in his ribs like a knife. "I never told you Volsky arranged Galena's visa."

"Listen," said Boyko. "If the computer inside the plant

doesn't read my card in five minutes, an alarm goes off. Where is Boyko? You don't think someone is watching? Someone is *always* watching. What do you want from me, Delegate Nowek?"

"The truth. You didn't leave Mirny when you could. Kristall is selling off diamonds to the cartel. They're keeping the miners like prisoners. Your son wanted to do something about it. Volsky wanted to do something about it, too. You didn't help your son. You made some bad choices. Maybe it's time to make a good one."

"And cut my own throat?"

"No," said Nowek. "And stand by your son."

They didn't move. The gate beeped impatiently. The green light flashed.

Boyko took a long, long breath, and let it out slowly. He held up his hand, short, powerful fingers stretched straight and taut. They tensed, curled into a claw, a fist. Just when Nowek thought Boyko would hit him, the pit boss slammed his fist down onto the steering wheel so hard it made the van shake.

"Fuck."

Boyko jammed his boot down onto the accelerator. The van skidded, gripped, jerked into motion. Instead of going straight to the ore plant, he turned right.

"They'll shoot me," said Boyko. "Maybe first they will beat me. People work. We mine ore. We deliver diamonds. Not to Moscow . . ."

"To Irkutsk. To Golden Autumn."

"On paper we're rich. All those dollars, just waiting for us at the end of the rainbow. It's all a fantasy. But when reality looks like *this,* fantasies look good. We know the system was invented to pick our pockets. We know we're just the fools at the end of the line. What do we do? Nothing."

"Your son tried to do something."

"Yes, he did," said Boyko. "And I'm proud."

A dirt road circled Fabrika 3. Security lights bathed every square meter of its skin. Curtains of snow billowed through the yellow beams. Cameras on poles peered down. But the island of light was surrounded by more than double fences. It was surrounded by darkness, too.

They came around to the side of the building that was scorched. Boyko turned away from it, bounced off the road, onto the open marsh. The van lurched over uneven ground.

It came at them unexpectedly, a ruined concrete building, small, barely a shack. There was a metal door set in one side. The roof was partly collapsed under a pile of junked steel beams and crumpled metal. Boyko urged the van over a pair of deep ruts. The van tipped down, then up. The headlights swirled with confetti snow.

They stopped on a giant wheel half sunk into the ground. Twenty blackened bolts orbited a charred cinder of an axle. A ladder, its rungs and railings distorted by intense heat, draped down to the ground from a platform that projected from a shattered, glassless cab. The number 7530 could still be read on its side.

Not a junk pile. A burned Belaz.

Boyko switched off the engine, but left the lights and wipers on.

"Volsky told me that the miners were being murdered," said Nowek. "The fire was no accident."

"It was a *Zabastovka*. A strike," said Boyko, staring at the burned ore truck. The windshield wipers swept dry snow off in clouds. "It was nothing new. Someone would gripe, there would be some whispers. The next thing you knew, the complainers were gone. But Alyosha? He did things in his own way."

"With an ore truck?"

"A computer. That's what he was doing in the middle of the night. Sending messages. Organizing everything."

"By *elektronka*?"

Boyko nodded. "In Mirny, computers are toys for children. Kirillin had no idea what they could be used for. It must have driven him crazy. He couldn't read Alyosha's messages. How could he stop them?"

Nowek wondered how much of the five minutes they'd burned up, how much time they had left. "How many people joined the strike?"

"The entire third shift from the mine, most of the workers here at the plant. The girls of the diamond line. Even some of the militia. They stopped work at the same moment. It was like a military exercise. The Belaz was waiting for them when their shift ended."

"At Mirny Deep."

"They were going to take their demands to the city. Right into the central square. Right up the steps of the fucking *apparat* if they had to. What could stop a Belaz?"

"Kirillin."

"They were waiting for them." Boyko switched the wipers off, then the lights. "It was an aviation flare. The bastard tossed it into the fuel. The first explosion burst the tank. Fuel was everywhere. The second explosion was the bad one."

Nowek saw the ruptured tank. It was peeled open, a jagged hole in its side, as though a giant had gnawed at it with a can opener.

"I was at home and I felt it. *Boom, BOOM!* Two. I knew it couldn't be from the *karir*."

"You knew the pit was already abandoned."

"Why blast tons when you can take a shovel and scoop up all the diamonds you'd want in an hour? Anyway, I looked out the window, I thought it was the end of the world. An atomic bomb." Boyko turned. "Fire was everywhere. Alyosha could have jumped for it. Instead, he backed the Belaz away from the plant. There were people who would have burned to ash if he hadn't. He made it this far before the fire got him. Maybe he was already dead when the truck ran into the ventilator. We'll never know."

Ventilator?

"It was August. People weren't even wearing work jackets. The women's dresses melted to their skin. They looked like black garbage bags piled up on the catwalk. You couldn't pull them apart. They didn't even know how many there were. You could tell the miners, though. They were cinders with aluminum hard hats, and the hard hats had all melted down over the faces like masks. They had to wait until the next shift to see who showed up to know the names of the dead." Boyko took a deep gulp of air. "When I got here the ground was still smoking. I found Alyosha's hands on the wheel. No flesh. Just bone. When I touched his shoulder, my hand went right through. He was hollow. My son's bones were hot to the touch."

"Boyko . . ."

The pit boss opened his door. Snow swirled in. So did the loud hum of a powerful motor. He sat there for a moment, then reached into a pocket for a cigarette. He patted his pocket. "Match?"

"Here." Nowek fished Chuchin's lighter out, flipped the cap back, and snapped a pale blue flame to life.

The cigarette flared red. "That afternoon we had lunch together. A picnic. We drove out to the observation platform at the *karir* and spread a blanket. It was the last time we were a family. You know how a big space swallows sound? I remember how quiet it was."

Boyko took a deep drag, then let the smoke out. "Some white cranes flew over. Snow cranes. People say they fly to America. Like your daughter. It was so quiet you could hear wings beating the air. Alyosha told me what he was going to do. I said wait. There's a better way. He let me see the demands. There was nothing out of the ordinary. Pay us normally. They were willing to take *veskels,* but they wanted their names on those dollars."

"How did Kirillin find out about the strike?"

Boyko took a sudden breath, a half-choked sob. He sucked the cigarette down to ash, then said, "At the *karir,* I told you there were no *stukachi* here. It's not true. There was one."

Stukachi. Pigeons. Informers. Nowek read Boyko's face, saw what was there, and wished he hadn't. *"You?"*

"Now you know."

Nowek looked at the ventilator shack. He could see another one in the dim light, dark against the drifting snow. They lined up perfectly with the headworks tower over Mirny Deep. "There's a tunnel connecting Mirny Deep and the ore plant. It's why you don't need ore trucks. There's a buried conveyor system."

"The real diamond line." Boyko faced Nowek. "You put things together, Delegate Nowek. You see under things. I understand now why Arkady Vasilievich chose you."

Arkady Vasilievich. It was not the way a stranger spoke Volsky's name. "You said you came here from the Kuzbass."

"From Anzhero. Three generations. Coal runs in the blood."

"Arkady Volsky came from Anzhero."

"We were different. All I wanted was sausage and beer. *He* was like Alyosha, he always wanted to change things. Where did it get either one of them? You tell me."

"His connection in Mirny," said Nowek. "It's you."

Boyko flicked the dead cigarette out into the snow. He checked his watch. "We still have a couple of minutes before they come for me. Let's walk." He got out and walked straight for the door in the concrete shack. Nowek followed him.

The air was filled with invisible crystals of snow.

They were under the wrecked Belaz. Though it had been months, the smell of the fire was strong and powerful. Up close, Nowek saw what he had not seen from the van; one wall of the shack was made up of metal louvers, and there was a faint light coming through the narrow cracks in the vanes.

Boyko pulled at the door handle, leaning back, using his legs. It opened, squealed, then stuck fast. Dim yellow light showed at the crack. "Go on. Look. You've earned it."

Nowek wedged himself through the opening. There wasn't much to see. Faint light came from a manhole in the floor. It barely illuminated unpainted concrete walls, crude graffiti scrawls. It was just a few steps to the hatch. Nowek looked down.

It went a lot farther than he'd imagined. Or perhaps the darkness gave it depth. A ladder, and at the bottom, Nowek saw the conveyor.

Boyko heard a sound and turned. A pair of lights appeared. A car was coming. Maybe Kirillin himself. Boyko didn't care. "We drove the tunnel through permafrost with a steam lance. A hundred meters a day. The pilot drift was done in three weeks."

The two headlights slowed, then turned their way.

"I figured that once we were in full production, everything would fall back into place. Then they started handing out those fucking *veskels*. Fuck. We were getting screwed and Alyosha had the balls to say so. After they murdered him it was *We're not so sure about you, Boyko*. After twenty fucking years, they weren't *sure* of me? I informed on my son, and I couldn't be trusted? They pulled me out of Mirny Deep and sent me back to the pit. *Pit boss*. A joke." He heard the thump of car doors. He turned.

It was the militia jeep. The spotlight blazed to life and caught him square in the eyes. "Tell them I went crazy. Say I forced you to come here. Say anything you want. Either way, it's finished."

Nowek didn't answer.

"Who's there?" A shout from the jeep. *"What are you doing?"*

"Nowek?" Boyko wedged his massive chest through the slim opening. *"Nowek!"*

The vent shack was empty.

CHAPTER 23

The Flight

To: wizard-private@russiamail.com
CC: <gnow@russet.ru
From: ivl-private@russiamail.com

If you are still in Irkutsk, stay there. If you are in Mirny
leave quickly. I am in Moscow, in Hospital 31. I won't be
coming to meet you. I was attacked and you can say
the only accident is that I am still alive. I think it was
arranged by someone in our own department. Maybe
by an amphibian we both know. Until we speak, trust
only the Delegate. And be cautious. If they would do
this to me here, what would they not do in Mirny?
There's no time. I'll explain later.
Levin

YURI DURASHENKO PUT THE SHEET OF PAPER
down and turned on his desk lamp. He'd arranged for the
local Internet company to make copies of anything coming
or going from Nowek's e-mail account. A friendly girl had
fished it out. But what did it mean?

The low afternoon sun sent a weak shaft of light through the cavernous hangar below his window. It was growing cool. His stylish Hilfiger sweatshirt, jeans, and Adidas, all Chinese copies of the real thing, were not enough to stop the invading cold. "When did this arrive?"

Plet shrugged his massive shoulders. "She didn't say." Plet wore a silver-gray blazer over a black silk turtleneck and jeans. The effect was like chrome plating a tank. Decoration only accentuated the underlying menace. Plet was well over six feet tall. His hair was black as sable and cut very short. Before prison he'd been an interrogation specialist in an elite unit of the Red Army.

"What's her name?" asked Yuri, reaching for one of his five desk phones. "I'll call her."

"Sabina. She won't be there," said Plet. "She works nights."

Yuri read the *elektronka* again. A message from someone named Levin, to "wizard." Who was this wizard? A colleague? Someone who'd come from Moscow, had been in Irkutsk, and was heading for Mirny? Like Nowek. But not Nowek.

Wizard could only be the young FSB lieutenant who had been Nowek's militia repellent. That meant that Nowek, the lieutenant, and this Levin, were working together on something, and with millions of carats of gem diamonds missing, wasn't *that* interesting? "It says *don't go to Mirny*. Who else left with Nowek?"

"His driver and the fucking KGB." A prison doctor, a KGB officer, had erased Plet's anti-Party tattoos with acid. Plet had them redrawn, only to have them blotted out again. When he put them on a third time, right over the scars, they finally left him alone. For Plet, *fucking* and KGB went together naturally.

"So Nowek really is working for the FSB."

"What difference does it make?"

"You're missing the point," said Yuri. "If Moscow is worried about one of their own, what does that mean for Nowek?"

"That Mirny's a bad place to go."

"Right. So how much is it worth to have the new Delegate in our pocket?"

"He's not in our pocket."

"I'm thinking ahead. What's the weather?"

"Snow by tomorrow."

Yuri picked up a Mont Blanc pen and tapped its heavy, reassuring weight on the polished desk. "You know the Siberian Delegate reports directly to the President."

Plet's blank look went subtly, and sarcastically, blanker.

"I know. But Yeltsin won't last much longer. Maybe not even until the election. Maybe there won't even *be* an election. Someone will make a move. Right now, that's Putin."

"Fucking KGB."

"*Right.* The guy who ran the agency Nowek is working for now. It means Nowek has a solid line to the top and if we help him now, he's going to owe us forever. It could be our big chance."

"Mirny is a long way to go for a chance."

"Then there are the diamonds. I wouldn't mind being around when they're found. Would you?"

"Finding is one thing. Keeping is another."

"Plet, you've become very negative." Yuri sighed and reached into a drawer and pulled out a small black instrument about the size of a flattened brick. A screen occupied one end, a keypad the other.

"What's that? Another cell phone?"

Yuri held it up. "Global Positioning. Satellite navigation.

A Garmin. Brand new. Point-to-point steering from this desk to the runway at Mirny. You know what this costs?"

"I'm not buying."

Yuri switched it on. A small screen glowed. "One thousand and ninety-nine kilometers to Mirny." He tapped a few numbers, a few letters, waited, then said, "Two hours and twenty minutes if I take the *Okurok.*"

Okurok meant *cigarette butt,* an unflattering but universal nickname for the small, stubby Yak-40 jet. The Yak was the jewel in White Bird's crown. Three powerful engines gave it the ability to land and take off from short airstrips. Its fat fuselage was perfect for outsized goods. A cargo ramp built into its tail could handle anything from reindeer to oil drums. Even people. It was a rugged machine perfectly suited for Siberian conditions.

"What about fuel?" asked Plet.

"They have fuel in Mirny."

"For us?"

"We might have to negotiate something," said Yuri. "What do you think? Is it worth it?"

Plet considered the question professionally. "It depends on how happy Nowek is to see you, and how long he remembers."

"Let's assume, very happy and long enough." Yuri sat back in his chair. "Two and a half hours there. Refuel. We find him. Mirny is small. An hour on the ground. Then two and a half back."

"The jet's expensive to fly."

"Plet." Yuri tossed the pen to the desk. "Putting a price tag on friendship. I'm disappointed."

Plet's expression underwent another fractional alteration.

"Especially when he works for the FSB. Especially when the next president of Russia is also FSB. And most of all, *especially* because our friend the Delegate knows a lot more than he's saying about four million carats of diamonds. It makes my blood boil to know they were running them right under our noses. We should have been in on that opportunity from the start."

"Like the dog skinner."

"Never mind. Who is this Sabina anyway?"

"A student during the day. A dancer at night."

"Dancer? What kind?"

"At *Night Flight*."

Yuri's eyebrows went up. *Night Flight* was an expensive club. It hired only the most beautiful women "associates." He checked the time. It was almost five o'clock. They could be back before midnight. "Have them pull the jet into the hangar and warm it up. I hate cold seats." Yuri rummaged in his desk and unfurled a spaghetti tangle of wires, the cables that connected the satellite navigator to the jet's autopilot.

"Nowek might not even be alive, you know."

Yuri gave up and balled the wires up, then snapped a rubber band around the mess. "He's only been there a day. How much trouble could he find so quickly?"

Plet blinked, looked up at the ceiling.

"True. He has a talent for it." Yuri thought about it and said, "Better tell the Brothers I'll need them tonight." He reached down into the desk drawer and pulled out a small, yellow box. The label said CHANEL NO. 6. He tossed it to Plet.

Plet examined it closely. The printing was fuzzy and the label proudly proclaimed it a *Product of Malaysia*. "It's a fake."

"You're an expert on French perfume now?"

"Number *Six*?"

"It's the new model," said Yuri.

———

"NOWEK!" Boyko's shout echoed off walls of ice.

Boyko. Volsky's inside contact. Boyko, a father who had informed on his own son, and by doing so had killed him. Nowek felt for the next rung down. His boot found only air. He stopped and looked. The conveyor belt below was still a good five meters down. A long jump. He shifted his weight to get a better view, but the ladder began to slide, carrying him down, the metal squealing with rock dust and disuse. He stepped off the last rung directly onto the ore belt. Without his weight, the ladder retracted back up like a fire escape.

It felt warmer down here, and it was. The belt was woven metal, spun from steel wire. The surface was covered with a half-frozen sludge of gray rock paste that crunched under his boots. The tunnel was big. You could almost run a metro train through it. The walls were all rough-hewn and jagged, as though they'd been cast from poor, crumbling concrete. Pale and dry, studded with ice wedges, glittering with crystals. Permafrost. Siberia's "eternal ice."

"Nowek!"

He looked up. A light was sunk into the ceiling of the tunnel. Heavy cables were strung up there, too. Blocks of blasted ore had gouged the walls. A frayed cord dangled from the final rung of the ladder. He could reach it, pull the ladder down, and climb back up.

Or not. Volsky had said, *Go to the horizon.* Mirny Deep had *eight* horizons. It was his chance. His last. Tomorrow would be too late.

Kirillin is connected with Hock, and Hock is connected with the cartel. Who else was bound by a chain of diamonds four million carats long? *Boyko's son. Sherbakov. All dead. And if the IMF turns away? Russia will die.* It was a chain that wound its way to Moscow, maybe to the Kremlin itself. Wherever its ultimate end might be, that chain had its beginnings just ahead.

A steady breeze flowed down from the vent shack. A distinctly stronger wind came from behind, from the direction of the ore plant. A deep mine had to breathe. Somewhere, fans were drawing fresh air into Mirny Deep's lungs.

Nowek put the wind at his back and started walking. The feeble light soon gave out. The belt barely deflected under his boots. What was Nowek's weight compared with boulders of ore?

Ahead, another dim glow marked the next light, the next vent shaft. Would someone already be there, waiting? Nowek knew that by running deeper into the mine he was only complicating Kirillin's job. Not altering the outcome. One way or another, sooner or later, he would be found. And then?

The glow grew nearer, brighter; he stopped and listened. The whistle of air, and now something else. Not the hum of a fan, nor the steady rush, rush, rush of blood in his own ears. Something more like the soft crunch of a boot in refrozen snow, coming from behind. Someone else was in the tunnel.

If the computer doesn't read my card in five minutes, an alarm goes off. Where is Boyko?

He walked under the glow of the next light. Another ventilation duct, another ladder, another dangling rope. Another downward rush of icy wind. The flood of air pushed him deeper. He kept it at his back. Except for the vent shafts, lights, ropes, and ladders, it could be a treadmill. He was walking, sure. But where? The sheer sameness of it lulled him. Perhaps that was why the meaning of all those deep scars in the walls didn't register sooner.

He ran his hand along the side wall. The cuts had been dug by tumbling boulders of ore. The ore plant didn't send rock to the mine. The mine sent rock to the ore plant. Nowek was walking up a one-way street, headed in the wrong direction. All someone would have to do was turn the conveyor on and wait for Nowek to be spit out of the tunnel at the plant like a piece of errant luggage.

Ahead, the next vent shaft grew brighter.

He could hear the hum of fans growing, as though big rapids on a wild river were drawing near. The flowing air urged him on. There was no reason to be cautious. No reason to be slow. He could run and the sound would be swallowed by the fans. He started jogging. He'd taken only three loping steps when, with a *snap,* the distant glow marking the next shaft went dark.

Nowek glanced back in the direction he'd come from.

A spark of white light flared. A flashlight, moving in slow confident arcs, the beam growing brighter. Whoever held it had the easy pace of a hunter with his quarry already cornered, who knew there was nowhere for Nowek to go but where he wanted him to be.

YURI THOUGHT OF THEM simply as "the Brothers." Anzor, Aslan, and Mahmet actually were. Mahmet was the eldest, Anzor the baby. The fourth, Bashir, was a cousin who'd made his living as a locksmith. His services were in great demand after the Russians were thrown out of Grozny the first time. There wasn't a safe, abandoned, buried by rubble, he could not open.

Then the Russians came back. The Brothers escaped the doomed city under the thunder of artillery. Instead of melting into the mountains, they took the last train north to

Moscow. The militia stopped them and threw them onto another train, this one heading east. They tried to get off, but no city wanted them. Six days later the train neared Irkutsk. They were hungry, broke, desperate. They jumped off before the station and wandered to the airport, thinking they might hijack a flight back home.

Yuri hired them on the spot.

The four Chechens had dark, ringletted black hair, sharp, angular features, black eyes, and volcanic tempers. They acted like a family. An incautious slur tossed at one in the Irkutsk bazaar was promptly answered by all.

The Brothers sat in a huddle beneath the Yak's high tail, smoking potent tobacco and drinking equally smoky black tea from a metal thermos. The jet's tail ramp was down. They were dressed in mottled green, tan, and white camouflage jackets and pants. Winter garments for the Red Army, except that the Red Army couldn't afford them now. They wore dark karakul hats. Mahmet had pulled his down almost to his eyes. Anzor adored him, and wore his the same way. Bashir and Aslan wore theirs pushed back at a jaunty, less threatening angle. Thirty-round AK-102 magazines were stacked nearby like dominoes.

Yuri did a quick check of the jet, pausing, probing, making sure that all the critical items were attended to. The Yak had once belonged to Aeroflot. It was taken over by a Siberian oil company in exchange for a mountain of unpaid fuel bills. Yuri had acquired it in a complicated deal that gave him possession without having to list it as White Bird's property. He painted out the old name, the old registration number, and replaced them with pure white-and-blue WHITE BIRD AIRLINES lettering.

No matter that its ownership was muddy. The Yak was

tangible evidence that if Yuri worked hard good things would come his way. People called it "Cigarette Butt." It *was* stubby, and the wings had none of the elegant sweep of more modern business jets. And when all three Ivchenko turbojets were in full cry, the roar was all but deafening. Even in the cockpit. But to Yuri, it was a mark of his achievement. He could scarcely believe that he'd begun with an old biplane covered with fabric measled with silver tape. It was an affirmation that Yuri Durashenko had what it took to make his way through the chaos that was Russia.

He walked over to the Brothers' huddle. "Everyone set?" Yuri waited. No one moved. "What's wrong?"

"There are diamonds in Mirny," Mahmet explained. "Winter is coming. Life will be difficult in the mountains."

Sometimes the Brothers seemed as impenetrable as the Siberian forest. "*What* mountains?"

"*Kavkass.*" The Caucasus. "Sending money to our families is like sending ice cubes. A little bit melts at every step. The banker, the agent, the courier. By the time it arrives, not much ice is left."

"And?"

"Diamonds don't melt."

Yuri did the simultaneous translation. "Okay. Let me get this straight. You want to be paid in diamonds so that you can send some back to Chechnya?"

Mahmet shrugged. "As you like."

"What if there aren't any diamonds?"

"We trust in God," said Mahmet.

Dealing with the Brothers was like negotiating with a band of pirate clerics. Pious men who lived by the teachings of the Koran and would slit your throat if they felt like it, but then feel obliged to find religious justification for it. Yuri looked at his watch. He didn't have time to haggle. "Suppose we run across some loose diamonds. If we do, everyone gets a share. But no guarantees."

"As God wills."

"*I* will that we get moving. I have to be back by midnight."

The Yak's cabin contained ten seats, a sofa mounted along the side, a VCR, a bar. Even a samovar. It left plenty of room in the aisles for the Brothers' carry-on luggage: four *Kalas,* AK-102 assault rifles, were piled against the arm of the sofa, their slings brightly decorated in tribal weavings. The short, foldable 102 was the weapon issued to Russia's elite airborne troops. Two RPG rocket-propelled grenade launchers were secured by seat belts. The seat sagged under the weight of a canvas *sumka* filled with conical grenade rounds. A PK machine gun on a bipod squatted in the aisle, with boxes of ammunition stacked around it.

Yuri tugged the explosives-laden *sumka* to be sure it wouldn't move with turbulence. The last thing he wanted was a rocket going off. They'd brought enough firepower to stage a modest invasion, which a simple flight to Mirny surely would not be. Satisfied, he pulled the tail ramp up and locked it.

Yuri settled himself into the cockpit's front left seat. The business end of the Yak was a tight fit. It seemed to have been designed by an indecisive committee. The seats were bright red, the armrests green, the ceiling tan, the instrument panel pastel blue. Three yellow throttles sprouted from the center console. He gave the ready signal to the waiting tug.

The Yak emerged from the heated hangar, out into the night. Yuri looked up at the cold, brilliant stars, then snapped the master battery switch on, bringing his own galaxy of lights blazing into existence on the instrument panel.

His hands flitted above the toggles, the dials, the handles. In a moment, a loud whine and a rumbling roar announced the awakening of the first turbojet. The cockpit lights blinked, went out, then came back brighter than before. The second and third engines joined the first. Yuri gave the signal, and the ground crew pulled the tow bar away and fled, their hands over their ears.

Yuri advanced the three yellow throttles on the center console. The engines built up to a thunderous shout, and the Yak began to roll. He touched the windshield. The glass was already cold. He hoped there was an extra parka on board.

He steered the Yak out onto the runway and ran all three throttles forward, and the little Yak climbed into the cold night, streaking over the dark expanse of Lake Baikal.

Yuri retracted the flaps, switched the autopilot on. If the GPS was healthy, if the cat's cradle of wires was hooked up right, he would have nothing to do until it was time to land.

The nose wavered, then swung decisively north. He smiled, sat back and watched as the faint lights of the tiny fishing village of Lystvyanka fell beneath his wing.

CHAPTER 24

The Ore Chute

NOWEK CONCENTRATED ON KEEPING HIS FEET beneath him. It was impossible to say how much ground he'd covered, how much remained. His boot caught on some irregularity and he fell. Sharp-edged rocks slashed his knee. He got up and took another step.

And fell. This time, not against rubble, not against the diamond line's conveyor belt. But against a steep ramp of smooth, slick ice. He needed a light. He remembered that he had one.

Nowek pulled out Chuchin's cigarette lighter, popped it open, struck a fat spark, and a blue flame glowed.

Nowek was at the bottom of a wide, icy chute. Triangular, broad at the top, narrowing down to the dimension of the ore belt at the bottom. Liquid water trickled down, freezing to lumpy milk before it made it halfway. He snapped the lighter off, put it in his pocket, got to his knees, and scrabbled up on all fours.

His hand struck something hard, something irregular at the top. Not steel. Not ice. Cold, wet stone. He found a crack, wedged in two fingers, pulled himself up and snapped the lighter back on.

He was no longer in the tunnel. The acoustics were different. He was in a room too large for the feeble fire of a cigarette lighter to reveal. In Mirny Deep, or at least the ore chute where rocks blasted from the mine were dumped onto the conveyor.

Dark boulders huddled at the top of the chute. A small tracked machine, a kind of miniature bulldozer, was parked behind them, and behind it Nowek could just make out a wide garage door. Leading where? Outside? If so, then what? Walk back into town and find a sympathetic ear? Across the tundra to the nearest railroad and catch a train? Hardly.

He looked back down. The flashlight beam that had followed him through the tunnel glinted on the steel chute. He killed the blue flame and dropped down behind a boulder. Nowek put his shoulder to it. It shifted with a gritty sound. It probably weighed more than he did. Another push. This time when it moved, its neighbor shifted. One more shove and he'd send it down the chute and bury whoever it was who was coming. A sharp *clack* from behind and overhead made him freeze. The whistle of moving air died away. The pressure changed in his ears.

The next instant, the room filled with blinding white light.

"Are there more lights?"

A man.

"Shut your mouth and open your eyes."

Two men. Nowek crouched lower.

"There's nothing to see."

"Slava, if you say one more word, I will kill you myself."

They were above him, standing on a kind of balcony overlooking the ore chute. They both wore white hard hats.

Their shoulders were dusted with fresh snow. The first one carried a stubby rifle. No. Not a rifle. A shotgun. Nowek crouched lower as the two men clambered down a ladder, jumped off, and began to pick their way through the boulders, heading his way. He held his breath. A puff of condensation would give him away. He took sips of air and exhaled them into his parka ruff.

"Anton. Look."

"I said not one more word."

"Down there. What is that?"

Nowek froze.

A pause, then Anton chuckled and said, "It's my villa in Sochi." His words were followed by the sharp *clack clack* of a shotgun shell being racked into the loading port.

Nowek's blood pounded. Then he heard something else. The sound of boots on gritty, frozen rock.

"Stop right there!" Anton yelled.

A voice from the tunnel called back, "Who is it?" A light flashed bright across the boulders. "Anton? Slava? I can hardly believe it. You two? Underground? What happened? Did you get lost?"

Nowek listened. *Boyko!*

"Where is he, boss?"

"I never thought I'd see you two ladies back in a mine. I thought you'd retired and gone shopping. Wait. I'll be right up."

"Stay right there. What are you doing?"

"The same as you. Looking for our distinguished guest. You haven't seen him?"

Slava began, "We just got here a—"

"Shut up!" Anton commanded. "Where have you come from?"

"Where do you think? If you two aren't hiding him

under your skirts, he's crawled up a vent shaft. Come on. We'll find him together."

"I said don't move!"

"Piss off. I'm not some farm boy you can push into a pulley."

"I'm warning you, Boyko."

"Like you warned that kid today? Like you warned my Alyosha? Don't move, or I'll throw a grenade into your fucking fuel tank? Or did you just creep up and do it like a saboteur? Tell me. I'd like to know."

"It wasn't a grenade. It was a flare. And if you take one more step you can ask your smart little boy all about it."

"So. I thought it was you. You and Kirillin make a nice couple. You embarrass me. You used to drive an ore scoop pretty good. Now what are you? A slug with a gun. And Slava. Forgive me, but the best part of you dribbled down your mother's legs. You're not miners. Who are you to warn me about anything? *Fuck* your mothers. This is *my* mine."

Anton said, "You'll die in it." He clambered up on top of a boulder not three feet from Nowek. His partner joined him.

Nowek put his shoulder to the boulder and shoved. It slid, then began to roll. Another one followed it down, then a third. More. A scream cut through the avalanche's thunder. Nowek hoped the one with the shotgun had ridden it to the bottom. His hope didn't last long.

Anton had jumped clear. He landed on his feet, the shotgun still in his hands. He saw Nowek. The shotgun began to rise.

Nowek dove for Anton's knees as the gun erupted in a brilliant flash, a tremendous detonation. The stream of pellets rocketed by so close he could feel their heat on his face.

Anton was already racking another shell into the breach when Nowek hit him. They toppled back together, sprawling over wet, cold boulders of diamond ore. Anton's hard hat flew off. He tried to bring the gun barrel around, but Nowek was on him.

The barrel was hot. Nowek grabbed it, pulling with all the strength he had, all the will he could muster, images of a dark Moscow alley and Mirny Deep mingling, overlapping.

Anton let go. Nowek slipped back, his grip on the barrel loosened, and Anton snatched the weapon away and rolled, then stood. Nowek clawed a chunk of ore loose and threw it. Anton batted it aside. The barrel came even with Nowek's head.

Nowek eased forward on the balls of his feet.

"Don't," said Anton. He was breathing hard, his eyes strangely empty. He slid his finger through the trigger guard.

Nowek jumped, not for Anton, but for the ore chute. His boot caught in something. His ankle twisted, but his momentum carried him through the air and down, down against the icy steel. He slid, rolling as he went, arms flailing, tumbling, caroming against the boulders at the bottom. At such close range, a moving target was only slightly more difficult to hit. How long before the pellets found him? Before they blasted him open just like they had with . . .

A white flash, and metal hail spattered off the ramp in a blaze of bright sparks. Something stung his arm, his shoulder, his arm. Three hot staples driven into his skin. Nowek slid, the time elongating, the sparks flying, dimming, yellow, then gone. He threw out an arm to stop. He struck something soft, bounced, and stopped. A body. The rolling thunder of the detonation went silent. Blood streamed down Nowek's wrist. He stared as it fell in thick drops to the milky white ice.

The unmistakable sound of another shell being rammed into the pump gun made Nowek look up. A figure stood astride a pair of boulders, heroic, triumphant. *Colossus at Mirny Deep.* The barrel slowly lowered, lowered, stopped. It was dim and Nowek's eyes wouldn't focus, and in a moment, it would no longer matter. What difference did it make where his investigation came to its end? Tomorrow morning in a plane? Tomorrow afternoon when the Moscow militia would arrest him again? Or right here? Right now?

A blast of hot light, another peal of thunder.

Then a brilliant beam of light lanced through a cloud of burned gunpowder.

"Nowek?" Boyko jumped off and slid down the ramp with the easy grace of an expert skier negotiating a gentle slope. He stopped right at Nowek's feet.

"Boyko? How did you . . . ?"

The pit boss pulled Nowek to his feet. "You're hurt?" He examined the holes in Nowek's parka. "Not so badly."

Nowek's left arm felt like he'd been stung by angry wasps. There were just three small punctures in the arm of his parka. Holes rimmed in wet blood. He saw the body at the foot of the ramp. Not Boyko, but Anton's partner. "How did you . . ."

"I didn't. *You* pushed the rocks from under Slava's boots. While he was sliding down, I climbed up. This was for Anton." He showed Nowek a flashlight. There was blood on it.

Boyko bent down and tore the plastic identity card from Slava's neck. "They'll be watching for my card. Not his."

Slava stirred, groaned. His eyes fluttered open. He saw Boyko, opened his mouth to scream. He started to scramble away when Boyko's boot caught him in the right temple. Slava's head snapped to the side. Stunned, he didn't even flinch when the pit boss kicked him again, hard enough for Nowek to hear the soft crackle of neck bones breaking.

Boyko picked up Slava's hard hat and tossed it to Nowek. "Let's go. We've got a chance."

A chance for what? Nowek flicked the helmet light on and looked down.

Slava was dying. His eyes, his brain were cut off from his body at the neck. His mouth gaped open as he tried to gulp air down into his lungs. A slender thread of spittle draped from his chin to a chunk of ore. His eyes were wide and desperate, pleading for just one more breath, one more minute of life. "He's alive."

Boyko drew his boot back and staved in the side of Slava's head. "Not now." Boyko turned and swarmed up the slick ramp with astonishing speed, like a ghost flying up an invisible stairway.

Nowek tried to follow. His boot slipped.

"Over there." Boyko pointed to the edge of the slick chute. A ribbon of rusty metal no wider than a boot ran up the edge.

Nowek put one boot on it. It held.

Boyko was already bent over Anton's body. He stood, clutching another identity card.

How did Boyko do it? Somehow, as Anton had fired the shotgun at Nowek, Boyko had flown up the chute and struck him from behind with his flashlight, hard enough to send him tumbling facedown between a pair of boulders. Now Anton's arms were bent back like a swimmer executing an elegant dive. Centered on his spine where Anton's shoulders would join, a ragged crater slowly filled with blood.

Boyko got the small bulldozer running. It chuffed asthmatically, then roared. Boyko maneuvered the blade up, then crawled forward. He dropped the blade level to the deck, then, with a second roar, he shoved the remaining boulders, along with Anton, down the chute. An avalanche of rocks sealed the end of the diamond line.

Boyko was at the ladder at the back of the ore room. "Hey Nowek. You want to get out of here or not?" He swarmed up the rungs.

Nowek had more trouble. His left arm was swelling. He could feel the skin growing taut and hot. Warm blood trickled into his armpit, cooling. Boyko reached down and hauled him up.

There was a door, open to a lit passage.

Boyko killed the lights over the ore chute and pulled open a metal box mounted by the door. Inside was a card reader, two buttons and two lights. The red lamp was on.

Voices rose from the tunnel. A beam played across the jumble at the bottom. They were close.

Boyko slid Anton's card through the reader. The red light went out, the green flashed. Boyko jammed his fist down on the topmost button. A warning horn blared.

Whoever was coming up the conveyor belt from Fabrika 3 knew what it meant. There was another shout, then the sound of running boots, and then the low hum of powerful electric motors drowned out everything. The belt jerked as the gearing drew up the slack in the mechanism, and then it began to move. Slowly at first, but then faster. The boulders at the bottom of the chute were drawn in, allowing the ones piled up behind to take their place.

"The belt travels at three meters per second," said Boyko as the boulders jostled into the tunnel and vanished. "They'll be back in Fabrika 3 a lot faster than it took us to walk." Boyko stepped through the hatch and into the gallery beyond. "We may be able to waltz right out of this hole if we're quick." Boyko slipped Slava's ID card next to Anton's under a strap on his hard hat. "Let's move it."

Like the tunnel and the chute room, the passage was cut through permafrost, with light fixtures at regular intervals. At the end was a surprisingly normal elevator door. A single round window set in the center of a tan metal panel trimmed in chrome. It wouldn't have seemed out of place in a Moscow office tower.

Next to it was a much larger door, the ore skip, big enough for a small truck to drive through, clearly made for transporting equipment down, loaded ore trams up.

Boyko stood next to the small elevator. Another card reader was mounted beside the door. A yellow light blinked. Then the yellow light went out. A green light came on, the door slid open.

Boyko motioned for Nowek to wait. He went in and started beating on something with his flashlight. Plastic crunched. Glass shattered. He looked out the door and nodded.

When Nowek joined him, a blinded security camera hung from the ceiling from its wires.

The car was lit by a single cold blue fluorescent tube. There was a control panel with buttons to open the door, to close it, to ring an alarm. The emergency stop button was the largest, and painted bright red. A vertical row corresponded to the working levels of the mine. The horizons. At the bottom of the row, blank holes to allow new buttons to be installed, corresponding to deeper horizons. The topmost button was marked SURFACE. The next down ORE BELT. There were eight buttons below it.

A fan blew cool, dank air across his face. He looked down. Black drops marred the floor like spilled ink. His blood. His left sleeve was starting to soak through. He knew he should put pressure on the wounds, but the thought of grabbing his hot, swollen arm stopped him. He wouldn't bleed to death.

Boyko stabbed the button to shut the door. He turned and held out his leathery hand. "Maxim Ivanovich. Thank you."

"Gregori Tadeovich," said Nowek. "You're welcome."

Though they weren't exactly friends, they were no longer enemies.

"When we get to the surface, follow me," said Boyko. "Don't look too interested. Don't ask questions. Just do what I do. There's a scanner we've got to pass through. You'll need one of these." He tapped the ID cards. "Who do you want to be? Anton or Slava?"

"Someone will see and know I'm not either one of them."

"The topmaster likes to drink so he might not. Besides, there's no other way. You take Anton's card." He jabbed the topmost button. "I don't want to even . . ."

With a lurch, the elevator car began to drop.

"Boyko!"

All thought of ID cards vanished as Boyko punched the button again. The car had a mind of its own. It continued to descend. He hit the emergency stop.

It had no effect.

Nowek stepped over to the control panel. "Circuit breaker!"

Boyko pulled open a hinged door. Inside was a reset switch that should stop everything. He threw it. The fan stopped. The light went out. The elevator continued its smooth descent.

Boyko smashed his fist against the red stop button again, then *all* the buttons. He stood back. "What's it doing?"

Taking us to the bottom, thought Nowek. The round window flashed with light as they dropped by the first horizon. The cab continued its measured descent.

The window flashed again as they dropped through the second horizon. Nowek got an almost subliminal view of lightbulbs receding into the distance.

He'd been in mine hoists before. Some dropped like they'd been pushed off a cliff. Your feet levitated, your brain swam with images of an endless fall, though more miners died when their hoist went out of control on the way *up.* Others were slow, jerky affairs that plunged ten meters, hung up, squealed, then dropped again. This one was swift, purposeful, eerily smooth.

Deeper, the air coming in from the vents in the wall grew wetter, warmer. It carried the smell of live rock, a smell Nowek had almost forgotten. It was to a miner what the smell of the open sea was to a sailor. Not earthy, not rich, but a pure, elemental smell unlike anything from the normal world.

They dropped through Horizon Three. Three hundred meters underground, not yet as deep as the open pit. The shaft was still encased in ice born of a thousand Siberian winters.

The Fourth Horizon. The Fifth. Five hundred meters below the surface. Down, away from the air, the light. Horizon Six. Beads of water condensed on the cold walls of the elevator. Seven.

"Don't worry," said Boyko. "We'll stop before we hit bottom."

The automatic controls should also be taking them *up.*

The lights of the Eighth Horizon filled the window.

Nowek looked at the control panel. There were no more buttons. "You said there were eight horizons."

"There's still something you don't know?"

"There's a lot I don't know."

A low, powerful throbbing made the walls of the car vibrate, as though they were approaching an enormous, beating heart.

"You've heard of diamond fissures?" asked Boyko.

Nowek had. They were veins of diamond ore extending into the native rock, rich and highly prized. Diamonds were starry messengers from deep within the earth. The titanic heat and pressure that created them lasted longer in fissures. Up in the throat of the diamond pipe, pressures eased, allowing most of the gems to burn up like lumps of crystal coal. But they survived down in the fissures. The largest, purest, most valuable gems were fissure diamonds. "There's a fissure system in Mirny Deep?"

"On the Ninth Horizon. Fissures so big you can stand up and walk in them for *kilometers*," said Boyko. "I told you it was possible to shovel up diamonds? It's no joke. Mirny Deep is the richest fucking diamond mine on earth."

A cable brake began to grip. They were slowing, slowing. Rivulets of condensation ran down the metal walls. Gravity began to reassert itself, pushing up on the soles of Nowek's field boots, as the hoist slowed. A final lurch, and the cage bobbed to a stop. The stink of hot iron flowed in with the warm, wet air. A curious combination of smells. Smoke, cinder, fire, water. Like being dropped down the flue of a recently drowned blast furnace.

The window was black. Big machinery was running somewhere nearby. Boyko pounded the proper button. The door opened. The chamber beyond the door was dark. Boyko paused for an instant, then said, "Wait." He stepped out into the Ninth Horizon, his headlamp a flashing comet receding into deep, limitless space.

CHAPTER 25

The Storm

YURI SETTLED BACK INTO THE PILOT'S SEAT with a cup of tea. The Brothers had seen him leave the cockpit to fill his cup. They'd craned their necks to see into the cockpit. They *knew* there was just one pilot on board. So who was at the controls?

He would have told them that the autopilot was on duty if they'd asked, but they wouldn't. They were too fearless. It was worth leaving the cockpit empty for a few minutes just to see them exchange questioning glances and turn slightly pale.

He took a sip and glanced at each of the instruments. Airspeed. Altitude. The three engine displays. Navigation. His eye came to a stop on the directional gyro. It was a good ten degrees off. Had it failed? Compass systems were unreliable so far north.

He looked out over the blunt nose and knew at once that something was wrong. Polaris, the pole star, was no longer in its proper place. A compass might wander. But Polaris? The jet was pointed too far east. It sent a shot of cold adrenaline straight to his heart, because in a place as empty as Siberia, not knowing where you'd been going was the same as not knowing where you were, and that meant you could be anywhere.

He checked the GPS. It was on, it was still flying the Yak through a pair of wires connecting it to the autopilot. The display showed him on course, just under two hundred kilometers south of Mirny. Then why was he pointed at Alaska?

Then he saw the speed he was making over the ground. The Yak cruised at nearly five hundred kilometers per hour. How could he be crawling across the ground at *three hundred*?

The engines were in order. Either the satellites were lying, or else a wind, a very *big* wind, was blowing from the northeast. What had Plet said about a storm? Didn't he say that was tomorrow?

Was there enough fuel to make Mirny? They were still forty minutes away. A quick calculation showed that if nothing else went wrong, they'd arrive in Mirny, though they might taxi up to the fuel pumps on fumes.

A new sound got his attention. A rasping hiss. It was coming from the windshield. He looked out. The nearest clouds were well to the north. They looked like distant mountains that blotted out the horizon. He flicked on the jet's landing lights.

Two beams lanced ahead into the darkness, filled with bright streaks of blowing snow. They were flying at ten thousand meters, clear of any cloud. How could there be snow?

The GPS screen was showing more wind. His ground speed had dropped below three hundred kilometers per hour. Mirny was now forty-seven minutes away.

His three engines pushed the Yak along at better than

five hundred kilometers an hour, yet somehow Mirny was growing more distant by the minute.

BOYKO MOTIONED for Nowek to come out.

Deep mines are wet mines, and the Ninth Horizon of Mirny Deep was both. Nowek's headlamp reflected off a shallow pool of standing water. The chamber looked more like the blacked-out bilge of a sinking ship than the ante-room to the richest diamond mine on earth. Everywhere was water. Raining in big milky drops from the roof, running down heavy electrical conduits, streaming to manhole-size floor sumps where it swirled and vanished. Empty ore trams were parked in a row in front of the ore skip. The water was deep enough to cover the rails, making them look like barges waiting for a tugboat.

The water was melted ice from above, and numbingly cold. But the walls radiated heat. The air was hot.

Boyko splashed over to a security camera. He used his battered flashlight to blind it, then slid his ID card through the reader and punched the ore skip's call button.

Nothing happened. The light above the wide door stayed red. Whoever had sent them down here was not going to let them leave. He let his flashlight linger on a bundle of cables that emerged from a conduit beside the elevator. The wires fanned out, draped from hangars pinned in the roof. They vanished into five tunnels set in the far wall. Detonator cables. The tunnels were drifts drilled into the ore body. Heavy blast curtains were rolled up above each one.

Nowek pointed his headlamp up. The low roof was supported at regular intervals by stout pillars of unexcavated ore. The kimberlite was dark blue and wet, veined with white quartz, cobbled with rocks caught up in the same flow of magma that had brought diamonds up from the basement of the earth.

A thousand meters underground. If this were a submarine, it would be a very deep dive, though a submarine wouldn't leak this badly. At least, not one that was coming back up.

Boyko pointed at the cables. "They're set to blow some rooms down. They could do it whenever they felt like pushing the button."

Nowek could feel the rush of air. "Not with the fans running."

Boyko gave Nowek a nod. "You've been in mines, Delegate Nowek. I keep forgetting."

"Never with the blasting cables connected." Nowek saw something move. He turned.

The red light burning above the door had gone out. The yellow lamp was lit. The ore skip was coming down. "Boyko."

The pit boss saw it, too. He pointed at the far wall. "Get inside a drift," he said. "Not too far. They turn into fissures at the end. If you do get into a fissure, keep the breeze at your back and walk. It always brings you back to the main shaft."

"Boyko, it could be—"

"*Now,* Delegate Nowek."

THE CLOUDS ON the northern horizon were no longer distant. They were growing alarmingly fast. Yuri would have to penetrate them, to find the runway still fifty kilometers away, buried somewhere underneath them. What choice did he have? Mirny was ten minutes away, and he had fifteen minutes of fuel. He would find the runway and land, or become one of the thousands of planes to vanish in the vastness of Siberia, to be discovered by some Yakut herder, a hunting party, or, more likely, not at all.

He brought the three yellow throttles back to idle. The nose dropped. There would be no second attempts. No groping for an unlit runway in the middle of a bastard of a snowstorm. He would have to fly to the airport at Mirny directly, and land as though it were a clear, sunny day in June, as though he could look off the nose and see it. The little GPS knew where the runway was with astonishing precision. If only it could land the plane, too. But it couldn't. That was a job for the pilot.

Yuri could see the rising summits of the cloud mountains. Eight thousand meters. Seven. Six. Now those mountains were a wall, solid, vertical, near. They grew texture, billows, canyons. The wind became fitful, more violent in its veerings. He switched on the wing and engine anti-ice, the igniters that would keep the fires lit. The wall of cloud towered. Any second now. Any second.

He called back to the Brothers to warn them to hold on, and then the Yak slammed straight into the clouds, the wind, the snow.

The jet was thrown to one side, tossed up, then mashed down. The wings seemed to tumble. Yuri was a daring pilot. Daring to even be here at all. But he let the autopilot fly. He let the GPS navigate. On its screen, the tiny dark line that was the Mirny runway crept down from the top of the screen with terrifying slowness.

Altitude, five thousand meters. Four. At least there were no mountains around to hit. The Siberian Plateau lay beneath them, high, but almost perfectly flat, minus a few man-made obstacles. Buildings, antennae. Luckily, the mine at Mirny was a pit. How tall could a *pit* be?

He was still in solid clouds at two thousand meters. He

switched the landing lights on. The beams were swallowed by heavy snow. He switched them off. The satellites were leading him to the runway, but at an angle made even more acute by the crosswind. Somehow he would have to line up properly. Somehow he would have to see the earth before he collided with it.

One thousand five hundred meters. Mirny sat at an elevation of six hundred forty meters. The ground was less than nine hundred meters straight down, and the snow was falling more heavily.

Five hundred meters to the ground. He turned the landing lights back on and let them burn. They showed only whipping clouds and slanting snow driven sideways by the wind.

Four hundred meters to go. There were probably ten-story apartment flats at Mirny. Maybe right below him. How tall was a ten-story building anyway?

He risked a quick glance at the GPS screen. The airport was dead ahead, five kilometers, the runway angled to the left. The wind was from the right. How the devil was he going to even *see* the runway, much less land on it?

He reached over and pulled the gear handle down. With a heavy *thunk*, the nose wheel popped out, followed by the mains. Three green lights. Three good wheels. Fuel? The gauges were in the zone of uncertainty. The engines could flame out at any moment. He selected landing flaps. Two hundred meters. Two kilometers to the runway. It had to be there. It *had to be*.

Mahmet entered the cockpit. He had a cup of tea with him. Remarkably, it hadn't spilled. "Would you like some tea?"

"Get back in your seat!"

"Are we getting ready to land?"

"Get back now!"

A rogue wind sent the Yak skidding. Yuri switched off the autopilot. He fought the skid with rudder and yoke. He looked down again at the screen. One kilometer. Then back up.

The landing lights pinned a tall black building. A tower. At its top, a red beacon flashed weakly through the storm. The beacon was *above* them.

Yuri yanked the yoke full over, knowing that he was giving the wind a fat target. Left wing down, down, then vertical. The black tower swept by beneath his belly. How close? Close. He fought the jet level, and when he did, the lights framed a white trapezoid of level, even ground, covered with snow.

Mother of God!

It was a runway.

He nosed over, knowing it was awful technique, but he wouldn't have a chance to try again. The snowy runway rushed him. He pulled back an instant before the nose wheel would have struck. He dipped his right wing down, down, shouldering the Yak into the howling crosswind, feeling for the ground, feeling for *anything*.

The snow was light and dry. Powdery. The landing was soft, imperceptibly gentle. It was a landing that violated every one of Yuri's hazy rules and, in the end, was one of his smoothest.

"Mirny?" asked Mahmet. Somehow he still had the teacup.

"I hope so." Yuri throttled the engines back and kicked the jet around in a pivot, using the powerful landing lights to hunt for something that looked like a building. A hangar. Even better, a gas truck. The beams swept over a long, low structure. The windows were dark except for one at the far end. A light burned over a door. A bus was parked in front, its side plastered white with blowing snow. And on the roof of the building, MIRNY.

IT WAS ABSOLUTELY BLACK away from the elevators. Only the small circle of light from Nowek's headlamp gave the space any dimension. His eyes were growing wider, more adapted. What was dark before became shadow, and shadow took on form and texture. He headed for the drift Boyko had pointed out. The floor of the main chamber was sloped for drainage. There wasn't much standing water now. It barely covered the ore car rails.

He turned and saw Boyko standing in front of the elevator doors. The light above them was still yellow. But then it flickered, went out. The green lamp came on. He ducked into the drift.

The roof was low enough for Nowek to touch. It was very quiet here, away from the hoist, surrounded by solid rock. A stiff, cool wind blew against his face as he walked deeper into the drift. He stopped and held up a hand to it. His palm grew cold. The back of his hand stayed warm. Fresh air was reaching the ends of the drift, flowing back into the main chamber and then up the shaft. If fresh air was making it down, didn't that mean there was another way, an air shaft that went back up?

He looked at his left hand. It was caked with dirt and dried blood. His sleeve was black. He tugged at the wrist. A drop of bright red fell, then another. He switched off his headlamp and put his ear next to the rough wall. He could hear the hum of the pumps again, and then, startlingly clear, Boyko sneezed.

Air pressure changed. His ears popped. Elevator doors

were opening. He heard Boyko say, "I thought it would be you."

"We found Anton and Slava. Did you think we wouldn't?"

Hot light washed across the wall of the tunnel, almost blinding bright. Nowek froze. Kirillin. Was he alone?

"He murdered my son, Kirillin. But then, you knew."

"You could have stopped him. You could have saved him. It was your own fault, Boyko." His bright light sent Boyko's shadow slanting across the inner wall of Nowek's tunnel. "You're injured?"

"Why don't you come close and see?"

The light shifted. "You used to be loyal. Everyone said so. It was something to count on. Then things began to happen."

"Alyosha happened."

"You started talking to outsiders."

"Long after you started working for them. How is it that *you* bent over and *we* were the ones to be fucked?"

"You didn't think we'd know about Volsky?"

"You didn't know about the strike until I told you."

"You should have left Mirny while you had the chance."

"You're the one who is going to be running. The FSB is after you now. That boy you murdered in DRAGA 1 was one of them."

The light swept the cavern again. "Where is Nowek?"

"In your pocket, taking a piss." Then "What's that?"

"A Makarov pistol, but let's not get ahead of ourselves. Here."

The light swung away. Boyko's shadow shifted.

"What are you doing with *these*?"

Kirillin said, "The question will be, what were *you* doing with them? The answer will be clear enough. A man who murdered his boss. An employee of Kristall with a grudge. An argument over a few hundred carats of smuggled rough. I wonder what will the FSB make of *that*? Careful how you handle the diamonds, Boyko. They're excellent quality and they belong to someone else."

"You won't find Nowek."

"I already have. Who left those drops of blood? You aren't bleeding."

Nowek heard a splash.

"That's close enough. You've done us a favor by bringing Nowek down here," said Kirillin. "You can decide where you will take your bullet."

Nowek expected the pit boss to leap at Kirillin. Instead, Boyko's shadow shifted, but only a little. He didn't leap. He didn't run. Nowek watched his shadow change shape as the pit boss raised his arms, stretching them out wide at his sides.

He'd turned his back to Kirillin!

"There's only one right way for someone like you to shoot a man," said Boyko. "And that's—"

A white flash, a *crack* that came as a sharp pressure wave, a surprised grunt as Boyko's breath was blown from his lungs.

The light pointed away from the drift. A second flash, a second sharp *crack!*

Then "Nowek?"

Harsh light flooded into the drift where Nowek crouched. He moved back, away, looking for something, anything he might use as a weapon. Bare rocks. Cables slung under the roof. He reached up and tried to pull a metal hanger free, but it was pinned well. There was nothing. All he could hear was the drip of seeping water. The rattle of falling pebbles. The subliminal groan of the earth pressing in all around. There was a low opening in the side of the drift. A stope, where ore was actually collected. He bent his head low and slipped into it as Kirillin's beam poured light into the drift.

"Are you down this drift? Of course you are. I can see your blood. There's no back door, so you can relax. You'll be in there for a while. I knew right away that working with you was not going to be possible. You weren't after money like Volsky. How could we conduct business on such a basis?"

The light shifted. Kirillin spoke again. "You came to Mirny to learn why Volsky died. You came so much closer than I would have guessed. You could have had lunch with the man who arranged it and you turned him down. So whose fault is it that you failed?"

Hock. Nowek held his breath, moving back into the stope. It was like crawling into a stone coffin.

"You wanted to find out where those missing diamonds went?" Kirillin laughed. "Your Moscow friends have been selling them all along. Every gem we've mined for the last year has gone to Irkutsk, then out of the country. Is it *our* fault Petrov chose an unreliable partner? Should *we* suffer because Moscow sent stones to Golden Autumn and no money ever came back? Of course not."

Kirillin was standing in front of the drift, letting his light follow the red drops of blood. The beam stopped at the stope. "You were going to fly to Moscow tomorrow morning with one million carats of gem diamonds. True, you'd be arrested and the stones were going on, but it's an irony I feel you would have appreciated."

Nowek heard a new sound. A metallic rattle.

"Your friends in Moscow are in trouble. They've stolen from us for years, now someone has stolen from them. Bad things will happen to them, but we'll survive. Why? Because our relationship with the cartel is stronger than promises.

It's made of diamond, and nothing is stronger than that. London has ordered the Ninth Horizon closed. But one day it will be opened again. One year, two. Maybe a hundred. We'll dig you up and you'll ride the ore belt to Fabrika 3 with the diamonds you were hoping to discover. Of course, they'll still be perfect. Well, I'm taking up your time and you don't have much left. I'll leave you to your own thoughts."

The metallic rattle echoed down the drift, followed by the *click* of a lock. Kirillin had rolled the blast curtain down.

Total blackness now. Nowek scrambled out of the stope. He switched his headlamp on and rushed to the blast curtain. It was made of thick rubberized fabric sandwiched between heavy steel netting. Kirillin might be on the other side. It didn't matter. He shoved it hard, again. He wedged his fingers around the edge. It wouldn't move. It was locked down tight. How long did he have? One minute? Two? As long as it took the ore skip to go far enough away for Kirillin to be safe. And how far was that?

Nowek's thinking slowed down, mired. Spinning in something he knew was close to panic. He was a thousand meters under the ground, trapped in a mine wired to explode.

Wired! He looked up at the bundle of detonator cables. They were stiff and well armored. Cut through them? With what? His teeth? Burn through them with Chuchin's lighter? Be serious.

Nowek's brain stumbled, faltered like an engine barely running on a winter's morning.

Then it caught.

Blow down some rooms. That's what Boyko had said. It meant that the explosion was going to take place on this level, but that the rubble would be collected *below*. Nowek turned his back to the blast curtain and ran deeper into the drift.

The passage stopped at a tee. The detonator cable split; three red cables went left, three right. He turned right, pushing the darting white circle of his headlamp forward, stepping over piles of fallen rocks fractured loose from the walls, the roof.

The drift narrowed as it plunged deeper into the ore body, the roof slanted down, lower, lower, until it scraped the helmet off his head and he had to stop. There was no reassuring flow of air now. The fans had stopped. He could be going in the right direction. Or not. One line of the red cable veered to his left, into another stope. Two continued deeper into the mine.

He followed the single red cable over a tongue of loose stones that extended halfway across the drift. He was down on his knees now. There had to be just seconds left. He kept one hand on the cable, feeling for an end, feeling for something. . . .

Nowek crawled over a sheet of heavy plywood. Above it, the blasting cable burrowed up into a drilled hole. He pulled. Something gave, slowly, reluctantly, like gum stuck to a shoe. But it moved. He pulled harder. Taffy too cold to work.

A fat purple sausage appeared, emerged, dropped into his hands. On it, the word DYNAGEL.

The blasting cable was attached through some sort of one-way fitting. A Chinese finger trap. He yanked at it. It wouldn't pull out. He attacked the plastic skin with his teeth, ripping at the sausage until he tasted bitter explosive gel. He spat it out and squeezed. Purple gel thick as toothpaste.

He squeezed again, but there was no time to get it all. He dropped the charge and grabbed at the sheet of plywood on the floor, thinking to use it as a shield.

It covered a hole in the floor large enough to slip through. But where did it go? He peered down into it and saw a rivulet of water running across a rough floor studded with boulders.

A fissure.

The shot might bring it all down on his head. But then, it might not. How much time did he have? He lowered his boots into the hole. He started to slip, to fall. He dug his fingers in for grip, kicking his boots, wedging his legs wide.

He heard a sizzle. The blasting cable shot out a fat spark.

As he hit the floor a hot white light filled the space, a sharp blow knocked him down to his knees, then rammed him back against a boulder. A tremendous *crack!* came from somewhere inside his head. It was drowned by the rumble of falling boulders, the gagging smell of explosive, dust. The ground rolled. The blast was endless. The white light faded to orange, to yellow, to black.

His helmet was no longer on. The light was smashed. The blackness was absolute. But in that first dazzling instant, he'd seen the walls of the fissure glimmer, nailed with the pinpoint brilliance of crystal. Nowek was at the core of a galaxy of stars. A million, million stars.

NIKOLAI TERESHENKO had been night manager at the Mirny airport for three years. For eight months of the year, it was a position that demanded little more than staying awake. The airport was closed to the outside world, and all night flights, even Kristall's, were prohibited. True, there was the occasional emergency, and in the short summer there was no night at all. But winter was back and Tereshenko could sleep through it like a bear.

He leaned back in his swivel chair, half-watching a re-broadcast of *Baywatch*. He had the sound turned off. He didn't want to wake up the denizens of the monkey house, the night maintenance crew sleeping in the bunk room next door.

He could hear wind shrieking across the open runway, the dry spatter of snow raking his window, the steam radiators ticking, the snores of men who drowned the day with the help of a bottle.

His sole duty tonight was to determine when to wake the crew and send them out to plow the runway. There was an early flight scheduled for tomorrow morning. A Yak-40 trijet to Moscow. Moscow meant big shots. The runway could not have so much as one flake on it when they arrived at first light. *Give it half an hour,* he decided, *and I'll rattle the bars of the monkey house.*

Bright lights swept across his windows. His window faced out onto the runway. He got to his feet and went to the window. *Who's out driving on a night like this?* The frost was too thick to see. At least the ice was still on the outside. Let another month go by and the inside would be coated, too. He had a series of nails hammered into the floor. When frost reached the fourth nail in from the wall, he could offi-cially close the airport and . . . a soft *click* came from behind.

Nikolai Tereshenko turned.

Two men in black karakul hats and mottled snow camou-flage stood at his door. They were dark-skinned. Each of them carried a stubby automatic rifle. Both were aimed at him.

A third person appeared, shouldered by the two gunmen.

"Good evening," said Yuri. His leather jacket was zipped up tight to his chin. "I'd like some fuel, please."

Tereshenko could scarcely push the word out. *"What?"*

"Jet fuel," Yuri repeated. "And also a car."

CHAPTER 26

The Crystal Garden

BLACK, THE FISSURE LOST ALL DIMENSION. Nowek might be standing on a sheer cliff at midnight. He might be drowning, sinking down to the cold, silent depths where light never penetrates. He might even be a dead man looking out at eternity, except that his scalp itched.

He reached up and found the hard hat gone, and with it, the lamp. His hair was powdered with rock dust. The air was thick with it. Like breathing glass. His forehead felt hot, as though he'd been working too long in the sun. A flash burn. His ears felt plugged with water. More likely a ruptured eardrum. It didn't take long before Nowek realized that waking up at the bottom of a mine, surrounded by rubble a thousand meters under Siberia's frozen skin, was not necessarily good news.

He moved a foot, a leg. The other. The blast had thrown him back against the fissure wall. But it hadn't buried him. Amorphous shapes, billowing, ghostly sails, washed across the darkness. Phosphenes, illusions. They only made Nowek hungry to see something, anything, real.

He hunted for the helmet, dislodged a silent stream of

loose pebbles. They pelted down and kept coming. He was sure the whole mine would follow, but then, the rain of stones stopped. He felt for the hard hat and its light. How could it just disappear? He thought that Chuchin would say the same thing about *him*.

His fingers became his eyes and ears. There was a boulder to one side. The other side seemed clear. What had Boyko said? Some of the fissures were big enough to stand up and walk in, that they went on for kilometers.

Slowly, dizzily, he got to his feet, keeping an arm out against a wall for balance, ducking away from a roof he sensed but couldn't see. But he could reach it. He tried to find the hole he'd dropped through just before the blast, the flash, the moment of painful white light. . . .

Light! Chuchin's cigarette lighter. He pulled it out of his parka, flipped back the cap, found the thumb wheel, and snapped it.

The spark was fat and impossibly bright, the blue flame a glare he could hardly bear to look at. He held it up to his hungry eyes. The hole in the roof was plugged with rubble. A pull would bring it all down. He turned.

The walls. My God. The walls.

The color of the exposed ore was deepest midnight, the smell subtle, almost organic, nearly sweet, like sawn lumber so new the cut still dripped sap. Nowek put his hand out to touch the wall of the fissure, as though it might vanish. Ice-clear diamonds shimmered in the blue light of his flame. Slender triangles. Doubles. Rounded cubes and dangerous-looking shards. Diamonds in impossible profusion. Diamonds enough to collect with a shovel and a pail.

Diamonds didn't come like gumdrops in a glass jar. They came by the point, by the carat, each the precise weight of a tiny seed from the carob tree, wrapped in special papers, guarded with guns, locked away, meted out with microscopic care. Here were diamonds by the kilogram, by the handful. Diamonds by the *ton*.

He took a step closer and kicked something, a loose pebble. There was something in the way it skittered across the stones, something almost musical in its clarity and tone. He held the flame of his lighter close to the floor. It took a few seconds to realize what he was seeing. He'd almost stepped on it.

A perfect crystal, blasted free from its prison of ore. A clear octahedron the size of his thumb, its points new and wickedly sharp. He picked it up and felt the characteristic cold of tightly packed carbon atoms sucking heat from his skin. Even unpolished, it captured the light of Nowek's flame. Worth what? Millions? Maybe in Antwerp, in New York. But what did it matter down here?

He put the diamond in front of the blue flame of his lighter. The crystal filled with blue light, scattering it throughout the fissure. Shimmering images of the flame were projected on the walls.

Shimmering?

The blue flame was flickering. A faint breeze was blowing again.

Nowek carefully pocketed the crystal. He could feel the air now, cool on his burned forehead. Turn, it disappeared. Turn back around and it flowed over his face like water.

Keep the breeze at your back and walk. It always brings you back to the main shaft.

Somewhere, a kilometer overhead, the ventilators in the headworks tower were running. Fresh air was reaching him here at the bottom of the world, in this impossible crystal garden. If it was reaching him, then there was a way up. A way out. He held out the flame and started to walk. Ten steps and the fissure angled off in a new direction.

A maze that goes on for kilometers . . .

Fifteen more and the roof necked down low, lower. The fissure made another twist, and he came to a wedge of rock, a keystone that had broken loose and fallen almost, but not quite, to the floor. There were cracks above, hinting at a way through. Air whistled through them. They were too narrow for even his hand to pass. He dropped back down.

At the bottom, a narrow opening, a slot. The blue flame was pulled horizontal by the wind. He got down and looked into it. The narrow opening went as far as he could see, which wasn't so far.

Hock. Volsky's death. The diamonds leaking out from Irkutsk to Golden Autumn. Everything Nowek knew would die if he didn't make it through. Those men and women, burned up to keep the cartel's grip on Mirny Deep, on the Ninth Horizon, intact.

The way out lay beyond that slot. Nowek got down on his knees, then his belly, the flame danced as the moving air accelerated through the gap. It was his rush light. With it, he could break the back of any winter's dark, even here where the night was eternal, where the icicles were made from diamonds.

YURI STOPPED AT THE DOOR to the maintenance crew's bunk room. He listened to the snores. They were deep, loud, untroubled. "How many are in there?" he asked the terrified airport manager. "It sounds like a dozen."

"Only three," said Tereshenko. "They'll give you no trouble. Trust me. It usually takes an explosion to wake them."

"We can arrange that, too." Yuri nodded for Bashir to wait by the door. "Where's the fuel stored?" he asked Tereshenko.

"The truck is in the garage. Straight ahead. Through that door." Tereshenko was trying hard to sound helpful, but he was running out of room. At some point Kirillin would be more of a threat than these terrorists. You *helped* them? You *gave* them fuel? Who are you working for, Tereshenko? It was a conversation Tereshenko wanted very much to avoid.

Mahmet motioned with the AK and said, "Open the door."

What was he going to say? No? A Chechen with an assault rifle was very convincing. How was he going to deflect the blame? Who would have expected a plane to land in the middle of the night, in the middle of this bastard of a snow? Chechens, in *Mirny*? He opened the door, reached in, and switched on the lights.

The garage was cold, but not bitterly so. A single hot radiator kept the fuel tanker from freezing, but you could still see breath.

A row of heavy arctic oversuits hung from hooks on the wall. Each had a blazing orange panel sewn on the back, with smaller stripes on each cuff. Designed to allow outside work in a Mirny winter, they looked like space suits.

"How much fuel is in the truck?" asked Yuri.

"It's always kept full. How far are you going to fly?"

Yuri jumped up into the cab. "All the way. Let's go."

Tereshenko climbed in after him. He opened an air valve to engage the starter.

Mahmet opened the outer doors. Snow swept in on the wind. If anything, it was coming down harder.

Tereshenko reached down to switch on the headlights. As

he did, he saw the tiny red eye of the portable radio glow from beneath the dashboard. *The radio!* He'd been lost at sea in a raging gale. Rocks here, towering waves there. But the radio was his lighthouse. His salvation. His way into a safe, snug harbor. He put the truck into gear and moved out into the storm.

Mahmet jumped onto the truck as it rumbled by. The wind buffeted them.

Tereshenko saw the jet. A Yak-40.

"The fuel point is under the left wing," said Yuri. He got out and Mahmet eased in to take his place. "Watch him."

Tereshenko knew that it took two men to fuel a jet. One at the nozzle, one at the pump control panel. He reached down to find a pair of heavy gloves kept under the seat.

"What are you doing?" the Chechen demanded.

"It's cold." Tereshenko showed him the gloves, and then pulled them on. There was no more reason to mention the emergency pump cutoff located below the seat than there was to call attention to the radio.

Yuri pulled the black hose out to the wing. He jogged back quickly, his leather jacket no match for the wind and snow. "Ready!"

"Someone has to operate the controls at the pump," Tereshenko told the suspicious Chechen. "Do you know how?"

Mahmet seemed to be looking at something inside Tereshenko's head. "Go," he said. He opened his door.

Tereshenko put up his hood and trudged back to the rear of the fuel truck. At least he was protected from the wind. Still, snow swirled over the top with enough force to sting exposed skin. He engaged the pump clutch. A red light burned. He closed the switch, then flipped it again. Still red.

Yuri opened the fuel port and thrust the nozzle up against the seal. His ears were burning with cold. He looked back and saw the red light. He pulled the trigger. Nothing happened.

Tereshenko pointed at the light.

Yuri's fingers were going numb. "What's the problem?"

"The emergency cutoff switch. It's stuck."

"Where is it?"

"In the cab." Tereshenko stood stock still.

"What are you standing there for?" Yuri was shivering. "Hurry up!"

"Absolutely," said Tereshenko. "It will only take a second." Mahmet watched him closely when he reached his right hand under the driver's seat for the cutoff switch. A gust filled the air with fine snow. Tereshenko used his left hand for balance, brushed the radio with his glove, and switched it on.

NOWEK SLIPPED OFF HIS PARKA, balled it up and shoved it into the slot, then crawled in after it. The roof pressed down on him. One tiny shift, an inconsequential shrug of the earth, and he would be pinned here until someone mined the fissure and found him. Of course, the cartel had no reason to mine the fissure and flood the market with gems from the Ninth Horizon. It would be Nowek's grave.

His chest was hard against the floor. He let his breath out. The rocks dug at his ribs. He no longer felt the buckshot in his arm. He turned his head sideways and pushed, like a baby struggling to be born. He moved, gained ground, pushed the parka ahead. The rocks scraped his cheek. He could feel the wind blow over fresh blood.

Keep the wind at your back. . . .

It was odd how Boyko's voice came to him, how he and Volsky seemed to merge in Nowek's memory. Nowek had been so sure the pit boss was an enemy. And yet he'd been Volsky's eyes and ears in Mirny. Two men, two miners. They'd faced death courageously. With dignity, with purpose. Both had died in different ways, different places, by different hands. But behind that hand?

A million carats leaving for London in the morning . . .

Somehow, he was going to stop them. Somehow, he would rise from this mine, pass all those scanners, even without an ID card. Somehow he'd live.

Nowek tried to bring his arm around, but it was stuck. He stopped his brain from racing to obvious conclusions. He slowed his breathing. He couldn't go back.

Nowek turned his wrist, flattened his arm, relaxed his shoulders and squeezed a few millimeters of freedom from his aching joints. It was enough to free the arm. He brought it up to his face, then squeezed it ahead. His fingers found his parka, the ruff soft as sable. He pushed it ahead. It moved more easily. He reached for it, and it was gone.

He strained his fingers out and came to a ridge, an edge.

Nowek got his hand around it and pulled. He won half a meter and felt like cheering, felt like he'd run a marathon. He pulled again, and his head was free. A kick, and he was through.

His parka was a heap beside him. Ahead, the fissure narrowed to an impossible vertical crack. It was a dead end. The fissure had closed off. He'd sit here and wait, using his light sparingly, but all the same it would run dry. Then there'd be nothing left but the hope that he'd die before going mad from the dark.

But it wasn't dark. Chuchin's lighter was still in his parka pocket but he could *see* the walls, even the soft, nebular glow of exposed diamonds. He looked up.

A golden outline, a soft rectangle of light.

Nowek stood. His hands were shaking. There was a way out. How far didn't matter. There was a way. He reached up and pushed the plywood hatch open.

Golden light flooded down. He tossed his parka through the open hatch, then pulled himself up into the light. He wasn't out of this mine. For now, being alive was enough. Nowek had been swallowed like Jonah. And like Jonah, he was coming back.

THE RAW KEROSENE gushed out over Yuri's hands. He tried to release the trigger on the hose, but his fingers refused to cooperate. The jet fuel felt warm on his skin. "Stop it!" he barked at Tereshenko, who was only too happy to comply.

The gusher ebbed. Yuri was shaking as he carried the nozzle back. He couldn't close the fuel door. He'd have to get warm first.

The winds were really picking up, tearing black holes in the clouds. A few cold, hammered stars burned down through the rips.

He hurried back to the truck, blowing warm breath into his cupped hands. They felt like claws. "I'm going inside. You're okay watching him a little longer?"

"The *Kavkass* are much colder," Mahmet said disdainfully.

"Keep looking on the bright side." Yuri hurried back into the warm terminal building.

The hose stowed back in the truck, Tereshenko climbed into the cab with Mahmet behind him. "So," he said to the Chechen, "you've made an illegal visit to Mirny. You've taken me prisoner, you're holding my men. What will you do now?"

"Drive the truck into the garage. Don't talk."

"It isn't every day four Chechen terrorists visit us. Me, I'm from Angara. Three years ago I came to—"

"Is that where you want the body sent?" Mahmet noticed the red light below Tereshenko's thigh. It was blinking urgently. "What is that?" He reached down and spun up the volume control.

". . . the devil is going on out there, Angara Three?"

Mahmet looked up at Tereshenko, who was properly terrified. *What have you done?*

UP FROM THE COLLAPSED FISSURE, through the hatch, down a drift that grew wider, the flow of fresh air stronger, cleaner. There had been five tunnels radiating out from the main chamber of the Ninth Horizon. Nowek had escaped down one and now he was emerging from another. The naked bulbs strung along the roof were almost searingly bright. Ahead, the drift opened onto the main chamber. The growing breeze urged him on. He came to the mouth of the tunnel. The blast curtain was up. He stopped.

Someone had switched on the lights in the main chamber. He wished they had not. They burned hazy and yellow behind gauzy veils of smoke and dust, dimmed, but plenty bright enough to see Boyko's body.

He was facedown in a growing pool of water. His head was turned to one side, away, thank God. One arm was trapped beneath him, the other stretched out. A white bag had been placed between his fingers. Blood swirled black in a milky suspension of powdered ore and melted ice. Nowek couldn't hear the pumps, but then he couldn't hear anything.

Boyko's hard hat was gone, and with it the two identity

cards Nowek had hoped to find. The pit boss had been shot twice. There was one small hole down from the shoulders, left of the spine. Another at the back of his head, behind an ear, surrounded by charred hair plastered to the scalp with blood. A doctor he once knew had a name for it: the gray tattoo. The pattern left when a gun is thrust against skin and fired.

Nowek couldn't bear to see Boyko's face under the dirty water. He gently turned him over.

Entry wounds are almost always small. Exit wounds are another matter. A fist-size hole in Boyko's chest exposed a sharp broken rib and lung tissue already gray, already dead. The part of his face that had been underwater simply didn't exist. Nowek saw something else.

In the hand he'd kept under him as he fell, Boyko's gray fingers clutched a plastic identity card.

He pried Boyko's fingers away and took it. Slava's face stared belligerently up from the card. Nowek let the body down softly. The pit boss had turned his back to Kirillin. Insolence? Maybe. It was also possible that Boyko and Volsky were more alike than even he knew. Volsky grabbing that shotgun. Boyko protecting a card Nowek would need to escape. Each one had died trying to save Nowek's life.

Nowek opened the diamond pouch. They were smaller than the huge gem in Nowek's pocket. Ten ice-clear, perfect diamonds. He carefully tucked the giant in with the lesser crystals and thrust the pouch into his pocket.

A pistol lay on the floor, already underwater. He picked it up, found the safety was off, and thumbed it closed. There were six rounds left. It felt heavy, like cast iron. His fingers left perfect prints in the dust.

With Slava's card in one hand and the Makarov in the other, he splashed to the elevator. The water was up to his ankles and rising even as he looked. The blind security camera stared down as Nowek swiped Slava's ID through the reader.

A red light burned above the door. There was a soft *click*. The yellow light came on. The hoist was coming down.

"TO BE FRANK," said Yuri as he put his feet up on Tereshenko's desk, "I'm disappointed. I thought we had an understanding. I thought you were part of the team."

Tereshenko looked at the radio and shivered. The red light was blinking furiously. Someone was trying to contact him. That would have been good news except that one of the Chechens had a very sharp blade almost, but not quite, pricking the tender skin of his neck. "You don't know what it is to live here," he said. "You don't know Mirny. *Everything* is watched. *Everything* is monitored. *Please*. It's the *diamonds*. He'll . . ."

"Mahmet?" said Yuri.

Mahmet barely twitched, and a thin stream of blood ran down Tereshenko's collar.

The airport manager screamed.

"Quiet," said Yuri. "You should be glad it's Mahmet. My other business partner is a professional. Mahmet might accidentally kill you, but Plet would make you *wish* you were dead. So who's monitoring that radio?"

"This is *Mirny*. You can't fart without Kirillin knowing."

"Kirillin?"

"The mine director. He's going to find you one way or another, and the sooner you leave, the better."

"I agree," said Yuri. He looked at Mahmet. "So?"

The Chechen said, "I have seen no diamonds."

"They're not scattered on the street like plums!" Tereshenko shouted.

Yuri thought, then said, "Mahmet, give him the radio."

"Please!" Tereshenko pleaded. "You're in enough trouble...."

The blade dug in another millimeter. Tereshenko went white.

"Now listen," said Yuri. "You're going to say you had too much to drink, that you and your boys were playing games, and everyone here is very, very sorry. You won't even have to pretend."

Mahmet held up the portable radio. He dialed up the volume.

"... airport? Angara Three, come in. This is Pine Tree."

Tereshenko's hands shook. Say one thing and Kirillin would call him a hero, though he'd be a dead one. Say another and this madman would let him live long enough to face Kirillin. Tereshenko had two options. Two ways to die. One tonight. The other tomorrow. And so he made the natural choice.

"Angara Three. Listening."

"This is Pine Tree. *What's going on out there?*"

Pine Tree was militia headquarters. "Nothing. The maintenance men had a little drink. Everything is normal."

"You'd better tell them to be more careful. I was just about to send word that someone was playing with the radio out at the airport. You know what that would mean."

He did. "They won't step on the same rake twice."

"Well, just watch it. Pine Tree out." The red light went dark.

Yuri clapped his hands. "Very good."

"What do you want done with him?" asked Mahmet.

"He can wait in the garage with his sleepy friends. Have Anzor guard them. Bashir can run a snowplow?"

"Without doubt."

"Have him clear the runway. Nobody gets near the jet. I want to be ready to go at the jump of a flea. You'll be coming with me." He looked at Tereshenko. "About that car we discussed?"

Tereshenko stumbled on his words. "A militia jeep. It's parked by the entrance. The keys are in the desk. The *top* drawer."

Yuri pulled them out. "We're meeting an official from Moscow who is visiting your lovely town. Where might we find him?"

"There's just one hotel. The *Zarnitsa*. In the main square. Across from company headquarters. The road outside goes straight there. Don't turn off to the pit or the mine. They're guarded."

"Thank you for your cooperation. Just so you understand, if we don't return in a few hours, Bashir and Anzor will be very upset. Is there anything else you'd like to tell us before we go?"

"The company building is guarded. The hotel is not."

Yuri got up and walked to the window. He said to Mahmet, "Those arctic suits in the garage? We'll borrow them. It's getting cold. If we don't come back in—"

"Wait!" Tereshenko shouted. He reached into his pocket.

Mahmet was faster. The Chechen plucked a wallet from the manager's fingers and tossed it to Yuri.

"There's a card inside," said Tereshenko. "There are magnetic readers all over Mirny. An alarm goes off if you don't have it."

"Thank you." Yuri slipped the card from Tereshenko's wallet. "And allow me to say, welcome back to the team."

CHAPTER 27

The Soldier's Story

THE MINE ELEVATOR WAS ALREADY THROUGH the Seventh Horizon. Rising, Nowek thought about *A Soldier's Story,* a folktale about a Russian soldier who trades his violin, his Russian soul, to the Devil for a book of knowledge.

The Devil takes him home for three days to explain a few details. But when the soldier returns home, it's been three *years,* not three days, and he's long been given up for dead. Now in his own house, in his own country, and soon in his own mind, he's just a ghost.

Nowek looked at his watch. The crystal was shattered. It had stopped the instant of the explosion: four forty-eight. Nowek had visited the Devil's garden for only three hours, not three days. But time already felt elastic, stretched out of shape.

Had he only arrived this morning in Mirny? Was it just yesterday that he found that dog skinner dead in a jet of live steam? Had only four days passed since Volsky was standing in a shower, telling him that things were looking up?

The Fifth Horizon flashed by as a line of flickering, smoky lights. The air reeked of explosives and dust. Nowek's ears still felt plugged by thick wool. When he tried to clear one with a finger, it came back bloody.

The Fourth Horizon. The air was getting cold again. The rock outside the elevator wasn't rock, but Siberia's eternal ice. It made him think of Galena and her diamond earrings. The thought that he might never see her again was more painful than the pellets lodged in his arm.

A shudder, a pressure wave pulsed through the elevator. It was like the quick, violent gust that precedes an express train barreling through a station. Nowek could feel it. *Wham!* Then gone. The car swayed against its guides, then continued up.

The Third Horizon. Would Slava's ID get him out of here alive? Or had Kirillin placed Slava's name on a watch list? He decided no. They'd already found him, dead. Kirillin had already solved the problem that was Boyko. He'd thought he'd solved the problem that was Nowek, too. He'd been wrong twice. With a little more luck, he might be proven wrong again.

The Second Horizon. The next would be the ore chute level, the tunnel that would lead to Fabrika 3. He thought about the ventilator shafts. About walking back to town. He thought about the cold and the snow and the burned Belaz and Boyko's son, his bones too hot to touch. He thought too long, because the hoist was already starting to slow as it neared the top.

The richest fucking diamond mine on earth.

The pistol. He already stood accused of murdering Volsky. There was no reason to be found with the weapon that had killed Boyko, too. He opened the door of the circuit

breaker box, stuffed the pistol in, and closed it as the elevator came to a stop. He remembered where Boyko wore his
ID card, and shoved it into a pocket.

The door slid open.

Four men in black smoke hoods, clear face masks and ear
protectors. They were breathing oxygen from tanks strapped
to their backs. A rescue team. Two of them rushed into the
hoist and grabbed Nowek. His lips were moving. Nowek
couldn't hear. He tapped his ears.

The man in the mask shouted in his ear, *"What
Horizon?"*

"Nine," he said weakly, then his knees buckled.

Someone thrust a clear rubber mask over his mouth and
nose. He drew in a lungful of sweet, pure air. He realized
why the others were wearing hoods and breathing from
tanks. The air was thick with dust and smoke.

"He's bleeding."

"Check him through."

Nowek sagged against them as they dragged him into a
brightly lit corridor that was ribbed with girders, throbbing
pipes, rust-riveted ducts large enough to vacuum up a small
car. Nowek spotted the topmaster's booth. It was surrounded
with thick, soundproof glass. There were two men inside.
One was the topmaster, charged with logging in miners
heading up or down.

The other was Kirillin.

Steel bars herded the miners through a scanner station.
Nowek recognized an X-ray machine. It was the same model
he'd seen in Sib-Auto's repair yard.

Diamonds glow blue under X-rays.

With all those diamonds in his pocket, he'd light up like a
neon sign. If not, the scanner would read his identity and
someone would know that Slava had been on the diamond

line, was dead, and had not been down at the bottom of Mirny Deep. One way or another, in the next few moments, the alarm was going to sound. It was only a matter of seconds before he would become that wounded soldier in Stravinsky's tale, rising up from the earth with precious knowledge, a ghost.

"THAT'S THE THIRD," said the topmaster. "He must have been near the blast. You want to stop him for a body search?"

Kirillin looked at the whole-body scan on the X-ray monitor. The injured man glowed from head to toe. The finely powdered residue from the Dynagel blast reacted to X-rays even more than diamonds. "The health of our miners comes before matters of security," he said gravely. "Let him pass."

The topmaster punched a button and the outer gates opened just as one of the rescuers slid the ID card into the reader. A name flashed on the topmaster's screen, but by then the injured man was already on his way out to the ambulance waiting in the Dead Zone.

LAKES IN THE DESERT. A warm cabin in a blizzard. Dollars in an overseas bank. Boyko had been right about hallucinations. When you run out of hope, they looked pretty good. Nowek was sure this had to be one. He'd been carried right under Kirillin's nose with a pocket full of diamonds. No alarm had sounded. If that was possible, what was not?

Now he was looking up at a dense cloud of steam billowing out from the top of the headworks tower. The snow had stopped. Clouds raced across the sky. The stars burned with an unreal intensity. Half a meter of drifted snow was on the ground. A path had been cleared from the tower all the way to the Dead Zone. They carried him to the back of the militia ambulance. It was painted the usual dull, army green, distinct from all the other dull, army-green vehicles by a red stripe painted on its side. It was small; two stretchers left only a narrow aisle for the nurse to stand and work.

There was already a miner inside having his wrist bound. He had an open bottle of vodka clasped to his chest. They installed Nowek on the other stretcher, slammed the doors, and the ambulance began to roll.

The miner took a long look at Nowek, then said, "You know what happened?"

Nowek pointed to his ears and shook his head.

"Who set off that fucking charge without clearing the mine?"

"That's enough," said the nurse as she tied off the last strip and pinned the arm and wrist to the miner's jacket. She shifted around to face Nowek. "Now what's wrong with you?"

She looked at Nowek's forehead, poured some raw alcohol on a cloth, and wiped away the dust.

Nowek felt the alcohol bite. He turned to look at the other miner. He was asleep. The bottle on his chest was empty.

She examined his left ear. "Blood. The eardrum is damaged." She stepped back. "Let's get you out of your parka."

A COMMOTION from the mine hoist caught Kirillin's attention.

The rescue team hurried through the ore skip door

carrying a miner slung in a heavy canvas tarp. They were soaking wet, as though they'd pulled a shipwrecked man from angry surf.

The topmaster had a microphone on his desk. He leaned over and keyed it. "Who is it?"

"It's Boyko!" said a voice muffled by an oxygen mask. "He's dead! He was shot!"

"Boyko?" said the topmaster. "What was *he* doing down there?"

"A good question," said Kirillin. "That makes three dead with Anton and Slava. It seems we have a killer on our hands."

"But Slava's not dead."

Kirillin turned to the topmaster. "What?"

"He's alive. He came up from Horizon Nine. You cleared him through yourself not five minutes ago."

Kirillin swung. He couldn't see outside the headworks tower. *Nowek?* He hesitated for less than a second, then mashed his hand down on the red button that sounded the alarm. He swung on the topmaster. "Notify the militia *now*. Have them stop that ambulance wherever they find it. *Now!* Is there a radio in it?"

The topmaster already had the handheld radio out, tuned to the militia frequency. He gave it to Kirillin, thankful to all the gods and devils that the mine director had been the one to allow the *other* Slava through.

"IT'S ALL RIGHT. I'm fine," said Nowek, holding on to the sleeve of his parka. The nurse was trying to pull it off.

"What's wrong with you? You think I'd steal your coat? It's ruined with blood already. Stop acting like a baby."

Just then Nowek felt the ambulance veer to one side.

The nurse grabbed a strap and hung on as the brakes locked and the van skidded sideways. The van was gliding silently across fresh snow. It struck something and came to a stop.

"Don't move. I'm not done," she said to Nowek, then walked up the narrow aisle to the front. A partition separated the rear from the cab. There was a window, and it slid open.

A face peered back, then away. "Yes. We have him."

The nurse was about to ask what he meant, when a thump made her turn.

The rear doors were open, swinging in the biting wind. One of her patients was sound asleep. The other was gone.

THE AMBULANCE HAD COME to rest against a decorative fence made from welded steel circles. A four-story building lay beyond, with some rusted playground equipment in front. A school.

Nowek jumped the fence and ran. The snowdrifts came up to his shins. He left a perfect trail.

The school was elevated on concrete pilings to keep it from melting the permafrost. He dodged under the cracked concrete stairs, then down a dim corridor of pilings. There were only a few windblown drifts under the school, with plenty of bare earth. He might not be getting anywhere, but at least he wasn't leaving a trail.

A flashlight swept across the snowy school yard behind him. Nowek hid behind a pillar as the light probed for him. A second light flared white. He waited while the beams were looking elsewhere, then ran farther under the school.

On the far side was a large open plaza facing a wall of apartment buildings. Their walls alternated in a pattern of light and dark. Nowek was breathing heavily. He stopped. No. Not light and dark. They were white and blue.

Liza . . . eats her lunch at school. It's nearby. . . .

It was the row of apartment buildings that lined Ulitsa Popugayeva, Larisa's street. The first blue building on the left was hers. He looked back. The flashlights were under the school.

He took off across the snowy plaza. Not for her building, but for the end of the row. He ran into a drift and fell. When he got up, he saw a car slowly making its way down Ulitsa Popugayeva. A militia jeep. Its searchlight was swiveling, hunting the entrances to each apartment building.

Nowek got to his feet when it passed. He didn't have much energy. He was running on will, on stubbornness. But the snow seemed so warm, so inviting. It would be easy to simply sit down in a drift, to fall, to rest.

His run was more of a lopsided walk. His feet felt wooden, his knees rubbery. Who knew how much blood he'd left at the bottom of Mirny Deep? One hundred meters to go. Fifty. The last twenty steps. He couldn't think about diamonds, about Volsky or Boyko. Not Hock. Not even about himself. Just the next step.

The Hotel *Zarnitsa*, Chuchin, his home in Irkutsk, they all might as well be on Mars. He stopped, and when he did he could hardly muster the energy to look up at the stars. He could see the future clearly now. Nowek would become a "Snow Flower," a body that emerged from the ice after the first thaw of spring.

One more step. Then another.

And then he was at the sidewalk. It was a jumble of footprints, and the walking was easier. He turned right and made his way to the first blue apartment building. Somehow, he climbed the four stairs to the front door. He tried to open it, but it was so well locked it didn't even rattle. He turned around, reached up, and pushed the buzzer next to the name Arkov.

He sat with his back to the door, looking out across the same snowy street he'd seen when Boyko had picked him up. The same, and completely different. Nowek felt the cold reaching for him. The stars were very bright. A bag of loose diamonds in his pocket. The giant crystal from the bottom of the Ninth Horizon. Boyko's body, the Makarov in the elevator panel. He'd done a good job of establishing his guilt. Even *Levin* would have to believe he was helping Volsky deal in dirty—

The door clicked, then pulled open.

"You can't drink here! Get moving or I'll call the militia!"

Larisa was wearing a long coat and slippers on her feet. He looked up into her face.

She looked down at Nowek, then up the street. The militia jeep was working its way back in their direction. Her expression was that of a chess player weighing moves. Nowek and the militia. Threats and opportunities.

The patrol's searchlight swept a bright white path over snow.

"Hurry," she said, and reached down to help Nowek stand.

CHUCHIN HAD FELT the hotel room floor shake, the windows rattle. He didn't need a phone call from that woman to know that a blast had been set off someplace, and that, as usual, Nowek had been in the middle of it. What did he expect? That Kristall would pin a medal on him for taking over Volsky's job of twisting their pricks? Did he think they'd give him the key to the fucking city?

He pushed a heavy dresser in front of the door. It wouldn't keep someone out of the room forever, but they'd make noise when they came for him. Chuchin knew they would come. They had to. The boy, Sherbakov. Now Nowek. He was the last detail.

He rummaged in his cardboard suitcase and pulled out a paper bag stained by fish oil. The smell of ripe *omul* was overpowering in the enclosed hotel room, which, after all, was the point. He shook the rotted fish into the toilet, then pulled out a small, plastic bag. He ripped it open with his teeth and poured seven Nagant 7.62mm cartridges into his palm. Their unique recessed tips gave them the appearance of turtles pulling their head into a shell.

Chuchin took them back to the bed and loaded them into the reassembled revolver. You weren't supposed to be able to break down this model Nagant into such small, easily hidden pieces, but Chuchin was a master at hiding things. After twenty years behind the gulag wire, they could blame themselves for *that*.

His old Nagant was an officer's model, a double-action gun. When cocked, the cylinder moved forward against the rear of the barrel, forming a tight seal, making optimum use of the exploding gunpowder. It gave the pistol the punch of a much larger weapon.

He slid the last bullet into place, then spun the cylinder, and sat back against two propped-up pillows. He'd been Nowek's driver, his confidant, his friend, since the election for mayor of Markovo. A long time, too long to slink away even if there was a way to do it. Chuchin hadn't begged those bastards in the camps for his life. Not once. He wasn't about to start now. And when they came for him? He placed the cocked pistol on his lap.

They'd learn what friendship was all about.

SHE OPENED THE DOOR, turned on another light, and helped Nowek inside.

The apartment still smelled of cooked mushrooms. The kitchen table was still set, though now there was a child's plate and a plastic Mickey Mouse cup that had tipped over and spilled red juice onto the cloth. The normalcy of it gave Nowek strength.

"Let's get this off you," she said, tugging at his bloody parka.

Nowek saw that her face was different, paler, slightly puffy, and red around the eyes. She'd been crying.

"Kirillin called," she said. "He said there'd been an explosion in Mirny Deep, that you and Boyko had disappeared. I said, disappeared? In Mirny? How is that even possible? He said that you might have been down that mine with him."

"I was." He let her pull off the coat, then his shirt. His chest was scraped from slithering through the rock slot at the bottom of the mine.

"I called your associate right away and told him. He said—"

"I'm not surprised?"

Larisa nodded. "What were you doing with Boyko?"

"Going to the horizon." What would she say if she knew what was inside the parka's inner pocket? Ten perfect diamonds, and the giant crystal from the Ninth Horizon.

"You're delirious." Her long blond hair was pulled back. She tossed his bloody shirt to the floor and clucked her tongue when she saw his arm.

Nowek got a look at it for the first time. Three hard, painful mounds painted in dried blood and a black bruise.

Larisa took her long coat off. She was wearing a dark green robe, hooded, made of plush, velvety fabric beneath it. It gave her an almost medieval air, a princess in disguise. It had a zipper that went from waist to throat. She looked at his arm, then at him. "Who shot you? Was it Kirillin?"

"Anton."

"Then it might as well have been Kirillin. And Boyko?"

"He's dead. We tried to get out, but the mine hoist took us down . . . to the bottom. Kirillin came for us. He killed him, Larisa. I saw it."

"But he let you live?"

"No. He thought I was dead. Listen to me. This is dangerous for you. You and your daughter. I just need a place to stop for a moment and rest. . . ."

"Liza's asleep. You'd prefer to go to the clinic and have them look at you? What about the explosion?"

"Kirillin. He thought I was trapped."

"How did you ever get out of the mine?" When she could see that Nowek wasn't sure himself, she said, "It doesn't matter. We'll use the bathroom. I'm sorry, but this is going to be messy."

The small bathroom was sandwiched between her bedroom and the large closet that was Liza's room. In it, a tub sat on a sea of cracked tiles.

"There was a militia patrol on the street," she said. "What were they looking for?"

"Me."

"You said Kirillin thinks you're dead."

"He knows I'm alive."

The tub was stained from the hard minerals. She opened the tap and let it run until the hot water came and the small room filled with steam. She let the tub fill while she hunted for the appropriate tools: a razor, a tweezer, towels, tape and bandages, a bottle filled with pale green liquid.

"What's that?"

"For the pain. It's medicine. Take it." She unscrewed the cap and handed it to Nowek. "Can you sit with your arm over the tub?"

He took a sip. Vodka, but with something else. He thought of the bottle his father kept by the chair. It was fiery and herbal at the same time. He sat on the floor as she took a washcloth and delicately began to clean his wounds. When she dabbed at the swelling, a shot of electricity sizzled up his arm, his neck, and discharged into his brain. He sucked in his breath.

"It's going to be worse. Drink."

He did, deeper, letting the liquid fire run down his throat. Thick as molten glass. "Boyko told me about his son. About the strike. I know why Hock is here. He's got to—"

"Quiet. I have to dig."

He closed his eyes and felt the tweezers probe for the lead pellet. They'd felt like staples going into his arm. They felt like boulders coming out. He drank, and drank again. Larisa was right. It was medicine. The liquid poured life into him.

The first pellet emerged. She let the wound bleed until Nowek's arm ran bright red, plunged it into the hot water, sponged raw alcohol on, let it dry. She bandaged it tight.

"Done?" Nowek asked.

"The first. There's two more. Drink."

He did. The second pellet fell to the tiled floor with a *clink*.

"Larisa, I have to see Chuchin. . . ."

"You might as well go to Kirillin's office. You can't go to the hotel. They'll be watching. We'll think of something."

She had to probe deeply for the last pellet. She used the razor to open up the wound, then pulled the edges apart with the tweezers. She saw the black metal ball embedded in pink muscle. She got a grip on it, but it slipped. She went in after it. The pain broke down the door and rushed Nowek's brain. He tensed.

"Almost out. Don't move."

Another *clink* of lead on tile. She sponged off his skin with alcohol, bandaged it like the others and used a fresh towel to make a kind of sling.

The tub seemed to be filled with his blood, like an animal had been killed, then butchered. "The diamonds," he said. "They're leaving Mirny tomorrow morning. They're going out on the same flight I was supposed to take. They can't—"

"Later." She helped him to his feet. "There's nothing you can do about it now."

Nowek felt the room swirl, the blood, the steam, the herb-laced vodka. He began to shiver.

"You're cold?" she asked.

"You've been crying. Why?"

"Does it matter?"

It was a complicated question. "Yes."

"You were honest with me. I know it's not the same as trust, but you were honest and I wasn't. Now look at me." Her slippers were smeared with blood. She kicked them off. She had long, narrow feet, a high arch. "I even look like a murderer."

"I'm alive. You knew Kirillin was going to do something?"

"No. I swear it. I thought Hock would try to buy you.

It's the way he likes to work. I knew he couldn't, and it made me happy to imagine his face when you said no. Hock isn't used to surprises."

"Did you tell that to Kirillin?"

She wrapped a dry towel over his bare shoulders. "Come on. You'd better rest."

She led him out of the tiny bathroom, switched off the overhead lamp, then opened the door to her bedroom. "Wait." She went ahead and turned off the light.

Pale, snowy light streamed through the window from the street lamp. On the bed, a stuffed bear.

"Larisa . . ."

"You can stay here. I'll sleep with Liza. I'll think of something to do about tomorrow. I don't know—"

She was interrupted by three insistent buzzes, like a large angry wasp trapped behind a screen. The telephone.

"Wait," she said, and went out to the main room.

Nowek followed her to the door.

"Larisa Arkova listening."

Nowek saw her posture change. Straighter, respectful. He'd seen it before when she'd opened the door to Kirillin's office.

"It's not possible. Never." She turned and saw Nowek in the door, then looked away. "Of course. What should I do?"

No, thought Nowek. *What will you do?*

"Absolutely. I'll be very careful." She hung up the phone.

"Well?"

She put her finger to her lips, then urged him back into the darkened room. "They found Boyko. He was shot."

"I told you that already."

"Kirillin said diamonds were found on him. He said that you did it."

Nowek thought of the gems sparkling from the fissures

of the Ninth Horizon. "And so what will you do now, Larisa?"

"I'll help you if I can. Can you believe that?"

Was it the drink, the shock, the absence of alternatives? Whatever, Nowek said, "Yes."

She shut the door and walked to the window. The curtains were open. She was looking down on the street. He joined her.

The gray world of Russia lay beyond the icy glass. The snow might as well be swirling clouds of ash. A militia patrol sat parked at the corner, more shadow than substance. "Now you're shaking," he said.

"Thinking makes me afraid. Doesn't it do that to you?"

"It's only in the movies where you can be shot and blown up and feel nothing."

She turned to him. "You hurting?"

"To be honest, it hurt a lot less when they just shot me."

She smiled. "You need some more to drink. I'll get it."

"No. I've had enough." *Inside, outside,* he thought. *A spark of life buried by Mirny.* He could feel the cold of the glass, and also her warmth. The silence, the space between them grew electric.

Finally, she said, "You shouldn't trust me, Delegate Nowek. If Kirillin walked in this instant I don't know what I would do."

"My blood is all over your bathroom. You can use my name."

"Gregori." She moved against him, her head on his shoulder, her arm carefully around his back, light and tentative. "I don't know what's going to happen. I can't think about tomorrow, about Liza and Kirillin. When I do, it terrifies me."

"Then stop thinking." He put his right arm over her and

felt the bones of her shoulders through the thick robe. She
curved her body against his. He felt the soft warmth of her
breasts through the fabric, against the skin of his chest.
"You don't have to explain." He stroked her back. He could
feel each vertebra.

She pressed against him. The movement surprised him,
almost knocked him off balance. They swayed, not quite
standing alone, not quite together. Her robe had a nap like
heavy velvet. She looked up at him, her face ghostly in the
pale streetlight coming through the window. "I don't even
trust myself. How can you?"

Nowek lived in a world of reason. But reason couldn't
span every empty space. There came a point where reason
stopped, where faith took over. "My best friend died at my
knee. He'd already been shot once, and then the murderer
pointed the gun at me. Volsky grabbed the gun and took
the second bullet. He did it because it was what he had
to do."

"But I . . ."

"I could have come to Mirny, seen nothing, asked no
questions. It would have been smarter, but like Volsky, I did
what I had to do. It's the same for you," said Nowek. "You
live here. There's nothing you need to tell me. There's
nothing you have to apologize for."

"I wish that were so."

"It is."

She shook her head. "It's easy to forget, being trapped
here, that there are different kinds of people in other places."

"You mean America."

"I mean you." She pulled away from him, reached for
her throat, and pulled down the zipper. She was naked
underneath. "You make me feel clean. It's something I'd almost forgotten." She took his right hand and pulled it inside

to her breast. Her skin was hot, her nipple firm as an unripe berry. A warm, delicate scent came from her scalp.

She shouldered out of the robe and let it drop at her feet.

In the snow-gray light her muscles were less distinct, more blended. Her arms, her legs were slender and athletic. Her hips were boyish, her breasts firm, full.

She helped him to sit down on her bed, moved the stuffed bear, put a pillow behind Nowek, then gently guided his head down to it.

She undressed him, then covered his body with hers. She let him breathe deeply from the warm, fragrant skin between her breasts.

He looked up. "I can't let you . . ." he began, but she put her finger to his lips.

"You're not. This is also medicine." She kissed him, letting warm breath flow into his mouth with her words. "Take it."

CHAPTER 28

Ashes

YURI LOOKED UP AS FLAKES BEGAN TO FALL around a streetlamp. They were parked under the great black bust of Lenin. "Can you believe this? It's snowing again."

"As God wills," said Mahmet.

"So if God wills that we're stuck here until July, that would be okay with you?"

"Over there." Mahmet nodded at a militia jeep prowling the empty, snowy street. It wasn't a tank. His *Kala* could take it apart, though noisily. But that would be a battle, not a diamond hunt.

"All right," said Yuri. "We're not going to hang around until the militia gives us a parking ticket. Let's get going."

"Back to the airport?"

"No. The hotel."

Mahmet hid his surprise, put the little jeep in gear, and drove around the perimeter of the square. He stopped under the *Zarnitsa*'s overhanging concrete awning.

"I'll try to find Nowek. If I'm not back in . . ."

"You're the only pilot, boss," said Mahmet. "I'll find you."

He trudged up the steps, went in, and walked straight up to the desk. It had a sign across it that proclaimed it closed. But there was a woman behind the glass. She made the mistake of looking at Yuri before turning her back. He rapped on the glass.

"Closed," she said, pushing the sign closer to Yuri's face.

"For your sake it better not be." Yuri looked around the empty lobby. "We're scheduled to leave in an hour. Where is he?"

"Where is who?"

"The Siberian Delegate."

"Where did you come from?"

"Moscow. Maybe you've heard of it. Now answer my question or else call your superior. I don't have time for conversations."

Moscow? "The Delegate's room is 322, but . . ."

"Call him."

"The telephone system is under repair."

"Then send for him."

"There's no one to send."

Yuri fixed her with his most determined gaze. "Call your superior *at once.*"

The woman looked terrified. Yuri had hoped his words would carry weight. He was surprised to see how much, but then, he didn't know Kirillin.

"It's not my fault!" she pleaded. *"Go up yourself!"*

"I will. You can notify the kitchen that we'll require a small snack. Tea. Bread. Cheese. Some sausage. Be quick about it."

"The kitchen is closed for the—"

"You have five minutes. Not six. Understood?"

Her lips continued to move, to protest, but the words didn't come. Finally, she said, "Understood!"

"I *hope* so." Yuri left her and made for the stairs. He didn't have time for the elevator.

CHUCHIN HEARD THEM COMING down the hallway. He sat back against the headboard of the bed, the Nagant in his lap.

Footsteps outside the barricaded door. Then a knock.

He expected them to rattle the locks, to pound on the door, to smash it open. He didn't expect them to knock. "Who is it?"

"Is Delegate Nowek in there?"

"You've come to the right place." Chuchin quietly got up and made his way to the door. The Nagant would fire a 108-grain lead bullet with five grains of smokeless powder. A big, fast bullet that traveled at better than two hundred meters a second. It would go through the door like tissue paper. He pulled the dresser away.

"Nowek?"

"Almost ready." Chuchin reached up and unlocked the door, then stepped back. "All right. Come in. I'm ready for you."

The doorknob turned, the tongue clicked.

Chuchin's finger curled around the trigger. The mechanism was stiff, reluctant. He wished he'd oiled it. A point of pride.

The door began to open. A hand appeared around the edge. A head. "Nowek? Are you . . . ?"

Chuchin pulled the slack out of the trigger mechanism.

Yuri didn't see Chuchin. He saw the gun. "Fuck." He dived for the carpet as Chuchin fired.

"PULL OVER HERE." Kirillin got out of the militia jeep. The ambulance that had taken Nowek away from the mine was long gone, but the tracks he'd left in the snow were still there. They were beginning to soften, to fill. He walked very slowly, very deliberately, to the school, then ducked underneath and walked straight to the other side. He found Nowek's prints again, saw where he'd stumbled in a drift, where he'd fallen, even where he'd put an arm out to push himself back up. The snow was pink.

Where was he going? The trail headed in the general direction of town. Where was he now? Dead in a snowbank? Walking out of Mirny on a road? That would mean the same thing.

The jeep's horn sounded. Kirillin hurried back. A militia officer met him halfway.

"There's been a shooting at the hotel," he said, his breath white as steam. "The *babushka* at the desk called the militia. They're going there now."

"A shooting?" said Kirillin. "Why wasn't I notified directly?"

The militiaman chose his words carefully. "Most probably she thought you already knew about it."

Kirillin didn't. "Is there anything *else* I should know about?"

The officer shook his head, but then he thought there was more risk in withholding even trivial reports than in letting the mine director in on everything. "There were unusual signals from the airport earlier in the evening. But . . ."

"What kind of signals?"

"The maintenance crew was raving about terrorists. They'd been drinking and . . ."

Kirillin hurried to the jeep and snatched the radio. "This is Kirillin. What's going on at the airport?"

You could hear the officer at the other end stiffen. "Someone used a radio call sign inappropriately and made a false report of—"

"Who? Tereshenko?"

"Yes. He took full responsibility."

"No," he said. "*I* am taking responsibility. I don't know what's going on. Until I do, the city will be shut down. The roads. The airport. Nothing moves through any gate without my authorization. Is that understood?"

"Understood. What about communications links?"

"Cut them all," said Kirillin. "Now."

"YOU DUMB *MUZHIK*! What did you do *that* for?" Yuri was on the floor. The door was splintered. The opposite wall had a crater in it, and from the wind whistling through, the bullet had hit the outside wall and kept right on going. It was probably halfway to Irkutsk by now, which was more than Yuri could say for himself.

"Who are you calling a peasant, Thief?"

"Where is Nowek?" asked Yuri. "I came for him."

"You mean you came to steal something." It wasn't one of those diamond bastards, but Yuri was close enough.

"There's no time to argue. You've fired off your stupid cannon and they'll be—"

"Delegate Nowek is in no hurry. He's dead."

"Dead?"

"An explosion at the mine. So whatever you came for,

you can turn around and leave. There's nothing for you here."

A long pause, then, "Fine. It's my mistake. You can stay and freeze for all I care. I'm going back to Irkutsk."

Irkutsk? "Hey. Wait." He pulled open the door and saw the hole in the wall across the hallway. "You're going to Irkutsk?"

"If you don't kill the pilot."

Downstairs, the two hurried by the front desk. A plate of cheese, bread, and sausage was there, covered with enough plastic wrap to protect it from the elements for a hundred years. A silver samovar sat steaming on a cart surrounded by snowy china cups bearing Kristall's diamond logo.

They ignored it.

The woman at the desk stood. "What's going on? I heard a shot. Is Delegate Nowek . . . Hey!" she shouted when they didn't stop. "What about the food?"

Yuri paused at the door. "Charge it to the room."

NOWEK LISTENED TO Larisa's breathing deepen, slow. Twice he heard the slap of tire chains as militia patrols moved along the snowy street beyond her window. One way or the other, Kirillin knew that Nowek was trapped in Mirny. There was no other place he could be. He wouldn't stop looking until he found him. How long could that take in a city where everything, and everyone, was connected? Where the web was drawn so firm and tight that the slightest quiver would summon him?

He turned to look at her. The light coming in from the street-lamp illuminated the tips of her hair from behind. It was golden, like soft tassels of ripe corn lit by a full moon. They'd each made a bargain, a deal. She'd left him feeling almost painfully alive. His brain was like some finely tuned receiver, picking up everything, flooded with signals, information, impressions. What did Larisa get? His forgiveness, his reassurance that she wasn't beyond the redemption of love. Even the kind that comes in the brush of a hand, the interlacing of fingers, the quickening of breath, and leaves only bittersweet traces behind.

His arm felt stiff as plaster and just as brittle. Move too fast and he was sure something would crack. He got to his feet. His head swam with the liquor, with the shock of being alive.

Nowek walked to the window and watched the snow drift down. The flakes slanted down through the golden halo of a street light. The wind had shifted. It was now from the northwest, meaning the worst of the weather had passed.

A million carats to London in the morning. . . .

Nowek had to get word to Levin tonight. Because Mirny was small and Kirillin was determined. A telephone might work, except it would be the same as pointing a gun at Larisa and pulling the trigger, and Nowek wouldn't, couldn't, do that.

Alyosha was organizing the strike with his computer . . . Kirillin couldn't read the messages . . . it must have driven him crazy. . . .

Larisa had a computer.

He found it out on a table in the living room. An older model. It made him think of Sherbakov, how his eyes had lit up when he'd seen Nowek's new laptop. There was a phone line connected to it. He found the power switch, flicked it, and the screen snapped and buzzed to life, filling with a picture of Larisa's daughter, Liza. She was holding a flower up to the camera and, on her face, a look of bright expectation.

The familiar Internet globe icon appeared. Nowek moved the mouse over and clicked on it. The computer dialed out with a series of beeps and hisses. The connection was made. He typed in his password. A message was already waiting for him.

> To: wizard-private@russiamail.com
> CC: <gnow@russet.ru
> From: ivl-private@russiamail.com
>
> If you are still in Irkutsk, stay there. If you are in Mirny leave quickly. I am in Moscow, in Hospital 31. I won't be coming to meet you. I was attacked and you can say the only accident is that I am still alive. I think it was arranged by someone in our own department. Maybe by an amphibian we both know. Until we speak, trust only the Delegate. And be cautious. If they would do this to me here, what would they not do in Mirny? There's no time. I'll explain later.
> Levin

Levin wasn't coming. What was left when the fire died, when the last hope burned to ash? Cynicism? Bitterness? Resignation? The very qualities that made playing *The Fool,* the card game with no winners, only losers, Russia's favorite. A million carats of gem diamonds would be leaving Mirny tomorrow. So would Hock. They'd go where all the other millions had gone: to the cartel. With Levin in a hospital, what would stop them?

The only accident is that I am still alive.

Nowek sensed that same high-voltage hum of an electrified web plucked, of another victim hopelessly snared. Here in Mirny. In Moscow. Who could say how far it reached?

Nowek had gone to the horizon. He'd seen its crystal gardens. Who ruled it?

There were levels to this game. At the very top was the oldest, wealthiest cartel on earth. A diamond empire happy to buy the enemies it could, and destroy the ones it could not. The empire had Hock. It had Kirillin. It had men in Moscow who would act on their behalf, in the corridors of power and in the alleys and streets. Against all of that, what did Nowek have?

He clicked on the Reply button.

> To: ivl-private@russiamail.com
> CC:
> From: <gnow@russet.ru
>
> I don't know if you'll ever read this, ever see it. But I am writing it all out anyway. Think of a man shipwrecked on an island. I'm keeping a diary. I'm putting it in this strange, electronic bottle, and throwing it into an invisible sea in the hope that someone will pick it up one day and read it. It's everything I believe. Everything I know. Sherbakov is dead. He was murdered by Kristall, a man named Kirillin arranged it, but he was doing it for a South African named Eban Hock. Hock was in Moscow when Volsky was murdered. He bragged he was at *Ekipazh* that night. He is here now. By this time tomorrow he will be out of your reach. But first, the diamonds. A Kristall airplane will leave Mirny tomorrow morning with one million carats of gem rough on board....

When he was done, when it was all said, not with beautiful words, not with grace, not even with much skill, he pressed the send button. The message vanished, followed by a sound, an odd *click*. A message box in dull, aching gray materialized.

CONNECTION TERMINATED. RECONNECT?

As Nowek wondered whether any of his words had escaped Mirny's gravity, there was another sound. It was the *click* of a key being inserted in Larisa's front door. The lock opened, so did the door, but only a crack. A chain was in place. Then a voice. "Larisa?"

Nowek switched off the computer. The screen went dark.

"Larisa?"

It was Eban Hock.

MAHMET SAID, "Behind us."

Yuri turned and saw two yellow headlights where there had been none a moment ago. They were out of the city, halfway to the airport.

A third light flared bright white.

Chuchin said, "He turned on a spotlight."

"Then we'll do the same." Yuri switched the light mounted on his side and swept the sides of the road. Tall reeds poked their heads up from new snow. In the distance, a tall building set out in the middle of nowhere. It was a strange place to build an office tower, but he recognized the red beacons on top. He'd almost flown into it on the approach to the airport.

The light from behind wavered, then an instant later, it swept back in their direction. The jeep was flooded with light.

Mahmet instinctively floored it. The engine coughed, caught, and the *bobyk* flew down the road, its front tires riding up over the snow like the bow of a speedboat.

"This is not good," said Yuri.

Their pursuer kept an ominously even distance, not closing, not falling behind.

Chuchin measured the situation with a very practiced eye. "He's sending word. They're going to trap us."

Yuri wished he'd brought the GPS navigator. It was a joke. He could fly to Mirny from a thousand kilometers away, land with pinpoint accuracy and some luck, but now that he was here, on the ground, he wasn't sure where the airport even *was*. The road made a wide, sweeping curve. Yuri wished he'd paid closer attention. "We could leave the road and go straight to the jet."

"If you can make this jeep fly," said Chuchin. "The airport is on the other side of the open pit." He looked off into the darkness. "It's two kilometers across. Five hundred meters to the bottom. This road goes around the perimeter."

Mahmet saw lights out ahead. "There's his friend."

"All right," said Chuchin. "Turn left."

"You said the pit was—"

"Turn left now."

Mahmet spun the wheel. The *bobyk* jumped off the road and into untracked snow, riding over rolling mounds of frozen marsh.

"LARISA? Open the door."

Nowek felt his heart sag. Hock. What did it mean that he would come here now? What did it mean that he had a key to her apartment? What *else* could it mean?

Nowek had just shared a woman with the man who murdered his best friend. In *A Soldier's Story,* a violin, a soul, buys a book of knowledge. What had Nowek bought?

In the bedroom, the light still spread the same glory over her, but now it looked like gray ash falling. He woke her.

"Gregori? What—"

"You have a visitor." His words were cased in crumbling rock and frozen soil. Eternal ice a kilometer deep and growing deeper.

"What do you mean? Who is it?"

He tossed her the heavy green robe. "Eban Hock."

She stared at him, then, with the same look of calculation, of appraisal, he'd seen when she let him in to her building, she threw the robe over her head. "Stay here. I'll talk to him."

THE RED LIGHT on his radio blinked. Kirillin picked up the microphone. "Well?"

"There's a report of a vehicle out on the ring road. It's beyond the gate to the *karir,* heading for the airport."

"What have you done?"

"The road is blocked ahead. There's a patrol in pursuit."

"And the airport?"

"Two more patrols are leaving now."

"Box them in. I'm on the way. Kirillin out."

THE *BOBYK* SCRAMBLED up a frozen mound of ore tailings, then slid down the other side, and onto another, more narrow, road.

"Left," Chuchin ordered. "Turn *left.*"

The Chechen swung the wheel hard left and urged the jeep onto the mine perimeter road. He gunned the engine. A fence appeared in the headlights. A fence, and a gate. *No. 5.*

"You want me to break through?" asked Mahmet.

"No," said Yuri, fishing out Tereshenko's ID. "Stop."

They pulled up to the gate. Yuri handed the plastic card to Mahmet, who slid the night manager's credentials through. Headlights appeared behind them. The gate remained closed. The lights stopped, found the tracks they'd left, then turned.

"Again. Slower."

Mahmet did as he was ordered, though it was obviously a foolish thing to trust a piece of plastic to do what . . .

The gate began to slide.

"Drive!" yelled Chuchin, "But not too far and not too fast!"

Mahmet rolled through the gates with one eye on the—

"*Stop!*" Chuchin yelled.

Mahmet jammed on the brakes. The jeep skidded sideways and bumped to a stop.

"You two. *Out,*" Chuchin told Mahmet. "I'm driving now."

"THEY'RE HEADING FOR GATE 5," the militiaman reported to Kirillin as his partner jammed his boot down on the accelerator.

"Did they break through?" Kirillin demanded.

"I can't tell yet."

"It doesn't matter. Stop them."

"Understood." He reached back for the Kalashnikov. It wasn't the new model. It was scarred, the wooden stock was taped together where cold had split it, but it was an old and trusted tool. He checked the clip. *Full.* The casings gleamed a muted gold.

They turned left onto the inner ring road. Now, at the

mit of their headlights, the *bobyk* appeared parked at the gate.

he militiaman said, "The gate's open. How did they—?"

"Don't worry about it. Just move us in a little closer."
he sergeant rolled down his window and leaned out. He
rought the Kalashnikov up and centered its iron sights on
ie parked *bobyk*.

Chuchin waited as long as he dared. The lights were
oming on fast. He waited, counted one second, two, then
ammed the gear selector into first and tore off down the
oad to the open pit.

The first burst was high. Chuchin ducked as the big slugs
ore through the *bobyk*'s rear window, punching into the
eats like sledgehammers, shattering the windshield. He
ooked down for an instant to see if he was still alive, then
ecided, who cared?

The road began a slight rise. He knew what it meant,
hat lay beyond the rim. There was nothing he could do
bout it except go faster. He swung the wheel, weaving
ack and forth to make himself harder to hit. The second
urst smashed into the tailgate. A rear tire exploded. Then
ie next. The *bobyk* sagged, running on steel rims. Not that
had much farther to go. The jeep roared up the final rise.
he headlights tilted up. At their end, the beams faded into
pen space.

Chuchin reached for the door as the third burst struck.

THE TWO VEHICLES were connected by ropes of yellow
acers. Mahmet didn't think there was any chance the old
aan could be driving. He didn't think there was any chance
e'd be *alive*.

The militia jeep tore past him. Mahmet tracked it, whis-
ered, *"Allahu akhbar,"* and squeezed the trigger.

The rocket grenade whooshed out into the night, trailing orange sparks, red sparks, white and gray streamers of smoke.

The militia jeep seemed to move slowly, the rocket swift. The warhead struck the passenger window, met a momentary resistance, then a greater one sufficient to crush the impact fuse.

The jeep's roof flew into the air, the wheels, still spinning, broke free from their axles and rose in incendiary arcs. A ghostly carriage bound for heaven. The four wheels stayed together, ruled by the laws of momentum, stabilized by their spinning, until gravity reasserted its authority. They tipped down and followed Chuchin's *bobyk* over the edge to the bottom, half a kilometer straight down.

CHAPTER 29

The Firestorm

LARISA SAID, "WHAT ARE YOU DOING HERE, Eban?"

Nowek listened with his forehead against the door. His fists were balled up. The pressure electrified the three pellet wounds on his left arm, and the burning, the pain, felt good.

"Why?" asked Hock. "Are you busy?"

"I was asleep. You woke me."

"It's awfully early for sleeping. Is something wrong?"

"Eban, no. Just tell me what you've come for."

"I'm leaving again in the morning."

"So where will you go? Angola? Sierra Leone?"

"To London," said Hock. "With a rather large shipment. Our friends think there could be some rough weather coming and they'd rather not leave a lot of loose stones around. Too tempting."

"So? Why tell me?"

"If you like, you can come with me. You and Liza both."

Nowek closed his eyes.

"I don't have documents. No visa. How could . . ."

"We won't be going through the regular procedures."

Not with a million carats in Siberian rough diamonds.

"What does that mean? You'll smuggle us in?"

He could hear Hock say something too softly to make out. Then, "Eban. Liza's asleep behind that door."

"Let's talk privately. Better yet, let's not talk at all."

"Stop it. This is *serious*. I have to hear more."

Hock sighed. "We're leaving early. There was going to be a stop in Moscow. It's not necessary now. We'll arrive in London in time for breakfast."

"Kirillin will permit it?"

"He's got some problems to solve. You know about Boyko?"

"I heard he was found."

"At the bottom of Mirny Deep. Your friend Nowek shot him."

"Has Nowek been found?"

"He will be. About London. You don't seem very pleased. I thought it was your dream to leave Mirny."

"Dreams aren't real. I'm trying to believe in this one."

"I'm glad. Leaving would be a smart move. Kirillin wanted to talk to you. I told him I would see you first."

"What about?"

"I imagine you'll find out if you decide to stay. Naturally, it's your choice."

Nowek knew how she would answer.

"What choice?" asked Larisa.

MAHMET PUT the launcher tube down and picked up the AK-102. He unfolded the stock, clicked off the safety and pointed it at the man walking toward them.

Yuri saw who it was, and motioned to Mahmet. "You weren't supposed to leave the *bobyk* behind, old man."

"What's the matter, Thief? You don't have legs?" said Chuchin. "The airport's not far. If I can walk there so can you."

HOW LONG HAD Hock and Larisa stood together, sealing their bargain? Long enough for Nowek to think about finding something heavy. Long enough to realize that there were other, more important things left to do than smashing Hock's skull in.

He heard the apartment door click shut. The chain rattle across the catch. One second, two, and then she was standing there.

"Gregori," she whispered. He was getting dressed. "Gregori."

"You should be getting ready to leave." He could smell Hock's cologne on her.

"Look around." She swept her hand at the walls. "You think I want to live like this forever? To see Liza live like this all her life? I won't say no. How can I?"

He was having trouble with his boots. How do you tie boots on with one hand? "Hock told me that Mirny is Africa. I wonder. What does that make you?"

"Where are you going? You can't even get dressed."

"I'm leaving Mirny."

"On foot? It's a hundred kilometers to the next town."

"Then I'd better get going. Like you, I have one chance. I can't afford to turn it down." He couldn't tie his laces, but he didn't have a long walk in mind.

"Please don't do this."

There was something in her intimate tone that infuriated

him. "What would you have me do, Larisa? See you off in the morning? Kiss you good-bye? Shake his hand? You and Hock The truth is, I don't know who to feel more sorry for."

"I'll think of something. Just don't leave."

Nowek reached for his parka and draped it across his shoulders. It was stiff with dried blood. "There's no reason to stay." He walked by her to the front door. He unhooked the chain. Unlocked the lock.

"Where are you going?" It was half scream, half sob.

"Mommy?" It was a sweet, tiny voice.

Nowek turned and said, "Good-bye, Larisa."

TERESHENKO SHIVERED. The metal garage was not *quite* freezing. He and the three useless men from the night maintenance crew were sitting on the cold cement floor, tied tightly together with a rope looped around their necks, strung between steel posts. They were guarded by a Chechen with a very big gun.

A *crack,* followed by a longer rumble, echoed through the empty space. It wasn't blasting. You felt those through the ground, first. "You heard that?" Tereshenko said to the Chechen guard. "Maybe that was your boss. You should think about what will happen now if it was."

Anzor, the youngest brother, knew the sound of an RPG round going off. What Chechen didn't? It had to be Mahmet. He looked at the radio. It was blinking almost constantly now with traffic. "We *both* should think about what will happen."

NOWEK OPENED THE DOOR and stepped out into the cold. The snow was still falling, but with none of the drive, none of the interest, it had shown before. The clouds were old and tired. He nearly slipped on the first step, and unconsciously made a grab for the railing with his left hand. He heard the soft ripping of bandage, then skin, felt the blood. Well, he wasn't in this for his health.

At the bottom of the stairs and he was already breathing heavily. To the right, he could see the red beacon atop Mirny Deep. To the left, beyond the Bulvar Varvara, lights burned in the windows of Kristall's headquarters.

The parka was stiff with dried blood. A shell. A carapace. Like some marine creature, he would very shortly shed it. There was a kind of freedom in what he was doing. And madness, too. But that was Russia, wasn't it? And what was Siberia if not the most Russian place of all? He stopped directly under the streetlight that had turned Larisa's hair to gold. He looked up. Her curtains were drawn. His head was light with possibility, with knowing that he'd left reason behind.

A militia patrol prowled down Varvara, slowed, then turned up Ulitsa Popugayeva. A searchlight blazed to life. It swung his way and caught him. From beyond the light, a voice. "Who are you? What are you doing out here?"

It was a good question. The diamonds were leaving tomorrow. Even if it meant riding with Hock and Larisa to Moscow and into the hands of the militia, even if it meant standing trial for the murder of his best friend, it was Nowek's final hope. And like Larisa, how could he say no? He held up his right hand to shield his eyes, then said, "I'm the Siberian Delegate. My name is Nowek."

WITH A PK MACHINE GUN, if you could see your target, you could kill it, and Bashir saw his target. Two men moving laboriously across snow at the bottom of a shallow slope. They'd have to run uphill, through snow, to get close to the terminal building, and they would never make it. He pulled the charging lever back, tugged at the cartridge belt to take out any slack that might turn into a kink at the wrong moment, and settled in behind the PK. He'd piled extra snow around him, snug in the white arctic suit they'd liberated from the garage. They really were very good.

The Chechen locksmith had expected them to come in trucks, maybe in tanks. Certainly not on foot. But you killed the target that presented itself, and right now these two men were well inside the PK's three-kilometer lethal reach. He pulled a woolen muffler over his mouth to keep his white breath from betraying his position too soon, and placed the PK's sights on the figure to the left, the one moving more nimbly. Kill that one, and the other would . . .

"Am I waking you, cousin?"

Bashir jerked. "Mahmet! I didn't hear you!"

"Some *mujahedin*." Mahmet had the rocket launcher over one shoulder, the AK slung over the other. Yuri and Chuchin came huffing up the slight slope. "Go inside," said Mahmet. "I'll take the watch."

THE LIGHTS INSIDE THE HANGAR weren't bright, but Chuchin slipped on his dark glasses anyway. He took over guard duty while Yuri left to preflight the jet, taking Anzor, the youngest brother, along with him.

"What are you, a rock star?" one of the prisoners asked.

Chuchin barely turned.

Tereshenko watched the red light on the radio blink furiously. You could hear the tension in the transmitted voices. They were shouting over the radio as though trying to be heard without one. A shooting at the hotel, a chase at the open pit. Security patrols everywhere. It brought to mind a wasp's nest swatted down from a limb, buzzing, boiling with angry insects. Now the night manager prayed for two things: that the terrorists would leave, and that Kirillin wouldn't try to rescue him before they did.

"*Angara Three! Angara Three!*"

Tereshenko looked up. He recognized the voice of the mine director.

"*Angara Three! Answer!*"

Chuchin brought the radio to him and held the microphone up. "Talk."

Tereshenko took a deep breath, then said, "Angara Three. Listening."

"Where were you?" Before Tereshenko could reply, Kirillin said, "Listen carefully. The city is sealed. Have you seen anything out of the ordinary?"

Tereshenko looked up into Chuchin's dark lenses. He held a very large, very black, revolver. "Please repeat."

"Have you seen anything out of the ordinary? Strangers? Vehicles?" asked Kirillin, then, to seal Tereshenko's fate, "Unauthorized aircraft?"

Lie and Kirillin would make them all pay. On the other hand, there was this maniac with a gun who would—

"*Tereshenko!*"

"It's been snowing," he blurted.

"Thank you for the weather report. Never mind. The patrols will be there shortly. Is Omsk 7 there yet?"

Omsk 7. A militia patrol. "I haven't seen him." It was even true. "He's definitely not here, Mister Director."

"Is the runway plowed?"

"Yes." Also true, though a Chechen had done it.

"The snow's stopped for the night. Bring in all the vehicles and lock them up. Then lock all the doors. Don't open them for anyone until you see me or a militiaman you personally know. Is that understood?"

"Count on me, Mister Director! I will open no doors."

"All right, Tereshenko. Kirillin out."

YURI TOOK THE DIRECT ROUTE to the Yak. Instead of going through the offices, he went through a side door in the garage. But it didn't lead outside. Instead, it opened onto another hangar. He felt around for the lights, found a switch, and flipped them on.

He whistled softly.

A gleaming Yak-40, white with two bold stripes on the side, one blue, the other gold, and the blue diamond in a circle logo painted on the tail. If his *Okurok* was a cigarette butt, this was a fine Havana cigar.

Kristall's Yak had three new turbofan engines. They made more thrust, pushed the jet higher and faster, and used less fuel to boot. It even had extra fuel tanks, "slippers," under its wings to give it continent-spanning range. If he'd had this beauty instead of the Cigarette Butt, he could have flown from Irkutsk to Mirny and back without having to stop for gas.

He checked the sight gauges mounted on the external tanks. Brimming full. Wherever they were planning to go, it was a long way from Mirny. He thought, *If I don't find a single diamond tonight, pocketing this jewel would make it all worthwhile.* But how? He could just fly away with it. One coat of new paint and it would be White Bird International's flagship. But there was Kristall to consider. Dodging the tax man in Irkutsk was one thing. Pissing on Kristall was another. Still, it wouldn't hurt to look inside, would it?

The rear ramp was up, but not locked. He pulled the handle. A stairway covered in plush red carpet magically, silently dropped. The interior lights came on automatically, revealing a small aft compartment with just two seats. The plush jet smelled of leather and money. Yuri filled it with rich American phantoms, winging across Siberia to save some endangered arctic mouse or photograph some scrawny plant.

He found a vault built into the tail compartment. It was bigger than the lavatory that usually was installed in the same space. It was open, so at least he didn't have to torment himself with the possibility that it was stuffed with diamonds. The main cabin had all the trappings of a well-appointed corporate jet.

Wasn't there *some* way to close this deal? With Nowek's protection he could thumb his nose at Kristall. But without Nowek, there was no way he could grab it and—

"Boss!"

Yuri stopped and peered under the Yak's tail. It was Anzor.

"Patrols are on the way!"

Yuri gave a wistful look at Kristall's jet, then said, "Let's go."

"SO HOW DID YOU get involved with these pirates?" Tereshenko asked Chuchin.

"I'm just a pensioner getting a ride back home."

"Why do you wear those dark glasses at night?" asked one of the maintenance men.

"You didn't know? I'm blind."

Another of the prisoners was emboldened. "What have you got in your jacket? A bag of diamonds?"

Chuchin opened his coat and showed him the Nagant. "My hearing aid. It works in reverse. When I use it, everything gets quiet."

Just then, an excited voice reported a fire at the bottom of the *karir*. Omsk 7, the lost patrol Mahmet had rocketed, had been found.

Then a new voice.

"We have him!"

"Who?" asked the man at militia headquarters.

"The Siberian Delegate! We have Nowek."

Chuchin stared at the little radio as though it had just called him by name. *What did they just say?* He ran up the volume. *Alive?*

"We're bringing him in now! He's wounded and carrying contraband!"

"Contraband?"

"Diamonds!"

Yuri poked his head in. "Okay, grandfather. We're leaving."

Chuchin shook his head. "No. We're not."

KIRILLIN LOOKED at Gate 5. It was in perfect working order. "Someone let them through. Whose card was used?"

"Tereshenko's," said General Stepanov, the commander of the Mirny militia. "The terrorists ambushed our patrol. It looks like explosives were used. Perhaps a rocket."

Kirillin turned. "Really? You can just look at a hole in the ground, some scattered pieces and four tires that flew a kilometer and a half, and come up with such a conclusion?"

"Well," said Stepanov, "it was *probably* a rocket."

Kirillin started walking back to the jeep, thinking out loud. "Boyko. A single shot in the hotel, fired out of Delegate Nowek's room. Your men ambushed. Tereshenko's card." He looked off in the direction of the airport. "It's clear these saboteurs flew in. That's where we'll have to stop them."

"Sending two jeeps against rockets is slaughter, Mister Director."

He faced Stepanov. "We'll use the snow tanks to push them back into their airplane. We'll encourage them to go."

"*Encourage* them? They've killed—"

"We'll station sharpshooters off either end to make sure they don't succeed, of course."

CHUCHIN MADE HIS CASE to Yuri. His breath smoked white in the chilly garage. Mahmet and Anzor, the eldest and youngest of the Brothers, stood silently. Aslan was guarding the plane. Cousin Bashir was back covering the road to the terminal with the PK, hyperaware of every sound now that he'd been surprised once.

When Chuchin was done, Yuri said, "Not a chance. I'm not sticking around another minute."

The five prisoners watched them argue, their eyes going back and forth like spectators at a tennis match.

"But he's alive," said Chuchin. "I heard them say it."

"They're sending a fucking army in our direction. Did you hear that, too?"

"Pah." Chuchin pulled out his Nagant. "I'm staying."

Mahmet's rifle seemed to materialize out of a white cloud of breath. It was pointed at Chuchin's head, safety off.

Chuchin paid no attention to the AK. "You came to pick him up because you thought there was trouble. Now there's trouble and you're running. If I'm the only one with balls, then go. All of you. Get out of my sight." Chuchin turned his back on them in disdain.

Tereshenko said, "He's right. You'd better go while you can. You may stop a militia jeep, but you won't stop tanks."

Chuchin turned. "Tanks?"

"The security office uses them for transporting diamonds to the airport. Believe me, if they don't come for you tonight, they'll be here in the morning. There's a shipment of . . ." He stopped himself, in time he thought. But he was wrong.

"Diamonds?" asked Yuri.

THE SNOW TANKS looked like eight-wheeled turtles painted white. They weren't true tanks, just obsolete BTR-60 armored personnel carriers Kristall had acquired from the army. Too slow for a modern battlefield, their armor and gun turrets made them excellent mobile diamond vaults.

First one, then the second tank started up with a clatter of cold engines and clouds of oil smoke. No diamonds were brought on board through the rear doors. Only belts of heavy machine gun rounds, each bullet as long as a man's index finger.

When they were ready, the driver settled behind his bulletproof prisms, and moved off, heading north.

"MOMMY?"

Larisa closed the small suitcase, locked it, then put it beside her bed. "What are you doing awake?"

Liza wore a one-piece suit in a waffled pink fabric. "I heard you yelling." She saw the suitcase. "Are you going away?"

"We're *both* going away. Tomorrow morning."

"For a long time?"

"If we're lucky. Now back to bed with you."

"Can Misha come, too?"

Her bear. "Of course."

She ran to the bear and grabbed it, hugging it close. "Why were you yelling?"

"Sometimes people say bad things that can hurt."

"You mean when they lie."

"Yes." She stroked Liza's wheat-colored hair. "But sometimes when they say something that's true, it hurts even more."

"Mommy? Misha has a bump."

Larisa looked. It was true. There was a hard lump under the bear's brown scalp. The seam in the back was loose. Torn.

"I hear a snowplow!" Liza jumped to the window, excited.

Larisa probed the lump in poor Misha's head. Her finger came up against something cold and sharp. She drew in a quick, startled breath when she realized what she was feeling, then another when she felt the crystal's size. She joined Liza at the window in time to see the first snow tank rumble by. Then the second. "The snowplows are gone. Now go to bed."

"Mommy?" Liza looked up. "Why are you crying?"

"Please," said Larisa. She clutched the torn bear to her breast. "Just go to bed."

THE STARS WERE OUT AGAIN, the clouds driven off by the wind, and the temperature was plummeting. "What do you think?" asked Yuri.

"It's possible," said Mahmet. He peered down the shal
low slope at the road to town. It was very quiet, which wa
not good. It meant they wouldn't come in stupid.

"That's all you have to say?"

"If you want something sure, boss, we should leave
now."

"You heard what he said. The tanks are coming in the
morning with diamonds. How many diamonds fit in
tank?"

Mahmet considered it, then said, "Enough."

"Exactly. There's something else, too. In the hangar nex
to the garage. A jet. A very *nice* jet."

"Two jets and one pilot is a problem, boss."

"Maybe not," said Yuri.

PAVEL WAS A SERGEANT in the Mirny militia, and an
avid gunner of eiders. Like mushroom hunters with their
secret glades, he had his secret lakes where he would build
hideout, sit behind a good mosquito net with his shotgun
and wait.

What he was doing tonight was the same. Pavel sat in
semicircular snow cave off one end of the runway. Someone
else, he wasn't sure who, was waiting at the opposite end
An airplane flew faster than an eider, and it might have daz
zling lights to blind him, but unlike a shotgun, his snow-
white SK self-loading carbine gave him ten chances to hit
target. By any reasonable count, that was six more than he
would need. He had no doubt who would bring the plane
down. Having no doubts was the key to accurate shooting.

The first bullet would go through the jet's left windshield, the next through the right. He'd send a third and a
fourth through the eyeless frames just to make certain. I

would be embarrassing if it took any more than that to kill them.

MAHMET SAW THEM FIRST. A fan of dark moving figures strung across the road. Behind them was a vehicle. Then another. Not jeeps. Not trucks. He whistled to Anzor. He was standing in the terminal door.

"*Tanks!*" he shouted in to Yuri.

"Slow them down!" Yuri yelled. "Then meet us at the plane!"

Anzor ran outside to join Mahmet at the machine gun. He slid behind the PK. "Slow them down?"

"They're Russians." Mahmet took command of the rocket launcher. "Just shoot. Let God decide who lives." Mahmet eyed the approaching tanks. They were at extreme range. A hit would be an accident, but it would make them think. He elevated the tube, whispered a prayer, and fired.

The rocket whooshed up and away, arcing high, tipping over, a falling star accelerated as it neared the ground. The round went long, exploding behind the rearmost tank, sending a column of white fire, red flame, gray smoke, and snow into the air.

The figures dropped and began firing blindly. Supersonic bullets cracked overhead, smashing the terminal windows, cratering the concrete walls. Mahmet loaded another spindly rocket and dropped it between the two tanks. The return fire grew in intensity. Bullets sent innocent puffs of snow into the air in front of where they lay.

"Answer them, brother," said Mahmet.

Anzor pulled the trigger bars and the PK vomited a stream of bullets. He walked tracers through the prone soldiers, and sent their bodies tumbling back over the snow, loose-limbed as dolls. Bright sparks spattered off the nearest tank. "God is making good decisions!"

The tank turret swiveled, the main gun rose.

"Anzor!" shouted Mahmet. "Get—"

A stuttering white flash, and the world vanished behind an avalanche of snow. A second burst punched a chain of fist-size craters in the concrete wall behind them.

Mahmet grabbed his youngest brother by the shoulder. *"Let's go! We've got to—"*

The tank fired again. The first round amputated the machine gun from the tripod and sent it flying into the air. Anzor still had his hands in front of him, holding the vanished handles, when the second round struck.

"Brother!" Mahmet dropped the RPG and dove into a sea of red snow. Anzor's legs, his hips, were connected to his chest by slender blue sinews. Anzor stared at his ruined body in wonderment, then recognition. He blinked, looked up at his older brother, and said, "God ..." His eyes went wide, dimmed, then shut.

Mahmet stared for perhaps a second, oblivious to the fury erupting around him. They were a family. A blow against one was answered by all.

He crawled back to the RPG. The figures down in the snow were coming again. They were close. He stood with the tube over his shoulder. He put the first tank in his sights, and as the crackle of automatic fire rose to a crescendo, he screamed *"Allahu akhbar!"* and pulled the trigger.

The rocket tore across the open space, flying almost in a flat trajectory. It struck at the joint of turret and hull, lancing through the thin steel armor, blowing the turret into the sky, and igniting the gasoline in the fuel tanks.

A wave of fire broke over the troopers. Mahmet could see them running into the snow, guttering like so many human candles. He dropped the weapon and ran for the plane. Its three jet engines were already running, screaming for the dead.

PAVEL LISTENED TO the explosions, the growing storm of automatic weapons, and knew that his own moment was drawing near. It was quickly confirmed by first the sound, then the sight, of a jet moving away from the terminal. It wasn't showing a single light, and the flashes and *crumps* coming from beyond said that whoever was flying was leaving someone, maybe everyone else, behind. It was a cowardly thing to do, and it made Pavel feel better about killing them.

The jet swung out on the runway and pivoted, pointing its nose right at him. The shooter at the other end of the runway was firing now. He could see the muzzle flash, but the report was lost against the thunder coming from the jet engines. The turbines throttled up to a roar. Pavel felt vibration in his belly as he lay flat to the ground. He brought the SK up, relaxed, checked the safety one more time, then placed the sights on the cockpit windows.

The Yak began to roll. It was coming straight at Pavel's eyes.

Not too soon. There's no hurry. No reason to rush.

The jet was gaining speed. He moved his sights slightly to the left, took up the slack in the trigger mechanism, and fired the first round. The explosion of windshield glass came at the exact same instant Pavel sent the second bullet flying, this time to the right. He sent a third round into the cockpit, a fourth, and because he wasn't sure, a fifth.

The Yak lifted its nose and ramped up into the sky.

Pavel squeezed a sixth shot off into its belly. He didn't

fire a seventh, because he was flattened by the thunder of three turbojet engines passing over his head.

He spun and brought the SK to his shoulder and sent a seventh, an eighth, a ninth, a tenth bullet into the bright red eyes of its fiery engines. He squeezed the trigger again, but the SK was empty.

KIRILLIN WATCHED IN HORROR as the plane took off, then banked gently to the south. "Your men have failed!"

"No! Look!" General Stepanov pointed. The Yak was still in a banked turn, no longer climbing. The angle grew steeper, steeper, until the wings went vertical. Vertical, then beyond.

The nose dropped, lower, lower. Straight down. An instant later the Yak buried its nose in the snow.

Kirillin saw the plane become a sphere of white fire, the fuselage vanishing like a dry log pushed into the eager, open mouth of Hell.

CHAPTER 30

The Spark

NOWEK WOKE UP, UNSURE OF WHERE HE WAS
and what had happened. He rolled over on a bare wooden
plank until he faced a cement wall. It could have been his
cell in Gagarinsky 3, except the graffiti was different.
Instead of TECHNOROCK RULES!, someone had written,
simply, FUCKED. Nowek understood the sentiment. He sat
up and looked around.

They'd taken his belt, his boots and socks, the towel
Larisa had used for a sling. Even the bandages were un-
wrapped and paper-thin gauze applied over the wounds in
his arm. It was encouraging. He wasn't going to be found
dead in his cell. It meant they had something more long
term in mind.

Boots scraped down concrete stairs outside his cell.
Nowek sat on the plank, waiting, listening. They'd taken his
watch, too, as though he might hang himself with it. It had
to be dawn, the traditional time for prison departures. To a
camp of corrective labor, to a hangman's noose. With luck,
to Moscow. With even more luck, the *elektronka* he'd sent
last night had been read by someone, the right someone,

and they would be at the airport, waiting. But then he thought, *Luck? No.* Hoping for even *some* of that put Nowek far into the zone of miracles.

He heard the rattle of a lock, the slide of a steel bolt. The tiny window in the door slid open, revealing two eyes. It snapped shut. The door opened.

A militia sergeant. He'd brought handcuffs and a friend with a rifle. "It's time," he said. "You're going on a trip." He was short, thick of neck, small of eye.

"Where to?" When there was no reply, Nowek asked, "What about my colleague? His name is Chuchin. He was with me when—"

"All your friends are dead. Their plane was shot down last night." He held out the steel rings. "Kirillin's waiting. Let's go."

Plane? It couldn't be Levin. His message said that he was in a hospital, only accidentally alive. Had he sent someone else? Nowek held out both hands, the steel cuff clinked around his wrists.

Up the stairs, through the entrance, and out to a waiting van. Outside, a pale, frigid dawn. The hairs in his nostrils froze. Nowek guessed it was minus ten. His paper prison slippers kicked up powdery snow. The eastern horizon was frosted white, like warm breath on cold glass. He climbed into the van. The rear door slammed shut, and they were moving.

THE CONVOY DEPARTED from the rear of Kristall's headquarters. Two jeeps in the lead, followed by the surviving snow tank, its flanks bearing scars of last night's battle. Two more jeeps fell in behind and, last, the company van with Hock, Larisa, and her young daughter inside. Liza and her stuffed bear were both wrapped in a cocoon of blankets.

As the little convoy approached the airport, Larisa saw the blasted, smoldering snow tank, the cratered walls of the terminal, shell casings strewn like bright coins. A swath of snow painted in frozen red.

Kristall's white, blue, and gold Yak-40 had been pulled out of its hangar. The runway was cleared. Snipers were on the roof of the terminal, and armed militia formed a *cordon sanitaire* around the plane itself. The flight crew was on board making final checks.

Kirillin paced the ramp with a handheld radio in his fist and with the commanding general of the Mirny militia on short tow.

A patrol had been sent to inspect the wreckage of Yuri's plane. They returned to report total annihilation. The plane was just a scorched crater filled with charred, shredded aluminum so sharp a touch drew blood.

The surviving snow tank rumbled up to the Yak. Kirillin waved the cold, unhappy militia aside. It backed into position. Kirillin gave the order, the steel ramp dropped.

The cold air transmitted a kind of electric tension, though even a close observer would see nothing more than men in winter coats carrying brown boxes up into the Yak's baggage hold. The boxes weren't especially noteworthy. A bakery might send you home with a cake in one. Cardboard, split at the middle and lined with foam. Each box contained nearly seven million dollars in gem-quality diamonds.

One million carats. Two hundred kilos by Mirny's measure, four hundred forty pounds of diamonds by London's reckoning. Thirty cake boxes to the men who had to carry them, and nearly two hundred million dollars by the most widely accepted measurement system of them all.

The boxes were stacked in an armored vault in the Yak's tail. The interior quickly filled to capacity. The last box was gently placed, the door swung closed, the locking bar turned, the combination pad spun and scrambled.

The snow tank rumbled away. Hock led Larisa up the ramp. Liza had one hand clamped on her mother's long coat, the other clutched her brown bear. She wore a blanket around her shoulders like a shawl.

Larisa got Liza settled into her smooth, gray leather seat. She looked out through the porthole.

Kirillin was staring up at her from the ramp below. He turned his back on her.

"He can't stand the thought of someone leaving," she said to Hock. "He can't stand losing control of even one person."

"Kirillin's got more to worry about than you, my dear."

"You said he wanted to talk to me. What about?"

Hock hung up his overcoat and blazer in the closet and sat down beside her. "He shut the city down yesterday. Microwave. Satellite. Phone lines. Just before everything went dead a call was routed through the exchange to a number in Irkutsk." Hock smoothed Liza's hair. "It came from your telephone."

One of the pilots pulled the forward cabin door shut. The rear ramp was still down. Two of the jeeps flanked the plane, ready to escort it to the runway.

"That's ridiculous. I don't know anyone in Irkutsk."

"It went to a computer. It was an e-mail message in code. Kirillin couldn't read it." Hock took Liza's chin. "You didn't send any *elektronka* last night, did you?"

"No," she said, then moved away from his hand.

He looked up at Larisa. "Kirillin hasn't a clue what was in that message. I told him it had to be Nowek."

"I fixed him lunch. I didn't give him a computer."

He patted her knee, letting his hand linger. "Nowek was

wounded in Mirny Deep. Someone patched him up. Not in the mine. No medical supplies were missing. And where was Nowek found? Right down the street from your flat. Kirillin's not entirely stupid."

"Mirny's a village. Everything happens near everything else."

"The world is like that, too. The diamond world."

"What's going to happen to Nowek?" She asked the question, wondering whether she really wanted to know.

"You didn't know? He's coming with us."

"To *London*?"

Hock chuckled. "To Moscow. The police want him." He peered at her face. "Something wrong, Larisa?"

"What could be wrong?"

"Quite a lot, depending on what Nowek says about last night. Do you have any idea who helped him?"

"Why should I know anything about it?"

"If you do, you'd better tell me now. You see, as far as the diamond world goes, London and Moscow are the same. Loyalty is rewarded. Disloyalty is punished. Severely."

"Eban," she said, moving close to him, "how can you even think I've been disloyal?"

"I'd hate to. You remember that little story I told at the hotel? About the UN fellow and the spear?"

She sat up straight. "Eban!"

"Most of what I said was true. Phillipe *was* working for the UN, only he was supposed to be working for us. Instead, he was sending reports out to them on private matters. Diamonds for weapons deals. Where war diamonds go to get a clean pedigree. Which African warlord was in our pay, how much he was getting. Very sensitive stuff these days. The cartel could hardly sit by and allow it to go on. Phillipe was setting a terrible example."

"You said the cartel doesn't operate that way."

"But they hire people who *do*. The rebels taking him for ransom was the one bit that wasn't entirely accurate. Oh, they ran him up the pole and stuck a great spear up his bum. But you see," said Hock, leaning close, lowering his voice so that Liza wouldn't hear, "*we* paid them to do it."

Larisa cupped her hands over Liza's ears. *"Stop!"*

"I remember when I first joined the company. They gave us our orientation down in Pretoria. Standard stuff. But at the end, there was a videotape. The diamond world, how the pieces work, how the market is maintained. Why it's a damned good thing all round that it is. When it was done, the screen faded, and up came six words: NOW YOU ARE ONE OF US. It gave you the shivers. Like seeing the words of God up there in black and white."

His eyes, one green, one blue, seemed to belong on different faces. "I hope you slept soundly last night, Larisa. Soundly and alone. Because if something awkward *does* come up, Kirillin won't be your problem. Neither will Moscow. *We* will."

NOWEK WAS LED to the tail of the Yak and through the cordon of militiamen. Kirillin was waiting at the boarding ramp.

"There you are," he said. "The Siberian Delegate. Didn't I say you'd be leaving on the first flight out?"

Nowek's feet were numb with cold. "You have remarkable powers of prediction, Mister Director."

"It's a shame you didn't listen to me when you had the chance. But crime has a way of catching up with the criminal."

"That's my hope, too. I wonder. When it happens here,

where will you run? Moscow? London? The Cayman Islands?"

Kirillin's mahogany cheeks colored a deeper shade. "No one is running. I'll be here, toiling shoulder to shoulder with the men and women of Kristall."

"I'd reconsider that if I were you. The last time your miners demanded what was fair, you had them burned. Now you're shipping a million carats of diamonds to the cartel and has anyone been paid?" Nowek looked at the stony faces of the militia. "Have any of you seen one dollar from your overseas account?"

Kirillin took a deep breath that flagged white in the cold. "You've caused enough trouble, Nowek. We have no use here for troublemakers. The Moscow militia is anticipating your arrival. I see no reason to delay them." He turned on his heel and left.

The sergeant urged Nowek up the ramp and into the Yak. A curtain was pulled across the aisle, isolating the main cabin. The tail was blocked off by a massive steel door. A vault. Two seats were to the left. A galley and baggage bin were to the right. The aisle was narrow. There were no windows. Nowek sat down, glad to be out of the cold. The sergeant unlocked one cuff, then refastened it to the rail under Nowek's seat.

The engines lit off with a whine, a *whoosh,* a rumble. Nowek felt a jerk, and the Yak began to move, flanked by two jeeps.

KIRILLIN RETREATED into the militia jeep with the commander of the Mirny militia, General Stepanov. An AK-74 Kalashnikov was mounted on a rack behind the front seats.

"Any trouble?" he asked the militia officer.

"Boyko. He's not like the others."

"The miners will understand what was going on. Boyko was under stress after what happened last summer. He was found with contraband," said Kirillin, slowly, deliberately, as though speaking to Stepanov in dialect. "The miners will wonder how much money Boyko pocketed to betray us. What did he have that I don't? Soon, that's *all* they'll remember." Kirillin watched the jet move out onto the runway. He picked up a microphone and the transmit key. "Mobile One. Move out now. If you see anything, even a rabbit, shoot it."

"Mobile One, understood."

"Mobile Two, park halfway down the runway and off to the side. Keep your eyes open. Your directive is the same."

"Mobile Two."

The lead jeep sprinted ahead. When it reached the end, it circled around to face down the runway. The trailing jeep stopped, moved off to the side, climbed a snowbank, and parked.

The Yak, heavy with fuel, trundled to the end of the runway and pivoted. It moved forward slightly to keep its jet blast from blowing Mobile One into the weeds.

"Kristall Six," said Kirillin. "This is Control. You're cleared for departure."

THE PILOT CHECKED the engine instruments one last time, then said, "Flaps?"

"Set."

"Speed brakes?"

"Stowed."

The runway stretched straight ahead, black between two

hills of plowed snow. The pilot put his boots on the toe brakes, then placed his right hand across the three yellow throttle knobs. "I hope the militia enjoys the heat," he said as he started to push them forward. The engine needles surged around their dials. The three turbofans moaned, crackled, roared. The Yak began to roll.

And came to a sudden stop.

"Get your feet off the brakes," said the captain.

"They are," the copilot answered, confused. He looked up. "Captain!" A red light blinked on the overhead panel. The boarding ramp at the tail was open.

KIRILLIN SAW THE YAK move forward, then stop. "Binoculars."

Stepanov handed him a pair. Kirillin trained them out onto the jet, furiously spinning the focus knob.

"There's a man down by the nose wheel!" Kirillin was reaching for the radio when a white flash erupted behind the jet, a boil of orange flame rose up, and a heavy concussion rumbled through the frigid air.

YURI WATCHED pieces of Mobile One rise, then scatter and tumble like dry leaves before the jet's hot exhaust. A fender, a roof, a wheel. A man. The chock he'd thrown in front of the nose wheel was slipping. Three jet engines at takeoff power was more than it could stop. The rear ramp was down. Aslan swarmed up. Chuchin was next, then Bashir. Finally, Mahmet, still firing at his AK, waved at Yuri to come *now*.

The engines were thundering, their blast blew the smoke from the rocketed jeep away in a hurricane of heat. Yuri yanked the stiff nylon rope he'd tied to the steel chock. The Yak needed no more encouragement. The jet started to roll.

"GET US OUT THERE!" Kirillin shouted. He threw the glasses down and snatched the radio. "Mobile Two! Intruders on the runway! Stop them!" He yanked the Kalashnikov out of its rack.

Stepanov jammed his boot down on the gas pedal. The tires slipped, skidded, then caught. The Volga shot ahead.

THE MEN OF MOBILE TWO had seen white-clad men top the mound of plowed snow on the far side of the runway. They'd seen one of them dive under the nose of the Yak. Given another half second they might have been able to bring them under fire. But in that half second, Mobile One vanished, and now they had more important things to consider.

Automatic weapons fire erupted. Bullets spatted angrily against their jeep's thin sides. Short rounds burrowed into the snowbank. The air was filled with invisible droplets of death. They did what anyone would do given the circumstances. They dove and rolled down the far side of the bank, then crawled away as fast as their knees and elbows would take them.

THE JET WAS ROLLING, faster, faster. The airspeed indicator came awake. Close to flying speed. The pilot was leaving whatever had blown up behind. He pressed the transmit button on his yoke. "Mirny Control, this is Kristall Six! What's going on?"

But there was no one able to tell him. At least, not before he heard a shout from the rear cabin, followed by the hammering staccato of an assault rifle firing on full automatic.

THE MILITIAMEN OF Mobile Two cautiously poked their heads up above the snowbank. The shooting had stopped. The Yak was hurtling down the runway, dragging its tail ramp, trailing a stream of sparks.

Kirillin was screaming over the radio: *"Shoot! Shoot them!"*

Yes, but who were they supposed to shoot?

The Yak roared by, accelerating.

General Stepanov's black Volga fell in behind. Kirillin was leaning out the window with a rifle in his hands. It was a race, and the car was swiftly losing ground.

YURI WAS ONLY HALFWAY UP the ramp. It was grinding itself into oblivion as the speeding jet dragged it across the runway.

"Let's go, boss!" shouted Mahmet.

Yuri reached up to grab Mahmet's hand when, with a sharp *pop,* a ragged hole appeared next to his head. Then another. He crouched down and looked back. A series of white puffs erupted from the side of a black Volga that was chasing them. He felt something cold and wet flood over his face. He screamed. He'd been shot.

"Boss!" Mahmet tried to grab Yuri's arm but his hand slipped. The Chechen took hold of the collar of his white snowsuit and hauled Yuri up the ramp like a freshly caught fish.

The jet's nose wheel broke ground, and the world tilted. He slid back down toward the open ramp. Something stopped him. A foot, clad in a paper slipper. He looked up. It was Nowek.

KIRILLIN SHIFTED HIS FIRE to the engines, aiming into their hot exhausts.

"They're taking off!" Stepanov shouted.

With our diamonds. Kirillin couldn't stop them from taking off. But he might be able to keep them from getting very far. He pulled the old clip out and rammed a fresh one in.

He swung the black snout of his Kalashnikov to the wings and emptied the whole clip into the fuel tanks. Kerosene billowed out in a white mist. Oily drops spattered the Volga's windshield.

YURI WAS THRASHING AROUND as though he'd been riddled with bullets. Chuchin didn't know what he was screaming about. There was no blood *he* could see, just a lot of jet fuel covering his oversuit. Chuchin tried to get around him to pull the lanyard and close the ramp, but Yuri kept rolling in the way. He reared back and kicked him, hard. Yuri was on his feet in a flash, fists balled and furious.

Chuchin shoved him back against a metal box attached to the cabin wall. It was hinged, and now it flapped open. An emergency kit, filled with bandages, ointments, aspirin. Three red cylinders fell out with the rest.

Flares. He scooped one of them up and slid down the oily ramp to the bottom step. The concrete below was falling away fast. As the wings took hold, he twisted the cap and tossed it out.

It struck the concrete once, bounced, tumbled, then vanished behind.

THE FLARE ERUPTED with a hard, brilliant light. General Stepanov saw it through the oily windshield as a glowing cloud that flashed bright, then brighter.

The air reeked of raw fuel. Kirillin was slick with a kerosene glaze. He watched the flare bounce up, then tip. "Turn left!"

General Stepanov swung the wheel. The front wheels moved, but nothing happened. They were skidding down the runway on an oil slick.

The flare was no longer a point of light, but a red-hot sphere.

"Left! Turn left now!"

Stepanov jammed his boot on the brake pedal. The Volga swerved sideways until Kirillin's open window faced dead ahead.

The alchemy of fire is surprisingly picky. Too much air and nothing happens, too much fuel and nothing happens. But in the invisible world where molecules meet, there is a favored place, a precise point, where very big things happen.

The flare burst through Kirillin's open window and struck him in the chest. It blossomed into something he could no longer explain. Something like pure light.

MAHMET DISARMED THE militia sergeant and found the keys to Nowek's cuffs. Freed, Nowek kicked off the paper slippers and yanked open the curtain to the main cabin.

Hock sat in the gray leather chair. He'd swiveled it around to face backward, and had his hands in plain view. He beckoned Nowek to come, as though he were intruding on a busy schedule.

Nowek looked for Larisa. He saw her on the deck at

Hock's feet, covering Liza with her body. She raised her head and looked at him, but nothing, not surprise, not even recognition, registered. Her eyes were like those of the birds in Kristall's book. They might have been made of glass.

Yuri and Mahmet continued up to the cockpit. Nowek and Chuchin stopped in front of Hock. Chuchin had the big Nagant pointed at the South African's chest.

"You know," said Hock. "None of this was necessary. We could have reached an understanding. Maybe we still can."

"You're too late. Volsky only wanted money for the miners," said Nowek, feeling something inside him give way and break like a dam releasing a raging, unstoppable flood. It ran beyond reason, beyond anything. "I want more."

"What, justice?" said Hock with infuriating calm. "In *Russia*? You're too intelligent for fairy tales. You know everything is for sale here. Everything is up for negotiation. Even now."

"Mister Mayor," said Chuchin. "Let's throw this fat bastard out of the plane and let him negotiate *that*."

"It wouldn't change a thing," said Hock.

"It would change *you*," said Chuchin.

"You're wrong, Hock," Nowek said. "Something big has changed. The diamonds were going to London. Now they're not."

"Perhaps not right away," Hock allowed. "But unless you plan to eat them, they're going to be sold. When they are, they'll go to the highest bidder. *We* are *always* the highest bidder."

"Petrov didn't think so."

"Petrov was a fool. He thought he could play around us by sending stones to Golden Autumn." Hock smiled. "Well, what did he accomplish? Golden Autumn sold the stones to *us* and kept the money for themselves. Not one ru *ble* came back to Russia or to Petrov. *That's* what he accomplished. Then your President pledged those diamonds to the IMF, and Petrov knew they weren't there. Neither was the money. He was about to run for some nice, warm island when your friend Volsky showed up. Really, who could turn his back on a gift like *that*?"

"What is he talking about?" Chuchin said with an impatient wave of the Nagant.

"Petrov had Volsky murdered?"

"Who else?" said Hock. "It wasn't difficult. Petrov has a lot of friends. More than you. But let's talk about you. The diamond world's a circle. The only meaningful question is, are you in or out? Like Volsky, you're in way over your head. Like him, you're in trouble. You can still do something about it."

"*Fuck* him." Chuchin held the Nagant out to Nowek. "Give him nine grams of trouble. It's already more than he's worth."

Nowek's blood answered *yes, yes, yes!* What could be more satisfying than to see Hock's smile fade at the *click* of the Nagant's trigger? It took all his will, all his resolve, to push the revolver away. "There's one thing you've overlooked," he said to Hock. "Volsky had demands. I have the diamonds."

"But not nearly enough of them," said Hock. "That might be important in a few weeks. How will you fix *that*, Delegate Nowek? Frankly speaking, I'm your only hope. You may want to keep that in mind."

"I know where to find more. Enough for the IMF. Enough to break your cartel."

"I wouldn't count on things that are out of your control."

"We'll see what happens when Mirny Deep goes into

full production. When diamonds become cheaper tha
eggs. We'll see what the cartel finds more valuable. Yo
or the richest diamond mine on earth." Nowek turne
"Chuchin? Take him back. Use the cuffs and make sure h
doesn't fall out of the plane unless it's *absolutely* necessary."

Chuchin prodded Hock to his feet with the barre
"There's a Russian card game," he said as he herded Hoc
back to the tail of the plane. "It's called *Durak. The Fool.
think you'll like it."

Nowek looked down at Larisa.

"Gregori," she said, "I know about the—"

"No," he said to her. "Don't talk. Listen."

When he was finished, she said, "Are you sure? Yo
could come with us. We could—"

"No," said Nowek. "Hope is your diamond, Larisa. N
mine."

YURI OPENED THE COCKPIT DOOR with Mahmet be
side him. He took in the instruments, the fact that the
were making wide circles over Mirny airport, that dow
below a fire was sending greasy smoke into the air from th
middle of the runway.

"Good morning, gentlemen," he said to the two pilots.

The captain said, "Are you the leader of this gang
Before you make demands you should know there's n
much fuel."

Yuri glanced at the gauges. One of the slipper tanks ha
leaked dry. How big a hole could drain that thing so fast?

"Let's be serious," said the captain. "We're going t
land."

Yuri peered down through the window. "I don't think so

"*You* don't think so? *We're* the pilots."

"Pilots," Yuri said with a snort. He reached up to the overhead panel. "What's this?" There were three red levers. The fire handles that would shut down the fuel to each of the engines. He picked the middle one.

"Get your hands away from that!"

Red flashing lights erupted as the center engine, the one mounted in the tail, starved for fuel and sputtered out.

"Are you trying to commit suicide?"

"We're all breathing. We're still flying." And they weren't using so much fuel. Yuri turned. "Mahmet? Take them back."

"Stand up," Mahmet ordered. "Both of you. Move."

The captain stiffened. "You won't fly a jet with a rifle!"

"Are you afraid to die?" asked Mahmet.

"Absolutely!" the captain said with a vigorous nod.

"Then you better start walking."

The pilots exchanged looks of perfect terror. They unbuckled their seat belts and slowly got up.

Yuri saw the captain casually let his finger brush against the autopilot switch, triggering the wing leveler. The Yak immediately stopped its gentle turn. "What's the big deal? It's just like a car, except that it flies." Yuri settled into the left seat and clicked the wing leveler off. He grabbed the yoke. "You steer with this, right?"

"Don't! That's the—"

Yuri threw it hard over. The wings dipped, the horizon tilted crazily across the windshield.

Yuri smiled. "See? Just like a car. It's only a matter of—"

"Boss!" Mahmet's eyes were wide. He was looking straight down the wing at the ground below.

An enormous yellow cloud had erupted from the top of the headworks tower over Mirny Deep. As Yuri watched, it grew, turned black. A sharp rumble shook the air. The ten-story tower began to shed its skin in giant panels. They fluttered away like petals, leaving only the tower's steel skeleton behind, engulfed in bright flame and dirty smoke.

"Tell Nowek to come up here," said Yuri.

MAHMET LET NOWEK THROUGH the cockpit door. The view from the cockpit was panoramic. The destruction below, complete.

The entire tower was a naked chimney. A blast furnace.

Nowek thought of the fissures of the Ninth Horizon. The looted Closet that could be refilled with its treasure. Not now. Now the IMF would turn its back on Russia. Never mind the miners of Mirny. The banks would fail and the nation would shatter like an egg. Petrov might have murdered his friend, but the cartel had just put a torch to Russia. The cartel, and *Hock*. "Let's get out of here," he said to Yuri.

Yuri leveled the wings and pointed the Yak south for Irkutsk. He pointed to the copilot's chair. "Have a seat, Delegate Nowek."

Delegate? Fugitive Nowek was more like it. Nowek settled himself into the copilot's chair. The open, empty land scrolled beneath them, quilted in patches of white and green. It reminded Nowek of the flag of Siberia. The snow. The taiga forest, an ocean of trees, rolling unbroken as far as Nowek could see. "So White Bird flies to Mirny now?"

"We make exceptions when a friend needs help," said Yuri.

"How did you know I needed help?"

"A businessman develops a sixth sense about these things. You don't seem so pleased."

"Who was flying the jet they shot down?"

"The autopilot. I hooked it up to the satellite navigator, pressed execute, ran up the engines with the brakes on, and jumped. When the brakes couldn't hold, it took off by itself."

"So coming up here had nothing to do with diamonds?"

"How can you put diamonds and friendship on an equal basis?" Then "Naturally, there were costs." A pause, then Yuri said, "How many diamonds are back there anyway?"

"It's difficult to say," said Nowek carefully. He didn't want Yuri to have a heart attack at the controls. "They're all going to Moscow, you know."

Yuri blinked. "All of them?" Nowek might have suggested feeding caviar to chickens.

"Every carat." *And it still won't be enough.* One million carats wasn't four million. "I need to call Moscow. Will your radio reach?"

"Not even to Irkutsk. But there's a satellite phone you can try." He reached back to a surprisingly ordinary-looking handset mounted to the cabin wall, lifted it off its hook. "You have to know the number, though."

"I know the number." Nowek's birthday, Galena's age, the year his wife, Nina, had died. He punched in the proper sequence, pressed send, waited while the whistles, squawks, and sizzles resolved into a ring, another, and, finally, a sleepy voice.

"Kremlin Duty Desk."

Nowek took a deep breath, then said, "This is Gregori Nowek. The Siberian Delegate." Another breath, then *"Buran."*

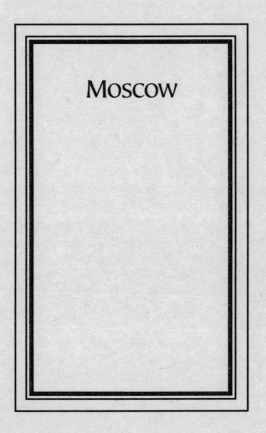

Moscow

CHAPTER 31

The Dacha

"I DON'T UNDERSTAND." GENERAL GOLOSHEV
checked his watch. It was half past eight. "Yesterday it was
rush rush rush. Today he's thirty minutes late," he told the
doctor.

An early-morning departure roared overhead from
nearby Shermetyevo airport, making the glasses in the bathroom jingle.

The doctor cracked open his briefcase and let it rest on
the bed next to Levin's thigh. "I can administer the first in-
jection right now if you're willing to approve it."

The Toad watched Levin's chest rise, fall, as he slept. The
hotel room reeked with the sour smell of sweat-drenched
sheets and urine. "I suppose that would be best."

The first syringe came out. The doctor threaded a long
needle onto it, then uncapped a vial of scopolamine. He
plunged the needle through the rubber seal and began to
draw the straw-colored fluid into the cylinder. He pulled
enough for one, two, three times the usual dose. Colonel
Chernukhin of the Presidential Security Service wished to

crack Levin's head open like a chestnut. He would get his wish. "I hope you understand what's going to happen."

"How soon will he be ready?"

"Give him ten minutes." The doctor squirted a bit of the sedative out to eliminate any air, though why he should bother was a good question. "He'll be able to answer questions for an hour, maybe two. No more."

"And then?"

"Drowsiness, dizziness. His breathing will become irregular. People panic when something so normal as taking a breath is no longer so normal. He'll become agitated, fearful, which only makes things worse. In the end, seizures, then full-body convulsions."

"You can stop them?"

"Here?"

Goloshev pursed his heavy lips. "Levin is my subordinate, and also my friend and comrade. But we must set aside personal views. We must proceed. The highest authorities have requested it. No. Not *requested*. Demanded it."

"As you say." The doctor rubbed Levin's arm to find a vein. He found the telltale bulge, saw its soft, regular beat. He was about to kill this man, he knew. And whether the highest authorities had requested it or demanded it or whispered it into Goloshev's ear, would shortly make no difference at all.

Goloshev heard a car door slamming outside, then a shout. He walked over to the window and pulled the shades. Three floors down on the street, a man was sprawled on the sidewalk facedown. A thug was standing over him with a gun.

Both victim and robber wore military fatigues, so which was which? Was the hotel security team stopping a crime, or committing one? Was the *mafiya* that ran Shermetyevo enforcing its law, or breaking someone else's? These days, the line between legal and illegal was impossibly blurred.

All of that would soon come to an end. Poor, befuddled Yeltsin would be out, the new president in. Naturally, he'd face a difficult time. But the last Russian collapse had been a crisis managed by democrats, who were, frankly speaking, amateurs. This time would be different. Starve in chaos or eat in the shadow of the iron fist? Russians were familiar with that kind of a choice. Goloshev was confident Russians would slip martial law back on like a pair of comfortable old slippers.

The doctor slipped the needle through Levin's pale skin as another jet thundered low overhead. Its roar faded. As the doctor pressed the plunger down, a loud knocking came from the door.

Goloshev unhooked the security chain, threw the dead bolt, and opened the door.

The Cleaner's eyes were even more baggy, even more red, this morning than yesterday. He hadn't come alone.

He was flanked by two men in fatigues and black balaclavas. The insignia on their arms said *ALFA*. The elite unit of the Presidential Security Service. They carried assault rifles, and both rifles were pointed at Goloshev.

"Good morning, General," said the Cleaner. "I'm sorry to be late. There have been developments that required our attention."

"What do you mean coming here with—"

"Your colleague Petrov found out about them even before we did. He was on his way to Switzerland, but we stopped him."

Goloshev's cheeks puffed as though he couldn't get enough air. His face was splotched red. "Colleague? Petrov?"

The Cleaner pushed by the sputtering Toad and walked to Levin's side.

The doctor had frozen at the sight of the ALFA soldiers,

the syringe still in Levin's arm, the cylinder still three-quarters full.

Chernukhin pushed him aside, then pulled out the needle. He threw it to the floor, then said to the doctor, "You brought some more, I hope?"

"Yes, but—"

"Good," said the Cleaner. He smiled at the Toad. "General Goloshev and I have a lot to talk about."

IT WAS THURSDAY NIGHT, the seventh of October, and a black Volvo glided over the smoothly paved streets of Moscow's Krylatskoye district, winding through hilly terrain. They were barely beyond the Ring Road, fifteen kilometers from the Kremlin, but you'd think you were out in the middle of the *glubinka*, the deep countryside where the Devil threw pancake parties. Big houses glowed brightly through the forest like illuminated cruise ships.

Nowek sat in back with Chuchin. Their driver was an Interior Ministry officer. The Volvo was a big step up from the Chaika he'd last ridden through Moscow. But then, so was their destination.

"Some neighborhood," said Chuchin. "I always wondered where my taxes went."

"What taxes?" asked Nowek.

"These thieves don't need my kopecks. They've stolen enough on their own. Just look at these houses."

"They're not houses," said their driver. "They're all *dachas*."

"Each one with its *sotka*," said Chuchin acidly. *Sotka* meant "strip," a garden plot used to raise potatoes, cabbages, turnips. Survival vegetables. At least, that's what it meant in Siberia.

The road passed through long stretches of dark forest broken by rustic stone walls, high gates, and lanes over-arched with trees. A place where the clean, white birches of the honest north met guarded compounds more typical of Medellin than Moscow.

At an unmarked drive, they turned right.

The lane curved in a series of winding, graceful esses for no obvious reason other than it could. The Volvo slowed and came to a white steel barrier guarded by officers of the Naval Infantry. They wore gleaming white belts over long, dark blue winter coats. Two of them had Kalashnikov rifles, and both muzzles came down as the Volvo drew near.

The third guard rapped on Nowek's window. The driver pushed a button, letting in icy air and a glove holding a flashlight. The beam stopped at Nowek's arm. Nowek allowed his arm to be scanned for weapons.

They were waved through. Soon, a three-story beige house appeared from behind a dense stand of birches. Other than a roof studded with satellite dishes and antennae, Boris Yeltsin's *dacha*, his country home in Moscow, was surprisingly ordinary.

The Volvo pulled in front, then stopped. Chuchin got out, came around, and opened Nowek's door. There was snow on the ground, but this was clearly not Siberia. The air was still rich with the lingering smell of wet, decaying leaves, spicy with wood smoke.

Chuchin slammed the car door. "Now what?"

Nowek had expected more of a reception. "Go knock."

Chuchin seemed dubious, but he obeyed.

It opened. A golden light spilled out, bright and cheerful, silhouetting the very identifiable shape of the President of the largest country on earth, dismantler of empires, sheller of recalcitrant Parliaments, heartsick, weary Boris Yeltsin.

He wore a dark blue cardigan sweater, buttoned almost to his neck, dark pants, and his trademark scowl.

Nowek could see the gray pallor when the light fell across his face. His hair was full and silvery, but Nowek could hear the wheeze and rattle of labored breathing. Boris Yeltsin was alive. Just.

"You're going to stand or come in?" Yeltsin's voice still rumbled like tanks tearing up bricks. He waved a hand slowly, deliberately. "Delegate Nowek? I have someone anxious to see you."

Inside the front door were muddy boots, a scarf, a stern young man seated at a desk with an earphone. A man sat on a simple wooden bench. Yeltsin retreated down the hall. "Take your time," he said with the wave of an arm. "You're keeping only the President of the Russian Federation waiting." With that, Yeltsin doddered down the corridor like a pensioner hunting for his glasses.

"Major Levin?" said Nowek. At least, Nowek thought that's who it was. His face was an atlas of bruises and swollen enough to pucker the stitches that ran in a jagged line from his ear to the corner of his lip. His hair was cut very short and he wore a large black patch over one eye. His mustache used to be full, almost dashing. Now it looked like a poorly applied disguise.

"Zdrastvootsye, Delegate Nowek," said Levin. He stood and clasped Nowek's shoulder and whispered, "And it's Colonel Levin, now."

"What some people won't do for a promotion."

"The half blind, the half lame, in the service of the half dead," said Levin. "You had the President's private number all along. Why didn't you use it?"

"I didn't have anything to tell him."

"I hope you do now."

So do I, thought Nowek. "Let's not keep him waiting."

They walked down the hall and into a large, bare room that shouted *state function*. It was sparsely furnished, though what was there was deeply Baroque: a black velvet sofa edged with gold, a small, oval table with ornately carved legs, four matching chairs. A television on a stand of Finnish birch. A fireplace blazed. Embossed white paper covered the walls. A window hid behind thick gold curtains.

Yeltsin sprawled on the sofa and indicated that the others were to sit. "Delegate Nowek," he said, "before you begin, first let me say that I knew Delegate Volsky. I am here today, Russia is here today, because of what *he* did then. There's nothing you can add to my sorrow over what happened. Moscow loves rumors. There have been some unpleasant ones about Arkady Vasilievich. They will stop."

"Thank you, Mister President. I know that—"

Yeltsin continued as though he hadn't heard. "Second, the International Monetary Fund will arrive in three days to inspect the state diamond stockpile." He looked at Levin. "My aides have informed me that Petrov's plan to sell Siberian gems to the world has not worked out in accordance with our hopes. Is that so?"

Levin nodded. "Yes, Mister President. That's so."

"Then the diamonds are gone, the money is gone, and the Closet is truly empty?"

Once more Levin spoke. "Yes."

"And there's no possibility of recovering them in time?"

"Not in time, Mister President. We know how the stones have been getting out. We have nearly a million carats in hand. They were stopped on their way out of the country. They were—" Levin searched for the right word. ". . . *impounded* by Delegate Nowek. They've arrived from Siberia and are under close guard. But the vast majority is missing."

Nearly a million? thought Nowek. *What happened to th* rest? Then a name: *Yuri!*

Yeltsin took a deep breath and said, "Then there's noth ing to be done."

"There might be, Mister President," said Nowek.

Yeltsin gave him a baleful look. "There's no time fo word games. If you have something to say, say it."

"I've been thinking about this all the way from Irkutsk. A Levin said, we stopped a million carats on their way to—"

"*Almost* one million. And it's not the same as four mil lion. If I know the difference, the IMF will also know it."

"But we can borrow the rest."

Levin leaned over. "Nowek."

"*Borrow* them?" asked Yeltsin.

"The South African, Eban Hock, said that when it came t refilling the Closet, we'd have to look to the cartel. Well, h could be right. They maintain the biggest stockpile of gen rough in the world in London. It can be here in a matter o hours. They have a *hundred* times what we kept in the Closet They've soaked up every loose diamond on the planet for th last hundred years. Every diamond that went to Golde Autumn, every stone that was never paid for, is sitting there Mister President. All we have to do is ask for them back."

"Why would they agree?"

"Because we still control Mirny Deep."

"I'm told it will be years before the mine can be repaired.

"But it *will* be," said Nowek. "And what will happe then? The cartel knows what's down there. It's a swor hanging over their heads. They can't afford to lose contro of it. Not and remain a cartel."

"But they *have* lost control of it."

"Not if we sell it back to them."

"*What?*" Levin exclaimed. "But you told me . . ."

"Listen," Nowek explained. "In three days, the IMF will be here. If the Closet stays empty, it will be 1998 again, only worse. We could *give* the cartel Mirny Deep and it would be a bargain next to that."

"What kind of a deal are you thinking of?" asked Yeltsin.

"We give them exclusive rights to Mirny Deep once the mine is back in operation and they send us a few million carats to parade in front of the IMF."

"We sell them the future in exchange for the next few days?"

"We have to *survive* the next few days to *get* to the future. We just have to find a way to contact the cartel quickly. Tonight, if possible. Perhaps our ambassador in London can call—"

"Excuse me," said Chuchin. "But don't we have one of them in a cell? *He* would know how to make the arrangements."

"You mean Hock?" asked Nowek.

"He's at Lefortovo," said Levin. Moscow's main prison. "Along with Petrov and the ... with General Goloshev. He's going to stand trial as an accessory to Volsky's murder."

"Maybe he shouldn't," Chuchin said with a shrug.

"Chuchin," said Nowek. "You know what Petrov has admitted. Hock—"

"Excuse me. *You* know your way around mines, but when we speak of cells and jails, forgive me, *I'm* the expert here. I was two tenners *na narakh*." Twenty years behind the wire. "So Hock is an *accessory* to murder. Is that even a crime? You can't put Russian *murderers* in prison. How long do you think Hock will be there before his friends buy him a key? A week? I say send the bastard back where he came from. Let *them* cut his throat."

"Eban Hock is the key to our investigation," said Levin.

"*Fuck* investigations. You already know he's guilty. It only gives the eel more time to slip the hook. I say let his own friends put his head on a pike. They'll do a better job of it."

Yeltsin's face was animated. He didn't often get the chance to hear someone like Chuchin, and it took years off his face.

"I'm just a pensioner who drives cars and raises flags," said Chuchin, "but even I know you can catch big fish in muddy waters. You think the cartel wants the world to know how dirty their precious diamonds are? We'll promise to keep it to ourselves, give them Hock, and borrow those diamonds for the fucking bankers to see. And if they don't like the deal, *fuck them*. There's always Mirny Deep to hang over their heads."

"Go on," said Yeltsin.

"Let those foreign bastards come look in the Closet. They'll see what they need to see, and then you can pack the diamonds and Hock into one box and kick his ass over the border."

Give them Hock? "Why do you think they'll put his head on a pike, Chuchin?" asked Nowek.

"Because when he takes back the diamonds we borrowed," said Chuchin, "they won't be the *same* diamonds. I'll tell you what I mean. . . ."

When Chuchin was done laying out his idea, Yeltsin looked at Levin, then Nowek, and let out a laugh that was so loud it brought his guards running, fearing the worst.

"No, I'm fine!" he said when he caught his breath. He waved at the door, and a steward brought in glasses of tea, some bread, wild berry preserves, and a silver pot filled with Vologda butter, the finest in the world.

"Tea?" said Chuchin with a look of distaste. "Is someone sick, Mister President?"

Yeltsin looked into his teacup and roared, *"Bring us something proper!"*

A frosted bottle was brought in, and glasses all around. "About the diamonds," said Yeltsin as the glasses were filled with fiery liquid. "We'll do it."

"There's one matter left," said Nowek. "The miners of Mirny have been paid with *veskels,* plus a promise of dollars. The dollars are being held in an overseas account."

"That's completely illegal."

As if you don't have such accounts, thought Nowek. But he said, "And that's the last thing we must fix. As part of the arrangement with the cartel, those dollars must be brought home. They must be made available to the miners. It comes to only a few million. It's nothing to London and everything to them."

"A lot of people haven't been paid," said Yeltsin.

"This is what Volsky wanted," said Nowek, wondering whether he'd stepped over an invisible line.

"Can it be done quietly?" Yeltsin looked to Levin.

"The *mafiya* sends money overseas every day," he said. "And no one hears a thing. I think we can bring some of it back."

"Then it's done." Yeltsin held up his glass and said, "To Arkady Volsky, our hearts. To the new Siberian Delegate, our hopes. *Sto lyet!*" A hundred years.

It was a very short toast, shamefully so by Russian standards, but Yeltsin was flagging.

Chuchin, Nowek, and Levin stood with their glasses raised and shouted,

"Sto lyet!"

THE BUSINESS WAS CONDUCTED with the same exaggerated solemnity of a Cold War spy swap. The prison vans. The stony-faced guards. But when Eban Hock passed through the gates at Vnukovo 2 airport, a facility reserved for state visits, and saw the British-registered Hawker jet waiting for him, he knew he was safe. He knew he'd been absolutely right. Warlords, despots, presidents came and went. But the cartel would always stand.

The driver stopped on the ramp. Hock got out into the chill, gray light of early winter, and walked up the stairs with a lightness of step known only to the truly, reverentially grateful.

He settled himself into his seat as an armored truck pulled up, flanked by motorcycle outriders. He'd told Nowek it would happen, that the diamonds would go to 17 Charterhouse Street, one way or another. Forget the blizzard of criminal cases surrounding Petrov, Goloshev, and Kristall. The stones would go to London the way a ball rolled downhill: by natural law. What was Moscow's law against *that*?

The familiar brown boxes were carried up the steps and into the Hawker. But soon, Hock found cause for surprise.

There were too many of them. He made a quick count, and after the thirty he expected, he sat back in his seat and reevaluated. He'd expected the one million carats. Where were all these *others* coming from? Forty boxes. Fifty. One hundred. More. The chain of bearers seemed endless. They finally stopped at one hundred and nineteen. *Four million carats?*

The hatch was sealed. The jet turned west, leaving

Moscow's grizzled haze behind, climbing to where the sun burned with the yellow fire of a faultless canary diamond. Four hours later, the jet came to a stop at a private hangar located in a reasonably inconspicuous corner of Heathrow's air cargo facility. Another armored car, another endless procession of boxes. It was the entire picture at Vnukovo 2 run in reverse.

A black Mercedes was waiting for him. Together with the stones, Hock left the airport for Charterhouse Street, a district known in the eighteenth century as the hangout of highwaymen and villains. The procession arrived at Number 17, a six-story building clad in white stone and warm bronze, with stout gates and armed guards pacing the street with drawn guns.

Hock was given a room on the south side of the fifth floor. It had a lovely bank of windows that offered a glimpse of the Thames. While he showered off the accumulated filth deposited by a week in a Moscow cell, the diamond boxes were taken to the sorting rooms on the north side of the building. There, beneath tall windows, in cold, shadowless light, one hundred and nineteen containers were opened and the stones plucked from their foam nests.

One thousand seven hundred pounds, four million carats, of gem rough worth three quarters of a billion dollars had been loaned to Moscow to parade before the IMF auditors. One thousand seven hundred pounds of industrial diamonds, sixty million dollars' worth, and Eban Hock, had been returned.

THE BRIGHT OCTOBER LIGHT faded to dusk, and streams of traffic glowed like strands of pearls. A yellow crescent moon burned like kerosene. The London sky was soft, almost feminine, compared to the unearthly glint of starlit Mirny.

Two managers from the Russia desk told him the news. "We've lost Russia," one of them said.

He knew these two men by name. He knew them by type even better. Hock thought of them all as *Jesuits*. Serious, intelligent, iron-gray hair, polished shoes, their faces full of the moral certainty Hock could never afford.

He'd worked with their like in a hundred dismal spots. Sierra Leone. Congo. Angola. Zaire. Moscow. Like missionaries, they lived to impose a kind of order on a chaotic world. Once they'd been adventurous young men in khakis and pith helmets with trains of native bearers and sacks of cash. They'd march off into the bush, unfold their tables, set up their beam balances, and wait for the diamonds to arrive. Their buying table was an altar to something greater, something pure. Something almost like religion.

Now you are one of us. . . .

Tramping through the bush was too dangerous these days. Now the cartel's missionaries floated above the foul streets of Africa, the urine-soaked alleys strewn with garbage, the crushed, immense cities where old cars honked their way through crowds of vendors selling peanuts, pineapples, bright plastic sandals.

Somewhere above the reeking mess there would be a hermetically sealed chamber, an air-conditioned suite, sleek with black leather and chrome, shielded behind thick steel doors, bulletproof glass, security cameras. An outpost not so much of empire, but of order.

Mombassa, Moscow, Mirny. They were all outposts. All messy spots where the natives were free to lie, to steal, to wage war in whatever horrible form they wished, so long as the cartel ended up with the rough. It always came down to that. The natives did the work and the dying. The cartel got the rough.

We've lost Russia. Apparently, the natives had decided the old rules no longer applied. They might have said, *We've lost gravity.* The ball no longer rolled downhill.

Hock let the curtain fall shut and went to the door and locked it. He picked up the wet towels, the filthy clothes he'd worn in Moscow, and placed them in a plastic bag someone had thoughtfully left.

The cartel was more than just a business, more than a profession. It was a faith, a religion that offered the world but demanded in return both loyalty and results. What was one without the other?

He walked to the bath, switched on the light above the washbasin, plugged it, and ran the water scalding hot. It wasn't quite boiling. He watched it fill.

Russia was Africa with snow. The cartel had always played it masterfully, and easily. Mirny might have enough gems to drown London in diamonds, but Moscow could be bought for pennies. Now something had changed. Now *Russia* was playing the *cartel.* Russia, a vast clock slowly unwinding, its gears slipping, its springs rusted. Russia, a consignment shop, not a nation, where everything was for sale on the cheap. *Nowek.* Could one man have found a billion-dollar key and, instead of trading it for pennies, stayed to rewind the clock?

He stared at his reflection in the mirror. They'd left him with a toiletries kit. Soaps. Colognes. A toothbrush. A simple, old-fashioned straight razor. He pulled it out and tested the blade against the edge of his thumb.

A red thread of blood welled up.

He plunged his right hand into the scalding water and

grimaced with the pain. Looking down, his hand seemed to branch off at a ridiculous angle, no longer part of his body at all. A refracted object. The pain eased, and he pulled his hand out and dried it with a snowy-white towel that was almost impossibly thick. He pulled a wooden chair next to the sink, folded the towel neatly across its ladder back, and sat down.

Grasping the blade in his left hand, he drew it slowly, deeply, surely across the burned, red flesh of his right wrist, pressing down hard enough to make certain.

The hot water in the sink instantly swirled red as his heart pumped, pumped, pumped. There was no pain, only a slight stinging where the razor had done its work. He looked up into the polished mirror. As he stared, tendrils of steam rose from the water, misting the bright glass, obscuring his face, his eyes, one green, one blue, now gray, now both lost behind a curtain that reminded him of an aurora, shimmering, dancing in the black winter skies of Mirny. A curtain of ice, of fire, of spectral light. Shimmering, fading, then gone.

CHAPTER 32

Hope Is a Diamond

THE OLD SIBERIAN TRADERS' GUILD ON Gorky Street was a jewel of a building on the Irkutsk riverfront. Made of soft, honeyed sandstone flecked with bright mica, a hundred winters had rounded its edges until it looked like a melting ice cream cake. The walls hadn't felt a paintbrush in half a century. Its pale, dusty pinks, its parchment yellows, its faded creams glowed warmly in the cold, slanting light of an October morning.

The office of the Siberian Delegate was on the second floor. You could see the Angara River through its tall windows of arched glass. Nowek sat at the desk and watched gunmetal-gray water sweep north. He still thought of it as Volsky's desk.

There was a faint ringing. The fax machine began to buzz.

Chuchin poked his head in. "It's time to go, Mister Mayor."

"I'm not the mayor," said Nowek. "And there's a fax coming."

"You want to be late meeting your own daughter?"

If she'll be there at all. Galena was coming in today from America. He hoped. "Are the flags up?"

"Pah," said Chuchin, and disappeared.

The machine hummed, then beeped. A page fell out as a second page began to print. Then his telephone rang. Typical. Nothing had happened all morning, and now that he needed to leave, the world wanted to speak with the new Siberian Delegate.

He snatched the page and picked up the heavy black phone. "Delegate Nowek listening."

"Colonel Izrail Levin speaking."

Nowek looked at the time. Nine-fifteen in Irkutsk. Four-fifteen in Moscow. "You're up early."

"Who's been to bed? I just came from the concluding ceremonies. I thought you'd like to know how it all went."

The IMF's inspection team had spent the previous day counting diamonds in the Closet. "So?"

"There's an American expression. *The check is in the mail.* You've heard it?"

No, but he understood it. Nowek let his breath out. Russia had run right up to the edge of a chasm far deeper than the *karir,* the open pit, up in Mirny. "Then we dodged the bullet."

"This time. Did you read the fax I sent? You should."

Nowek picked up the first page.

Mister Delegate:
You see how our positions have reversed? I pulled you from a cell and now I have to be polite. I'm writing because there are drums being beaten in the Kremlin, and you should know what they mean. It's about our new President Putin (yes, I know the election is still months

away, but it's going to be a coronation, not an election).
Putin feels the regions are growing too powerful. He's
setting up six more Delegates for all of Russia. A few
might actually be honest. They will all be under his
thumb, even you. As Siberian Delegate, you will have to
be the President's man. After everything I can say that I
know you a little, and so you may want to think about
whether you want to be *this* President's man. By the
way, a clipping came from the Foreign Press desk. I'm
sending you a copy.
Levin

The second fax sheet. Nowek found it on the floor.

(NY, Oct. 19, 1999) The William Goldberg Diamond Corporation, renowned for cutting nu-
merous majestic stones, including the *Premier Rose*
and the *Guinea Star,* announced the purchase of a
magnificent piece of rough: a 48.90-carat octahedron with the obvious Russian name of *Zvyezda
Nadezhde,* or *Star of Hope.* The sale was private and
the purchase price was not revealed, but seven
figures would be in line for a flawless crystal of
such size. According to the Gemological Institute
of America (GIA), the stone is "the largest, most
perfect single crystal diamond we have graded as
of the date the report was issued." The report
went on to say "Its condition, with points and
edges undamaged by the usual extraction and
sorting processes, suggests new mining technolo-
gies, long rumored to be under development in
Russia, may have borne fruit."

"Any idea where the diamond came from?" asked Levin.

Seven figures? Larisa Arkova and her daughter had left Moscow for Stockholm the day before Hock had been returned to London. He had no idea where they'd gone from there, and if he did, he wouldn't have told a senior officer in the FSB's Investigations Directorate. "If it's a Russian diamond," said Nowek, "it probably came from Mirny."

"I thought you'd say something like that. And the rest?"

"You mean about our new President? You're suggesting I quit?"

"God knows if you do, Putin will pick someone worse. But you have to be realistic. You won't be able to steer your own course for long."

"Realism is overrated. At least in Russia. What about you? You're staying on, aren't you?"

"I don't have to work with him. I just investigate official corruption. I'll *always* have something to do."

Chuchin poked his head in. He was wearing his dark glasses and heavy felt jacket. "You want her to stand in the cold?"

Nowek said, "I'm supposed to protect Siberia from the kind of people you investigate. I'll keep busy. But thanks for the warning."

"Don't mention it. I mean that literally. Not to anyone. Winter's coming back. Even in Moscow. Sometimes I wonder if it ever left."

Nowek knew what Levin meant. "If you want to understand winter, come to Siberia."

"No thank you. Did I tell you about my new dog?"

"Another basset?"

"Feliks is still a puppy, but from his paws he's going to be a big one. You have my number. Call if you get in over your head, Mister Delegate. Or should I say, *when*?"

"I won't wait so long next time." Nowek hung up and grabbed his coat.

Outside it was cold enough to kill, but not yet cold enough to freeze the Angara. A hundred rivers small and large flow into Lake Baikal, but the Angara is the Sacred Sea's one outlet, and the surging water seemed sure of itself, impatient and unstoppable.

Two flags snapped straight out from their poles on the brisk wind. The white, blue, and red of the Russian Federation, and the Siberian banner. White for the sky and snow, green for the *taiga*.

Hope was a diamond, a great blue gem tucked away in a museum. Hope was a jet touching down in Mirny, filled with dollars transferred from a bank on the Cayman Islands. And hope was a 48-carat crystal tucked into the head of a stuffed bear. Maybe it would take a thousand years to make Russia a normal place. Maybe Moscow would *never* join the civilized world. But if there was any place big enough for hope, Siberia was surely it, wasn't it?

Chuchin pulled up in the white Toyota. The Land Cruiser was looking frail. Nowek wondered whether it could live through another winter. Whether *he* could live as the new Siberian Delegate, working for a President who didn't mind the company of spies and thieves, and perhaps preferred them. He got in and they headed off for the airport.

Chuchin lit a cigarette. In deference to Nowek and despite the cold, he opened his window. "The call. It wasn't good news?"

"What do you think? It was from Moscow."

Chuchin offered a sympathetic, understanding nod. "Well, you'd better get used to them."

Nowek had uncovered one deal with the Devil. He'd

smashed it by making one of his own. Mirny's miners woul[
live, but only because its diamonds would keep going to th[
cartel. Nowek was the Siberian Delegate, but only so lon[
as he agreed to be the new President's man. Nowek wa[
Siberia's *kryusha*. Its "roof." He could keep it dry when [
rained. He could keep the Devil from the door, but only b[
doing his bidding.

They turned onto Derzhinsky Street, then up the acce[
road to the terminal. Nowek could see Yuri's old hanga[
He wondered what the difference between one million cara[
and *nearly* one million would mean for him. Was skimmin[
a few thousand carats from the back of Kristall's jet lega[
Was it right?

Once, Nowek would have had an answer. Now it took [
genius to figure out what was right. Or a fool to ask. Winte[
was back, and what worked seemed to be all that counte[
Was this what being Delegate meant? No certainty, n[
right, no wrong?

Was that a country worth fighting for? Worth *living* in? [
Chuchin said, "There she is."

Galena stood outside the terminal hall despite the win[
and cold. She wore a long camel coat, boots with high heel[
She seemed astonishingly tall, topped with a flame-red woo[
beret that only made her dark hair look like sable. She had [
wrapped package under her arm. It was large, but thin.

Nowek thought, *She found it.*

She saw the Land Cruiser, and waved, girlishly.

Chuchin pulled over. Nowek was out before they stoppe[
He took her in his arms. Two workers passed, their expres[
sions said, *He's lucky!* He felt a quick, shivering shock, lik[
diving into cold water. She wasn't a child. She was a woma[
and despite too much lipstick, a disturbingly beautiful on[
"I thought you might not come."

"I can't believe I'm here, either. Careful," she said, holding her package up for Nowek.

He took it. "The Dvořák A Minor?"

She nodded. "It wasn't that hard to find. America is filled with music. Even old music." She looked around, nearly distressed. "I'd forgotten how everything is so gray."

Nowek smiled. "Only on the outside." He stood, quietly drinking her presence in. Her eyes were his. Dark, dark blue. The blue of Baikal. Her hair, that was Nina's. She put her cheek up to be kissed, and he saw the earrings. Diamonds. They were at most a quarter of a carat. Pinpricks, compared with the gems he'd seen flash from the walls of the Ninth Horizon. It stirred up a ghost of the old fear he'd had for her safety, and also the anger. "The diamonds. They're the ones . . ."

"Uncle Arkasha sent. I'll wear them forever. For him." She turned and the diamonds caught the sun, flashing fire. "Diamonds are forever. Isn't that what they say?"

Nowek thought, gray sky, gray buildings, gray people. A weak, desperate country that could fall backward, stumble ahead, collapse entirely, and most likely all three. But standing here next to Galena, he was filled with a delirium of color, with faith, with unreasonable hope. "It's too soon to tell."

Galena rolled her eyes, exasperated. "What's *that* supposed to mean?"

Chuchin honked the horn. Nowek had left the door open. There was no one more Siberian, and *he* was getting cold.

Nowek put his arm around her shoulders. "Let's go before Chuchin freezes," he said, "and I'll tell you the whole story."

About the Author

ROBIN WHITE has been an oil-well rough-neck, oil-well-logging engineer, science writer, community energy planner, and architect by vocation, instrument-rated pilot by avocation. He has lived all over the United States and in Europe, including Russia and Siberia. He now lives near Monterey, California, with his wife and daughter.